DOOR TO DARKNESS

U. S. A.
UNHOLY SLAYING AGENCY
BOOK THREE

GUY QUINTERO

Sinister Raven Publishing LLC

DOOR TO DARKNESS

Book Three of Unholy Slaying Agency Series

Copyright © 2024 by Guy Quintero

First edition: September 2024

All rights reserved. No part of this book may be reproduced in any form or by any electronic or mechanical means, including information storage and retrieval systems, without written permission from the author.

This is a work of fiction. All characters in this publication are fictitious, and any resemblance to real people, alive or dead, is purely coincidental.

ISBN: 978-1-958828-06-9 (Ebook edition)

ISBN: 978-1-958828-07-6 (Paperback edition)

ISBN: 978-1-958828-08-3 (Hardback edition)

This novel is dedicated to all the individuals out there battling demons in silence, not matter what form they come in. Stay strong and remember the words of the wise magician King Solomon. "This too shall pass."

ACKNOWLEDGMENTS

I want to thank all the brave men and women that I had the privilege to serve with during my tours in Iraq. Especially the bad ass recon soldiers of 7-10 Ghost. Thank you to the bookstagram community for all the love and support. You all have helped this washed-up old soldier live out my dreams of entertaining you with my stories. Thank you to my editor Sally Odgers, and my manager Simone. Thank you to actors Carl and Gavin Manes for starring in my book trailer. Thank you to Jeff Fox and Nashelle Brown of Star Fox Media, the most talented video production group in San Diego.

A very special thanks to my ARC/Beta Team:
    Agent Kelly Horrocks @Kelly.the.Jabberwock
    Agent Tera Dugan @TheBookishAbyss
    Agent Katie Stewart

*Let me warn you
Against the nightmares that await this dive.
You may suffer a fate worse than death,
And still remain alive.
Oh, what I say here
And what I say there.
May seem as I'm simply rambling
Without an aim or a care.
But you'll know my words ring true
When your widened eyes see.
The Pale Furnace in its horrific glory,
Cooking screaming souls with glee.*

You should be going now.

CHAPTER 1
GRASP FROM BEYOND

PRESENT DAY: SANTA FE, NM - 2200 HOURS

Young Joey Ridgemont lay staring at the dark ceiling of his bedroom. Tension melted away from muscles roiling with the ache of fatigue. His eyes drooped to half-mast. The sweet aroma of green apples and cinnamon diffused throughout the two-story home, permeating into his room from the kitchen, where his mother had labored. He rubbed at his bulging stomach, filled to capacity with celebratory pizza purchased by his coach, and the pastries that awaited his arrival home.

The loud crack of his homerun swing resounded in his memories. A smirk arose through his weariness, his vision carried away by imagination. He felt his heart racing with the clamor of excitement from the surrounding stands. The wooden bat's throbbing bite resonated in his palms after it rolled out of his fingers, clanging with the home plate. Wind rushed over his face, whisking under the visor of his helmet during the mad dash to first base.

"Keep going!" his coach urged. "Dig! Dig!"

Cheering rose from the crowds as Joey gained control of his breath, gazing across the brown sand that morphed into the shining grass of the outfield. The ball landed on the outermost fence that shuddered as it bounced against it. Fervor swelled in him, pumping his legs across to the second, then the third, his cleats stomping into the dusty base pads.

The white spot of the ball rose high in Joey's peripheral, gunned by a desperate outfielder trying to salvage his team from the magnificent play. Arms and legs pushed through the expanding weariness of heaving lungs, driving Joey closer to home plate. The catcher positioned along the baseline, impeding his path in a squat stance with her wide glove centered for the speeding ball.

"Run her over, Joe!"

Joey collided with the catcher, breaking through the blockade of humanity as his feet scampered over the plate. Squeals erupted as they both toppled to the dust. Clouds of brown rose around them, staining their white uniforms in faint traces. The ball missed its mark, colliding with the backstop, and rattling its chained links. The two little leaguers groaned, rising to their feet. Joey reached out to help the catcher.

"Sorry, Wendy," he said.

"Don't be." The girl took off her mask and cap, setting free long brown locks sprinkled with sand. "I would've done the same."

"Sophomore year is right around the corner..."

"Yep. Don't remind me." Wendy paused, taking a deep breath. "I was wondering. If you weren't doing anything this weekend, my folks are going to the movies and said I could invite—"

Cheers grew louder with scrambling cleats and his giant

The door closed, pinching away light until there was only the illumination from his computer and the glowing moon. Faint rays beamed through branches and leaves from the oak tree looming in the front yard.

A loud and hoarse cawing whisked his attention to a raven staring through his open window. The haze of slumber melted away. The boy's eyes widened then narrowed on a tiny black face staring back. The gleaming pupils of its big eyes locked with Joey, who rose from his bed, yawning while he lumbered to the sill.

"Dang thing woke me!" Joey grumbled. "I should've closed this window."

A shifting commotion lowered Joey's attention to the base of the tree. Staring up at him was a tall silhouette draped among the shadows. Its narrow face remained obscure within the night. The boy felt the figure's attention bearing up at him. Black feathers spiked along its crown. The silhouetted presence lowered its gaze, fixating through the sprawling front windows of the living room.

"Mom! Come quick!" Joey turned, screaming into the hallway.

The bedroom door swung open with Phyllis Senior rushing through. Her son wielded his bat, taken from its stand near the headboard. Joey cocked the weapon behind his frame with both arms, taking slow steps back to the window.

"What is it?" his mother inquired.

"There's someone outside, looking into our house!"

They peered around, staring down among the bushes lining the home's outer wall. Their eyes found nothing, but the shadows given shape with the contrast of moonlight and the evening gloom. The boy shook his head.

"I saw someone. I did!"

"I believe you. Go grab your sister and get your cell phone ready. I'm going to the safe and I'll check downstairs, then outside. If I'm not back in ten minutes, call the police."

"Yes, ma'am."

Joey rushed into Phyllis' room, his view washed from the blaring of her computer monitor, flashing with gunfire, and screaming mutant monsters. She turned in the computer chair with wide-eyed dismay, before sighing in deflated relief.

"I thought you were Mom! Don't just rush in like that! So rude!"

"Philly, we got a problem. Someone's outside. Mom's going to check it out, but you're going to stay with me until this gets resolved."

"Drama queen. Probably just one of your jock friends playing a prank."

"No, this doesn't feel right."

"Whatever. Least you could do is hop online with me."

Joey shook his head.

"Oh-Em-Gee. You're seriously spooked? Joey, you're such a pussy." Phyllis stormed over, leaving the spinning chair for her window with an adjacent angle. "I don't see anything."

"There was a raven or a crow or something and a man. He didn't look friendly."

Phyllis rolled her eyes. "Good. Mom was a soldier. She'll toast that asshole. Just like I'm smoking these monsters!"

"Don't use language like that!" Phyllis Senior barked from the doorway, a .38 revolver in her hands.

"Sorry, Mom."

"It's fine. We're all a little worked up. Whoever was outside is gone now. Probably just a vagrant looking for an easy mark. I'll call the police and put in a report, then notify the neighborhood watch."

"Come with me, child," the voice demanded from a mouthless and unmoving countenance.

"No!"

With teeth gritting, Joey swung his bat for the being's head, only to watch it pass through. Energetic residue sparked from the strike, dissipating into the surrounding world, leaving the entity's form pulsating. White eyes continued staring at Joey, an incandescent hum tethering his attention.

Nana appeared in view behind the being. A wave of her hand saw the figure erupting into a geyser of blackness, the particles of its essence showering over the room.

Ripples flowed through reality, warping all that Joey witnessed. He shrank back, his legs colliding with the bed and toppling over. His grandmother walked to him, the glistening of her oversized dentures usurping his attention from the rest of her darkening presence.

"That mean ole bird trying to take my precious child away from me. Look at you, Joe-Joe. So yummy I could just eat you up." Nana extended her delicate and smooth hand, the elongated fingers awaiting his grasp. "Your place is with me. I'll protect you."

Scuffing from plastic and wool slippers dragged through the hallway behind him. Joey turned around seeing another image of his grandmother. She continued past the doorway muttering to herself, a paperback novel hugged tight, pressing into her thick robes.

"He's not in bed," his grandmother murmured. "How odd... Must be out playing sports...Yes... He likes baseball..."

"Nana..."

Alarm raced through the boy with gripping apprehension slowing his limbs.

Joey's vision bounced between the two images of his

grandmother, matching the pace of his thumping heart. The fingers before him extended and widened. The former visage of Nana stormed forward. Plodding steps pounded on the floor with a weight greater than her tiny frame. In a quick scoop, the large hand latched around the boy's head.

"Clueless and pathetic." A voice carried hoarse scratchiness with each straining syllable ending in sharp contempt. "You've no idea where you are, child. Such innocence to devour."

Tight darkness wrapped his vision. Surges of pain shut down attempts to resist. Deep and racing gasps grew thicker with each breath, weighed down by tension through his nose and chest. Heartbeats rose to his ears, drumming inside his skull. Efforts to resist melted away in the authority of his assailant. A hum resonated around his core, growing until reaching levels of body quaking convulsion.

Paralyzed! Can't... do... anything! A pop echoed in his mind. His presence drifted upon the currents flowing around him as the familiarity of grounding slipped away. Joey's limbs writhed and kicked in open space, until his weariness left him a flaccid husk. Only the dark remained, with his subjugator's heavy rasping breath brushing against his ear. The being drew closer with the masquerade of Nana melting away to a towering figure possessing a pale countenance and a crooked dead man's smile. The wide brim of a large black hat emerged from the darkness that surrounded the being.

How? What's happening?

"Mine!" a voice wheezed.

I'm drowning!

"To the Pale Furnace. Your nightmare is just beginning. Suffering beyond comprehension awaits, until there is nothing left but the ashes of your burning soul."

No! Mom! Someone! Please! Nana... Please...

CHAPTER 2
BIRTH OF A BUTCHER

PRESENT DAY: COLORADO SPRINGS, CO - 0300 HOURS

The little girl's eyes crept open to her bedroom, despite weariness weighing heavy on her drooping face. Her legs shook. Her mind strained to command them, but the impulses failed to reach her limbs. Pounding from her escalating heartbeats climbed into her ears.

A second attempt also failed, leaving her petite body locked in place on her bed. Rapid and blurred movements snatched her attention toward the ceiling. The star projector on her nightstand rotated images of space upon her ceiling. Twinkling spots of light competed with sporadic flashes from her computer monitor.

A towering silhouette emerged from the shadows, looming over Penny, blocking the glowing light on her face. The little girl fought to direct her gaze at the presence, convulsing with failure as her body resisted. Her heartbeat escalated with the cold chill of fear clinging to the back of her neck, spreading down her spine and into her frozen limbs. The presence leaned forward, bringing into view a large top hat. Hot breath contrasted against Penny's skin, ushering away the chill, leaving a clamminess sticking to the girl.

"Back to the table!" a frantic voice called from a third presence. "We must make haste, or we'll never make it back in time! There's no one to watch him! Blood will flow! It'll flow like the rivers upon us!"

"It'll all be over soon," another hoarse voice said, registering more within Penny's mind than her ears. "A rebirth into a new home for you. Now it's time for an unbirthday, little one. Such sweet and pure energy coming from you."

Penny whimpered. Her nostrils dried and constricted, calling only shallow breaths into her gasping lungs. Shivers coursed through her limbs, until her fingers and toes twitched out of her control.

"Mother will cherish you," the Hat Man replied. "I'll surely be rewarded when I present your soul."

Penny leapt out of bed, reclaiming control. The presence vanished. Yet his laughter continued to weigh upon her thoughts, still echoing from a place beyond her sight. The warmth of his breath clung to her clammy skin, spreading through her limbs as the girl hugged herself. Penny sprinted for the door, then down the hallway to her parents' room. The girl burst through, sobbing to the ceiling while tears spilled like a fountain.

"What's wrong?" Her mother jolted awake. "Are you okay, Penny?"

"Mama!" Penny cried out, scampering to her side of the couple's king bed. "Someone was in my room. He threatened me!"

"Okay, baby." Lara hugged Penny, turning to her husband and shaking him awake.

"Wha—" her father murmured, his eyes struggling to open. "Honey, I had a long day of meetings, and I have another one coming tomorrow."

"Our daughter is having night terrors."

"Sweetie, you're eight now," her father muttered. "You're too old for this bullshit. It was just a nightmare. Go back to bed."

"No, Daddy it was real!" Penny sobbed. "I heard them! I felt them!"

"I know nightmares can be very disturbing, but I promise it wasn't real. We've been through this before many times when you were younger. Go back to bed, please."

"Peter, can't she just sleep with us?"

"No, because we'll be encouraging this wild imagination of hers. She'll never get over it. You have to face your fears, Penny. Then you'll understand they're not real."

"Please, Daddy!"

"No!" Peter snapped. "I have too much going on. You both know I have a hard time going to sleep. I have an early morning meeting after an hour and a half of traffic. I don't have time for this nonsense! Go to bed or you're grounded for the next two weeks, Penny! No computer! No friends! No dessert!"

Apprehension weighed Penny's steps with shaking reluctance. Head lowered; the tears continued to flow. She closed her parents' door, staring across the hall to her own. Quivering overtook the girl, before she rushed back into the room and dove into bed, hiding under the sheets

An hour passed, with the fear dissipating from her body. Weariness brought the girl drifting back to slumber. Through the limited visibility of her thin sheets and the light of her computer monitor, two figures emerged. A diminutive presence wore a coat, with large horns protruding from his tapered skull. Next to him was the tall man with his hat. Their noiseless steps brought them closer until both sets of gleaming yellow eyes bore down upon Penny. The Hat Man extended his lanky arms, unfurling wide hands with bony calloused fingers ending in sharp claws.

"You... belong... to us!" The duet of voices called out from the darkness.

PRESENT DAY: QUANTICO, VA - 1700 HOURS

A deep sigh deflated Carla Leonard, her face drooping with a frown. Glare from the computer monitor reflected along her thick glasses while she skimmed the lines of pages detailing the report. After another sigh, she pulled away from the keyboard, leaning into the maroon coat draped over the creaking chair. Her long fingers rubbed into the heavy bags underneath her reddish eyes, working the wrinkles adorning her once taut cheeks.

No sign of foul play, biological, or chemical attacks. This can't be a coincidence. Spinning my wheels here. Should I... Damn it. Can't fight my gut instincts, no matter how much my peers in the Bureau want to dismiss them. There's something here, but I don't have the resources to decipher it.

The small screen of her cellphone flared to life as she tapped away on it, scrolling through contacts, stopping at Katherine Howler. Her lips formed a smile at a picture of the two grinning women embracing. Long sleeves of their blue and gold alma mater sweaters extended beyond their hands, draping from where they clung to each other.

The phone entered its call screen, showing Katherine's name and rumbling with the dial tone. *Is that due to clumsy fingers or eagerness? Didn't even realize I was pressing the call button.*

"Been a long time, Carla." Katherine greeted her. "I'm surprised you still have my number. I take it this isn't a social call?"

"Not entirely. But, while I have you here, how are you? How's John?"

"Serving me with divorce papers."

"I'm sorry to hear that. Look, I know we didn't leave on the best of terms—"

"You know firsthand I'm not the type of person to let personal feelings get in the way of accomplishing a mission."

"Still talking like a soldier."

"You can take the girl out of the Army, and all that jazz, but you didn't call to hear tired cliches or to finally patch things up."

"Frigid as always. Well, Kat—"

"Assistant Director Howler. Let's keep it formal."

"Moved up quite a bit in the world since you took that demotion when you transferred to that top secret agency."

"You were saying?"

"An inexplicable occurrence has been unfolding within the last month. I've exhausted all my resources in the Bureau trying to find answers. My superiors and colleagues believe it's a dead end, but I don't agree in the face of these numbers. I'm emailing you the details—"

"Send it over TSIPR-net only. Too many holes in the non-secure side, especially in your networks."

"Ouch... Not much faith in us?"

"The FBI has caused us a fair share of problems in the past. Continue."

"There's been a massive spike in children and teens slipping into comas, with zero correlations between any of the cases. The victims are between the ages of four and sixteen. At first, it was a few hundred, but now we're up to thousands that are simply not waking up. We've been through all the proper channels and procedures on our end. No traces of biological or chemical attacks. No clues as to why it's happening, or even the means to triangulate the occurrences due to the randomness. Every state and major city has had a case. There is one lead though that we've gotten in the New Mexico region. AD Howler?"

"I'm listening. Go on."

"I forgot how quiet you can get when you're deep in thought. Well, the lead comes from several witnesses who spotted a man of native descent, wearing black feathers. Reports said he was seen prowling outside of homes or within neighborhoods before each incident."

"Now, that is piquing my interest."

"This perp is slippery. I've sent agents from the Bureau to track him and issued an APB to all local law enforcement. I even recruited the Marshals with a federal warrant that I managed to drum up with minimal details and the expense of many favors... but nothing. Not even a glimpse of our main suspect aside from the witnesses. As much as it's stinging my pride to say this... Everything has failed. I've exhausted all possible options. That's when I started wondering, despite my best attempts to rationalize the circumstances. So, you can see where this is going beyond the realm of my expertise."

"You were right to call. This sounds like something my agency deals with."

"That agency being?"

"I've gotten your email on the case. Looks as if all necessary details are attached. Thank you, Agent Leonard. Rest assured; it will be taken care of."

"Well, that was worth a shot. Be safe, Assistant Director Howler. Wait—"

"Yes?"

"I'm sorry for how everything turned out. I've missed you, all these years. I didn't mean to kiss him. I was just a young dumb kid. It's not an excuse. I know that. What I did cut deep, and even though I wanted to make it right, I never could."

"I forgave you a long time ago, Carla. I learned myself that people aren't perfect, and I've gotten mud on my soul, too. Lord knows, I'm no saint. I just never reached out because I'm a different person now. That was another lifetime."

"That's a relief to hear."

"Circumstances have taken me down a path of no return. Funny how I thought I knew so much in my youth, being resolute in my decisions only to find them changing in the years that followed. So idealistic and naïve. I don't have any regrets though because it's why I am the woman I am today. Would I do anything different? No. But, heed my advice. Take care of yourself, Carla. Life is too short and the factors threatening it are growing in number."

24 YEARS AGO: KALINGA PROVINCE, PHILIPPINES

The hums and chirps of cicadas played against the croaking of frogs, drowning away the footsteps of ten-year-old Gabriel Agapito and his parents trailing behind. Beyond the towering emerald trees and their branches of crisp foliage lingered a deepening orange sky, heralding the evening. Cool breezes ushered away the humidity, but not the sweat stains that remained along the boy's collared brown shirt and shorts. He stabbed at the ground with his walking stick during each step, bobbing along until a loud snap brought his attention behind him.

Both parents had stopped, his mother tossing away her broken walking stick into the bushes. She smiled, brushing away the free flowing strands of her long black hair, before stepping forward once more. Whisking breezes clung the woman's pink and white dress to her body, revealing a seven-month baby bump. Gabriel handed his walking stick to her and with a thumbs up, his grinning father reached out, ruffling the boy's shaggy dark hair.

"You're a good boy, Gabe. Isn't he, Alma?"

"The best, Jovan," his mother answered.

"I don't have to tell you to do the right things," Jovan continued. "Your heart and soul are pure. You always do the things you know are best."

"Thank you, Tatay." Gabriel strutted upright, cocking his head. His parents chuckled.

"You know why we walked all the way to Tabuk City today?"

The boy nodded. "So, the doctors can check on Nanay and my future brother?"

"Well, actually, sister," his mother interrupted. "It was

more than just a check-up, Gabe. God has blessed us with a little girl."

His father nodded. "That's right and to confirm just that with the ultra-sound. You're going to have a sister, Gabe. That means I'm going to need you to look after her when I'm at work checking on the boats going up and down the Chico."

"You can count on me!"

The two exchanged a high-five. His father took off the baseball cap, placing it on Gabe's head. "This is yours now. It's the only one I've ever seen in our village. Everyone's going to see this and know that you're stepping up, because it's what I wear when I'm out directing boats. My cousins brought it from America."

The boy removed the hat, staring at the design with its faded golden letters of 'SD' overlapping each other on the front. He nodded to his father, standing upright in posture, before placing it back on. Wetness from the band brushed his forehead as his hair compacted inside.

"You need a haircut."

"Who is this team, Tatay?"

"From San Diego, California. That's where our cousins are from. I like the team because they stand for Catholics; our faith."

Gabriel nodded. "Thank you."

The family followed the churning river until they turned down a trail leading into the banana grove. Within seconds the jungle canopy disappeared, peeling away to the dimming orange that morphed into the darkness of night. Little trees surrounded them, their tanned smooth trunks standing up to the height of an adult, topped by fluffy green leaves reaching in all directions.

Gabriel's head bobbed, remembering the radio in the

doctor's waiting room that blared with the joyous sounds of Korean pop music and American hip hop. The boy hummed, matching the tunes of soulful rhythms, his glance stuttering at a pair of legs standing among the trunks, deep inside the field. Giant leaves draped over them, blocking his sight of the torso.

Beyond the hips was nothing save for white shorts covered in stains of brown along the rim of wide feminine hips. The slender legs possessed a near perfect texture, shaped with contours of youth and beauty, into dainty and petite feet with toes sinking into the grass. The boy came to a stop, his attention locked on the vision, focusing through the foliage.

"Gabe," Jovan urged. "Why did you stop?"

"I—"

His father gazed at the rows of trees and shrugged. "Come on, let's get home for dinner. It's only about a mile more, I promise."

"Oh… okay."

"Ugh," Alma groaned.

"Almost home." Jovan encouraged, taking his wife's hand. "I'll do the cooking. You just rest."

"Thank you. Walking is good for the baby though. The change in temperature is probably causing the baby to be unhappy."

Jovan wrapped his jacket around his wife, holding her hand as they continued their trek. Frogs ceased their croaking. The clicking of cicadas came to an end. The flow of water from the river quieted, except for when the evening breeze caressed their ears. Gabriel peered around, finding the stars were now above them, sprinkling the skies with points of light and the crescent moon that illuminated their way.

Their steps crunched on the gravel of the beaten path.

Rustling leaves caught Gabriel's attention and he halted. With a gentle guide of his hand, Jovan urged the boy onward.

He looked back and saw his father rubbing his stomach.

"So hungry, Gabe. All I can think about is food. Let's hurry."

A powerful gust of air thrust overhead, flapping along the darkened skies. Gabe looked up again, finding only the stars gleaming beyond drifting clouds. A scream erupted from his mother. The boy spun around, finding his father with his arms reaching underneath hers, tickling at the pits. Squeals followed as the woman tried dashing away, only to be embraced by her husband's arms, sharing a giggle.

"Gabe?" his mother asked. "Everything's okay, your father is just being silly like always."

He nodded, before looking up to the skies once more.

"Awfully jumpy tonight—"

Hoarse screams of bestial fury stretched into the night, ringing eardrums with vibrations matching their throbbing hearts, escalating with a rapid pace. Wings and claws bore down upon Jovan from the rear, slamming the man face first into the ground. Dust clouds pushed out, with flapping leather appendages bringing mighty winds over their eyes. Gabe stumbled away, raising his arms in the calamity before falling on his backside.

A scream expelled from his mother, her mouth stretching, as she fell over. When Gabe's vision cleared, he saw the creature pressed upon his father. Withered skin covered the sinew of its thin arms, rippling with tension as it pinned Jovan. Pointed black nails extended from the long fingers as they reached underneath with a curled grip. The sharp claws clove away. The skin of Jovan's throat split with ease under its sharpness, pulling away like a rising curtain when the man's head knocked back from impact. Blood spilled from the gaping wound, pouring like a faucet from the hanging strands of meat that once formed vital muscles and veins.

Loud gargles erupted from Jovan, drowning away his cries of anguish. Gabriel gasped, his eyes following his father's convulsions. Blood pooled underneath his head in seconds. He reached out for Jovan, his sputtering breaths growing heavy, while the ground vanished until he was floating.

Perception slowed, holding the moment as Gabe watched the last movements of Jovan's body as animation ceased.

Long strands of black wiry hair dangled over large glistening eyes, narrowing with menace upon Alma. Another skin crawling howl came from its extended lipless mouth. Saliva flew from curved teeth, long as knives, jutting from black gums. It raced forward, with wings flailing, and arms slapping at the ground. The scrapes of its claws followed each movement as it galloped upon them.

Alma collapsed, the wind expelling from her mouth as her back hit the ground. The mass of limbs writhed until its arms locked over the woman, with its wings folding together along its back. Deep breaths expelled from the creature, and its teeth proceeded back into its mouth, reforming gentle feminine lips over a shrinking maw. From the bottom of its pointed chin, a slithering limb extended, reaching into Alma's belly button where it pierced into her stomach. Fluids traveled through the translucent appendage, slurping inward by churning muscles along its throat.

"Gabe... Run..." Alma murmured before her gaze turned statuesque to the stars above.

The boy stepped backward, his legs trembling with each step trying to push through. Blood flowed through the creature's suction tube, with small chunks of meat chugging through. First, a tiny foot, then fingers, until what followed was shredded beyond recognition.

The floating sensation faded from the haze paralyzing Gabe's thoughts, returning with the compaction of dust beneath his soles after every movement. Wind rushed over his face, gathering with the speed of his arm pumping dash. Blurs of the banana tree shadows raced from the edge of view as echoes of his mother's last instruction continued.

Run! Run! Run!

PRESENT DAY: SAN DIEGO, CA - 0200 HOURS

Agent Gabriel Agapito kicked away the sheets, his legs thrashing along the king-size mattress. Murmurs laced with desperation escaped from his quivering lips. Gabriel rotated, plunging his grimacing face into his pillow. Small and delicate fingers reached out into the dark, caressing his shoulder. He rolled away, the shallow utterance of his unintelligible words hinting at demands. The small hand reached out again, and Gabriel spun in place, with his elbow catching something soft.

A woman screamed. "Ah! Gabriel!"

When the agent awoke, he clicked on his bedside lamp, turning to his wife sitting upright. Her slender hands nursed a red swelling along the side of her face. Blonde strands broke away from her bob cut, mussed over her face.

"I'm sorry, Steph." Gabriel reached out only to have his hand slapped away. "Lemme see, baby girl."

"You think sweet talkin' me is going to make up for this?"

his wife snapped. She paused, seeing the redness of his tearing eyes and bags of weariness. "You were back there again?"

Gabriel nodded. "Yeah, it's been happening more lately."

"You've been burying yourself in assignments, Gabe. You're running yourself ragged. That takes a toll, even if you're tough as nails on the exterior." She fist bumped his bulging pecs. "The interior still wears thin."

"I know but—"

"Don't give me that tough guy Army soldier bullshit. I know, I've heard it before. Ugh, what time is it? 0200!" Stephanie sighed. "Tell you what, I'm going to make some tea to help us get back to sleep. I have to be at HQ at 0800 to take my shift at the comms station."

"I love you."

She smiled from the doorway. "I love you too, goof. And you just remember there aren't many wives out there that would take an elbow to the eye and understand."

Gabriel nodded. "I know I'm lucky. I tell myself that every day."

"You better!"

Rumbling from his cell phone swept his attention to the nightstand. Assistant Director Howler's name flashed on the screen. Gabriel cleared his throat, snatching the phone.

"Good morning, ma'am."

"I wish that were so, Team Commander Agapito. I know you were supposed to be on the range tomorrow but I'm pulling Butcher from Q-ing to focus on more pressing matters."

"Understood, ma'am."

"I'll brief you in the morning, just wanted to make sure that you reported to the war room and not gunnery. My apologies for the abrupt change of plans but I need my best sorcerer hunters on this one. They're hurting children, Gabe."

"We'll answer the call, ma'am."

"Outstanding. I'll get you up to speed when you get here. Rest up."

Clicks ended their call before Stephanie sauntered back in with mugs. Steam rose, carrying the aroma of fruit and chamomile through the room. Gabriel smiled, accepting the warm beverage with both hands.

"I heard you talking to Howler," Stephanie said. "I take it these next two weeks slated for ranges and home time is ending sooner than later?"

"Yeah. Something is going down. Sounds big."

"You can't say no? Alma's piano recital is Friday after school."

"They're hurting children."

"Oh..." Stephanie's brow rose in concern. "Someone's little girl or boy isn't coming home?"

Gabriel nodded.

"Alma won't understand right now. But she will later come to admire your passion for justice and the fight against darkness. I'll talk to her. Just come back to us in one piece."

Mugs rested on their separate nightstands as they embraced, bringing their lips together with hungry passion. "Nothing can keep me from you."

CHAPTER 3
A BASTION BEFORE THE SEA

PRESENT DAY: USA HQ WEST, SAN DIEGO, CA - 0900 HOURS

Coolness engulfed the war room from air conditioning vents. Gabriel sat upright, centered on the colossal table that usurped half the area with its polished length. His furrowed brow was surrounded by trails of wrinkles, leading to shining black strands of hair draping over them. The team commander's dark brown eyes burned with rising fury, held back only by discipline keeping his body locked and steady. In the corner of his view was Butcher Team seated next to him.

Forgive me, mahal. My little Alma. Gabriel pictured the cheeks of his daughter rounding on her smiling face flanked by pigtails. Her big brown eyes would search for him among the crowd. She'd sag back into her piano bench after failing to locate him. The team commander shook his head clear of the stupor, the warmth and love tingling within his heart shaking away. Gabriel turned to scan over Butcher. *I have no other choice.*

Light reflected images of the room on Mara Graves's glasses as she skimmed through her copy of the report. Thick and shriveled burn scars stretched from her fingers, disappearing underneath the long sleeve of her uniform. She turned, nodding to Gabriel, her dirty blonde bun staying affixed like stone.

"Where's the Assistant Director, Actual?" Leo's hulking frame came into Gabriel's view as he leaned forward. A few braids escaped from the operator's tight wrap, dangling over his forehead. "A brother's gotta get some breakfast before he hunts evil."

The Agency is running hot these days. So many simultaneous operations. Teams are being run ragged. Can't even blame Howler for showing up late to her own meeting. Probably has her hands full and then some.

"She texted me," Gabriel answered. "Trying to coordinate air support for Ghost Team's operation right now. Hang tight."

"Want to grab some donuts?" Portia raised her hand.

"Yeah, Doc. Sounds good. Let's go in on a dozen." Leo chuckled. "Gotta gets them cream filled. Can't do those old fashion."

"I'm fine with that. More old fashion for me."

"Not sure how you all eat those sweets," Kevin murmured from the far right of the table. "Count me out of that inevitable sugar crash."

"I like working with AD Howler," Portia said.

Leo and the medic nodded to each other.

"Meh, you like everyone," Mara jabbed.

"Better than dealing with the Curmudgeon." Leo sighed. "Dude is always mad as fuck. A lot like—"

The machine gunner looked to his commander. Gabriel

glared at him through the corner of his raised brow. *Don't you dare, Lion. Not today.*

"—heard he's balancing some major shit right now with Mustang, Rogue, and Honey Badger. Oh, and rumor is Raptor found something in the Jefferson Mountain Range, but all comms have been lost after going ape shit on a contact."

Clicking heels approached the door. Katherine Howler marched inside, slamming it shut. Her pants swayed as she rushed past everyone to the head of the table, nursing a sloshing cup of iced coffee. Butcher Team stared at the back of her black coat, lips pressing, postures correcting into an upright position, and chins raising with stiff lips. The Assistant Director swallowed deeply before turning around. Water rimmed the red tint of her eyes. Howler's face hardened into a stern gaze, meeting each of them.

Hope she didn't hear Leo running at the mouth.

"You are correct, Agent Mills," Howler responded, spotting Leo. "Thankfully for you, AD Hughes is busy at the moment. Now, if we're done with the scuttlebutt let's get down to business."

"Yes, ma'am!"

"Good. Agent Agapito, I thank you and Butcher Team for assembling on such short notice. As you're well aware by now from the reports, these bizarre happenings are occurring nationwide and at an alarming rate. Our only lead seems to be the sightings of a thirty-something, Native American man, wearing black feathers."

"Ma'am, are we to assume he's a rogue practitioner?" Gabriel asked. *At least this won't be a total loss. We'll get to smoke another damned sorcerer. Vile piece of shit is harming kids. No mercy when the time comes. I hope he resists so I can make it hurt before I send him to hell.*

"Precisely, Agent Agapito. Which is why I called upon your team specifically for this lofty task."

"Nice." Leo grinned. "We're up for it, ma'am."

"The lion roars. That's good."

"How do you know my nickname?"

"You're not the only one that gets the gossip around here." Howler grinned.

Gentle knocks shifted their attention to the opening door. Within the entrance was a tall smiling man with spikes of brown hair rising from a faded cut, dressed in the combat fatigues of the Agency. His chiseled cheekbones and toned jawline went into a thick neck and broad shoulders. He folded his hands while taking slow steps inward.

I don't like these jokers. Something isn't right...

"Gray." Portia read the newcomer's name tag.

"Pleased to meet you, Agent Portia Lawson," he replied.

Several boot steps trailed behind Agent Gray. The new arrivals followed him to the opposite side of the table, across from the narrowing glowers of scrutiny projected by Butcher Team, save for Portia who smiled and waved. Glances were exchanged with unintelligible murmurs before eyes clicked to Howler with quiet demand.

She's pulling some funny business here. Damn it, couldn't just be a normal bag and tag.

"Butcher, I want you to meet Diver Team," Howler introduced. "They are an experimental hybrid outfit, rigorously trained over the last four years in both duties as Agents and Scryers."

"I knew I didn't like these guys," Mara whispered to a nodding Gabriel.

Mara's feeling it too. Always in sync with me during operations.

There's no better second in the Agency. This is some bullshit. Time to measure dicks with the boss lady.

Curiosity morphed into lip curling glowers and grimaces oozing with disdain.

"Ma'am." Gabriel stood up. "We kill sorcerers. We don't work with them. Have them bother another team."

The door swung open again, followed by whirring motors and rubber pressing over the ground. Madam Simone Dupree passed through on her mechanized chair, stopping behind Butcher Team. Wrinkles piled together with her grin. Her gray brows arched with impish fervor. She winked at Gabriel, who rolled his eyes in retort.

"That is precisely the cold welcome I was anticipating, Agent Agapito," Madam Dupree jeered. "Sad to say, I see those apprehensions about the gifted are still at the forefront of your thoughts."

"Gifted... Yeah, right. Don't mistake apprehension for hatred."

"They read the same in the layers. And that's not a coincidence my dear angry Team Commander."

Stay out of my mind, witch.

"Gabriel, that hurts! Oh, and too late by the way," Dupree mocked. *"Such barriers inside of here..."*

"Team Commander Agapito!" Howler snapped. "I understand Butcher's reluctance all too well. But you will give Madam Dupree her due respect as a ranking member of the Agency's command staff, and the Grand Scryer of The Order."

"Acknowledged, ma'am."

Gabriel's hard stare fell upon Alexa Gray next, scanning over her dark curly pixie cut and navy blue eyes surrounded by a gentle face of porcelain, with a freckled button nose. The woman's lips pressed together with an uneasy smile under the burning examination. *She's pretty, but different...*

"I see those wheels turning, Butcher Actual." Alexa delivered a warm smile to Gabriel. "Let me save you from the awkwardness of having to ask, I am trans, and my pronouns are she/her."

"The fuck is a pronoun?" Leo scratched his head. "That sounds like some English class shit."

"It's how a person prefers to be addressed," Portia answered. "Be nice, Leo."

"I am being nice! I'm a street dude. You gotta explain these things to me!" Leo snapped, turning to Alexa. "Nice to meet you. My pronouns are bro/bruh/homie."

Portia brought her face into her palm. "I'm sorry, Alexa."

"What did I do now?" Leo asked.

"He's fine." Alexa chuckled.

"If I may introduce us, maybe break the ice," Gray said. "Agents of Butcher Team, I am Harland Gray, and this is my second, Rahaan Patel Diver12Bravo."

A bronze skinned man with a shaved head and pegged nose amongst a gentle smile approached. The uniform hung from his thin and short frame. He waved to the room.

"These are Agents William Travis and John Winston, our Golf and Delta," Harland continued.

The two men nodded in greeting.

"And this is my wife, Alexa Gray, the team medic," Harland replied. He placed a hand on the shoulder of the woman with a pixie cut. Their eyes met with a loving connection before turning back to the room full of glaring rivals.

"Tough crowd," Alexa replied.

"Mga bading," Gabriel murmured, shaking his head.

Mara nodded, Leo's eyes widened, while Kevin remained statuesque.

"That's so mean, Actual!" A scoff expelled from Portia's thin pink lips.

"I take it your entire team understands Tagalog?" Harland asked.

"And so do I!" Howler barked. "Knock it off, Agent Agapito!"

Gabriel shrugged. *I didn't mean that. But perhaps if I make them uncomfortable enough, they'll get assigned elsewhere and Howler will stop this nonsense. I'm not a fucking babysitter.*

Madam Dupree winked at Gabriel.

Fuck! She's still in my head, even with quartz in my pocket.

"That only protects from left-handed practitioners, Agent Agapito. I know your prejudice makes it hard for you to discern the difference. Your quartz only hinders negative energies. I am a witch of the right-handed path."

"Well, this isn't going as I had hoped," Alexa stated.

"Ditto," Gabriel replied.

"Put your egos and predilections aside, youngsters," Madam Dupree commanded. "Children need our help."

"That is what should be foremost on everyone's thoughts," Howler said. "Can we at least agree to that?"

Everyone around the conference table nodded.

"Good. Now let's get down to the important details. Butcher, with the scope of these occurrences, you need to be able to cover more ground and scryers may be needed. That's where Diver comes in to augment you."

"The victims are all comatose. That means their vessels are still alive," Madam Dupree stated. "While Butcher is hunting for clues to this perp, Diver's job will be to conduct etheric readings of the area and attempt to commune with the victims."

"With the permission of their loved ones of course," Howler added. "This means I want cordial behavior and bedside manner. These families have endured so much. Handle this situation with the utmost care."

Katherine gave Butcher's members firm glances, until they each conceded with reluctant nods.

"Understood, ma'am," Harland replied.

Gabriel met Harland's meek smile with an unwavering glare.

"The official nomenclature for this Operation will be Through the Looking Glass, because of the investigative nature of this mission. There will be more than meets the eye to what we are facing. I'm going to require everyone to be at their best. If there aren't any more questions for Madam Dupree or me, then I'm giving you the go for launch."

Gabriel and Harland scanned their respective teams, before turning to their superiors.

"Good to go, ma'am," they acknowledged.

"Excellent. Happy hunting, Agents. Your transport will be ready at 1300 hours. Dismissed."

Chair legs rubbed and screeched across the floor as agents filed out.

"Agent Agapito," Madam Dupree called.

"Yes, ma'am?"

"I understand. I do. But we need you to lend your expertise to my Warrior Scryers. For the good of the Agency."

"Acknowledged, ma'am."

"That's his way of saying he'll think about it." Howler smirked.

"Your tenacious nature has seen you through such arduous

ordeals," Madam Dupree continued. "I know of your incredible success record. Your anger has driven you through some dangerous missions that would've broken most. But it will be your undoing if you cannot discern beyond your rigidity."

"Acknowledged, ma'am."

The door closed, leaving the women commanders alone.

"You gazed into his mind?" Howler asked.

"Yes."

"What did you see, Simone?"

"Pain. After a bastion of discipline and anger was a broiling sea of agony, churning with memories locked away. We expect all agents to have it. Agapito's suffering is deeper than what you would expect, despite knowing the details from psych interviews. That man's willpower is strong, and if he were gifted, he'd rival the best scryers. He's taught himself to traverse the misery resonating within, but I doubt it will ever go away."

"I see."

"I only hope he comes to terms with it someday."

MOMENTS EARLIER

Madam Simone Dupree's vision penetrated the presence of Agent Agapito. Gray and white layers of thick fog immersed her mind's eye, slowing her pursuit of the man's psyche. Shrieks rang through the air with a predatory declaration, each inhuman wail succeeded by heavy and eager breaths.

"Run! Run! Run!" a woman screamed.

Slurping churned around her with desperate suction running through a thick straw. Adolescent whimpers swelled in Dupree's ears with sobbing mixed into oxygen deprived gasps. Her vision followed rapid steps tapping along the dust laden road, past the haze where it cleared into an open night sky.

Splatters of blood soaked into the road, trailing to a being held aloft by its arms rippling with thin muscles, pushing from paper-thin skin. Slime oozed from a long apparatus of flesh, extending from underneath the looming creature's chin, puncturing into the woman's abdomen. She writhed on the ground, her stomach flattening as a whisking force shredded tissue from within. The bloody slough of the unborn streamed into the abomination's hungry gullet.

Alma, his mother...

Writhing limbs struggled to find strength beyond the incoherent movements, with Alma's eyes rising into her skull, mouth agape with saliva dripping from her chin. Movement ceased and the woman lay placid, darkness immersing her closing vision. Her abdomen sank inward, below the rib cage failing in its movements for breath.

Skin and flesh gave as the fiend withdrew its limb, sending chunks of meat raining upon the woman. Blood rushed to the surface of the enormous tear, streaming out and drenching Alma's waist, until the ground could absorb no more. A lake of red formed around her corpse. With a flap of its giant wings, the assailant propelled into the air, screaming as it soared past the treetops, beyond Dupree's sight.

Pounding heartbeats whisked away the Grand Scryer's vision to the fleeing child. *This isn't what I'm looking for. There's a depth here that not even Kat knows about.* Mottled images twisted and blended. Madam Dupree raced past the moments she knew, to years later when the boy sat inside the room of a house. Gabriel sighed from the small bed, staring out his window at children playing basketball on a court across the street.

"Come on!" Their faint voices carried through the glass. "Shoot it! Don't miss!"

"Brick!"

Echoes of inflated plastic bounced on cement.

"Gabe," a woman's voice snapped.

"Tiya Analyn..."

She stood in the doorway, her smooth and thin face shining from the sunlight pouring into the room. The woman wore a skirt, wrapped snug around her pronounced hips and backside. Her legs remained poised on high heels, bringing a fullness to her sculpted golden brown calves, leading down to her feet where her painted red toes compacted. Gabriel turned to her, recoiling at the tight blouse she wore, buttons stretching with the material they held together save for the open ones displaying her ample and pert bosom.

His aunt married a naval petty officer after adopting him. Well, this is quite new to me. If memory serves me, she's ten years older than his mother but looks to be barely out of her teens, if that.

"You just going to sit around and mope all day? Go play with the other kids."

Gabriel shook his head.

"Fine, you wanna sulk? Fine. Sulk while you sweep the floor or there will be no supper!"

The boy nodded. "I'll clean it, Tiya."

"You better."

"Why are you dressed like that?"

"Don't go questioning me! You mind your business, or I'll slap the taste from you."

"When is Uncle Mark coming back from sea?"

"He's only been gone a week. You miss him already? You have six months left. So, deal with it." Analyn's hard disposition softened. "I'm just going to hang out with some friends tonight. That's all."

Gabriel said nothing.

"I don't care if you believe me or not!" Analyn snapped, slamming the door.

Dupree focused on the woman's presence. Her aura dimmed in comparison to the boy's. The dark grayish tint surrounding her body repressed the light that should have existed. Writhing waves of darkness crept from the silhouette of her essence.

CHAPTER 4
EYES IN THE WALLS

PRESENT DAY: SANTA FE, NM - 1000 HOURS

Phyllis sat at her desk in the classroom, staring at the textbook sprawled in front of her. The words blurred into unintelligible grayish lines, washed out by the surrounding whiteness. A long blink interrupted the attempt at following sentences to her teacher's monotone dictation. Another moment passed with her eyelids flickering, then drooping to half-mast. Spasms churned from her neck, popping her head up from the incessant bobbing overcoming her posture.

The view of her classmates returned, seeing their backs and lowered heads turning from right to left, tracking the words from their books. A tremble formed within the corner of her cheeks, crawling its way into her shaking jaw, and quivering lips trying to fight the impending yawn.

"Psst, Philly," her neighbor whispered. "Hey, you look bad."

"I feel bad, Consuela. I can't sleep."

"You been up playing those video games all night, haven't you?"

"Yeah, Connie. But—"

"You're the best in the clan but you need to chill—"

"Excuse me, ladies!" Mrs. Croaker snapped from across the room at a wide oak desk. Her glasses dipped from the tilted frown she bounced between the two girls. Students turned, their curious gazes guided by the reprimand to Phyllis and Consuela. The duo sighed. "Now I understand that your brother's ailment has been a stressful ordeal for you, Ms. Ridgemont. Joey is a talented and kindhearted young man, a real pleasure to have in class. So, I have shown some leniency to your dozing off and yawning. But do not interrupt the learning of others. Understood?"

"Yes, Mrs. Croaker."

"Good. Now where was I..."

"Here." Consuela rifled through her backpack, handing Phyllis a cold, shining can of Ripped Power Drink.

"Oh my God, I love you. You're a lifesaver." Phyllis embraced it with both hands, keeping it low behind their fellow students, watching the attention of Mrs. Croaker. "I owe you so big for this. You're the best, Connie."

"I gotcha back. Just be sure to help me slay the Omega dungeon boss this weekend, cool?"

Phyllis nodded. Consuela paused, examining the dark heavy bags draped underneath her friend's reddening eyes. Phyllis' head dipped, until popping back up, with her lids lowering just above her sea green irises. Consuela shook her head.

"Stole them from Pedro." Consuela shrugged. "He steals them from the store he works at. So, it's kind of all justified."

"Ladies!" Mrs. Croaker barked. "Final warning!"

"Yes, ma'am!" A simultaneous response came from the two girls, burying their attentions into their textbooks.

Trembles ran through Phyllis' mouth until a slow and long yawn forced its way out. Blinking caused glimpses of darkness within long pauses, the weight of her head dipping again. A jolt of awareness brought her view back, staring at the back of the student's shoes in front of her, tracing the dirty gray footprints on the white floors, until her view went up a chair leg, then back to normal level. After Phyllis' breaths slowed, her eyelids closed away the hazy view, until the drifting sensation of slumber wrapped around her body.

"Haaaa… Yess… dea… stea… your… sss…" Unintelligible words of monotone and listless rhythm invaded her ears.

Phyllis' eyes jolted open, peering around the class sitting motionless staring ahead at Mrs. Croaker, who never looked up from her book. The teacher's voice droned on, despite her lips not moving. Graying blurs pulled Phyllis' attention to the large area of the white walls where the posters of cartoon owls and artwork of the students were no longer displayed. Croaker's head moved. Phyllis stared at the woman, who was statue-still again.

What's going on? Phyllis peered over to Consuela, seeing her friend focused straight down on her texts.

"Connie," Phyllis called out. "Something doesn't feel right."

The girl waved a hand before Consuela's face, her view remaining with an unblinking stare into the pages. Phyllis reached out, tapping her friend's shoulder. Consuela didn't move.

"Weird. Am I like dead or something?"

"Not yet," a voice answered.

A shifting silhouette of gray formed upon the wall. Shapes

and shadows converged and pressed outward, pulling the churning pale surface closer to the girl. Phyllis' vision narrowed on a forming visage with a hooked nose protruding from a tall figure. Slender feline eyes peered from the textured wall's surface, gleaming with the essence of a nocturnal predator around its thin pupils.

"Almost time, little one. Oh, the plans I have for your innocent soul."

Long fingers reached from arms stretching across the distance. The massive shoulders of the being shifted, wresting from the reality that held him away. An alarming heat rose into Phyllis' ears, gathering beads of sweat along her forehead. Youthful voices carried murmurs crescendoing around her.

"What's wrong?" A child's voice materialized and boomed around her. "What is wrong with her?"

"Wake up!" another exclaimed.

"No!" The being hissed, stepping forward with a liquidity that tugged on her view. "Stay with me, little one. Time to sleep forever."

Phyllis racked in her chair; body unable to move save for the convulsions of her legs. Desperate breaths expelled gibberish, toned with pleas and whimpers.

"I can feel your soul," it continued, rasping each word. "Why are you fighting it, Phyllis? Your kin is here with us, inside of the Pale Furnace. Can you hear him?"

A whining frequency grew, its pitch fluctuating with a resonance through her ears that pushed out from the presence. Phyllis' eyes widened as the hands gripped at her shoulders. Chills ran through her body. She hollered to the ceiling. The force grasped her, shaking harder. Heartbeats pounded in her chest with a deep drum that traveled into her hands. Her vision shook, until slow blinks ushered away the white silhouette, and there was only Mrs. Croaker looming over her.

"Phyllis!" the teacher urged. "Are you okay? Please say something!"

The girl's scream rang in Mrs. Croaker's ears. Phyllis launched from her chair, hugging her teacher. A wide-eyed Mrs. Croaker wrapped her arms around Phyllis, patting her head. Sobs came from the girl as she burrowed her face into the woman's cotton dress, her little body trembling inside Croaker's arms, leaving wet stains from spewing tears.

"Oh my!" Mrs. Croaker sighed. "It's okay. I know you've been through a lot. Phyllis, you need to go home and get some rest. I want you to head to the nurses' office. Have them check on you, then call your mother. Consuela, can you please walk her over there and make sure she's okay?"

"Yes, Mrs. Croaker."

"Good." The teacher lowered her gaze to Phyllis'. "Please get some rest. No video games. I'm not oblivious. I remember your gaming aspirations from your class journal. Ambition is good, but not at the cost of your health. Gather your things and go see Nurse Lenly."

Phyllis shook her head, apprehension settling into a wide-eyed frown.

"Young lady, this is not up to you anymore! You're in no shape to attend class. Those screams frightened us all. I'm going to call your mother tonight about this incident. Now go on to the nurses' office and not another argument out of you."

With trembling hands, Phyllis grabbed her book, then her backpack before heading to the door. She turned, seeing Consuela shuffling between the other students. Their classmates displayed a mixture of cringing grimaces, weak sympathetic smiles, and gawking. Whispers passed from leaning classmates, their mouths covered, muffling their words. Phyllis' vision went past them to the whiteness along the wall that called to her. A chill crawled down her back.

"Go on now," Mrs. Croaker urged. "I know you want to stay with the others, but sometimes we have to make decisions for your well-being."

PRESENT DAY: SANTA FE, NM - 1100 HOURS

Phyllis stared out the car window at the mesh of tan, brown, and green racing in and out of view as her mother zipped along the streets. Images of the hooked nose and glowing eyes festered in her thoughts. Echoes of the voice called to her, with its raspy tone scratching in her ears. The touch of his hands lingered on her skin with the clammy imprint of lengthy fingers permeating into her soul. Phyllis' spirit weighed on her mind, the presence of which seemed unaligned with the rest of the girl's existence.

It felt like it was pulling me away from my body...

"Mrs. Croaker texted me about your outburst, Philly," Phyllis Senior said. "You have everyone worried, kiddo."

"Mom..." the girl's voice cracked. "I'm s-scared."

The car slowed, jostling as they exited the freeway merging onto a narrowing road surrounded by two-story homes with manicured lawns. Towering trees lined the road, providing a measure of shade.

"What's going on? I know you're taking Joe-Joe's situation really hard. We all are—"

"Mom, just listen, please. I know I'm just a kid—"

"But you're smart like I was at your age. Just talk to me." Phyllis Senior caressed her daughter's cheek.

Smooth, soft tan fingers went into Philly's view. A long blink saw them turn pale white. Hard calloused skin scraped against the girl's face. Another long pause and the sway of the vehicle's travel melted away. There was no longer the cool breeze of air conditioning, nor the gentle hum of the engine. A tepid cloud of smoke-laden breath replaced the scent of strawberries from the car's air freshener. Claws extended into view as Phyllis Junior opened her eyes.

"Phyllis don't be scared," Joey called out from the beyond. *"They're our friends. I promise. Don't you go being the pussy now. Just relax and trust me."*

Joe-Joe? I can't... This isn't real...

"Time... Time... Only a matter of time... You will be ours, little one." A voice drifted into her ears. *"Joey is waiting for you."*

"We await!" another stated.

Philly screamed, filling the cabin of the vehicle with piercing shrieks as she climbed to the far corner of her seat, pressing into the door as she trembled. Her tiny hand batted away at Phyllis Senior, scratching across her mother's knuckles.

"Philly! What has gotten into you!"

The girl sobbed. "I don't want them to take me, too!"

Shining black polish from three large SUVs came into view. The vehicles were extended in length with thick tires possessing deep treads. Several individuals paced the area, dressed in long dark coats and military style boots. Phyllis Senior drove closer, spotting a woman with gray hair, and a thin wrinkled face seated in a large electronic wheelchair. The wizened lady smiled and waved at them as they approached.

Next to her was a man of Asian Pacific Islander descent, scowling and examining the other buildings. The smooth churning of mechanisms brought the car window low, with Phyllis Senior looking directly at the older woman in the middle of the squad.

"Hello, Ms. Ridgemont? My name is Madam Simone Dupree of the Department of Homeland Security, and this pleasant grump is Agent Gabriel Agapito. We need your help. May we have a word with you regarding the welfare of your son and possibly your daughter?"

Phyllis Senior sat on the loveseat adjacent to the couch with the agents. Gabriel was poised upright, his glare tracing over the big screen television across from them to the large window behind it, darting over to the fireplace, along the wall that led into the kitchen. Madam Dupree and Harland were seated next to him. The Diver team commander was at the far side with his hands folded into his lap, smiling at the woman, while the Grand Scryer positioned herself close to Gabriel, brushing with the pillowy armrest of the brown sofa.

The energies of this place are different. There's a dim frequency, radiating upon the girl and the home. I would have likely missed it, had I not been so adept with navigating the layers. Trying to key on it is difficult, it slips from the grasp of my will, outside of the conscious psionic measure. There are tingles upon my back like spider legs, gentle and subtle, but with an ominous aura.

"First, let me start by saying thank you for allowing us into your home and cooperating with our investigation, Captain Ridgemont," Madam Dupree announced.

"Wow, you people really did your homework," Phyllis Senior replied. "So, you already know I was a captain in the Army. I try to leave that chapter of my life in the past."

"I understand. It hurts. That wound will never heal and understandably so. Your husband was a good man."

"How did you—"

"That's not what's important. As much as I would love to engage in casual chat with a woman of your caliber and experience, we aren't here to talk with you."

"Oh, then why the federal shakedown and intimidation?"

"I apologize if we seem heavy-handed. But these measures aren't for you. On the contrary, it's to protect you and the other innocent lives within the neighborhood. But we are actually here to interview little Phyllis."

The girl remained quiet. Deep breaths climbed with her heart rate.

"You're making my daughter nervous," Phyllis Senior replied.

"You are mistaken, Ms. Ridgemont. It's not us that she's afraid of. Is it, Philly?"

"No, ma'am," the girl replied. "I keep seeing them."

"Who?" Phyllis Senior demanded. "What's going on? Please talk to me."

"I don't want anyone to think I'm crazy and take me away. I've seen what happens on TV to people who get labeled crazy." Phyllis Junior's reddening eyes swelled with tears.

"You're not crazy," Madam Dupree assured. "Try me, sweetie. Just close your eyes and relax. Let me see—"

"No!" Phyllis screamed, her mother put an arm around her,

pulling the girl close. "No, ma'am... I can't close my eyes. I'll fall asleep..."

"I understand. Your spirit seems weary, little one. How long have you been without rest?"

"A week and a half, ma'am. Every time I close my... I see them. Tall... pale... cat eyes..."

Madam Dupree reached out with her willpower to the waning energies that comprised Phyllis Junior. The weight of weariness locked heavy on her limbs, gripping at her face, pulling her head downward. Zaps of adrenaline spiked through her with a racing heartbeat each time she caught herself bobbing and blinking. Hazes of gray emerged, clouding moments of her vision that sprang back to reality with waking gasps.

Memories of the girl's week played within Dupree's psyche. A baseball field appeared, its grass shining in the bright afternoon sunlight. Rushing colors and speeding images brought Madam Dupree back to the girl's home. Sweetness hovered in the air with a warm aroma rising from the stove.

That itch is looming with the hint of something more. But where? Think, Simone... It's here. I can feel it. Guide me, Great One. Help me defend this innocent life. Reveal to me the intentions of our opposition.

Flashing images of gunfire and monsters played along a computer screen, with girls sharing giggles over headset communications. Within the unlit halls of the second story a man walked. Long black feathers lined the cowhide band tight around his head. Heavy wrinkles stretched underneath it as he grimaced from an immersion of shadows. The intruder reached for the sleeping Joey.

A presence traversing the layers. Not the usual pesky ghost or little nasty. I sense the breath of life within this one. Madam Dupree pondered.

Veins stretched along an arm reaching for the boy. Heavy graying callouses lined from the crevices of his thin fingers, inches away from Joey's forehead. The man rose upright, speeding from the limits of the home's frequency, his large frame whisked away in hovering motion, howling with a deep voice of lamentation.

Madam Dupree guided her sight to another bedroom. The currents of time raced around her. Sunlight drew from the darkness until it set again with the return of night. Mother and daughter walked through the home, paramedics passing them, rushing Joey away. Red-faced and watery-eyed, Philly crumpled in the hallway outside his door, bawling into her palms.

The days passed, until the night's darkness contrasted with the light of the computer monitor in Philly's room. Shadows boiled along the uneven surface of the room's paint, along the areas untouched by the posters of gun wielding heroes and boy bands. Motions peeled from the unseen, writhing over the opaque wall ornaments. A ringing grew, continuing in a dull sequence until it drowned away Philly's heaving gasps.

Eyelids opened along the walls, with feral unblinking gazes staring back at the girl as she trembled underneath the sheets. Her hands convulsed, gripping the blanket to pull over her head. Heavy breaths flowed against her with a tepid caress, drawing closer from all directions, brushing against the thin shield of material. Their unwholesome intent carried with the escalation of tooth filled panting. Loud pops and snaps faded in and out as writhing white light reached the height of the ceiling. Whimpers and cries echoed through the walls, drowned away by the sinister laughter of a woman in the distance.

A woman's presence? Dupree pushed outward, the vision slipping from the grasp of her will. *That type of power... Never have I felt something like that from a scryer, let alone an uninitiated human being. She cut me off with little effort. But how?* Dupree's reach went through the girl, her essence vanishing from the ether. *I see her in the material, but I cannot commune with her anymore upon the etheric layers... She's slipping away. What is this?*

Philly screamed, bouncing from the sofa, and swaying as she walked over to Gabriel. The agent rose catching the staggering girl before her balance gave. The weariness of her eyes met his. Streams poured from her tear ducts with rapid abandon. Philly buried her head into the agent, his grim disposition melting during their embrace. The small, soaked face looked up to him with the gleam of wetness over shaking eyes.

"Help me, sir... Please." Philly begged. "I can't... much longer..."

CHAPTER 5
BREADCRUMBS IN THE DARK

16 YEARS AGO: NAVAL MILITARY HOUSING

Screaming jolted young Gabriel awake. His eyes popped open, staring at the dark gray ceiling of his bedroom while he took in cold breaths from the night air. Red letters of his alarm clock read '1:00 AM' from his small wooden nightstand. The coiled tension of his neck released, allowing him to melt back into his pillow.

Another nightmare...

Another cry rang throughout the house, climbing up the stairs from the living room, where it echoed into the hallway. Haggard shrieks of desperation mixed with the shrill cry of a voracious beast, growing deeper with each successive outburst. The woman's presence faded from the sound, her feminine cries melting into growls that passed through salivating and clamped teeth.

I know that sound...

Gabriel rose from his bed, stepping quietly with his bare feet over the frigid floor. Shivers rose into his thin frame as he cracked open his door to be greeted by the rise of another wail, ending with the gasp of Aunt Analyn.

Tiya Ana! It's got Tiya Ana! No! How is it here in the States?

Smooth and quiet steps brought the boy down the staircase where he crouched in the middle, gazing over the wooden beam, through the archway that led into the kitchen. Rapid movements carried across the floor, pounding from the dinette to the other side of the main partition, through the entrance leading into the living room.

Gabriel scampered over to the kitchen, dropping low behind the fridge, next to where the two areas of the house connected. Heaving breaths arose, each exhalation increasing with unwholesome fervor. Loud groans morphed into sobs. Gabriel leaned over to peer from behind cover, stopping once warm wetness squished underneath his soles. Warmth rose from the blood pool he stood within. The boy's sight followed a red trail of handprints and deep gashes that left splinters of debris from where long fingers had dug into the tiled floor.

I'm too late! It got her, too!

The boy covered his mouth, holding inside the deep gasp that wanted to escape. The quake of his heart drummed into his hands and grimacing face. The pulse of fear resounded from his chest, coursing through every fiber until reaching his cold fingertips and resonating from emerging goosebumps.

Howling sobs came from the living room by the sliding glass door leading out to the backyard. Gabriel peered out, seeing his aunt by the long white blinds over the back entrance. Analyn was upon her knees, a long rip carried up the side of her skirt, while the outfit's thin red top was wedged underneath her ample breasts. Blood soaked over her hands that possessed elongated fingers ending in sharp nails a quarter meter long.

Tears flowed down the side of Analyn's face, mixing with the red smears of gore that stained her mouth and cheeks. Her disheveled hair stuck to the rest of the macabre tapestry of vital fluid spotted across her shoulders. The woman's enlarged, shining black eyes looked up, connecting with the quivering Gabriel.

"Gabe!" she cried, before wincing. Analyn leaned over. Her head rose, releasing a long groan as her arms clamped around herself. "Hurts so much! I killed him... Gabe! I didn't have control... Help me!"

"What did you do, Tiya?"

The woman's gaze pulled away from the boy. Her lips came together in a frown. "I messed up. I was tricked."

"Who tricked you?"

"It betrayed me. Said that a little bit of its blood would make me pretty again, young again, if I put it in the elixir..."

"You made a deal with the manananggal? The same one that killed my parents?"

"It wasn't supposed to happen like that. She was just supposed to eat the fetus, leave the three of you be! I swear! I just wanted a second chance... I wasted my youth being a party girl... Then no man wanted to marry me when my looks were gone... It wasn't fair that Alma had your father! I had no one!" Screams expelled from the woman. She keeled over to the side. "Help... me... Please!"

"Tiya... I don't know what to do..."

Analyn sobbed, until her face morphed into a bestial grimace. Her wails of agony reignited. Her torso pulled upward, stretching the skin of her abdomen. Ligament and bone gave, snapping and popping as the woman's cries grew ever louder. Flesh ripped like fabric. Gaping tears lined her waist, extending as the rest of her body continued pulling away. Churning yellow fluid poured out, mixing with blood that streamed from the wounds. A small burst separated Analyn's spine, sticking upward with the strands of intestines and innards that seeped across the ground between the two halves.

She crawled forward, beating at the floor with her palms. Sharp nails dug deep into the ground, scratching with each desperate pull. Remnants of her interiors strewn before Gabriel festered and sizzled, melting into stains of pink and white that dissolved into a stinking foam. Grumbles rose from Analyn, her breaths growing heavier, shifting from lamentation to primal fury. She turned away, facing the thin images of the moon between the swaying blinds.

"Tiya Ana?"

The head of his aunt turned to him, grinding bone and meat as muscles brought Analyn's snarling visage staring behind her back. A roar bellowed from her fang filled mouth, where a long, black tongue slithered from a gash beneath her chin. The fiend stormed forward, smashing through the sliding glass door, sending debris jettisoning through the area. Gabriel covered his face, only to turn back moments later, finding nothing. The boy stared out into the night sky, shivering as bellows of hungering death ascended to the clouds.

PRESENT DAY: SANTA FE, NM - 1200 HOURS

Alexa Gray's fingers rummaged through an open wooden chest filled with shining hunks of raw quartz. The agent knelt over to place them around the bed in a circle. Alexa slipped another piece underneath the pillow, before turning to Madam Dupree seated beside the computer desk, nodding.

"Very good, Alexa," the Grand Scryer announced. "I can already feel it working. This room seems to be a major force for the conflicting energies I am sensing." Pops of gunfire and monstrous screams followed flashing lights and the chomping jaws of big red monsters over the computer monitor. "Oh my!"

"I'm sorry, Madam Dupree," Phyllis Senior said, rushing from the doorway, past Gabriel who held hands with Philly by the foot of the bed. "I'll turn off this ruckus."

"That won't be necessary, dear. It just caught me by surprise. During my youth, I read books and painted. I guess this generation has entertainment that's a bit more—engaging."

"It's just a screen saver," Gabriel noted.

"Yeah, it came free with the game," Philly added.

"Well, let's get on with it. Harland, would you like to do the honors?" Madam Dupree asked.

"Yes, ma'am. Quartz is a special crystal, capable of neutralizing negative energies—"

"The curtain of evil is being opened," Madam Dupree said, with Alexa nodding.

"We want Phyllis Junior to lie down and try to sleep with the crystals around—"

"No!" the girl cried out. "I can't!"

"Trust, little one. Agent Agapito, she seems to have faith in you, despite your perpetually dour disposition. Please try to negotiate with her about our process."

Gabriel took a knee, his face softening with a smile, looking into Philly's widened eyes. "It'll be fine. I promise. They may seem like an odd bunch, but they have an understanding of these things. Especially the old one."

"Well," Madam Dupree scoffed. "I prefer the term seasoned to old."

"I have a daughter, same age as you, with that same intelligent sharpness in her eyes. You're strong, Phyllis. Most adults wouldn't have the discipline to survive this. I'm going to need you to trust us, okay?"

Philly nodded. "Okay..."

The agent guided the girl to her bed. He stepped back as she kicked off her sneakers and settled underneath the sheets. Her head dropped back to rest on the pillow, where she gazed past the motionless fan with its long wooden blades, to the ceiling turning gray with the shadows that came after the lights were clicked off.

"You have a way with children," Madam Dupree whispered to Gabriel. "They can sense you are one of them."

"And what the hell is that supposed to mean," Gabriel paused. "Ma'am?"

"I rest my case," Madam Dupree quipped.

The Grand Scryer's lips closed, her face turning into a stony frown with eyes narrowing to pinpoint focus. The mind's perception carried her view through the levels of energy that hovered within the frequencies of the etheric layers. Negative and positive churned like oceans upon oceans, their waves flowing into her reach, sifting through the familiar world in the beyond. Attention went outside the immediate area to the regions of energy on the cusp of material and etheric, where the universal unconscious existed.

Why have I been guided here? This is but the level where the mind goes in dreaming, when tapping into the levels of consciousness outside of the cognitive process.

Passing currents rushed around Dupree, swaying the scryer as she traversed deeper, pushing back against the resistance.

It's so strong here. This is one of the resting frequencies, into the dimension of the dreamscape where we all go to slumber. But this hidden area is saturated to the brim in ruinous powers. A sliver of darkness among the ocean of the spiritual realm. This thin opening in the veil would be easy to miss, had the loving universal authority not guided me. How did it accumulate such force?

Rippling shadows underneath the curtain of reality formed a narrow path, ending with a thin black split between the worlds.

A doorway to another realm, where one can travel.

Steps carried her forward. The darkness encompassed her vision. Streams of energy poured into the realm from the material plane, feeding it with an expanding presence as a subtle undercurrent between the fabric of reality. Madam Dupree blinked, her eyelids beginning to weigh heavily as weariness clouded her spirit.

These are the same delta waves utilized during slumber. I should not be feeling this presence while conscious. It wanes my focus. My mind wants to set adrift despite the shadows that surround me.

Yellow glowing eyes popped open in the darkness, fixating on the scryer. Madam Dupree reached for the presence, her focus and intent slipping through the muck and grasping nothing. A grin flashed into view below the unblinking gaze narrowing with ferocity. The large maw of sharp teeth curved and pointed in all directions, their bladelike edges ending with points stretching into the unseen regions where the rest of its countenance should have appeared.

"Oh, curious to see, a soul arrives to the party without an invitation from the Queen." The visage spoke without movement, possessing a melodious tempo carried by a relaxed drawl. "Talented, you may be. I'm afraid you're quite out of your depth diving here, but I won't be mean."

"You're no demon. What are you?" the Grand Scryer demanded.

"Am I not? Oh, the names, the labels, the ideas that never rung. So many over the millenniums, yet I prefer the first tongue."

"Which is?"

"You should be going now, little one. Your gift won't be enough to protect you here. So far away from the world you know, with its open sea." The eyes gave a slow blink. "Not sure what fuels your journey. The others washed upon the shore, while there were those who smoked the cactus, and the ones that drank the tea."

"Peyote and Ayahuasca."

"If that's the name you call it up there. Your labels serve the purpose of grounding the rationale, which is why you strive for it, rather than just knowing the truth at last. Until your consciousness adapts, I'm afraid I cannot let you pass."

"Why?"

"Because you remind me of someone I once met. A delightful young lady with a gift like yours, save the poor thing couldn't control it, and wandered until luck released the vise's grip on her mind. She remembered me as I was and not like the rest of my kind."

"That didn't answer my question."

"There are things worse than death, little one. And that you will find beyond the door."

"And what about those that washed upon the shore?"

Cackles of delight resounded through the area.

Dupree smirked at the being and nodded. "Very clever, you roped me into that rhyme."

"Exactly as it seems, Diver. You know the waters and how they change. The spills that pollute it and endanger all. It's not far, just within range."

"That metaphor! That's the answer! Thank you."

"You should be going."

Lips pulled away, revealing more teeth, and stretching the grin. His eyes and mouth closed, leaving only the empty darkness before the Grand Scryer.

That was interesting.

When Madam Dupree's vision of the material realm peeled open, the blurred faces of Gabriel and Harlan peered in front of her. She nodded to the agents, who sighed with relief. The Grand Scryer extended her will, sifting through the frequencies once again. The crystals had banished the undercurrent of darkness from around them, save for the pulse coming from the small speakers on the computer desk.

Whirring motors brought Madam Dupree around, facing the wooden furniture structure with its three levels. The Grand Scryer's narrowing countenance shot upon the lower deck where the keyboard sat, up to the monitor blaring with images of a squealing, chubby monster flailing while being shot in the forehead. Triumphant soldiers raced over its corpse. Bright flashes of yellow and white flared from the screen as guns roared from the troops again.

Machine gun fire resounded through two speakers, resting on the top level above the monitor. Madam Dupree focused on the throbbing instruments as more noise reverberated through. The undercurrent flowed, carrying the frequency of the veil. Where it went, the energies lingered, festering between the material realm and etheric layers with its presence blending amongst them.

"There you are," Madam Dupree announced.

"Ma'am?" Gabriel asked.

The Grand Scryer pointed to the waste basket near the desk. Gabriel pulled out the black video game box. The side of it read 'Sons of the Apocalypse' in fiery letters, pronounced from the rest of the cardboard package. Along the bottom was a small square logo of a white rabbit with a black pocket watch centered on it. 'Partridge Games' sandwiched the entire emblem with bold print.

"I found the source of how the children are being abducted. This video game. We need to expand the investigation. I'm heading back to base to speak with Kat. We're going to need more resources and intel for the task force. I want Diver and Butcher teams to continue with our investigation. This situation goes deeper, and not just in the etheric layers. Mortal operatives are working with the other side."

"Acknowledged, ma'am," Harland replied.

Gabriel's view shifted to the corner, where Diver Team's commander stood on his flank.

"I trust there aren't going to be any issues with you two playing nicely?"

"No, ma'am," Gabriel answered. "Protecting the children, and neutralizing the vectors are my only priority."

"A good sentiment to have, Agent Agapito. Agent Gray, I want Diver doing a communion with me downstairs so I can transfer what I've learned. Sadly, we're going to have to wake the little one here and ask her if she has any friends who share the same enthusiasm for this game. I'll let you two coordinate that. Tonight, you set the trap."

CHAPTER 6
SHADOWS AMIDST THE CIVIL WAR

PRESENT DAY: SANTA FE, NM - 1500 HOURS

Alexa and Harland sat upright on one side of the vast maroon sectional, encompassing the living room. A glare shot from the New Mexico sun, reflecting from the unused television screen, shining over Gabriel's face as he squinted next to them. Their boots remained firm on the tanned carpet floor, while he leaned in with a smile to the little girl who was flanked by her parents.

Consuela smiled back and nodded, brimming with confidence and wide eyed eagerness. Her father, Tito, kept his chubby arm around the girl while scrutinizing the agents from behind his thick prescription lenses. Beads of sweat gathered along the sides of his head, lighter than the rest of his golden complexion due to a fresh faded haircut.

Tito cleared his throat, looking over to Blanka. The woman's bob cut wobbled in unison when she shook her head with doubt. Her pale complexion was lined with wrinkles that riddled her forehead and mouth when she frowned. Next to his wife was her mother, a shorter, graying version of the woman with long strands of hair and a thick red cotton coat. The matriarch sat hunched with occasional glances at her family, shaking her head in disapproval.

"Mama," Consuela pleaded between her parents. "I want to do this. Please. You didn't see Philly today. I believe them. Something is trying to hurt her. She's my bestie, like a sister. She's family. I have to try to help."

Tito nodded, tightening his arm around Consuela, and placing a kiss on top of her head.

"You are so brave." Alexa smiled. "We commend you for making this decision to assist us."

"For obvious reasons, we cannot use Philly as bait," Harland replied. "The girl's current state of fear will make her more susceptible to the dangers of the other side."

Alexa nudged Harland with her elbow.

"What he means to say is that there's a certain state of mind one must be in to ensure a better outcome," Alexa explained. "We believe that Connie's courage and great attitude will be exactly what is needed to assist us with apprehending these vectors."

"Vectors?" Tito asked.

"A nomenclature used for entities without a nephesh," Harland replied.

"A what?" Blanka's frown deepened. "What is that?"

"What he meant to say was it's the word we use for those we are apprehending," Alexa continued.

"I can do this," Consuela said.

"We believe so too," Alexa replied. "The sound on your screen saver will be turned up to permeate more of the frequency through your room. All of us have varying levels of resistance to the arcane. We believe that there's a certain degree of exposure required to be enticing to these vectors. Diver Team will be with you every step of the way. My husband and I, and our second will be upstairs with you in the etheric layers. The rest of our team will be downstairs monitoring for any other incursions."

"My team will be serving as a physical outer cordon," Gabriel interrupted. "The Ridgemonts reported an unsavory individual who appeared during the last unfortunate event. I promise that if he shows up at your house, we will apprehend him immediately and with extreme prejudice."

"I like this guy," Tito said. "Okay, knowing that kinda sets my mind at ease."

"I promise no harm will come to your daughter, sir," Gabriel added. "We'll be hiding among the bushes around your house, waiting."

"See." Consuela bobbed with glee. "We got this!"

Tito nodded.

"Okay," Blanka agreed. "This is my little girl. I don't know what I would do without her. I know there are other mothers suffering out there. So, we will help you."

"Excellent, ma'am," Alexa said. "First thing, understand that being in the dream state is another form of the etheric layers. Your mind and spirit create and project itself into an alternate dimension of existence. These frequencies blur the lines between those countless dimensions. So, when you sleep tonight, it'll feel like any other dream, but with the frequencies being used, you'll draw closer to the vectors. Remember, in a dream anything is possible. You need only have the willpower to project your desires. That is easier said than done. Fear cripples that, which is what these vectors like to prey upon. Being such a brave girl, I know you'll do just fine."

"Okay." Consuela nodded. "I think I can do this!"

"With that said, I'll inform the rest of the team and start the preparations for the ambush." Gabriel stood up from the couch, shaking hands with the parents. "Thank you again for your cooperation, sir and ma'am."

PRESENT DAY: SANTA FE, NM - 2300 HOURS

Night fell upon the neighborhood, bringing forth a cool breeze. Gabriel and Mara kneeled behind a row of bushes, across an adjacent neighbor's front yard overlooking Consuela's home. They snapped their PNVG-18 panoramic night vision goggles to the rhino connections that extended from the front of their helms, rotating the arms down into place. Moonlight shone over the row of four bluish lenses, bringing a wide field of view into their eyes. The devices gave faint hums when activated, hugging the agents' faces with rubber seals. Green illuminated their view, outlining everything they beheld with a clear and concise image.

They shifted upon their kneepads, their boots scraping across the soil. Mara nodded when she repositioned, tucking her M4 carbine deep into her shoulder, keeping the movable buttstock on its innermost setting so the weapon remained compacted. Gabriel peered through breaks between the leaves and branches, staring up to the window at the second story belonging to Consuela.

"All Butcher elements, this is Butcher Actual." Gabriel spoke into his communication bud that cupped over his ear, extending from the rim of his helm, and across his cheek. "Status check. Over."

"Butcher10Actual this is Butcher10Golf." Leo's deep voice came over comms. "We read you, Lima Charlie. Sweet Pea and I are set along the backyard. Over."

"Butcher10Sierra, status check. Over?" Gabriel asked. "Are you with us?"

A few seconds passed.

"Butcher10Actual this is Butcher10Golf," Leo replied. "Butcher10Sierra is performing security with the vehicles. Probably can't answer because he's dehydrated and incapacitated from watching Pornhub, again. Over."

"Fuck you, Leo!" Kevin's voice snapped over a quick transmission. "Butcher10Actual, this is Butcher10Sierra. Comms cut out. I have eyes on a dark figure moving along the front side of a neighbor's house. He's passed by me and creeping along the shrubbery."

Gabriel scanned the frontside of Consuela's home. A tall figure cloaked in shadow drifted past the trees and bushes. The broad-shouldered silhouette stepped through a surrounding rock garden lining the front without a sound. He peered into a wide window leading into the living room, before crouching beneath the sill and walking past it.

"We got eyes on the vector, Butcher," Gabriel replied.

Mara raised her carbine's barrel, bringing the dark feathered figure into sight alignment with the glowing red reticle of her holographic close quarters optic.

Gabriel placed a hand on Mara, who broke sight picture to acknowledge her team leader.

"Not yet," Gabriel whispered. "Let's see what happens first and get positive confirmation and try to subdue him at a closer range. I don't want to risk endangering any civilians."

"Roger, Actual," Mara agreed. "Good call. What do you think?"

"It's a fucking sorcerer," Gabriel replied. "At least that's what my instincts are telling me."

"Son of a bitch..." Mara's lips peeled back into a snarl.

Gabriel patted her shoulder.

Fluttering wings stole their attention, and they followed a large raven cawing and landing upon a towering tree in the front yard, planted among a square of soil in the rock garden. Sprinklers rose from the ground, spewing arcs of water across the bushes and trees. Gabriel's attention turned back to the vector as it slipped around the corner heading behind the house.

"Butcher10Golf," Gabriel called out. "We have eyes on the vector heading your way. Butcher10Sierra, fall in on us. We move in silence behind him. Do not open fire until I give the order. Let's try to subdue this fucker without terrifying the whole neighborhood."

"Roger, Actual."

Gabriel and Mara stepped out from behind their cover, jogging across the street, with Kevin catching up to them.

Consuela's dark brown hair gathered in a cluster behind her neck as she lay in her bed. The girl brought the blanket high, covering her head. Consuela remained on her side, her heartbeat quickening. A fog of weariness sent her vision fading in and out. Her gaze traced over a K-pop poster immersed in shadow. Moonlight escaped into her room, finding the glistening sheen of another poster with a masked blue and gold Luchador. Her focus settled upon the open laptop resting on a small glass desk as the screen saver blared to life.

Eyelids lowered, heralding the blurred haze of weariness and the drifting sensations carrying her thoughts to slumber. Tension left Consuela's shoulders, releasing the grip on her neck. Her head sank deeper into the pillow's softness. A moment of darkness flooded through her perception, before returning to a view of the room.

The dark figure raced down the empty dog run leading into the vast backyard with a tall wooden fence. His attention skipped over the bulky white shed with its cracked door, past the large stone-walled barbecue with its silvery lid and black handles. He peered up to the second story.

The raven cawed overhead, landing on the roof and peering down at the sorcerer, who nodded up to the creature.

The tall sorcerer tossed his long hair back over the black feathered tunic. He brushed through the raven-plumed headdress, stroking the feathers together while lowering into a cross-legged position. With a deep breath, the man placed both hands on his thighs, bringing the tips of his thumb and index fingers together. Darkness consumed his vision from lowering eyelids. His willpower projected forward, propelling a spiritual copy of himself through the sliding glass door of the house, where he whisked past the parents asleep on the sofa with the television running infomercials. Churning energies called to him from the screen saver's frequency, blasting through the second floor from speakers at maximum output. Ripples of darkness churned through the sorcerer's vision, terraforming the upper level into an unwholesome presence, running goosebumps over his skin. The sorcerer continued up the stairs, wading through the negative frequencies toward Consuela's room.

Miniscule red dots lined Consuela's perspective, moving with a slow drifting current through the vicinity. An obscure figure loomed within the corner of her eye. Cold gripped her back, leaving her legs and arms listless against the desire to curl deeper into the blanket's protection. The silhouette stepped closer, yellow gleamed from its eyes piercing through shadows and the distortion of its tall outline.

"Connn-nnnie," a rasping voice called between clamped teeth. Each syllable surged chills down her spine. "We have been watching. We have been waiting for the moment to invite you. I can sense your resistance. You need not be afraid. Joey and Phyllis are with us. Don't you want to join your friends? The games and fun are endless on the other side. We promise. And we never lie."

Shudders traveled through the girl's back. Consuela's heart raced from an unseen grasp holding steadfast to her trembling body. Pressure grew within her chest, rising into a throat lump that would not swallow away.

Black fog expelled through the room, enveloping the girl. A long whispering hiss rushed over Consuela. The presence vanished from her peripheral vision, along with the pressure from its ominous gaze. Her limbs pulled inward, curling into herself once the paralysis lifted. By the closed door stood a taller figure. Black feathers rose around its crown, above murky eyes that narrowed on Consuela.

Noiseless steps brought the presence closer, its towering dark visage brushing the ceiling with its dark plumes. Goosebumps rose high on her golden brown skin. Tremors ran through the girl's frame, vibrating into the blanket clutched within her fists. It stood before Consuela's view, revealing a raven standing upon one of its wide shoulders.

The bird leaned over, cawing with a thrust of its head.

A gasp escaped the girl. She rounded into a face scrunching fetal position. Her body convulsed, rattling through the mattress and into the creaking frame. A long arm reached from the figure of shadows, its black talons opening wide, the sharp hooked lengths drawing near as Consuela buried her vision into the pillow.

"Come with us!" the being demanded in a monotone voice. "Before they return with him. Do not resist for your sake."

"No!" Consuela screamed.

The bedroom door opened, slamming against an adjacent wall. Agents poured into the room, their boots clapping over the wood floors. Crisp black, gray, and white fatigues ruffled with their fast movements, as they formed a perimeter. Silvery auras of light surrounded their presence, pushing back against the frequency of darkness that permeated the room.

Its presence floats through the dreamscape with such ease. This is far different from the universal conscious layers. Had we not been poised and ready, it could've slipped by.

"No sudden movements, vector!" Harland ordered. "Or we'll toast you!"

Black wings flapped in fury as the raven squawked in outrage.

"Calm your familiar!" Alexa demanded.

"Cease this!" the being replied. "You are making a grave miscalculation!"

"No, buddy," Patel snapped. "You made the miscalculation!"

Light channeled inside of their balling grasps, crackling with the growing presence of bright energies. Consuela peeked over her blanket, seeing the specter turning to the agents, its cold stare locked on Harland as its head shook with doubt.

"Begone! I do not wish to harm you," the being retorted.

Flashes of light brought positive energy channeling from their grip, streaming through the shadowy being, where it arced into the etheric layers of the bedroom wall. They paused, their foe looking where the psionic attacks entered its large frame and passed. Big dark eyes stared back at the agents, motionless save for the ripples forming the outline of its presence.

The positive energies went through without effect. But how? We toasted demons during training with those. Had them withered and crying. Now nothing? Think, Harland...

"What the hell happened?" Alexa queried. "Those attacks did nothing!"

"One more go!" Patel barked.

The being shifted its massive frame, reaching out with the back of its long hand extending until it crashed against the side of Patel's head. The agent screamed, his presence blowing through the door until catching himself. The Grays turned, reaching for their teammate whose body flailed into the unlit hallway, pulled by a torrent of unseen power. Veins rose through Patel's forehead and neck, his face grimacing through the pressure.

"As I suspected," the vector said. "No experience within the confines of the sand. You amateurs are out of your element."

This practitioner is powerful! But why is it just toying with us?

Harland looked back to see the figure turning to Consuela. The raven screeched. Its master reached for the girl.

Gabriel crept down the dog run that opened into the backyard, maintaining a bend in his knees, with his chest protruding and shoulders squared, keeping the plate on his vest forward. His arms held tight to the M4 carbine locking into his right shoulder, with the infrared laser from the PEQ14 mounted on the barrel of his weapon guiding the way. The agent slowed his approach when arriving at the building's corner. Mara came close to him, the toes of her boot touching the heel of his own, while her attention shot over his shoulder, to the open field now at his flank.

Kevin brought his boot to touch Mara's, before turning his weapon sights upon the dog run, covering their rear.

Gabriel canted his body, maintaining a vertical line of cover with the building's corner, giving only a sliver of his profile as his view expanded, side-stepping to pie open his line of sight. The backyard came into view, seeing the shed with its cracked open door. Dual beacons of infrared light pulsed within the darkness of the fixture, signaling that Leo and Portia were hiding inside. Leo's lens peered out from the darkness, locking on Gabriel, before turning his sights toward a skittering in his periphery.

Gabriel inched over, opening his view of the area.

The sorcerer sat cross-legged on the grass outside of the light that emanated from the living room and draped within the night that blended with his outfit. Gabriel's reticle hovered over the practitioner, zeroing in on his torso. With his weapon barrel trained on the quarry, Gabriel stepped out from behind the corner, his team followed as he closed upon the sorcerer.

The shed door burst open with Leo aiming his M249 Squad Assault Weapon Light Machine Gun at the target. Portia trailed, carrying her M4 low and at the ready.

"Cease your channeling now, vector!" Gabriel ordered. "Raise your hands and do not make any sudden movements! Mara, search this fucker for any small arms or magickal implements."

"Roger, Actual." Mara shouldered her carbine. "Get on the floor with your hands out in front of you."

The sorcerer remained seated, his eyelids twitching with wild fervor.

"Son of bitch is still channeling!" Gabriel barked.

"Gotta hand it to these evil muthafuckas, man." Leo shrugged. "They're a determined lot. They never go easy, do they?"

"It's over!" Portia demanded of the sorcerer. "Leave that little girl alone and surrender!"

"Fuck this asshole..." Mara unholstered her M1911.45 caliber pistol, while Gabriel shouldered his M4 and balled his fists within resin armored gloves.

Mara cracked the solid metal frame of the sidearm across the sorcerer's head, sending him toppling over. Blood spilled from a nasty gash, pouring out and drenching his matted hair.

The man remained with his eyes closed, twitching despite hanging on to his focus.

"You must come with me, Consuela. I will show you a world where you can go outside of these confines."

"No!" Consuela screamed to the ceiling.

The dark entity withdrew its hand. Writhing shadows forming its presence peeled along the outer layers. Flakes of blackness drifted away, floating to the ground where they dissipated. The raven's screech resounded throughout the room. He flapped his wings, locking on Consuela with a firm glare.

"No!" A roar exploded through the room. "This cannot be! Interrupters are here! I haven't finished my work! Must protect the—"

Protect? Harland wondered.

Thudding strikes and scuffling echoed throughout. Shuddering ripples channeled from its body until the entity keeled over. The raven launched into flight, crashing through the window. Shards of glass rained upon the front yard, as the bird rose into the stars, flying away from the dream.

"Want another, fiend?" Gabriel's voice quaked through the room, shaking the foundations of the dream's layer.

"That's Agent Agapito!" Harland noted. "He must've found the sorcerer's physical body."

"You think I'm playing with you? I said cease your channeling, sorcerer!"

Another thudding strike reverberated throughout. The

cock of a pistol's upper receiver followed by the sliding of metal and the click of a round chambering into place. Ripples pushed through reality, peeling the being from their sight. The three agents plopped to the ground as the forceful current ended.

"Nice! Score one for the good guys!" Alexa smiled.

"I'm not so sure about that," Harland murmured.

"What do you mean?"

"The light passed through without harming the vector. And it mentioned protecting someone. Think about it."

"Not sure if you noticed, but it almost blew me into next Tuesday, Actual," Patel quipped.

"It obviously has exponentially more experience in the dreamscape than us," Harland noted. "Why not just kill us if it was that powerful?"

"Good point, my love."

"We need to stop Butcher. I think they're making a dire mistake."

Blood streamed down the native man's stern face, gushing from his broken nose, doubling in size from swelling. Droplets of red fell from the rim of his busted lip. He scowled at the surrounding agents.

Gabriel threw another punch. Knuckles crashed against the man's skin, digging deep with a hammering impact. The sorcerer toppled over, his crown of black feathers skipping across the back patio, rolling into the grass. Groaning, the man gazed up from wild strands of black hair, finding only the unyielding glower of Butcher's leader.

The others gathered around, their lips twitching with the rest of their sullen dispositions. Narrowing eyes beamed into the man with rays of hate.

There it is again... The manananggal's roar... And now my mother's cries... My sweet, kind, gentle, Ina... Footsteps pounded in Gabriel's thoughts. Whimpers and heavy breaths conjured from memories of his escape as a boy. His mother's shrill cries for mercy hounded behind him, growing more haggard and extended as the initial shock wore from her predicament.

Up for two days straight hunting this bastard. Adrenaline surged through his body, renewing the vigor of weary limbs with powerful tension. Aching faded from his knuckles. Gabriel stared into the dark watery eyes of his quarry, sadness and fear morphed into trembling ire. Lamentation moistened over his eyes.

"I told you to stop channeling!" Gabriel ordered. "Stop focusing! Stop exerting your will, and using your cursed powers, or else I'm going to start by breaking your ribs!"

"Break'em!" Leo urged, his M249 machine gun bobbing in his grip. "Dude's got a lot of sass in him, Gabe. Fuck him up!"

Kevin nodded, slinging his M16A4 with its ACOG scope around his back, then crossing his arms. "This should've been my tango. It's fine. I'm enjoying the show. But I get the next one, Actual."

Mara raised her M1911.45 caliber pistol, lining the weapon to the practitioner's chest. "Make a move, scumbag. Please resist so we can just call it an early night."

"Oooh!" Portia squirmed. Her thick medical pack with its red crosses bobbled behind her small frame. "This is the part I hate the most!"

"Not me." Leo shared a shrug with Kevin. "Dude likes hurting kids. He had this coming."

"Why are these sorcerers always such shitbags?" Kevin asked. "The one Ghost Team was tracking was also doing some unspeakable fucked up things."

The two shrugged again.

"Lemme get a pinch of your dip, Kev?" Leo asked.

"Nah, big guy." Kevin shook his head walking up beside Leo. "Used up my stash on vehicle guard."

"You better not be holding out."

"I'd never shit ya." Kevin smirked. "You're my favorite turd."

Leo's eyes narrowed on the designated team marksman before they chuckled.

Blood and saliva spat from the sorcerer's mouth, carrying words of heaving desperation. "You are misguided. I must—"

Gabriel climbed on top of the man. Rocky knuckles of his fists drove loads of crushing blows upon the sorcerer. A hook snapped his head to the left, followed by a hard right cross that bounced his skull on the dirt. Gabriel raised his trembling fists overhead, baring teeth, raining down swift hammering strikes, leaving the sorcerer wilted. "I said shut the fuck up!"

The agent flipped the man on his stomach, grabbing his arms. After a few clicks of steel notches, metal cuffs secured the sorcerer's wrists behind his lower back. Mara stepped close, delivering a skull jarring kick to the man's dome, splattering droplets of blood across the grass, and stretching to the patio. A red river snaked out from underneath the sorcerer's face, slithering through the grass. Gasping cries were the only movement from his limp frame.

"That's for all the children you terrorized, you son of a bitch," Mara snapped.

Gabriel and his second shared a nod.

"Stand down, Butcher!" Harland rushed through the opened sliding door, with Diver Team behind him.

"Stand down?" Leo raised a brow. "Are you crazy?"

"There's more here than what it seems!" Alexa halted, covering her mouth and gasping. "Oh my God, Harland. They beat him to a pulp!"

"You don't give orders to my team, Gray." Gabriel rose, his stained fists balled tight and convulsing with fervor. "Now, what's this crap you scryers are whining about?"

"I think he's innocent—"

"Bullshit!" Mara snapped. "We literally caught this asshole in mid-trance, doing his evil on that poor little girl."

"Have you lost your mind, Diver Actual?" Kevin asked.

"It's not what it seems."

"You guys, maybe he's right," Portia said. "He didn't seem to put up much of a fight."

"Hard to do that when you've got guns trained on you while getting your ass beat," Leo noted. "Actual hits hard as fuck. I remember from our sparring sessions."

"He's a coward, that's why!" Gabriel barked. "Like every dark practitioner."

Butcher Team nodded.

"Yeah," Kevin agreed. "Trust us, Diver. We know the fucked up shit they do."

"You didn't see what we did in there," Harland snapped.

"And we don't have to see it. We live in the real world, not your fantasy land. The place we dwell has consequences."

"You could be harming an innocent man—"

"Suffer not a witch to live," Mara replied.

"Words we live by." Gabriel bumped fists with his second. "There is no such thing as an innocent sorcerer."

"You're wrong! There are benevolent witches. You don't understand—" Harland pleaded.

"No!" Mara reprimanded. "You don't understand, rookies! And how could you? With your sheltered attitude, what hardships have you experienced? Everyone on our team has suffered at the hands of a sorcerer's bullshit."

Mara's gaze drifted. The curtain of reality peeled away to visions of memories within her mind's eye. Everyone around vanished. The grass morphed into sand. Ocean waves crashed in the distance, interrupted by the seagulls' cries overhead. Her toes sank into the beach, gripping at the granules as they curled with her shaking body. There was only blackness in view, brought about by the tight bindings of cloth over her eyes, soaked by a river of tears. Her head rocked back, the intense heat still sweltering on her locked and outstretched arms tied to the post they crucified her upon.

"You stupid, bitch." Chad's snickers mixed with several others.

She imagined him as she remembered when their date started. Chad's long and unkempt mane of dyed black hair flanked his strong jawline, dangling to his opened leather jacket, flapping with each movement over his bare and chiseled abs.

"Hail, Lucifer!" Chad roared.

"Konig! Konig!" others chanted.

"Continue burning her limbs slowly, until there's nothing left but ash. Negative energy will attract the masters. This cunt is going to be our ticket to the big time."

"Smells like bacon," another mocked.

Rumbling engines brought wailing police sirens, before handgun rounds popped into the night. A loud thump of a body collapsed nearby, the impact sending particles of sand brushing against Mara's bare feet. There it clung to the shriveled skin along the hot exposed flesh peeling up to her ankles. Dozens of rapid steps kicked and shuffled, as the surviving assailants fled into the distance.

Tightness from the bands lifted, the darkness giving way to an array of bright colors from the police SUVs surrounding the ritual site. The view from her mind's eye peeled away to the current moment. Mara's focus returned to the beige stucco walls of the suburban home she was here to defend. *Consuela...* Her thoughts went to the smiling face of the brave little Hispanic girl they vowed to protect... to the girl's peach cheeks that rolled upward and the small rows of teeth that flashed at them, with a hopeful glow of innocence within her brown eyes.

I will not let her, or any other innocent girl be harmed by sorcerers... Never drop your guard. A renewed focus brought clarity to her present surroundings. Mara's fellow agents reappeared within her peripheral. Heartbeats pumped through the woman with the heat of rage climbing through her heaving body. She stormed toward Diver Team, pointing in accusation.

"You see these burn marks?" Mara barked, rolling up her sleeves. "Sorcerers. I was just sixteen years old when this happened. So, you tell me again about innocence!"

Gabriel rose, placing a hand on Mara's shoulder.

"I'm sorry that happened to you, Agent Graves," Harland pleaded. "But we hunt the unholy not—"

"I'm thinking you should stay out of this one, Diver12Actual," Leo said. "You don't want to get in our way when we're on the hunt."

"If you don't have the balls to do what's gotta be done, why don't you take your asses back to the vehicles and handle the report to Tac-com," Kevin said. "This job isn't for the faint of heart."

"My boy is right, Diver Actual," Leo continued. "I feel your concern. It's your first sortie. Shit is getting ugly. So why don't y'all just go sit this part out? No shame."

The sorcerer groaned, shifting to his side. Mara turned, aiming her pistol. "We told you not to move!"

"Must... I must..." The sorcerer pleaded. "He's... coming..."

Alexa motioned close to her husband in a whisper. "Harland, they're going to kill him. It's all over their signatures."

"I'll back you," Patel said. "But please be right about this, Actual."

Harland's other agents nodded.

Diver Team stood in a line. Their leader moved, placing his hand on Mara's firearm, and pulling it away from the mark. "Stand down, Butcher Team!"

"Dude likes hurting kids." Memories of Leo's voice echoed in Gabriel's mind. Analyn's face appeared in glimpses, her mouth agape, retching howls to the sky. Her haggard voice repeated the phrase, leaving an open wound across his soul from the lash of words. Roars of the beast escalated, piercing until there was only the ringing pitch. *"It wasn't fair! Alma had your father! I had no one!"*

Gabriel's mind guided him back to his two-story home within the naval housing area. The tart pong of onions and sour meat hovered from the kitchen, up the stairs, and into his bedroom. The boy gagged into a thick textbook strewn before him on the bed, the black numbers within it blurring along the white pages.

"She knows better than to cook that foul stuff when Uncle isn't working overnight. He'd never approve. Ugh, the whole house smells like ass again!"

The boy sighed, finding his way downstairs where the

pungent odor grew thick until tears squeezed from his eyes. Another gag roiled in his throat, wanting to explode forth, bearing the contents of his lunch.

Analyn stood before a large pot boiling on the stove. She lifted the cooking device over the sink, pouring its contents into a funnel stuffed within an olive green glass bottle, before sealing it with a cork.

"It smells nasty," Gabriel said. "Why are you able to cook this weird stuff but only make a microwaveable pizza for me?"

"Shush!" Analyn retorted. "Not even your stupid questions can bother me right now. You're so annoying, Gabe! Why don't you just go back to reading your monster books like the nerd you are?"

The boy stared at her.

"Ugh! If you must know, it's my medicine to keep me beautiful. I'm stretching it. When I get low, I just add more, although the main ingredient is very diluted by now."

"You're not making any sense. Can I at least open the windows and back door so we can air this place out?"

"Do whatever, Gabe. I'm done."

"Finally."

"You would do well to respect me. I'm a witch now. Powerful too. I can make things happen." Analyn snickered.

"Yeah, whatever, Tiya. Stop being weird."

The manananggal's cry shifted Gabriel to reality, returning him to the warm evening at the back of the house. Mara's brows arched, shooting a sneer of contempt to Harlan as her aim was forced away.

"Damn sorcerers!" Gabriel bellowed, launching a punch.

A hard impact struck Harland's jaw, sending him careening into a wooden patio chair. The furniture collapsed under the agent, snapping beneath the weight of his combat armor and gear.

"Harland!" Alexa cried out, leaping forward to jab Gabriel in the nose. "Stop this!"

"You bitch!" Mara roared. Redness incapacitated all reason when seeing her best friend struck.

Butcher's second landed a ferocious head jerking hook that sent Alexa staggering before regaining her composure and launching a return shot, popping Mara's head back.

Harland rose to his feet, gasping as Patel charged forward, plowing into Gabriel, and knocking him into the grass.

The East Indian agent rose to his feet, only to be swept forward and lifted when Leo sped into him. The large Butcher agent carried the smaller man until slamming his back into a wall. Agents from both sides jumped into the fray.

"No, you guys!" Portia pleaded, fleeing into the shed, and peeking out. "We're supposed to be combating the bad guys! Don't do this!"

Fists launched without remorse, eliciting thumps and groans. Noses gushed forth like red waterfalls. Lips erupted, leaking like faucets down the sides of mouths. Eyes swelled with stains of black and blue permeating through tender skin.

"Why the fuck are you guys fighting us and not the soul-snatching sorcerer?" Kevin bellowed.

Leo delivered a hard punch, crashing his fist against a Diver agent's mouth. A loud crack signaled the separation of bone upon the hard impact, sending the man collapsing to the floor.

"Muh juw…" the agent whimpered and slurred, through the canted structure of his jaw.

"Aww, damn it!" Leo sighed. "I'm sorry, Agent… Fuck I don't know half your names."

"You bastard!" Patel cried out, charging into Leo. Both

agents toppled over while exchanging short jabs. Patel cocked his head back before lunging forward and biting Leo's bare forearm.

"Ahhh! You dirty motherfucker!" Leo screamed. "You got karma coming for that!"

"Oh my God!" Portia squealed. "See me for a tetanus shot after, Leo."

Amidst the chaos of flying strikes and barreling agents, Gabriel and Harland locked their indomitable scowls. They charged, the former leaping over Leo and Patel who wrestled between them. After landing, Gabriel ducked underneath a wide swing, rising with a leaping left elbow that turned Harland's face. A short right cross slammed into his cheek, knocking him back. The Diver team commander reeled until reclaiming his footing, springing forward with a wide haymaker. Gabriel extended his arm, blocking it, but not the front kick that followed, sinking Harland's boot into his stomach. Gabriel staggered, bringing his guard high. Harland swung again. Gabriel brought his body into the attack, catching the other agent's arm, before dropping his hips low, and turning.

Harland's body rolled off Gabriel's back, flopping to the ground from the toss. Groaning rose from the Diver team leader, silenced by a boot to the head. Harland's vision blurred. Pain channeled throughout his face, despite the empty floating sensation in his limbs. Strong hands gripped at him, the weight of Gabriel pressing down as he mounted and struck Harland.

Green resin knuckles entered the latter's vision, his head crashing back against the grass after each attempt to rise. Flashes of Gabriel's snarling visage appeared between thundering strikes. Harland's head sank back. The Diver team leader closed his eyes. Hard rattles continued through a drum of successive blows. The dull chime of white noise radiated through his mind, until there was only the darkness of fading consciousness.

Pressure on his sternum lifted when Gabriel stood from Harland's listless body. Flickers of light passed overhead from the porch, illuminating the blurring visions beheld by the fallen agent. Harland rose, swaying with the fight to remain balanced. His shaking arms raised into a guard, rolling his fingers into a fist once more. Gabriel's snarl melted, his lips covering the teeth he once bared. The Butcher Team leader's face elongated with a frown.

"You're tough," Gabriel said. "I'll give you that."

"I'm just getting started…" Harland replied. "I've taken worse… That all you got?"

Guards raised, their vision rose over the horizon of their fists. The agents leaned forward, bodies coiling with anticipation, shifting in and out of their centerlines, making themselves difficult for the other to time.

"Agents!" a short man cried out from the door, gasping at the writhing mass of humanity launching punches, kicks and grappling each other. "Stop it! Agents!"

Harland and Gabriel lowered their guard, finding Consuela's father Tito waving them down. Fists remained balled, and fierce glares were exchanged throughout the pleas. Gasps came from Tito's wife Blanka.

"Why are you fighting!" Tito exclaimed. "Consuela needs you! Something is wrong!"

Harland and Gabriel rushed over, following the couple as they raced up the stairs.

"You promised she would be safe," Blanka cried out. "We trusted you!"

They dashed through the bedroom door, finding the grandmother in her nightgown, shaking the young girl. "Consuela, it's Grandma. Wake up, Nieta! Por favor. We are worried!"

"Look, Agents!" Tito snapped. "She's not waking up!"

"No!" Blanka sobbed into her hands. "No, this can't be!"

Harland closed his eyes. The scryer's mind set adrift on the currents of the room, finding the shell of the girl, the energies composing her material presence solid, but hollow as her essence was missing. Crackles of negative energy traveled in waves underneath the layers, on frequencies between the physical and etheric. Reality's memory played before the agent.

Rumbling growls came from a mouth of sharp and curved teeth. Saliva dripped from the corners, glistening over its maw, as lips smacked before rolling open in a grin. Feline eyes narrowed their view onto Consuela, emanating a broiling presence of hatred, as the sobbing girl withered away behind the sheets that trembled with her. The being glided closer, his top hat mere inches beneath the ceiling.

"The Queen is ever right in her lessons." The being hissed each word with spite. "Mortal stupidity is the greatest constant that I can rely upon. These protectors were no obstacle. You cavorted with the usurpers. Therefore, you will pay the ultimate price. No longer shall you be an ingot, but a morsel. I will pressure dear ole Mom to make sure you are placed ahead of the line with the other bothersome ones."

Cackles more akin to whining grew around Consuela. Her fear guided her vision to each one appearing from the shimmering walls of the dream state. The thin pupils of feline eyes sprouted around the central hatted figure in the dim visage of several grinning faces. Whiteness from the walls pushed outward, stretching with the being's claws pressing out from the warp that churned through her perspective. The girl screamed, her body twitching each time the sharpness of their grip dug deeper into her etheric form.

"She's gone..." Harland lowered his head. "Something took her. Something more powerful than we anticipated."

"*I want to help them!*" Conseula's voice played back in the agents' memories. "*These things tried hurting Philly. You haven't seen her these last weeks! I have! Please, let me help, Papa!*"

Blanka stormed forward, slapping Gabriel and Harland across their faces. Swelling wetness gathered in her eyes. A fount of tears followed. The woman rushed past them, disappearing save for her bellowing sobs echoing through the home.

"Connie wanted to be a hero, like in those games she plays..." Tito sighed. "I don't know why I was so foolish to trust that you could protect her from something like this. You failed my little girl. Get the hell out of my house. All of you."

CHAPTER 7
THE WHISPER AND THE RAVEN

PRESENT DAY: USA HQ WEST, SAN DIEGO, CA - 0700 HOURS

The office door slammed shut with a thundering impact echoing through the headquarters. Faces rose from paperwork and folders slipped from hands, evaporating the moments of ruminations with eye gaping stares from those traversing the polished corridors.

Inside, AD Howler's heels smacked against the floor as she stormed around her desk, turning to face the two agents standing centered next to each other on the opposite side. A deep sigh blew through Howler's teeth. Her fingers stretched over the glossy deep brown finish to brace. She leaned over.

The woman's brows arched over her eyes, swollen with pink clouds and veins encroaching around her forest green irises. Convulsions of gathering rage ran through the woman's body, grounding into a twitching eye. A scrunched death gaze radiated from Howler, her eyes shooting like lasers, burning in their periphery. Loose brown strands bobbed on Howler's head when she jabbed a finger in their direction.

Howler's lips pressed together. Her fierce glare bounced between Gabriel and Harland. They stretched their bodies into a ramrod position, heads held upright. Their stares focused on the wall, tracing the spackle with all their attention. Thumbs remained along the outside of their rolled fingers, lining down the seams of their pants. Heels cemented together, with toes pointing outward at a forty-five-degree angle.

Small breaths escaped from their mouths, deviating from the usual tight lipped stance. Red spotted tissue remained jammed up each nostril. Dried blood and scabs ran as thin lines over Gabriel's forehead, the length of which dragged over the bruise that doubled his left cheek. Black and blue radiated around Harland's eyes, inflating the region around them, fattening the upper portion of his face.

"You imbeciles!" Howler snapped. "You let your dick measuring contest interfere with the agency's operation! This is my fault—"

"Ma'am, we—" Harland tried.

"Shut the hell up, Agent Gray! You will keep your mouth open only so that you do not suffocate! Remain at attention and say nothing! Zip!"

Harland reaffixed his stare to the wall, beyond the AD's glower beaming front and center within their mutual view.

"A little girl had her soul stolen under the watch of two teams! Her parents are distraught and even though I promised them we would continue the case, they didn't seem too confident in our ability to handle it. I cannot say I blame them."

A small black alarm clock at the center of Howler's desk buzzed next to a widescreen laptop with a thin keyboard. Snarling, the AD grabbed the device, hurling it against the wall. The clock's plastic shell split open, fizzing as the red numbers faded from its transparent face. Katherine shook her head, returning the ire to the team leaders.

"What the hell happened? All those agents, and you both still managed to fumble it? Most of Diver Team will be recuperating in the infirmary, save for Agent Patel and the Grays. All we have is a half dead perp that has been unconscious for hours, and Diver12Actual's psychometric recall of an unidentified alpha vector."

Howler leaned forward, her finger shifting between the two of them. Teeth bared from her rising upper lip. Wetness swelled in the woman's eyes. A shakiness rose within them, only to be erased by the firming of Howler's countenance.

"I just lost most of Ghost Team..." Katherine swallowed deeply. "There's too much going on right now for me to dispense the reaming you both deserve. If it wasn't for what Madam Dupree and I discovered, this trail would've gone cold, leaving the agency on the back foot right now, gentlemen. We would be meandering around and waiting until another victim is claimed, just for a chance at a lead!"

Katherine sighed, brows lowering. Her gaze found the computer's monitor, skimming through a report.

"After you two patch up whatever remains of the task force, you will investigate the company making this game. Our techs have been working with the scryers and discovered this is no ordinary commercial software. The program commandeers the computer's sound interface, constantly irradiating the surrounding area with a subtle arcane frequency. Madam Dupree discovered this during the initial consultation of your failed investigation. You are going to the manufacturing company's headquarters at the Carnival Ranch in Arizona, with the warrant I had hastily issued. Your mission is to search for and apprehend their CEO and owner, Meryl Partridge. Any questions?"

"Meryl Partridge the billionaire gaming mogul?" Harland asked. "I've heard of this ranch. They host world invitational gaming tournaments. The place is like an amusement park."

"Yes, Agent Gray. It will not be the normal locale that our agency is accustomed to visiting. We believe she has strong ties to whatever is happening with this case. Apprehending her will not be easy. First glances of Carnival Ranch would have one believing it to be a place purely devoted to cyber hedonism and fun. Intel reports it more like a fortress. These people believe they live outside of the law, even on a federal level. There is a private security force guarding the compound and surrounding land. So do not expect a warm welcome, if any. Run it heavy."

"Hope for the best, plan for the worst," Gabriel said.

"Exactly, Agent Agapito," Howler agreed. "As I am doing by sending you two on this mission. Do not disappoint me again, gentlemen. Anything else?"

"No ma'am," both agents responded.

"Clean yourselves up and get your teams refitted for deployment. Dismissed."

The agents took a step backward, bringing one foot behind the other, turning their frames in one swift and smooth motion before stepping off to the door. The presence of Harland's large shoulders came into the corner of Gabriel's view. The two halted, exchanging stares.

"Work together, damn it!" Howler snapped. "I mean it! Go through the door as a team or you won't survive this!"

The team leaders nodded, lips pressing together as their elevated shoulders and puffed chests began deflating. Harland stepped back.

"By your leave, Butcher10Actual," Harland said.

"Very well, I can respect that." Gabriel broke eye contact, zipping out of the room.

They hurried down the corridor, past the curious gazes arising from other agents and personnel. Gabriel shot ahead, meeting each of them with a frown. Fervor beamed through his eyes with each connection until their gazes pulled away. Harland sped through, nodding with an uneasy smile to each of them until catching up with Gabriel.

"Good afternoon, fellow agents," Harland said to another duo, bringing his attention to Gabriel. "You know, you walk fast as hell."

Gabriel's lips scrunched together, his fists balling while his shoulders stiffened. "What are all these assholes looking at?"

"You, my angry little fellow," a voice said from a doorway.

Gabriel and Harland stopped, turning to face a tall man leaning against the door frame with his arms crossed. A shine reflected from his clean-shaven head that canted with a smirk aimed at Gabriel. The agent's caterpillar brows inched together in scrutiny.

"This is Agent Brian Majors callsign Hitman10Actual," Gabriel said to Harland. "What are you doing here?" he added to Majors.

"Looking over intel for some shit going down in Seattle. Just taking a small break to listen in on Howler reaming your asses."

Gabriel shook his head. "I guess we're the only ones keeping busy?"

"Hardly." Majors chuckled.

"How are you?" Harland reached out, shaking hands with Hitman's team leader. "I am Diver12Actual."

"You really punched the perpetually angry man? Well, anyone who did that is a friend of mine."

Gabriel's frown locked on Hitman Actual.

"Oh, simmer down, Gabe." Majors smirked, turning to glance over Harland's name tag. "I've known this guy since we went through indoc together, Gray. He's a hard ass, but trust me, there's very few others I'd have watching my back in a fight."

"That's good to know."

"We have to get going," Gabriel retorted. "Wish I could say it was good seeing you again."

"Yeah, fuck you too, Gabe. Stay safe out there."

"Ditto."

Harland extended his stride to match pace with Gabriel. "You're pretty much an antagonist with everyone in the agency? Does anyone like you?"

"My family does." Gabriel pushed through the double doors with red crosses painted over the opaque white glass centered on them.

Gurneys lined the area in neat rows throughout the sprawling room. Each bay remained open with the curtains tucked away through a network of ceiling guides. Small computer monitors sat on the left side of each station, with rolling cabinets adjacent to them. Medics rummaged through jars and plastic containers gathering bundles of gauze and tape, stuffing them into the agent's hands.

Portia Lawson dashed between, hurrying over to Leo where her tiny delicate hands slapped away his attempts to stop her. The short blonde inspected the dark blemishes of residual iodine stains over a brow gash held together by two stitches.

"Looks like it's healing just nicely," Portia announced. "No sign of infection. I think you'll be fine."

"That's what I've been trying to tell you, woman!"

"Hush!" Portia stepped over to Mara. Butcher's second crossed her arms, shaking her head at the hovering medic. "Don't you give me any attitude either! This is my jurisdiction!"

"I wouldn't dream of it." Mara rolled her eyes.

"Why is it that Diver's agents were more cooperative than my own?"

"Portia, we appreciate the care, but sometimes you can be a bit of a—mama."

"Yeah, MILF." Leo and Kevin snickered until the medic spun around, jabbing the Lion's shoulder. "Easy! Easy! Good grief those boney little hands may not be able to knock you out, but they feel like needles!"

"Where was that animosity during our field expedient smoker?" Kevin smirked.

"I don't partake in things like that." Portia turned up her nose. "It's my job to fix agents, not break them."

"I see you're all lively," Gabriel said. "That's good."

"Bossman is here!" Leo cheered.

"How bad was it, Gabe?" Mara asked.

"We heard Howler, well—howling," Kevin smirked again. "But we couldn't make out what she was saying."

Gabriel shrugged. "Nothing I haven't heard before. But listen up. We're going with Diver Team—"

Alexa and Patel's heads rose from their rest, acknowledging the Actuals.

"—to investigate the source of this game."

"It's releasing a frequency that is terraforming the layers with a presence sustained and navigated by subconscious mental patterns," Harland added.

"In English there, fluffy," Mara jeered.

Harland's eyes widened before narrowing on Butcher's second. "Let's try to move past this nasty business."

"I'll brief as we're gearing up," Gabriel answered. "Go heavy. Full battle rattle."

"Whoa!" Leo replied.

Kevin grinned.

"Now that's what I wanted to hear!" Mara stated.

"Harland," Alexa called out. "Sounds as if things are getting worse."

"Diver12Actual," Patel inquired. "What's happening?"

"Butcher is the more experienced team, so we will follow their lead. We're going on a raid."

USA HQ WEST: SUBTERRANEAN HOLDING BLOCK

Rasping breaths carried from the sorcerer's mouth, between swelling lips, glistening in the yellow lights beaming upon them. Pain radiated through his face, rising with thick blackened portions swelling across his tanned skin. Strands of his dark hair pulled on his forehead, the tightness arising from the grasp of rubber bands around the midportion of his flowing mane. Wounds flared with sparks of agony arising as consciousness settled into the waking moments. They peaked into dullness and throbbing, biting at the man who struggled to push himself from the bed of cold metal.

Dreadful events have seen me cast here. Great Spirit, what have I done to earn your ire? Is this part of your grand plan?

Clouds of breath fluttered from his gasps, forced by the shuddering winces of each movement. A sheen reflected from a thick wall of glass that surrounded him, the light shining its presence off the countless slivers of translucent stone within it. His eyes turned to the door made of the same material. The view expanded as the weariness of sleep removed the fog that draped over him. Dozens of cells lined parallel forming a block. Numerous figures meandered about within the confines. Some floundered, while others flailed, the muffled echoes of their screams passing into his room.

A prison. Yet not a conventional one. With whom have I crossed paths, Great Spirit? I beckon you to guide me.

"Wah gwaan, you be interestin'." A voice tethered to his thoughts, dragging his focus to the cell adjacent from his own. "*Someone who be gifted, more den jussa dunce bat, like da othas.*"

Beyond the sparkles of the thick wall stood another man at the edge of his room. Dark eyes peered between long, gnarled dreadlocks dangling over his sunken and wrinkled countenance. They remained unblinking, with a twitch growing more evident as the seconds passed. A grin of ice-white teeth stretched over the man's face and raised his wizened features as they made visual contact. The man stepped forward, until his face pressed against the glass. The bare chest and rippling abs revealed within his open black coat disappeared as clouds of his breath fogged the view.

"Whey yuh name, roomie?"

"Corvus Gaagi," he answered. *"Where are we? Who are you?"*

"Seems like ya be taken by da agents too, Corvus. We be rottin' away in a prison meant for our kind, 'cept I dunna believe ya be one nuv us. I be tinkin' dey made a mistake capturin' ya."

"I sense ample portions of quartz around us. This is a prison for left-handed practitioners."

"Ah, ya be a quick one."

"You!" Corvus' hands wrapped around his bruised midsection, stepping away from the man who projected his voice. The etheric layers fluctuated around him, despite the presence of quartz holding back the negative energies. The small stones fizzled, turning white as they gave to the power beyond their consumption. A gaping hole appeared where his presence should have been, leaving a dull ache in Corvus' mind, tolling with a pulse through his psyche in a natural instinct to recoil. Darkness spread like writhing tentacles from an aura reading like a wound in the reaches. Whispers surrounded him, their unintelligible words oozing with venomous malice, stinging like a whip upon the mind's eye. Feral stares seethed with deep breaths, through glimpses into the material world, between flickering moments when the layers receded.

"I asked who you are," Corvus snapped. *"Or should I inquire... What are you?"*

"Nutten naw gwaan."

"What does that mean?"

"It mean I be sittin' 'ere jus like ya."

"You're a liar. I can read it all over you. The others around here are different. Not you. You're stronger than all of them combined, which is why you're able to slip past the warding measures even as a

dark sorcerer. Your presence is a wound, the greatest of a left practitioner that I've ever seen—"

There's a genius level intellect behind that cunning grin of his, calculating paths to the future at rates beyond what I can keep up with. His intentions stretch like roots deep into the earth.

"*—so I ask you to withdraw the pretense of playing coy. For I am no amateur either.*"

"Ah, wut ya be sensing, da last gifts of muh beloved Baron. Yuh see, energy neva dies, merely finds an'er place to go. Very well. I am simply Edjewale. Master of da practice udda saints but moved on ta bedda tings. An' you? Wut do you be?"

"I am Corvus Gaagi, last of the Chaktowi Tribe."

"Oooh!" Edjwale nodded. "I noe bout ya kind, da dream walkers."

"You do?"

"Oh yuh. Ya tink I don't be readin' n' researchin'?"

"I'm not as arrogant as society at large. To assume you primitive just because your accent and dialect are different. No, Edjewale. I can sense that your mind is quite expansive. Being a magician requires a studious ethic and tutelage."

"Right on."

"But I am not a minion of the dark, as you are. So, while you propelled your will through the protective confines of this prison with sheer force and talent, I do so because these parameters are not set against me."

Whirring motors grew louder with the treading of rubber against the floor. Denizens rose, closing to the edge of their cells, with gazes of arched brows and bared teeth flashing at the woman in the wheelchair rolling by. Flanking her on either side walked two men, dressed in black and gray fatigues; their combat vests decked with magazine pouches. The black M4 rifles they carried in their grasps bounced with each hurried step they took, their lowered barrels pointing outboard toward the prison cells.

The woman stopped before Corvus' door. She shot a warm smile at the dream walker, turning it to a sneer at Edjewale.

"It seems as though we've made a huge mistake," the old woman proclaimed. "I am Madam Simone Dupree, Grand Master of the Scryer Order. On behalf of the Unholy Slaying Agency, we hope you accept our deepest apologies and humble request for forgiveness."

"You've been listening the entire time?"

"Of course, Mr. Gaagi. In more ways than one."

"Very well. I can put aside our differences and slights. My concern is the—"

"The children. Yes, we share that exact sentiment. I think we can help each other. No more hiding for either of our factions. Let us reveal our hands, shall we?"

"That would be appropriate, given that we are working against time."

"Ominous words I relish to hear." Madam Dupree sniggered.

"Ya can go wiff dem, or stay 'ere wiff me," Edjewale countered. "Look wut tey dun. Tey gun use ya up n' spitcha right out."

"Hush, fiend!" Madam Dupree rebuked, shaking her head, bringing the fury of her gaze to his snicker. "You are responsible for the deaths of countless good people; many of whom I called friends—"

"I know. Doncha be takin it personal now, Simone. Dat was chus business."

"Edjewale, you will be transported by Sentinel to our maximum security prison, where I guarantee that smug grin will fade. Such a waste of talent. You could've been one of our greatest, but you're too far gone."

"Yah be right bout one ting, Scrya. I be gone soon." Edjewale turned his grin to the dream walker. "Tink on it, Corvus."

"So, what shall it be, Dream Walker?" Madam Dupree asked. "Do you wish to stay here with him or come with us? The choice is yours."

Corvus gazed around the prison. Across from him was a bald man of Eastern descent. Black Taoist robes hung loose and flowing on his body, while he remained statue-still in the full lotus position. He was completely shaven save for the thin graying eyebrows, revealing advanced years despite a flawless golden tan along a lean face. Movement whisked away his attention to a woman wearing a black cloche with a frayed peacock feather bobbing as she shuffled in a slow dance. A small and contented smile remained etched on her thin lips, surrounded by thick and cavernous wrinkles dotted in liver spots. A black velvet coat rested over her shoulders covering a vintage beaded La Garconne dress a size too large for her thin and short frame. His head turned again, seeing an emaciated Latin woman facing him with a frizzy bushel of curls extending over a faded Hair Metal Band's T-shirt. With rapidity, she waved at Corvus, who turned away.

"No wait!" Her muffled shriek carried through. "Look into my eyes. I want to try something with you! Please!"

"I choose to help the young innocent souls." Corvus turned to Madam Dupree.

"Ah, da pickneys. So be it. Walk gud." Edjewale chuckled. "I can feel da waves, eva-changin' as tey be. We be seein each other again, Corvus. Inna di morrows." The dark sorcerer turned his back to them, sauntering to his bed. An unblinking gaze and resolute grin lingered through an eruption of his cackles.

"Since we've concluded that unpleasant business, please release our new ally, Agents."

"Yes, ma'am," the guards acknowledged.

"We have much to discuss. Do you like coffee, Corvus? I have been partial to the cold stuff lately."

CHAPTER 8
FOLLOWING THE WHITE RABBIT

PRESENT DAY: WHITE SANDS, AZ - 0900 HOURS

Dozens of mirror black SUVs raced along the crumbling road. Their wide tract bodies reflected the morning sun's radiance as they sped along the middle of the two-way lanes. Passengers jostled against the deep padding of the seats as the vehicles' thick tires ran over stone and debris. Loud popping rose into the cabins from sand grounding beneath rubber and tonnage.

The calm, I've felt so many times, before...

Gabriel peered through tinted windows to fields of tan rocks and sand extending for miles around. The occasional towering cacti stood out among the blue of the open sky along with patches of golden yellow grass. The manananggal's roar echoed in his mind. Its ringing shriek left his psyche throbbing, drowning away the vehicle's engine and white noise from their comms. The agent's fingers tightened around his M4 carbine's resin pistol grip.

A stiff upper lip pushed from Butcher's team leader. A haze

trickled into his view, blending with the memory's perspective. Twitching eyes peered back at him from a reflection in the window, their thin pupils unwavering despite the backdrop's details passing through. Long strands of black hair draped around its sunken face. The lipless mouth of curved fangs sneered before a guttural wail rose from its quaking jowls. Gabriel turned away.

"Force Tracker is reporting that we are five klicks from the AO, Actual," Mara reported from the passenger's seat with Kevin driving next to her, nodding. "Monach2Actual reported that they're going to issue the warrant for civilian security to stand down. He's betting since it's so early there will be a minimal civilian presence, if any. Then he'll give us the go to infil the main building after the perimeter is secure, Actual."

"Very good, second. Everyone green to green?"

"Roger, Actual!" A unanimous reply followed.

"Ready to rock!" Leo patted his M249 light machine gun with its truncated airborne barrel.

A Ferris wheel's large circular frame protruded within the horizon. Long empty tracks appeared around it, hoisted many stories by numerous steel beams. The rollercoasters were devoid of speeding carts and screaming passengers that should've been racing down the neon painted slopes of metal. Large tents lined with stripes of white and red appeared inside tall gates extending outside their view range.

The road widened into a giant lot of sand and gravel. Fifty meters ahead stood the main entrance, its mouth lined with shining turnstiles adjacent to a small building with sprawling tinted windows facing into the lot. Men dressed in baseball caps stared at the agents. Deep brown stains of perspiration bled from underneath their pits and chests. The morning sunshine reflected on their large sunglasses.

The guards squared with the agents' presence as the hulking vehicles were evacuated, watching the men and women decked in tanned Kevlar helmets, matching the desert uniforms and combat vests. The guards' grip on their short and slender Ruger Mini-14 rifles fixed to ready positions. One placed his hand on the box magazine in the weapon's stomach, assuring himself it was well fed and ready.

"Those jokers trying to square up?" Kevin asked.

"Kind of ballsy for civilian security if you ask me," Mara scoffed.

"Yeah, dudes gotta be kidding." Leo chuckled. "Probably just flexing because it's their job."

Monarch's first squad stepped out from the assembly area. Curtis carried the rear. The tall black man looked back to Butcher Team and nodded as his first squad's leader, Mancini, presented a copy of the warrant to the guards. Gabriel's view narrowed on the gate security looking at the paperwork. The guard nodded while skimming through the lines, smiled, and handed it back to Mancini.

"Okay, let's fall in behind Monarch and—"

Gunpowder erupted, filling the sky with booming echoes and the twang of lead. Muzzle flashes barked out from the guards' rifles that were trained on Monarch. Casings flew from the weapon's receivers with each trigger pull, ringing along the ground where their tiny bodies bounced, spewing smoke. Carbon spat from the kicking weapons, barking violence with each shot that rattled Mancini. The agent collapsed to his back.

"Contact!" Curtis hollered into their earbuds. "Fall back! Enemy personnel are armed and extremely hostile!"

"What the fuck!" Leo screamed.

Butcher Team took cover behind their vehicle.

"Oh no!" Portia squealed. "We have to help him!"

"Hold!" Gabriel ordered. "That agent is still alive, they only hit his plates! Do not return fire while that friendly is between us!" *Something is not right. Why would such a small force preemptively strike at this range, against a much larger one with more firepower?*

Harland peered over to Gabriel from behind Diver's vehicle. The entirety of the hybrid team remained beside him, ducking low with their heads tucked as rounds flew against their cover. Curtis and the rest of Monarch's first squad dashed behind their SUV.

These rookies are deadweight. Gabriel shook his head. *Howler is going to have my ass if anything happens to them. Damn it...*

"Armor!" A guard's voice carried with a shrill roar. "It wears armor! Shoot it in the face!"

Bullets punched through the window of the small building. SUVs rattled with each shot bouncing off their armored hides where they popped into the gravel laden parking area. Cracks rose into the glass until its entirety crumbled forward as shards rained to the foot of the building. Five more rifle barrels pointed outboard, firing with rapid shots. Each hard and desperate trigger pull jerked the weapons off center from where the guards aimed.

"Linear ambush!" Mara yelled. "Stay behind cover!"

"Luckily these MFers can't aim for shit!" Kevin mocked.

Three turnstile guards stomped forward to where Mancini crawled, backs hunching with coiled tension. Their high-pitched cackles grew louder as they hopped onto the crawling agent's back. A cold barrel was pressed to Mancini's neck. The trigger pull sent a round puncturing through the exposed skin, where it erupted from the man's jugular. A shower of red droplets and threads of meat bedecked the walkway. Mancini's body crumpled, going limp as his blood pooled with granules of sand, beneath his face.

What the fuck!

"Those bastards!" Curtis bellowed. "Give them the business! Weapons free!"

M240B machine guns released thundering bursts, spraying across the guards' chests, ripping open cloth and flesh. Streaks of crimson squirted across the open desert air. The foes' collapsing remains piled at the entrance before the crew-served weapons turned to the building. The torrent of heavier firepower sent the guards inside reeling from the window, their discarded rifles cracking loud upon the ground.

"Tangoes suppressed!" Curtis announced. "Status remains unconfirmed. First and second squad cordon with me on near side. Third and fourth head around to far side!"

"Third squad leader acknowledges, Monarch Actual. We are en route." Four of the SUVs broke from the convoy, wheeling out of the parking lot into the desert terrain, where they raced around the vast perimeter.

Curtis' vision fell upon his friend and teammate, Mancini. A red lake of the man's life fluids formed at the entrance. Two of Monarch's agents kneeled beside their fallen comrade, lifting his body and carrying it back to the vehicles.

"I wasn't expecting this shit..." Leo murmured.

"Wake the fuck up," Gabriel grumbled. "We're moving in behind the cordon's advance. Let's go! Double time!"

Gravel and sand kicked from their pounding footsteps. Gabriel's stare turned to Harland and his team, nodding at them.

"We move, too!" Harland announced. "Here we go, Diver!"

"We're with you, Harry." Alexa patted her husband.

Harland led the sprint with Diver Team rushing behind

him, their legs churning to the turnstiles they pressed through. Butcher Team was ahead, the tip of the spear for their wedged formation led by Leo, who was flanked by Mara and Gabriel with the others carrying the borders. Behind them was Monarch, their agents taking cover in the prone, their bodies wrapping around the corners of tents, with weapons pointing down horizontal and vertical avenues that blocked off each section of Carnival Ranch. Music flowed from speakers high above on poles that dotted along the landscape.

"Mr. Sandman, bring me a dream—" The Chordettes' classic song played over the speakers. Soprano and alto voices harmonized with flawless precision, singing the lyrics in a dreamy composition that was unmatched by similar groups of their time. The catchy and melodious chorus continued on loop, with the signature barbershop quartet style relying purely on the surreal flow of their vocals, and minimal instrumental background.

The tuneful beat was interrupted by a dimwitted and clownish voice. "Hello, boys and girls! It's time to play! Step into a wonderland of possibilities! Let's have some fun!"

Heads turned to where illumination flared from the light bulbs outlining tents and stands. The Ferris wheel squealed to life, its gears whining as the massive bulk spun and swung the chairs within it.

"Damn it," Gabriel snapped. "This reeks of an ambush. Eyes up and call out what you see, Butcher."

"You heard the bossman," Mara said. "Don't be shy if you see some bullshit."

Rapid steps approached from the rear. Gabriel turned, seeing Diver Team forming a smaller wedge behind their own. Mara's lip curled, baring teeth through a grimace of disgust.

"Go easy on them." Gabriel's head shake melted away the

woman's ferocity. Mara turned her attention to the perimeter ahead.

"What's the word?" Harland asked.

"Glad you could join us," Gabriel quipped. "We're about to infil under the cover of Monarch. You sorcerers carry our six. Call out anything from the ordinary. Understood?"

"We got you," Alexa replied with Patel nodding.

"Good, because we don't have time to babysit," Mara snapped.

"On us," Gabriel ordered. "I want our heavy firepower upfront. Leo, take point with Kevin."

"Roger, Actual." The large man went forward in slow and cautious steps, gripping his light machine gun. "I'm ready. Nothing is getting the jump on us."

CHAPTER 9
ENTERING THE SANDS

Gravel crunched with Butcher Team's footsteps through the cordon of aimed weapons Monarch trained along the premises. Flakes of dust carried along the winds, cooling the beads of sweat gathering on their bodies from the growing brightness of the desert sun. Flags along the top of each tent flapped with the gyrating walls, the echoes of their movements contrasting with the wailing music carrying over the horizon. Gabriel peered over to Curtis as they passed. Monarch's team leader nodded from his kneeling position along the side of a gaming booth.

"Gabe, do me a favor?" Curtis asked.

"Whatever you need."

"Get revenge for my second."

"We aren't leaving this place until Partridge is in cuffs."

"Roger and thank you. We'll be ready with whatever you need, Butcher Team. Live up to your name on this one."

"Something isn't right, Butcher10Actual," Harland called out.

"Yeah, I can feel it too," Alexa agreed.

"What are you two sorcerers going on about?" Mara snapped. "This is for real, not a training course. Rounds are live. You need to stay focused!"

"That's what the fuck we're doing!" Alexa retorted.

"Gabe—" Harland tried.

"Dude, so we're on a first name basis now?" Leo mocked. "Are you trying to start another fight?"

Play nice; damn I can already feel Howler's reprimand on my ears. "Easy, Butcher10Golf," Gabriel warned. "What is it, Diver12Actual? And keep the interruptions to a minimum. We need speed and stealth on these SACs."

"SACs?"

"I don't say much," Kevin muttered. "But damn these Diver bubbas are stupid."

"Search and capture." Mara sighed. "Jeez, you guys are deadweight."

"The music coming from the air is a cover," Harland stated. "Butcher10Actual, we can feel it. There's a frequency in it; the same one used in the video games to terraform the etheric layers."

"Okay, fine. That doesn't stop us from the mission. Just keep me aware if it gets worse."

"Fair enough. Thank you."

Paced steps brought the agents maneuvering between pavilions, beyond the sight of Monarch's cordon. The ground popped and fizzed in dozens of locations around the teams. They halted, their rifles pointing to the numerous locations where dirt and rock gave way. Black sprinklers rose from the ground, their dusty heads clicking and spinning as nozzles hissed air from their dry vessels.

"Bitch tried turning the water on us?" Leo asked.

"Ooh, that's not good!" Portia exclaimed. "But water is better than bullets, I guess."

"You guess?" Leo chuckled and winked.

The medic shrugged.

"There's no water coming from them though," Kevin said. "Probably because there isn't any in this desert."

The sprinkler heads shuddered and rotated, clicking loudly with attempts that only spat more air. The agents continued, scanning along the main road, and hurrying past another row of unlit lifeless buildings. Gabriel paused, looking over to his team. Mara's head turned with grim resolve, the intense ferocity of her eyes morphing into a relaxed poise. They popped open before drooping with lids half down.

"Feeling like shit today, Actual," Mara murmured.

Whoa, I'm slowing too... We just started though...

Shots popped in the distance from the tents adjacent to the right of their position. Rifle barrels jutted from the shadowy mouths of interconnected pavilions. Traces of smoke wafted from the door flaps. Lead rounds sparked across a nearby gaming booth. A large light within the stall exploded and fizzled within, sending the rest blinking as the wooden frame shuddered with the arrival of more gunfire. Howls followed, soaring with a high pitch from their foes outside of view.

"Contact!' Leo hollered.

"One Alpha!" Gabriel ordered. "Mara on second element with me!"

Butcher's machine gunner raised his weapon, delivering a series of triple-round bursts ripping through quivering nylon. Team members scrambled, taking low positions behind gaming stalls lined parallel to the enemy tents. Leo continued the suppression fire. Portia and Kevin added to the salvo with their M4s. Mara and Gabriel swung wide around their sector of fire, stopping a few meters before the shining path of tracer rounds that guided the team's return punishment. Their attackers squealed, reeling into the depths of cover.

Mara is slowing to the limit of advance, not crossing into our team's sector of fire. Perfect as always.

Gabriel raised his fist, signaling the ceasefire. Loud giggles came from the tent when Mara and Gabriel closed on the entrance. Their M4 barrels guided the way with the illumination of their boxed holographic close-quarter sights, bringing the glowing reticle over the foes who were piled near the main support beam at the center. Blood streamed from their mouths, flowing down their necks. Gargles of red bubbled within their throats, choking away their laughter. Peppered across their abdomen were gaping wounds, spewing into dark stains in their brown uniforms.

Unblinking eyes and a grin peered back at the duo from one of the guards, his body heaving to breathe in its death throes.

"The party is beginning..." The man winked before the strength spilled from his body. A thud came from the back of his head hitting the ground. The expansive smile remained etched over his countenance even as the light extinguished from his eyes.

Giggles roiled from the other guard, his body curled in the fetal position. Rumbles of laughter churned his failing organs, the growing intensity sending the man wincing. The guard's twisted smirk fixed on the approaching agents.

"Oooh!" the guard mocked when their black rifle barrels trained on him. A shimmer of light from their close-quarter optics brought a red hue into the wounded man's view. "So scary with your big guns."

"What the fuck is wrong with you, assholes?" Mara

demanded. "Why are you interfering with a federal warrant? And what the hell is so funny about all of this? Stand still so I can administer first aid, damn it!"

Rasping cackles expelled from the man, his body convulsing with hard coughs interrupting the glee. "See you... soon... Agents..."

"Don't you fuckin' move!" Mara shouldered her carbine, taking a knee and rummaging through the large pouch clipped to her hip along the thick utility belt.

"Don't bother, Mara," Gabriel said. "He bled out."

Butcher's second nodded. "Never seen someone smile during death before. I'm suspecting drug use. How about you, Actual?"

"I think it goes deeper than that." Gabriel nudged a body with his foot. "Possession."

"They're not showing the usual signs."

"I know. But I can't—that feeling there's more going on here than—" Gabriel's eyelids drooped, and his head nodded, breaking the haze washing over his view. "Feeling like... crap. Let's Charlie Mike and finish this."

"Me too. Maybe I need to lay off the coffee. These crashes are getting worse." Mara turned her attention to her communications bud. "Butcher and Diver, this is Butcher10Bravo. We have two EKIA. Actual and I are exiting the pavilion. Two friendlies coming out. How copy?"

Mara waited.

No response. That's odd. I'll let Mara examine the situation. She's going to be having her own team soon. Best to keep letting her have point on some decisions.

"Butcher and Diver, this is Butcher10Bravo. We are exiting the tent. Two friendlies coming out. How copy?"

Gabriel shook his head before walking to the mouth of the

domicile. Brightness from the morning sun washed through his vision before the gaming booths formed in his view. Granules of sand blew across the ground, brushing against the downed bodies of Butcher and Diver team members, strewn over their positions.

"They're down!" Gabriel shouted. "Quick, Mara!"

"What's going on?"

Butcher's team leader raced from the tent, snapping his M4 into a shoulder, scanning from right to left. Within the transparent box was the reticle of his combat sight, tracing over the booth corners, then inside to the dart boards, still clinging with the projectiles from the previous day's games, and the ring toss with its round accessories hanging from protruding targets. Blurs of darkness whisked from the agent's corner view. Gabriel canted to the right, spinning on his heel as the left foot brought a firm step forward. His aim zeroed on waves of dust carried by a desert breeze until they splashed against the walls of a tent.

"It's clear." The coiled tension subsided when Gabriel rose from his ready stance.

"What the hell happened to them?"

Mara's knee pads squished with the ground as she lowered to touch Leo. Wheezing breaths expelled from the large man's nose and mouth, his eyes shut tight, the weight of his body sagging into an imprint on the ground.

"I don't see any blood—" Mara yawned, shaking her head in doubt. "—or signs of a wound, Actual."

"I'll—" Gabriel released a deep yawn, drooping his shoulders. "—cover you."

Mara yawned again. She placed two fingers along the side of Leo's neck. "Leo's pulse is still... strong."

Their eyelids drooped. A tingling cold crept through, the

tension of focus lifting from their shoulders. A numbness spread through the duo. Each step sent them floating in dysphoria, until their knees wobbled and ankles shuddered. Gabriel staggered forward with a drooping head. He fell to his knees, straining through the darkening of his vision, catching glimpses of Mara keeling over to her side.

Damn it... mind... fading... We're being poisoned. NBC gear out! Quick! Gabriel dug into the side pouch of his utility belt, drawing out his gas mask. Tossing off his helmet, he strapped the apparatus snug over his face. Fatigue shuttered his eyelids. Adrenaline and discipline forced them back open, only to cascade again. *Too late...*

Gabriel's weapon slipped from the limp fingers of his grasp, the weight of it swinging with a tethered pull of the guideline keeping it secure to his vest, along a Grimlock D-clip. Piling downward, the agent caught a glimpse of the rocks and sand below before his thudding collapse turned into the darkness of slumber.

CHAPTER 10
OF MADNESS AND MEMORIES

HIDDEN REACHES OF THE ETHERIC LAYERS - TIME UNKNOWN

Fingers tapped against Gabriel's forehead. The cracking of a slap followed with an impact in front of his face. Soft palms scented in lavender caressed his forehead. Dull blackness rippled away, formulating vision as Gabriel's eyes peeled open. His sight carried to the sky from upon his back, searching through the endless darkness of night. Brisk clouds of purple floated above, their bodies roiling with the giant mass of shapeless forms, blending together before continuing apace. Countless miniature red dots flowed within all he beheld, possessing a translucence that allowed the details of the world to appear through their presence.

"Portia!" Leo snapped. "What I tell you about slapping the top of the hand! That shit hurts even with these protective gloves!"

"I know it hurts, dummy! That's the point! You don't tap my patient's forehead like that," the tiny medic roared back.

Her piercing blue eyes connected with Gabriel's. "Actual, how are you feeling?"

"Better now, Doc." Gabriel rose to wobbling knees. "How long was I out?"

"I have no idea. It honestly feels like a few seconds. Time and physics don't seem to apply in this place."

"This place?"

Lurching forward, Gabriel's steps registered only tingles outlining the numbed lengths of his legs, despite being grounded. Weapons, armor, magazines, and utilities were as feathers upon his floating structure. The mechanics of muscle and pressure evaporated within the anticipation of tensed muscles, leaving an emptiness inside.

"Where are we?"

"A frequency extremely similar to the dream state," a voice answered from ripples of a view still forming. Harland appeared next to Portia and Leo. "Madam Dupree warned me about this in passing. This is where the children end up after having their mind, body, and spirit reformed by frequency saturation. That haze you're experiencing right now feels like REM sleep, correct?"

"Yes. As if nothing is connected, everything disjointed, but I recognize and acknowledge it."

"That's your mind formulating the reality here. This isn't easy. Whatever is happening in this plane is beyond just willpower and focus, which is something I'm discovering is difficult even with my scryer training."

"I'll manage. Where are the others?"

"No idea, bossman," Leo replied. "This place has a weird fog or some shit over it. Even though we can see around us, the details are constantly reforming, coming in and out of view.

Sometimes they leave us out of reach. Mara and Kev were here just a few moments ago. Now they're gone."

"We need to find them, and the rest of Diver."

Gabriel slid back the charging handle of his M4 a few inches, checking for the 5.56 round drawing with the bolt's grip before allowing the upper receiver to feed it back into the firing chamber. The others nodded, trailing close behind as they trekked between tents. Black and white stripes lined down the walls of the statuesque pavilions, their wide bodies remaining unfettered in the stagnant air. Gabriel scanned the first, walking its perimeter then halting after tracing nothing but the walls. He stood upright with a brow risen.

"Where the fuck are the entrances?"

"Good question, Actual." Leo shrugged.

"Just walls and roofs all around us," Harland noted. "Also, there aren't any stakes or ropes to help pitch them. Not like the ones we saw earlier."

"Whoa!" Leo exclaimed. "Check this shit out."

The machine gunner leaned close to the tent walls. Transparent ripples flowed through the material, distorting the view of their surroundings. The waves grew, until the foundations vibrated with noiseless fervor, liquidating the material before them.

"As if the tents here are made from—"

Lithe white hands reached out from the walls, grasping Leo's forearms. Black nails pierced through his sleeves, digging into skin that peeled with ease. A gasp came from the agent's mouth, becoming groans when he strained to pull away. Leo stepped backward, leaning with his weight. The hands tightened, nails stabbing deeper into the meat of his limbs, bringing the agent forward on trembling legs.

"Leo, watch out!" Portia squeaked.

The medic's carbine spat two shots within the confines of the tent. Holes ripped in the material, undulating with the liquid energies, before oozing lines melded its presence whole again. Leo bellowed through a face scrunching grimace. Another stammering step brought him closer. Gabriel reached for the back of Leo's vest, gripping the edges, and pulling back until veins pressed through his forehead.

A roar echoed through the clouds, carried by the heavy beat of wings generating flight. Churning air passed overhead with a guttural bellow pulsing down on them. Deep breaths seethed through bared teeth, between the reverberations of wind.

"Manananggal!" Gabriel let go, his vision darting around the stars and the clouds.

"What?" Leo pleaded. "Actual! I need you! Don't let go! Shit!"

Gabriel turned, his carbine sweeping the skies, spinning to track the flapping patterns, swooping low before rising away. "It's here!"

"Fuck!" Leo screamed.

Butcher's machine gunner let his weapon hang from the attachment cords on his vest, reaching out, bracing himself upon the wall to push away. Long veins pressed up from the skin of Leo's neck, a pinkish tint overtaking the white of his eyes. Wrinkles gathered over his forehead and eyelids, coming together over a trembling grimace. Beads of sweat rolled down his cheeks, disappearing into the uniform collar. A quiver of weakness pulsed through burning muscles, aching with the heat of fatigue.

"Let go of him!" Portia yelled.

The petite medic stepped forward, raising her carbine with both hands clamped around it. She reared the weapon overhead, turning it backward before slamming its thick buttstock against the knuckles of the being. Metal rattled with repeated thudding, until thin lines where lengthy hand bones protruded bent underneath audible cracking.

A grin of sharp fangs materialized within two inches of the sweat droplet at Leo's nose. Clouds of warm breath expelled from the shaking maw. Strings of saliva hung between sabered fangs that curved from the roof of its mouth, opening with a long hiss. The stale reek of corpses pushed out from threads of pink flesh lodged between its teeth and gums.

Deep stinging from the digging nails subsided when its grip loosened. Tension from the fingers lifted, with the heat of blood trailing from a multitude of tears. The lengthy arms slithered away and slurped into the liquidity of the walls. Its mouth clamped shut, into a grin shaking with glee. When its lips closed, it disappeared, until there were only the lined patterns of the tent and the sheen over its nylon material.

Leo gasped, staggering back to his rear. "The top of the hand—"

"Always works," Portia responded.

"Thank you, Sweet Pea! You saved my ass! I won't give you any shit for like... a week."

"Hold still, butthead!"

The medic knelt beside the machine gunner, tossing her pack next to them, rifling through it for gauze. Leo held up his arms with eyes darting to all the blood covered rips within his tan sleeves. Sweat and blood greased his arms around the stings of agony throbbing along it. A cool breeze carried away his attention to the shadows between the tents leading to the unseen.

"Where the fuck is Actual and that scryer punk?" Leo asked.

Portia shrugged. "Gone... This place swallowed them up like the others. Don't you leave me, too."

"I wouldn't dream of it." Leo smiled. "We stay within arm's reach of each other at all times."

"Agreed. But keep your hands to yourself."

"Hey, you're in my dream..."

Portia pressed the alcohol deep into the wound. It fizzled with increasing jolts of pain, rising with a pink foam around his wounds.

"Ah!" Leo yelped. "Okay, I'll behave. Sheesh..."

Mara's M4 carbine remained firm in her shoulder, her eyes narrowing down the glowing crimson reticle of her cubed holographic close-quarter optic. Fluttering clouds of fog intensified around her, its whiteness clogging the outer limits of her vision, fading the view of tents and stands, until only boxed shapes of gray loomed. Gravel crunched beneath light footsteps trailing behind the path she blazed. The woman stopped, spinning around with her stern glower to a tall figure whose gray outline stood within the drifting pale barricades.

Someone's behind me...

"Easy, Mara," Kevin warned. "It's me. Please watch where you point that thing."

Why couldn't it have been Gabe or Doc? Meh, I shouldn't be thinking like that. Kev is probably just as confused by this shit. "My apologies for flagging you, Butcher10Sierra. I'm standing down. Keep pace with me and drop the colloquial shit. You're not with Leo where you two can soup sandwich it."

"Yes, ma'am."

Gabe goes too easy on these boys, then they start talking like civilians. Mara's head shook, carrying a frown. "We have to link up with the others after we orient ourselves. Damn this fog."

Speckles of whiteness curled with a gust of air, whisking out of Mara's view. She pressed onward, transposing the aim of her intent with locked and steady rhythms scanning the fog closing around them. Kevin's steps hammered behind her, the tall man's big feet dropping heavy and uneven with solid stones caught in the boot tread.

"Damn it, Kev!" Mara's hushed snap launched over her shoulder. "What's wrong with you? Noise discipline!"

"Yes, ma'am."

Butcher's second continued, her steps finding resistance compacting around her boots with each movement plunging into the ground. With bent knees, she leaned over, peering down to countless thick granules of sand.

"We must've reached the outer perimeter somehow," Mara whispered back.

Salty aromas drifted along lazy breezes. Cries from seagulls echoed above. Churning waves crashed in the distance. The fog departed before Mara, giving a view of moonlight glistening along the ocean spilling into a damped and darkened shoreline.

This place...

Mara turned around to Kevin, approaching from the outer reaches of the fog.

"We have to get the hell out of—"

"You're not going anywhere." Chad's rasping tone came from the tall silhouette.

"K-K-Kevin..." The trembles transferred to Mara's thoughts. *No, that voice... It's my ex... But... Different...*

The tight embrace of cloth wrapped around Mara's eyes, fastened by a knot at the back of her head. Darkness covered all she beheld. Mara's arms shot back to the pillars of wood. Slithering ropes curled over the thick planks, scraping against the frayed edges as they coiled around her wrists and ankles, fastening the limbs. Convulsions rose from her gasping frame along with groans that shot between her clamped teeth. A cold ache drummed into the woman's hyperextended shoulders.

"You were always such a dumb bitch." Bellowing laughter exploded around her from closing voices.

"I liked you... I thought you liked me, too... Why?"

"This is bigger than you know, baby. My ambition is greater than nailing some pasty-faced geek. I came from shit. This is my ticket to the good life. Virgin sacrifices, you're suffering to feed the master's desires. Do you have any idea how hard it was to find a pure bitch these days? That's why I backed off after you gave me a peek between those thighs."

He never cared... "No—"

"What you think I was going to do, huh? You saw the tatts!"

Chad flapped his jacket, bearing his chest with a round seal over his heaving left pectoral. Within the circle was an inverted triangle, the lines of which intersected, careening at the bottom above a 'V' traced through it. To the right was a cross with parallel lines through it, the bottom of which connected with an infinity symbol. Upon his neck, above them both, an eye was traced over his Adam's apple.

"You thought this was a joke? I was just some poor lost soul playing the bad boy role for the validation of a dumb bitch like you? Nah, I'm about this life. I'm not playing pretend like some edge lord on the internet." Chad leaned close, the whiskey

CHAPTER 11
FOUNT OF DESPAIR

HIDDEN REACHES OF THE ETHERIC LAYERS - TIME UNKNOWN

T*he night I killed her...*

Young Gabriel's trembling eyes gazed past the bristling limbs of the cedar, towering in their backyard. Haggard cries bellowed with a deep guttural resonance through clouds drifting among the sparkling stars. The ring of a woman's pitch mixed with a gruff drawl, fading into the rolling hills outside the perimeter of the housing area. Lights turned on from the neighbor's windows as silhouettes of curious faces peered out into the night. They shuffled away, their illumination disappearing after minutes passed.

The shine of Analyn's skirt blared in his peripheral vision with the short stature of her lower extremities standing adjacent to him. Strands of meat writhed from the opening at her waist, flickering within slimy and clear mucus along her hips, dipping within the deep indentation of red where the spinal cord had once been. Her thin golden brown legs remained planted by her small feet that had pressed their arch flat, locking into the grass and dirt of the yard by the steadfast grip of her toes.

I remembered from the books...

Backward steps carried the boy to the sliding door's base. Heartbeats rose until pounding in his throat and ringing to his cranium. The cold breeze disappeared from the moment, along with the contrast of their home's warmth. Gabriel's slow and rigid movement caught his heel with the metal frame, bringing him to a seated tumble. The boy stared ahead at Analyn's legs, leveled to his position. He pushed off the ground, running through the living room to the kitchen. Swinging open the pantry door, he grabbed the long glass and metal sea salt grinder.

Gabriel found himself dashing back outside where the cold blades of grass crushed beneath his bare feet. The boy's shaking hands gripped with scratching and sliding fingers at the grinder's lid. His eyes carried back up to the sparkling stars overhead, sweeping until hearing the pop. The lid's muffled descent to the ground was followed by granules of white crystals. He dug into the container, sprinkling the contents along the folds of gaping flesh.

Glistening folds of blood covered flesh fizzled and popped with each bit. Pink tissue shriveled, crisping upward and chipping away. White minerals poured into the deep spinal crevice, drawing away blue veins that curled into dried strings. Smoke arose, laced heavily with the odor of burnt meat. The legs wobbled, then collapsed.

Gabriel stepped away as reddening foam and crumbling remnants spilled into the grass. The lower extremities twitched, jolts of movement coursed through the bending knees, down the bouncing calves, and curling toes.

Roars brought Gabriel's vision up to the sound of large

stench of his breath flying with spit from his screams. "The validation I seek isn't from you. Begin the sacrifice!"

I'm not just a victim. I'm no longe—

Wetness from oil poured down Mara's bare shoulders until its thick stickiness dripped from her fingertips. She convulsed in her constraints. The slick liquid worked its way down her other arm, a line diverging down the crack of her bare breasts.

Where is my gear? I am a former army ranger! This can't be happening! I am an agen—

"You're nothing, bitch," Chad declared. "You are food for the abyss. Nothing more."

Waves of heat grew on Mara's skin, gathering intensity until its presence stung over her breasts and shoulders. Smoke billowed into her face, passing with glimpses of light through the blindfold, bringing shape to figures closing around the one wielding a torch. High-pitched cackles surrounded Mara, growing louder with saliva droplets spotting the ground from their undulating jaws.

"König! Zi Dingir! Ie' König!" The chant grew.

"Cook this bitch! Burn away her pathetic presence from this realm, bit by bit! Scream for me, nerd girl! Beg for mercy that will never come! There is no one to stop us this time! Let the immolation begin!"

wings beating the cold night air. Heavy breaths expelled overhead, each successive pant whisking between Analyn's long fangs, growing faint.

Run! Run! The legend! Remember the warnings! Quiet before the kill! Their sounds lessen as they draw closer!

You aren't fast enough... You've seen how they move...

The walls of the house reappeared as Gabriel sprinted inside. Wind fluxed underneath the abomination as it touched down. Analyn's wings dragged as her arms hefted her torso, the razor-sharp talons hooking into the earth with ease as she walked upon her arms. Howling cries rang through the house, morphing into a shriek and deep panting.

"Gabriel!" Analyn screamed. "What have you done?! I'll tear you apart! Apart!"

The boy's eardrums rang with the shrill tempo of guttural cries, following her palms beating against the floor. Gabriel reached for the key rack mounted along the wall next to the kitchen counter, snatching away both sets. Coming through at a low profile in the doorway was Analyn's bobbing head. Her grimacing face scrunched together, compacting thick wrinkles around glowing yellow eyes.

Gabriel locked with the thin black pupils, convulsing with the rage swelling through her frame. Fangs bared from the monstrous being, her mandible stretching to the lower portions of her neck, fanning long canines, tipped with jagged barbs. A deep shuddering hiss followed as she leaned forward, the nocturnal sheen of her ire pinpointing upon the quivering boy.

You can't outrun her. You are going to die, Gabriel. A voice appeared in his mind.

No! Run! I must... run!

You die here, Gabriel—

Run, damn it! Gabriel pleaded through the fear creeping into his mind, slowing his limbs.

—weighed down by what has always hindered you. The voice continued mocking. *Thus as it has transpired, so shall it be.*

The rime of fear clung to Gabriel's legs, climbing into his heaving chest where shallow breaths expelled in rapid succession. Thoughts crumbled into nothing as he fixated on the black gums and daggerlike teeth glistening with saliva, the droplets dribbling to the floor. Audible ringing grew with Analyn's screams, climbing ever higher with shrill echoes resounding off the walls.

No! This isn't how it happened!

You're not going anywhere.

Who are you?

Gabriel turned, rushing down the narrow path, both sets of keys jingling as they bounced in his grasp. The roars trailed him, their reverberation shaking in his ears, as he sprinted through another door leading to the garage. The lights flashed on, illuminating the large emerald minivan parked inside. Two clicks of a button along the keyring, and the trunk to the vehicle puffed open, the whining gears pushed it outboard where it bumped against the wooden garage door, leaving a narrow opening.

Your uncle never did know how to park. Analyn was right about that much, eh?

Shut up!

The boy turned sideways, his torso squeezing until it wedged with the metal of the vehicle's door and frame. Steel crests scraped through his shirt, running on the ridges of his spine with sparks of pain forcing a grimace to the heavens. Analyn erupted through the door, hissing long and deep in the wake of her palms beating at the floor. The long black claws scraped at the cement as she closed on him.

You are food, boy. Nothing more to her.

This isn't right! They only eat the fetus of a pregnant woman! Who are you?

Is that so? Intriguing.

Skin pulled from the boy's back as he pushed inside the trunk. His shoulders folded, whimpers escaped from quivering lips, and the wetness of blood swelled with heated panic along the laceration staining his white shirt. He pressed the button again, hearing the whirring of the mechanisms and chirping of the vehicles' alarm engaging.

Black nails pushed through the closing door, their length grinding at steel through the carpet, inches from Gabriel's foot. The boy crawled into the corner of the trunk, bringing his knees to his chest, holding tight to them. A shrill roar flowed with the warm fog of Analyn's breath pushing through, contrasting against the coolness that immersed the garage. Bones from her wrists grazed against the metal of the door, her arm whipped away in retreat.

Now you've done it...

Shut up! Shut the hell up! She dies! That's how this ended! That's how it will all end again!

Don't be so sure about that, Agent.

Gabriel rattled as the van rocked. Claws scraped against the vehicle's body, with thumps from repeated blows. Dry skin rubbed against the metal and glass, as Analyn climbed up to the roof, scratching at paint that flaked in her claws. Her deep breaths and sobs carried into the confines of the trunk, where the curling synthetic gray fibers had worn thin.

"Gabriel!" Analyn's screams lengthened with harsh desperation. The van continued swaying with rapid and powerful motions above, hammering and scraping. "You ungrateful shit! You ruined everything!"

Sirens blared from outside, with the crackle of thick tires screeching to a halt on the street. Analyn's growls carried back into the depths of the house, the van's movement ceasing. Knocking pounded along the garage door.

"Master-at-Arms here!" a stern voice announced. "Open up, ma'am! We've gotten calls about domestic violence and child endangerment from your neighbors! Do not make us use force to enter!"

Oh, what happens here?

Nothing! Shut up!

The wide mass of the garage door lifted, carried by the creaking metal joints and hinges along its support extensions. Bootsteps tapped along the cement of the floors. The boy pressed his ear to the wall of the trunk. Distorted banter passed over quick transmission through radios secured to their utility belts.

"What the fuck happened to this vehicle?" the officer inquired.

"Wild animal, maybe?" his partner responded. They drew their M9 Berretta pistols.

"Ain't no cougars in these parts, Smithy."

"What about the SNCO's club, Michaels?"

"Stop dicking around," Michaels snapped.

Gabriel pressed the release button twice, opening the trunk. The men turned their flashlights, covering the boy as he rushed to hug an officer.

"Damn, kiddo!" Smithy patted Gabriel. "You scared the daylights out of me!"

"We've found a dependent minor that seems distraught." Michaels squeezed the radio's handheld transmitter attached to his shoulder. "We're going to secure him and proceed further into the premises—"

Don't tell them, Gabriel. They're going to think you're mad.

I said shut up! Why don't you shut the fuck up?!

"No!" Gabriel cried.

"He's shaken, bad. It'll be okay, little dude."

"You don't understand! She might still be here or even come back!"

"Who?"

"My aunt!"

"Calm down. We'll handle it. Now what's your name?"

"Gabriel, sir. Please—"

"Easy, Gabriel." Smithy patted the boy. "We need to know what's going on here. Now, can you tell us what happened to this car and why you were hiding in the trunk?"

"She turned into a monster! It's called a manananggal!"

"Okay..." Michaels raised a brow. "The boy is obviously delirious."

"Sir, please!"

"I'll secure Gabriel from the premises, in our vehicle," Smithy volunteered.

"Roger, I'm going to check to see if his aunt might be lurking around."

With a hand on Gabriel's shoulder, Smithy guided the boy outside to the black and white SUV with its flashing lights illuminating the windows and walls of neighboring homes. A cool breeze rushed against Gabriel's face. He peered up at the purple clouds, parting as beams of light flashed in the distance with the rising sun.

"Come on, kiddo. I think I have a candy bar in my snack box. It's yours. I just need you to stay calm."

"Sir, please! You don't understa—"

"Smithy! Come quick!" Michaels transmitted. "This shit is a mess!"

"Damn it, couldn't just be a normal patrol shift?"

Smithy jogged back, with Gabriel trailing behind in soft steps. Through the garage and back into the kitchen they moved, gazing through the walkway to see Michaels in the living room, near the back sliding door.

You killed the woman that adopted you, Gabriel. That's cold. Even for you.

Leave my thoughts, fiend! I banish you.

Oh, it doesn't quite work like that. My curiosity is piqued. All these walls, yet here it flows so freely. What's the matter, Gabriel? Never had a chance to tell your story to anyone else, besides that gullible uncle of yours?

He's a good man...

There is no such thing. Even in your attempts at retribution, you are tainted. You can't fool me, boy. I see everything from here.

Charred flakes arose with the morning currents, whisking before them from a crumbling trail of black and gray ashes leading through the grass. A twisting mass of a withered dried husk was poised before them, with arms outstretched. The knuckles snapped with residual tension where her long fingers had stabbed into the dirt, the shriveled remains pulling away from darkened bones. The torso was before the pair of legs, with the head twisted, having looked up into the sky, leaving its elongated maw locked open with distended shock.

"Whoever this poor sap was had been cut in half and tried crawling back to their legs..."

"Look at those teeth though... What the fuck..."

"And those damn fingers..."

"That was Analyn..." Gabriel interrupted.

"Kid!" Michaels gasped. "You're a spooky one."

"This is your aunt?" Smithy holstered his firearm, pulling the mic close to his mouth. "Dispatch, this is Unit 7. My partner and I have secured the residence in question, but we have what looks like a mutilated burn victim, an animal attack, and a traumatized minor. Please send backup and any available special units. How copy?"

"That's a solid copy, Unit 7. Backup is en route."

Oh, dear. They don't believe your story, despite their own eyes. Can't say I'm surprised. I'm not even sure I believe such extravagant tales.

Who are you? Get out of my head!

So you keep saying. And your thoughts continue to flow like cheap wine. Slaying that variant of vampire is quite the feat for a boy. I'd tip my hat to you, but for obvious reasons, I can't. Yet, all your endeavors seem to be going downhill after that. Never could shake that childhood trauma, could you? You know what they say about trauma right? These fragile human minds of yours never mature past that first major trauma, lest they overcome it. Here you are now leading an elite group of fellow veterans. But we both know you're a fraud, don't we? A petulant child with a gun and mommy issues. You're their leader, and yet you seem like the most malleable one. We are not impressed.

Once I find you—

If you find me, it's going to hurt. Best you keep your cool and join me for a cup of tea instead. I can be quite reasonable. Oh, something's happening, Gabe. Where are we going?

The green blades of grass, beige paint of the exterior walls, and purple clouds swirled together, clogging Gabriel's vision with an array blending into a bristling rainbow. Deep breaths continued, forced from his small chest by the fatigue of the evening. Flashing images of teeth and claws flickered within the mind's eye, until the realm of the physical was no longer registering to the touch of his soles.

Sirens blared, growing louder until throbbing in his skull with each strident beat echoing over the neighborhood's street. A ruffling breeze filled his ears, mixing with footsteps arriving in the living room filling with more shuffling officers. Their stern voices blended with static, competing with other transmissions passing over the radio.

"The victim—"

"Animal attack—"

"Has to be—"

"Units 12 and 18 please assist in the South Mesa housing area—"

"Take the kid. He's in shock—"

"No one touch the corpse—"

"Check upstairs—"

"Victim seems to have perished due to severe burns—"

"Have we contacted the servicemember—"

"Roger, we have more units on the way to assist—"

The voices melded into a ringing drone, hanging without pause until it resounded through quivering walls, forming squared tiles around the ground and walls. Gabriel's view trailed to the ceiling with its bumps and waves of paint, long dried from uneven brush strokes. The boy's toes touched the ground, a chill crawling up into his legs that swayed from the bed he sat upon with his head hanging low.

"He is my family and I want him out, do you understand me?" Uncle Garret's voice bellowed down the hallway. "Gabriel! Get your stuff!"

"Sir, your nephew needs hel—"

"Damn it, he's not crazy! He was traumatized. Locking him up like an animal and drugging him isn't the answer! Now you release him back to me, or I will be seeing the adjutant tomorrow and filing complaints! Admiral Finn is a friend of mine. I will pull strings to have you removed from base services."

"Chief Doucet—"

A fist slammed on the countertop, sending clipboards and pens flying.

"You quacks don't give a shit about helping others. It's all just following protocol and repeating procedures while casting judgment. People have real problems, and they need to be heard. All I need you to do is shut the hell up, give me the release forms, and my nephew. Do you understand me? I won't be repeating myself!"

Curioser and curioser! the invader's voice jeered. *Something positive shining through. We can't have that.*

Master Chief Garret Doucet. My uncle. Gabriel's thoughts fought against the mental intrusions. *He got me out of there... I'm remembering now...*

The details are convoluted, Gabriel. No one cares about you. Remember?

A large fist balled white knuckle tight hammered at the rattling bedroom door. Gabriel's head snapped over to the shuddering wooden entrance, its frame wobbling with each successive blow. Clicking metal filled the room as the locked bolt banged against the adjacent strike plate. Cracking streaked horizontal to the knob, remaining concealed under the white coat of paint.

"Gabriel!" Uncle Garret bellowed. "I smell it!"

Already experimenting with drugs at sixteen. My, my, Gabriel you are an early bloomer. Take a gander at poor dumb Garret, wasting his time and prestige on a lost cause like you, right?

Silence. Damn you.

You keep demanding that, as if these were my abysmal decisions, leading to memories that become dreams of failure. Oh, is this sacred? You cared about the chief? So be a man for once in your life, Gabriel. Answer, why didn't you ever tell him that, instead of always giving grief to the poor guy who already carried the weight of many lives on his shoulders?

I... I don't know... I failed... him and myself.

Finally, some of that—what is that word you service members like to say? Ah, yes. Integrity. I think we've seen enough, don't you?

No.

Yes. Time to go—

No! I'm remembering...

A cough expelled from the boy, tears swelling in his rosy eyes and the heavy bags below them. The rolled joint in his fingertips fumed with rising gray laces of a pungent skunky odor, blending into the room's tepid reek of soiled gym clothes and boyish flatulence. Gabriel's eyes widened as he turned on his bed, pawing at the space below for a bottle, before dunking the evidence, burning end first, into the shallow water within.

"Open this damn door! I smell it!"

"What do you mean, Uncle?" Gabriel murmured. He dished the bottle back underneath. "I was just napping."

"Gabe! Don't make me kick down this door. Now open up. We need to talk."

"I'm sorry, Uncle," the boy murmured as the door pulled from view.

Garret's countenance held like stone with bushy dark brows and piercing brown eyes narrowing over his pale wrinkles. The tall man strode inside, holding brochures with green and brown camouflage patterns running behind the information boxes written in solid black type.

"Have a seat, Gabe." The man cleared his throat, keeping

his stature tall and straight with both shoulders facing him. "There's no easy way to say this, so I'm just coming out with it. I've failed you, Gabe."

"Uncle—"

"Let me finish. I don't like this any more than you. But I have to do what's best for your future. The Navy has been my life, and it's been good to me. I don't know any other way. These are brochures for military academies. I want you to go over them, pick one by tomorrow morning, and prepare to join them next semester."

"Please—"

Garret's eyes remained locked with the boy. "No! I've failed at guiding you into becoming a man. You're sixteen years old and your grades are shit, even though I know you're smart. You've been suspended countless times and expelled twice from local districts. This is it. Your only chance at a decent future. More importantly my only chance to fix what I failed."

The brochures slapped on Gabriel's desk as his uncle walked to the door, where he stopped to look back at his nephew.

"You have damage, Gabe. The shrinks can't fix you. Neither could my love. And smoking that poison to escape your torment isn't the answer. It only masks the pain."

Gabriel nodded. His eyes lowered to the floor.

"I've never even seen you cry. You have to let it go if you're ever going to move on with your life. I believe it all, kiddo. Everything. It's all that makes sense of that crazy night. Discipline is the only answer I can think of. It's what got me through my shitty childhood. Service can teach this, even to the most broken of souls."

"Uncle, I can't. I'm not strong—"

"I believe in you, even if you don't," Garret announced, walking out.

He never gave up on me, and that's why I will never give up.

"You're wrong!" Gabriel barked. The drifting haze of thought ceased, evaporating into a singular focus on the moment. "Someone did care! And I see your little game now!"

Tension melted out of his shoulders, from the tunneled focus on the images of youth, pulling back to his own frame, witnessing the events from the outside. The bellows of his voice rippled with the walls, from the wardrobe where his small television stood, to the full-size bed with its wrinkled sheets and even the presence of his teenage self. Gabriel stepped forward, his boot heels going flat against a hard surface of drifting darkness. Attention was brought to the small images of red hovering throughout. A narrow focus was brought to floating red particles, the details around him remaining clear with their lucidity.

Weariness weighed on his neck as a tingling coursed through his limbs. Darkness descended with the fall of his eyelids. Smoke and shadow reformed the space around him, save for the crisp brochure in his grasp. Gabriel's head bobbed forward with a lurching step to catch himself, his vision jolting open.

Fight it... No!

Gabriel's presence pulled away, back to the outside perspective. Flashes of yellow stole his attention in the distance, appearing along the backdrop of the darkness adjacent to the theater of his mind. Thin pupils fixed upon him from incandescent eyes. The outline of a large top hat appeared over them. Gray lips materialized with deep cracks and thick callouses over them. They peeled upward and back, rolling above a set of long teeth, curving into a grin.

"You!" Gabriel sneered. "Nice try. But I'm on to your game."

"Can you hear their cries, Gabriel?" the being's hoarse voice uttered as if raking gravel with each syllable.

"What the fuck are you talking about?"

Gabriel raised his M4 carbine into a shoulder, poising his frame forward. He locked both hands into position on it. Quick trigger pulls sent muzzle flashes pushing vapors of carbon from the barrel with rounds speeding at the being. Its eyes and mouth closed, leaving only the darkness. Gabriel peered around as the shadow faded, the walls of his home disintegrating in seconds, replaced by tents and gaming booths.

We've been divided by enemy forces. I have to link up with the rest of the team. But where the hell do I start?

CHAPTER 12
CHAINS OF MISERY

Damn it! I'll never forgive them for ruining this! Don't these assholes have anything better to do than keep an eye on us? Our anniversary... ruined... Together since freshman year, but now the secret is out...

Blood streamed down the front of Harland's face, gushing from his reddened nose, widening with swelling. Warmth and salt poured into his mouth after flooding over his lip, leaving a metallic aftertaste melding with saliva. Deep breaths expelled from his mouth, a guard of fists raising into a locked posture. Guffawing surrounded Harland as he stared past his aching knuckles, peeling with flakes of skin, torn from the opening salvo of punches.

The team is all here... Fuck my life. Have to get Alex out of here. She's too small and delicate for this crap.

Several faces leered back, a mix of sneers and glares meeting them, seething with auras of rage. The boys shuffled in their baggy pants, sagging below their backsides, as they formed a bastion of hatred along the alley's exit. Scuffing steps echoed against the walls, growing louder when they closed past the dumpster.

Harland's attention shifted to the corner of his sight. Alex cringed to his rear, the soft palms of her thin hands shaking along his large back. Flared strands of her dark brown pixie cut dipped out of view, murmuring words in the familiar rhythm of a prayer.

"Hey J, looks like you got beat up by sissy!" Robert cackled with the others.

"That's what you get for starting the fun without the rest of us," Johnny mocked.

"So, which one kicked your ass? Lemme guess, the little one?"

"These fags got some fight in them!" Jeremy uttered, fingering at trickles of blood from his swollen lip. "But the gang's all here. So now what, Harland?"

"Just leave us alone!" Alexa pleaded. "We weren't bothering anyone!"

"Shut the fuck up!" Johnny snapped. "You poisoned our boy!"

"Don't talk to her like that!" Harland barked.

"Her? Holy shit! Have you lost your fucking mind, Gray?"

No point in reasoning with them. They wouldn't understand or care.

"You faggots think it's all good just walking around our town holding hands?" Jeremy continued. "Like we're gonna stand for that shit?"

"Maybe that shit would fly in California, but not around here," another jeered.

A taller, broad-shouldered boy stepped out, raising both hands and pointing at Harland. Head shaking, the boy's lips rolled back in disgust. "Harry, you butt pirate! I can't believe we shared a locker room with you!"

"Probably eyeing all of us, making plans and shit to convert us all with their degenerate ways. Motherfucker! Whup his ass!" Jeremy roared.

Harland turned over his shoulder, whispering, "Alex, once you see an opening, you run for it. Don't look back!"

"Harland, I can't leave you—"

"Do it! And you don't look back! I've gotten my ass kicked before." *The backyard kickboxing with Dad prepared me for this.*

Harland's vision turned back to the dragging sneakers, whose scraping closed over the pavement. A punch sent his head popping back. Vision blurred with an alarming ring blaring through his senses. The quivering surge of adrenaline brought an uncomfortable warmth over his ears. Tightness followed in his fists. Harland's arms whipped outward with retaliation. A hard right hand punch caught Jeremy, sending the teenager plopping on his rear.

Robert and Johnny raced around their comrade. In rapid blurs, Harland's vision switched between the two, his muscles firing in place with squeezing contractions, pulsing with adrenaline. An elevated haymaker came with a wide arc. Harland parried with his arm. Another wild shot went through the momentary opening, catching him in the face. A barrage of punches followed from both boys.

Thudding blows struck Harland over the back, shoulders, and head. Alex screamed, balling herself into the alley's corner, cradling knees to her chest. Her ivory skin reddened with a river of tears flooding down both cheeks. Alex quivered with each loud thump from the shuddering blows landing on her beloved.

"Stop it!" she screamed. "Please!"

The other boys joined the fray with successive blows striking down Harland's arms, finding their marks on his head and torso. Each wild assault sent his vision shuddering. Harland crumpled to the stiff asphalt. He curled on his side; eyelids clamped tight. He opened them for a moment, catching the glimpse of sneakers crashing across his face, head, and arms. A stomp found its way through his guard, sinking into the rib cage, sending him rolling over the pavement, gasping for air. Fragments of stone, dirt, and trash clung to his blue and white letterman jacket. Their silhouettes loomed over with hyena-like falsetto cackles elevating in pitch.

Done for... This is it... Alex... Run...

"Wait!" Robert hollered. The large boy leaned over, tugging on Harland's letterman jacket until stripping it from his body, leaving only a white shirt with darkening red stains. "You don't deserve this, Harry. You fucking disgrace."

Harland pushed from the pavement, with bits of dirt and rock crumbling off his body as he braced against the wall. Warmth and swelling grew over his right eye, bringing it to a squint. Blaring pain stabbed at his side, nursed by the arm he locked over it.

"Gray!" The stern voice of a man bellowed through the cackling around him. "Agent Gray!"

Harland peered through the guard of his arms, seeing the faces of those around him, locked in their diabolic sneers. His arms withered to the ground at his sides, the deep breaths continuing to race from his lungs, the flame of adrenaline continuing to surge through his firing muscles and throbbing heart.

"Diver12Actual!" the man bellowed. "Agent Harland Gray! Former United States Army Ranger. Two tours of combat, bronze star recipient with valor, graduate of—"

Harland's skinny frame widened as he rose from the ground, his brow line thickening. Bags of weariness developed underneath his eyes. The thin, soft face of his youth firmed with stubble, forging into the solid jawline of a man. Gone were the white shirt and skinny jeans, now replaced with a combat uniform and tactical vest. Bullies of memories past vanished as he spotted Gabriel at the mouth of the alley.

"Who are you?" Harland demanded. "Are you a friend?"

"No," another voice carried along the backdrop like the soft caress of a lover. "He's just like them, remember?"

Alexa gasped, cupping her mouth. "Oh my God, Harland. They beat him to a pulp!"

Alley walls peeled away from the tunneled vision narrowing on Gabriel standing over the beaten sorcerer. Lines of red crawled over the man's face, swelling with dark patches. Silhouettes of agents gathered around them, watching.

"I'll back you," Patel murmured, taking a stance next to Harland. "But please be right about this, Actual."

"Stand down?" Leo snapped at Diver Team. "Are you crazy?"

"What the fuck?" Gabriel peered around. "Fight it, Agent Gray! This vector is using—"

Currents of wind brushed across Gabriel's face. Rapid blinking blacked out his vision in momentary curtains of darkness. Harland's form neared each time his eyes struggled open, the glower of his face zeroing in on him. Diver Team's leader stood before Gabriel, with Alexa on his flank gasping. Gabriel followed her view to the sorcerer at his feet. Bloody trails seeped from his moaning face and over the agent's boots.

"Fight it!" Gabriel snapped. "The vector—it warps our memories and fears in this world! Fight it—"

Knuckles crashed hard across his face as Harland stepped

behind the punch. Gabriel's head jerked as he staggered, tipping back on the weight of his heels. Harland's boots clapped with the cement as he rushed forward. A sweeping strike came. Gabriel ducked underneath, spinning out when the larger man lost his balance, stumbling forward. Harland rose, bringing a death glare to the Butcher team leader.

"Gray!" Gabriel called out. "You're a good agent. Think back to that moment we shared in HQ, during the refit. The hatchet was buried. You're one of mine now."

Harland paused. Tension faded from his arms. Fists unfurled into shaking fingers. His brow scrunched in quizzical confusion. The blaring redness of anger evaporated from his mind. Sizzling fear subsided with the aching wounds spotted across his body. Dilated pupils quaking for retribution narrowed to normalcy as the firmness of his glower melted. The agent looked at Gabriel.

"Thank you..." Harland sighed. "None of this even happened. The guys gave me troubles but never like this..."

"Damn good to have you back," Gabriel said. "That's what these vectors are doing. Warping our memories and fears together. Some more than others. How's the other Gray?"

Alexa's stare went to the rifts of energetic currents flowing around them as minuscule red dots, their translucent state allowing the textures and colors to permeate through.

"It's all an illusion," Alexa murmured. She placed a hand on her husband's shoulder. He nodded as their eyes connected. "I—I'm good now, Butcher10Actual. Thank you."

"What now?" Harland asked.

"We find the others. We won't rest until everyone is accounted for."

"Agreed." Alexa peered down at their weapons, lying within their grasp. She cocked the charging handle on her M4 carbine, drawing the bolt back, and checking the ejection port's window for the round fed into the star chamber.

"This vector is using our memories and emotions to wear us down and kill our minds. I'm ashamed to say... it almost got me."

"As you can see, you weren't alone in that," Harland quipped.

Screams rang through the air, carried in a strident pitch. Desperation resounded in the echoes, spreading without pause. They turned, seeing endless mounds of sand lining the area, where crashing waves rose high to the dampened shoreline. Stars twinkled high above, among clouds of purple drifting among pale light from a full moon.

A young male stood before glowing light emitting from thick wooden beams facing away from the agents. He grinned, combing fingers through lengthy strands of hair, brushing them away from his chiseled face. Others gathered around, raising emblems of a goat's skull, along with a banner held high atop a staff. Flapping in the ocean breeze was the sigil of the dual cross curving into the infinity tail.

Flickering orange and yellow lights grew from the shadows of the evening, engulfing a person racking on the large fixture. The hearty aroma of cooking meat invaded their nostrils, contending with the tart saltiness of the ocean air. The putrid scent of char grew heavier with smoke. The agents stepped closer, their boots crunching with the sand, as loud chants continued.

"Konig, et Konig!" the men called with monotone unison. "Konig et Diingeer!"

Flames lashed out, devouring the skin with bubbles and boils. Loud thumps grew with the rapid movements, cries climbing to the heavens. Gabriel gasped, taking in the view of

Mara. Her face glistened around reddening tear ducts, as the woman's gaped mouth bellowed. Curls of sloughing flesh shed from her limbs each time she rattled from the fire's slow ascent.

"Mara!" Gabriel yelled.

The agents raised their weapons to inhabitants who ceased their chanting. Unblinking eyes fixed upon them as they grinned with sadistic glee.

"You're late, but I'm so relieved you could join us." Chad's mouth never moved from the wide smile. "Let's party!"

CHAPTER 13
COALITION OF LIGHT

PRESENT DAY: USA HQ WEST, SAN DIEGO, CA - 1300 HOURS

Whining motors powered the momentum of rubber wheels, passing over the shine of the corridor's wide floors. Madam Dupree raced along in her chair, humming quick jazz tunes while her head bobbed in rhythm. Corvus followed, his beaded obsidian necklace clacking together with each hurried step. He matched glances with those around them wearing combat uniforms, the heavy steps of their boots pausing to scrutinize the shaman. Others in suits stopped in their paces, bringing attention from clipboards and manilla folders to the native man, with his outfit of black leather, lined by long raven quills. Chilling tingles sizzled down his spine as goosebumps pressed up with the hairs down the back of his neck. The dream walker's eyes fixed on the Grand Scryer with locked circumspection, analyzing every inch of her.

"Coffee, I need coffee," Madam Dupree murmured. "Or maybe a nice warm tea with lemon?"

"Pardon me?" Corvus asked.

"Plotting my breakfast, Mr. Gaagi. Do not worry about the agents, they are simply curious and cautious."

"Where are we going? First, I must—"

"Ah yes, your familiar. The lovely bird that has been shadowing us since your erroneous apprehension. When the time comes, we will leave a window open for him to join us. There will be enough time for you to reestablish the link. I seem to have found myself a companion, too. It followed me from our mission to apprehend you."

Corvus closed his eyes, reaching his will through the layers. Rumbling purrs pulsed from a plump figure curled in Madam Dupree's lap. Gleaming serpentine yellow eyes materialized with two large pointed ears. A grin of sharp twisted teeth flashed before fading from his perceptions.

"So, that is the dread I am sensing. Simone, why do you have a cucuy in your lap?"

"He followed me from our first encounter. I must admit he has grown on me. If it wasn't for this one, we wouldn't have gotten far in our investigation. Although I'm afraid his intel is limited to the general information about what we're up against." Simone leaned away, whispering to Corvus. "Just between us, he seems a little unhinged. So, I am thankful for what he's able to articulate. What I want to know is the inner workings of their nefarious operation. Anyway, I trust you were given ample food and rest this morning?"

"Yes. Thank you. The healers in your infirmary are very kind and skillful. But I am sensing there is more to this assembly than us?"

"Correct, Mr. Gaagi. I have some of my scryers joining us, as well as guests from other disciplines. One that beseeched us on behalf of a victim's family and another who is concerned like yourself."

They approached a set of doors with a placard suspended over the top of its rounded frame, emblazoned in gold were the words 'Temple Site'. Smoke laced with the aroma of frankincense and myrrh hovered through the door with a warm embrace. Corvus stilled his thoughts, quieting the apprehension arising from the unfamiliar confines, wiping away the stares in his peripheral vision, along with the soreness that sparked from bruises dotting his body. The pull of weariness lifted from his baggy eyes and drooping shoulders. His senses floated away, into the presence of several positive energies shining as beacons amongst the etheric layers, with gentle caresses from minds bringing stillness to the waves of power around them.

"They're like us?" Corvus asked. "Practitioners who serve the Great Spirit?"

"Indeed. We all have different names for it. I reference it as God, because of my Christian heritage. While our Wiccan scryers refer to it as the Goddess. But I believe we all can agree that we serve the same benevolent power."

Corvus nodded.

"You will be welcomed among our ranks, Mr. Gaagi. And within it, maybe even find a home."

The doors opened. A smiling woman with gleaming chocolate skin and ivory white teeth greeted them. Long and thick braids were bound within the confines of her bandana. Loose strands extended down her shoulders, over the rounded frills outlining a beige dress on her voluptuous frame. Stones of ruby quartz and obsidian were embedded within the many silver rings and bracelets adorning her body. Shining upon the center of her forehead, within the confines of a chained circlet, stood a diamond-shaped lapis lazuli.

"Simone!" The woman's southern twang flowed with a soulful melody. "I was wonderin' when you'd show up! About time ya got here!"

The large woman leaned over, hugging the wheelchair-bound Grand Scryer in a long embrace, their hands patting each other with a familial kinship.

"It's been a morning, Mama Dinga." Madam Dupree sighed. "And my assistant messed up my coffee."

"Aww, Simone. I tell you what. After we sort out all this mess, I'll make you a big ole pot of my shrimp gumbo, and some lemonade. Make you forget all about that awful stuff."

"That sounds like heaven. I am partial to seafood. Oh, and I had quite the disparaging run-in with your rival."

"That boy. Edjewale. I tried with that one, but the demon sank its claws into him long before I came around." Mama Dinga turned her bright smile to Corvus. "And who's this handsome but scrawny fellow? Oh, my child. You look like you've seen better days."

"Mama Dinga, this is Corvus Gaagi, the last of the dream walkers, heir to the Chaktowi Tribe."

"Oh my!" the large woman exclaimed. "The native night magicians. I thought they went extinct."

"It's a pleasure to meet you, ma'am," Corvus responded, taking her hand, and kissing it.

"And manners, too!"

"Corvus, this is Mama Dinga, the foremost authority in America on Voodoo and the practice of the saints. She is heir to Marie Laveau's spiritual lineage. You've had the misfortune of meeting a more nefarious practitioner of the faith, but Mama Dinga is the most adept in the right-handed path of the craft."

classification. Your culture knows them as the boogeyman. A vile creature that feeds off fear. Pero, listening to the others, there seems to be many."

"Bloody oath." An Australian woman tipped her head of wild blonde strands as her suntanned cheeks rose into a smirk.

"This is my friend from Down Under," Madam Dupree announced. "The famed Pan Pacific devil hunter and honorary shaman, Pepper Morris."

"Thank ya, Simone. I'm rough 'round the edges. Might drop a clanger or two, so don't take offense, eh?"

"None taken." Corvus nodded. "I think we have bigger issues at hand."

"But we call those lot the featherfoot. Spirits of the malevolent kind. The only thing worse are pommies."

Madam Dupree snickered. "I shouldn't laugh at that one, seeing how we're on good terms with our English brethren and their agency."

"And in my home country, they are the rakshasa," a bearded man announced. He wore a neat Chand Tora turban, bearing the metal images of a prone crescent moon with a double-edged sword rising from the center.

"Everyone, this is Randeep Singh, a Granthi and warrior of the Sikh faith. He has traveled from India to assist us."

"Thank you, Simone. In my country, throughout the sea of my people, there are sparse reports about these beings. The rakshasa have existed in solid form before the great deluge."

"The cucuy must be stopped," Tía Hermosa announced. "And we shall do that."

"I'm afraid it's not that easy," Corvus declared.

"I want everyone to follow Corvus' lead with this," Madam Dupree instructed. "He has the most experience within their realm. I have delved in there for only a conversation's worth of time and can say it is no ordinary location within the etheric layers."

"A coalescence of energies is required to navigate the realm of the cucuy. Even with my training, I am no match for their alpha."

"Alpha?" a scryer apprentice asked.

"Yes, he is the dominant one of their pack; with a control over the sands beyond my comprehension. The fiend that many have reported invading their dreams."

"The sands?"

"That is the name given to the realm where thought flows during slumber."

"Mr. Sandman," Mama Dinga announced. "We know about him in the practice. The Hat Man utters madness to his victims. Fortune has always guided my path away from him. Guess it's time we finally met."

"He is Ravana among the Khalsa and Hindu people," Randeep answered. "The stories of ancient India claim that he was slain by the hero Rama. These sands, as you call them, must be where he resides in his disembodied state."

"A correct assumption," Madam Dupree agreed. "This Ravana, leader of the cucuy or rakshasa if you will, is a sect of the Nephilim. I wonder though, after they became disembodied, why weren't they relegated to the pit with the others?"

"Good question." Pepper shrugged. "Bloody neph derros probably wandered there to avoid the pit, with that Ravana bloomer leading them."

"It's not him that I worry about though," Corvus replied. "That hat wearing fiend is simply following orders. The one that he serves is far more nightmarish. I've only heard her voice from afar... Screeching like a thousand eagles. Such a jabbering mess. The pain was immense, shattering my grip on the sands. The pocket she dwells within is not accessible from the normal point of slumber."

"I surmise that is where the children are being kept," Madam Dupree stated. "That is why Kat has dispatched the task force to apprehend Partridge. We will wring the intel from her mind and know exactly what we need to do. I just hope that Gabriel and Harland are faring well in that mission."

"Thank you, for the lovely introduction, Simone. Indeed, I serve Bondye, the great all-encompassing spirit most of you probably know as God." Mama Dinga nodded. "But enough about me; come meet the others. We are gettin' this mission goin'."

Chatter filled the room, as a group of intuitives gathered around a wide copper plinth. Gleaming along the top of it was a massive hunk of amethyst, with a white sparkling base rising into angular protrusions of a glorious purple. A large man held the hand of an older lady, walking in tempo with her shaking steps as they approached Madam Dupree.

A lengthy head of salt and pepper hair curtained a wizened and craggy face, save for the momentary glimpses from sharp brown eyes peering between its sway. She reached up, revealing bony hands possessing gray fingernails more akin to claws.

"And this wonderful lady here," Madam Dupree introduced as she took her hand. "She is Tía Hermosa, the radiant heart of Mexico's 'El Orden' an offshoot from our own scryer order."

The woman bowed her head. "Thank you, prima Simone."

Corvus' eyes met with the man holding her hand, analyzing the thin mustache, and unwavering hardness within his stare. A shine rose from the pointed leather shoes he wore, below the cuffed tailored pants held up by a belt with a solid gold buckle.

"I know you," Corvus announced with sharp accusation, the pleasantries dissolving from his countenance and into a glower. "You're Javier Iglesias, the drug lord of the borders."

The man stepped forward, his stiff lip and chin rising to match Corvus' ire. The broad-shouldered Javier closed with the dream walker, their eyes deadlocking among firm brows.

"No," the man answered. "I am Javier Iglesias, the grieving father."

"Javier is a guest, under the agency's protection," Madam Dupree announced. "He beseeched Tía Hermosa for aid after his twin sons were taken like the others. Javier funded Tía Hermosa's trip here and is acting as her aid during this operation."

Corvus nodded. "I can put aside my differences for the sake of the children's souls."

Javier stepped away, retaking Tía Hermosa's hand.

"Mijo," Tía Hermosa announced with her cracking voice. "Everyone. Aquí. Aquí. Por favor."

Conversations died down, as the practitioners gathered around the graying woman, who turned to face the majority. Her gentle brown eyes connected with each of them, complimented by her wrinkled lips pressing together in a weak smile.

"Please listen," she continued. "We all face beings older than the great deluge. They have—"

Puffing coughs forced from the woman's short frame. Javier patted her back.

"Gracias. As I was saying. Our foe has haunted the children of our people for many years, feeding on their life force and using it as currency. Only in recent times have they expanded, stretching their efforts beyond a few unfortunate cases. Why they have decided to openly declare war on the innocent, yo no sé."

"What are these creatures, ma'am?" a young scryer asked.

"The cucuy is what we call them in my culture."

"There seems to be a mix-up, Tía Hermosa, ma'am. The agency has them classified as a goblinoid creature."

"There are many kinds of cucuy, these being the worst

CHAPTER 14
FESTIVAL OF FOOLS

HIDDEN REACHES OF THE ETHERIC LAYERS - TIME UNKNOWN

Chad's unflinching grin remained poised at the agents. Weapon barrels were trained on him and the others. The ocean breeze paused, ushering the arrival of a stagnant and tepid air. Black robed cultists flanked the leather clad bad boy. Their perfect white teeth glistened in the moonlight, matching their eyes, pronounced by the contrast of shadows spreading over them.

"Mara!" Gabriel cried out, rushing to her.

In unison, the cultists' gaze followed Gabriel with their locked expressions.

"You take one step toward him, and you die!" Alexa warned. "All of you, get on your knees and put your hands behind your head!"

"What demonic outfit are you with?" Harland barked. "Who are you?"

"Who are you?" Chad asked.

"I'm not playing games, buddy! You're about to get turned into a 5.56 pin cushion!"

"Who are you?" a cultist asked.

"Mara!" Gabriel pulled off his jacket, beating away the flames from the woman. "I'm here."

"We're all here now," another of their accomplices muttered.

"The Queen will be coming soon," Chad murmured. "To collect your heads."

"She's hungry."

"Of course. She's always ravenous."

"Shut the hell up!" Alexa barked. "Eyes on me, assholes!"

Stone-faced grins turned to the Diver agent. "It wants our attention."

"You want our attention, little one?" Chad asked. Their smiles unfurled into glowers.

Light from the stars and moon bent away from the cultists' presence. Shadows thickened around them, erasing all features save for their eyes. Side steps brought them behind each other in single file, until their silhouettes appeared as one. Rounds barked from the barrels of M4s, sending forth bright glowing lines of phosphorous from tracer rounds that were swallowed by the darkness.

Thick lips smacked, then peeled away from Chad's outline. Pointed canines lined his crescent smile. Glistening pools of saliva spilled over with droplets patting the floor. Seething breaths of eagerness set the figure's position bobbing. Its obscure visage extended higher.

"It wants us to cooperate," the multitude of their scratching voices declared. "It wants us to listen—listen, from the voice within—what better way—hear your pleas—from within us…"

"What the hell are they babbling about?" Alexa murmured.

"Gabe!" Harland called out. "Hurry up with Mara! We have contact! Unknown vector! Gargantuan class!"

Gabriel's fingers rifled and tugged at the bindings. Heartbeats resounded through his being, rising with each groan of pain from Mara. Her eyes rolled upward, behind drooping lids, with twitches of instability bringing back her vision in fleeting glimpses. Strands of Mara's long brown hair unfurled from the thrashing movements, the bitter reek of smoldering flesh clinging to it. A black elastic hair tie hung adjacent on a lower corner of her bobbing head. Rasping moans arose with smokey mutters from Mara's trembling lips.

"Hang in there!" Gabriel pleaded. "I'm going to get you out of here. Damn, these ties!"

Thick and blackened straps dug into Mara's shriveling skin, pressing deep into the caustic remains peeling from cherry red layers. Blaring temperatures rose from veins of blue and pink along withered lines drawing the flesh together. Whispers fluttered from her mouth, the words marred with elongated strains rising from her stomach.

What the fuck am I doing? Gabriel wondered. Butcher's team leader peered down to his vest, where the brown strapped handle of a combat knife materialized. Its scabbard bounced where it attached over his magazine pouches. *I always have my blade!*

Sliding metal, guided from Gabriel's vest, who brought the weapon over Mara's confines with smooth slices. Tightness from the straps loosened, and the woman spilled forth as a whimpering pile of humanity. Murmurs passed from her lips, fading with each repetition.

"I got you!" he exclaimed with arms around Mara. "What are you saying?"

"Be—" Mara's head rolled back. "It's... behind... you..."

Gabriel turned, stepping away from the glare of thin serpentine pupils. The gaze locked on to him from a towering height within a shroud of darkness. Glimmers of starlight pierced the veil with its incandescent reach, bringing glimpses of an outline within. Among the blackened reaches, a plethora of writhing limbs churned like waves from an elongated body, noiseless in their rapid motions.

"Who are you?" the vector called out. Its words traveled with a low and curling resonance, repeated by successive voices. Each grew quieter than the last, until they were as breathy whispers, passing into a reach beyond ears.

The being swayed from the length of its lower extremities, blending into the unseen reaches it slithered across. Long scrapes followed with the motions of churning muscles, propelling it forward.

Tracer rounds fired from Alexa and Harland's weapons, guiding a series of shots from their M4s. The creature continued as rounds sped into the morass of obscurity, its long silhouette wading through the hail of lead. Piercing bullets passed into the tall being, leading into view with its sneering feline face. The stripped orange and black muzzle rose with a sneer, revealing saber-like fangs, swelling at each tip with droplets of olive ichor. A nocturnal sheen passed over its predatory yellow eyes, fixated with Gabriel's.

"Damn it, rounds aren't doing shit here!" Harland snapped.

"Switch to etheric weaponry," Alexa suggested.

"They think they have authority within the sands." The fiend turned to the couple.

Carbines dangled from D-rings on their vests, as Alexa brought her hands together. Harland sidestepped, breaking away from his wife. With smooth trigger pulls, rounds zipped through the being's countenance. Thin pupils of the creature's glare fixed on the Diver team leader, tracing his movements along the beach, walking upward of the dunes lining the back end from the moist shoreline.

"Right here!" Harland yelled. "You're mine! Come on, demon!"

Alexa closed her eyes, ushering away the last images of her husband and the fiend from her mind. The woman's psyche began to focus on the singular breath running through her. Flickering particles called to Alexa's grasp, swirling until gathering into a ball of light. As she brought her hands forward, the energy shot out, guided by her vision, until finding its mark upon the slithering fiend.

Light smacked into the buckling creature. A grimace of teeth homed in on Alexa, its body rotating with the uppermost set of massive shoulders turning to challenge her. A gasp escaped Alexa, as it approached. Their eyes locked. The tanned hues of the beach were erased from her view, along with stars dotting the night sky. The crashing waves faded. Alexa's thoughts drifted back to the alley.

"Return to me," the echoes called. "Remember who you are."

Moisture lined down her face from reddened tear filled eyes. Salt from Alexa's cries soaked over her lips. Thudding fists smashed into a downed Harland, rocking with each fierce blow. The boys encircled him, continuing an onslaught of punches. Jeremy peered up at Alexa, his slender pupils locked with hers as a grin brought thick wrinkles creasing over his visage.

"Faggots!" The word left Jeremy from unmoving lips. "Send his boyfriend to the emergency room!"

"No!" Alexa screamed. "Stop it! Just leave us alone!"

"Alex!" Harland's voice rang out. "Move! It's coming right for you!"

"Agent Alexa Gray!" Gabriel hollered.

Concrete and walls from the alley disintegrated, the red particles forming Alexa's vision pulling away like a curtain, returning to the beach. Grimacing teeth bore down on her. Wind curled underneath the heavy lash of a tail, whipping out from the veil of shadow. Alexa dived, landing into a tumble before shooting back to her feet. The creature's large appendage slammed into the beach. A wall of sand jettisoned under the thumping crash, pelting the ground in a shower of granules.

"Gabriel!" Mara cried out. "I'm too far gone... Can't..."

"What are you saying?"

"Can't break free..." Mara's voice cracked. "I can't let it go..."

"I don't understand!"

Butcher's bravo reached for Gabriel's M1911.45 caliber sidearm, tucked away on his hip. Mara pawed with red, skinless fingers brushing against the gun. Heaving breaths deflated her frame. Winces arose from the blaring pain roiling through her limbs.

"Neither do I. I just know. Gabe, you have to let me go, because I can't... Or all of you will die in here..."

"No!"

"It's connected... Remember our training against the dark arts... The opening..."

"When there's an opening, it goes both ways."

"Do it..." Mara pleaded. "So that I know... you are going home... to your daughter..."

Gabriel rose to his feet. A slow and reluctant nod came, his eyes looking away to the vast ocean distance. He drew the pistol. "Goodbye, my friend."

Mara's eyes rolled up into their lids. Her head dropped back. The woman's shaking hands reached up for her friend, pleading with outstretched fingers. Gabriel aligned the front and rear sight apertures with Mara's forehead. A trigger pull sent the round punching through her skull. Laces of blood streamed from the gaping hole as Mara's head cocked back.

Thunderous shrieks reverberated through the area. Waves rolled through reality, shaking the foundations of all they beheld. The monstrosity screamed with his array of voices rising to purple skies, thundering overhead. The slithering form beat at the ground, a multitude of limbs peeling from its body, grasping at sand. Movement ceased from it, leaving a shadowed husk lying on the beach.

Gabriel carried Mara's body around to it, with the Grays following. They peered into the empty caves of darkened flesh where its eyes had once been.

"Thank you," Gabriel whispered, hugging Mara's body.

The purple skies brightened as the clouds peeled away. Their view carried up to cracks of light beaming through. An enormous face with a strong jawline peered down at them, its details washed out by illuminating whiteness.

"There you are," a voice announced.

CHAPTER 15
ROYAL FORK

PRESENT DAY: USA HQ WEST, SAN DIEGO, CA - 2200 HOURS

Yellow secretions clung to Gabriel's twitching eyelids. Flakes broke away from the crusty mucus as they peeled open. His mind carried from the tepid air and pallid hills of sand to the embrace of the air conditioner's whining churns, ushering forth coolness that encompassed the room. A whitewashing glare emanated from lights above, giving shape to the face transferred from the view of the mind's eye and into the material. Curtis, the commander of the Monarch Team loomed over the gurney. Other agents gathered around, with hands touching the metal rails flanking Gabriel. Portia's blue eyes focused with concern when they connected with Gabriel's blank stare.

"There you are," Curtis said. "He's coming to, Butcher10Mike."

"Roger! I'm on it, Monarch Actual," Portia replied.

"Good to have you back in the land of the living." Curtis patted Gabriel's shoulder.

"That accounts for everyone except Butcher10Bravo," Portia said. "Looks like Actual's vitals are perfect. I'm going to attend to—"

"Don't bother," Gabriel murmured.

"What, Actual? Why would you say that?"

Gabriel gazed across to where Mara lay. Her long dark hair had unfurled over her shirt to her forearms with layers of wrinkled scars. Next to her, hanging from the steel coat rack was her uniform jacket, the name label 'Graves' over her left pocket with 'Department of Defense' embroidered on the right. Gabriel turned away, sighing.

"She's gone. That shell is an empty vessel."

"What happened in there, Gabriel?" Curtis asked. "Your Mike and Golf spoke about their own contact, after the etheric ambush was sprung."

"They ported us to their realm, or at least something similar. I was a fool—"

"No one could've seen that coming, Agent Agapito," Katherine announced, her heels clicking with each step as the other agents parted for her. "I'm just glad we got you back in one piece. You have valuable intel on how that realm works. Madam Dupree is planning a major hop. Brought in some heavy hitters from the spiritual community to augment the scryers. Butcher and Diver are the most experienced now in that realm. I want the task force to go with them. If you're combat capable."

"Always, ma'am. I don't care how many bumps I take."

"Good. That's what I wanted to hear. Take the time you need to refit yourselves. I'll give the order to rendezvous at the staging point when it's time."

"Yes, ma'am!" agents from both teams responded.

"It's good to have you back, Agent Agapito. Great work with the mission." Katherine nodded before taking her leave.

"We apprehended Partridge while you were dealing with the vectors in the other realm," Curtis said.

"Great." Gabriel shook his head. "While I was napping, Monarch was stealing all the glory."

"I wouldn't say that. We wouldn't have fared so well in that realm. My agents are grunts, not detectives. You sprang their trap and cleared the path."

"Curt. I know what you're trying to do. It's not helping."

"Fair enough, hard ass."

"At least the boss lady is happy with the results. Except for... Damn, this operation has me twisted."

"Not going to lie. You're looking like a soup sandwich. Hey! You wanted me to drop the cordiality."

Gabriel peered over to his reflection in the glare of a monitor. Disheveled strands of black hair draped over his wrinkled forehead. Dark bags weighed heavy underneath bloodshot eyes. The reek of stale odor emanated from his breath akin to warm oatmeal and overboiled corn.

That place took its toll on me. Damn, it was only a day. Not even. How many hours? Maybe twelve? I can't. What the fuck. Barely able to do simple math...

"Good to have you back, bossman," Leo chimed in. "Even if you're grumpier than usual."

Gabriel murmured under his breath, rubbing the gunk from his eyes.

"The interrogation is going down soon," Curtis warned.

"And I want in on that." Gabriel hopped off the gurney, reaching for his combat jacket.

"Figured you'd say that. I'm going with half of Monarch to

augment Hitman Team. Monarch2Charlie will be taking the helm until I return."

"Understood. Thank you for having our backs out there."

The team leaders gave a firm handshake.

"You know the deal, a few cold ones during R&R and a good conversation."

Gabriel nodded. "Will do."

"Be safe, Butcher Team." Curtis waved, exiting the room.

The door opened again with Harland standing in it. "We're ready, Butcher Actual."

"Let's get this interrogation going."

I've failed every step of the way with this mission. I failed Mara. I failed my team. I failed the children. I failed their families. I've failed myself. Yet, I can feel this is just the beginning of our problems. How deep does this hole go?

Reflections of the room surrounded Meryl Partridge from polished mirrored walls. Unkempt strands of hair separated from the woman's shining and silvery bobbed cut. Red marks striped along her ashen pale face and forearms, humming with the residual bruises of the agents' apprehension. Meryl peered around at the reflections of herself, smirking before her attention darted to the towering geodes of shining purple amethysts standing in each corner. Windchimes dangled above her, clamoring with a smooth vibratory resonance bearing upon the room. Frigid air rushed from ceiling vents. The cold whisked through the thin and baggy clothing she was issued, slipping within her sleeves, bringing Meryl's thin limbs to shivers. Wrinkled and pale hands gripped at opposite elbows in a self-hug.

"*You were a beauty once, weren't you? Before those awful liver spots and wrinkles. I don't like to think back on my youth as much. Then again, I prefer accepting the present rather than dreading it,*" the monotone voice of a woman announced into Meryl's thoughts.

"Get the fuck out of my head, Dupree."

"I guess the reputation of your genius is deserved. Figured it out so quick? Most non-practitioners only catch on after the fact."

"Mistaken about so much in your arrogance, Scryer. You're not getting anything out of me. Now where's my lawyer?"

"Perhaps you're right and I am wrong. Someone else entitled to that credit?" Simone smirked. "Oh, I'm afraid it doesn't work like that. You see, you're no longer a citizen of the United States of America, once you have been classified as a vector. Those rights were erased the moment you sided with the hidden darkness. Now for the sake of national security, you fall under a special jurisdiction."

Meryl's eyes rolled. Her teeth started to chatter.

"You don't like the clothing we gave you? Not warm enough?"

"I will block you from my thoughts."

"You can try." Simone chuckled. "You're just an amateur, girl. That much is obvious. Took to the craft later in life? You're a disgrace to witches."

"Figuring it all out? Spare me any theosophical lectures of selflessness or the laws."

Madam Dupree pushed beyond swathes of fog, through chilling curtains of mist, and into the shadowed regions of Meryl's psyche. Patter from a quartet of little feet trailed the Grand Scryer in a lazy and curving gait. Thoughts whisked past in murmurs, garbled with red hot contempt that pushed away the cold. She continued until her steps were weighed by the grip of an unseen muck. The Grand Scryer waded, the pressure rising into her knees, then hips. Each movement brought a strain to her psyche, the resistance forcing a standstill.

What is this? Simone pondered. *A barrier. Not by her design. There's no way it was summoned by this pretentious woman-child. I can't bypass it. Whoever created this is extremely gifted. Yet, I sense it was done with casual effort.*

"The promise of eternity." Utterances of Meryl's psyche fluttered past Simone like the wind. *"Lies! She lied! I swear I just wanted to serve."*

Perhaps we've dived deep enough. Let's observe. Shall we?

Tiny paws split in their path, stretching around Dupree's presence with steps on each side, then closing again to normal width. The invisible being stopped before the wall. Licking noises proceeded, along with the swishing thump of a tail. It continued with soft steps immersing it, blending with the deep recesses of shadow.

"Oh, but no you didn't. You were scared." A rebuttal sparked from their quarry's inner doubts. *"Meryl, we only wanted what was lost to return forever."*

"The White Queen is no fool. Not yours. Not ours. Not anyone's. You knew this. We knew this," Meryl's psyche barked at herself.

"It seems my assumptions were correct," Dupree murmured. "The White Queen is your benefactor. But who is she?"

"No. The Queen just used me," Meryl uttered with reluctance.

"Because she knew we weren't loyal," Meryl's angry consciousness reprimanded. *She anticipated the duplicity of our selfish desires."*

"Your doubts about her intentions are wrong. She never cared. We had to worry for ourselves."

"I see." Simone nodded. "She used your company and programming skills in the creation of that awful game. Goading you with false promises, perhaps?"

"Get out of my mind, Scryer!" Meryl bellowed.

"No," Madam Dupree quipped. "I don't think I'll be doing that. I'm finding your rampant worries to be quite entertaining. Your mistress never taught you how to discipline the mind."

"Fine, Dupree. Don't even bother with that. I'll give you what you want. What you probably already know. First, I need guarantees."

"A deal then? I sense your fear, girl. Don't think that you have leverage here. State your conditions but do keep them reasonable."

"Protection and a pardon."

"The first we can do. The second, that's going to be a bit tough. See, you've helped set this nightmare in motion. Many families have suffered because of you. Even worse is the loss of innocent life. We do not abide by the corruption of the civilian justice system, where your affluence can buy or demand a slap on the wrist for even the most heinous transgressions. There's a penance that must be paid, child. It can be reduced though, depending on what you give me."

"We must tone down the ego which has left us bereft, for there are many outcomes worse than death." Echoes within Meryl's subconscious continued surging from the darkening regions of her despair. It crawled from the alcoves where the woman had tried to lock it away, inching toward the consciousness at an alarming rate. "You've seen the heavy tolls, what she does with the souls. The dust and the pain are all that ever remain. You've heard the screams, their wailing that shook your core. They feel it even after their presence is no more. The elongated agony can be heard through the millennium. Everyone knows them throughout Pandemonium."

"Who is the White Queen?"

"No idea."

"Don't try running this game with me, girl."

"You're looking for a specific name? I don't know, damn it! Not even the others dwelling there understand her origins. I was privileged to learn only a fraction more than them. She reached out to me! Promises were made..."

"Elaborate. No more stopping with half the truth, Partridge.

Don't think that I am not privy to your schemes. You wish to feed me to your master for her clemency? Trying to play both sides to see who comes out on top? I warn you that I will not be easy quarry."

"How did you—"

"Like I said. She should've taught you how to discipline your mind. Now continue."

"I hope you do find what you're looking for." Spite tainted Meryl's words. "All of you—"

"Out with it!"

"She promised me the secrets to eternal life. That if I helped her gather enough pure essence, she would teach me how to utilize it to craft my own world."

"So, you could prolong your miserable existence, at the expense of innocent children? You sicken me. What about these worlds?"

"I spent my life building a billion dollar empire in a world dominated by men. You think I want to give that up? These children won't amount to a fraction of my success—"

"You disgust me!" Madam Dupree snapped. "I don't want to hear your delusional reasoning. Spare me the nefarious cognitive dissonance, before I lose my temper and allow Butcher Team to use you as a punching bag!"

"The one with the raven felt their wrath." The voice carried from deep within Meryl's psyche. "Trails of blood were left in their path. You would be wise to heed her warning. Or I doubt you'll survive to the next morning."

"She told me a few things. Bragged about being the first wife. It never made any sense to me. The White Queen claimed to not have fallen because she avoided the quince, at least that's how she put it. She claimed to be a god because of that. Most people in that realm say questionable things."

"Go on. Why the children?"

"That I do know. The purpose behind the abductions. Fuel for *everything that she does. It maintains the dimension that she created, but most importantly they are utilized to keep most of her children alive. However, many others sought refuge within the realm that weren't the Queen's progeny. The innocent energy of a child's soul is the closest thing to Godly energy. Then we go off and let it become tainted by the interactions with the material world. You know, the inevitability of sin and all that jazz. Adult souls just aren't as useful unless you can trap them in abundance. Your God has a limitless supply of pure and positive energy used for creation. While the Queen had the knowledge and power to shape the energy and utilize it, she needed a source. The human soul has such tremendous power within it, Dupree. There's your answer."*

"Her children are dying?"

"They fade out of existence within any of the realms save for that cursed pit of the etheric layers. Where the dead go when they do not have a proper nephesh. To become—"

"Demons. Yes, I know. So, the door that leads to this realm—"

"Is a narrow frequency corridor, so small that even most of the best trained scryers will miss it. The energy fashioned from innocence reads no different than the upper levels to most. But, the frequency is always changing, hopping from one to the next, making it incredibly difficult to find the door. This is done to ward off intruders, mostly to protect the realm from the Red Queen. Finding the entrance will be your toughest endeavor. From there it expands into its own pocket of reality. I know you scryers can be slow. Don't be too discouraged. A little girl was able to find it once before, all on her own during a nap that became an inadvertent astral travel. I'm sure you've seen the movies or read the book?"

"That won't be of any consequence for me, Meryl. Because you're going to be helping us with that." *Don't want to reveal my hand just yet.*

"That wasn't part of the arrangement—"

"Our arrangement is you cooperate for protection. Or I can let Butcher Team in here, then release whatever is left of you for the White Queen to deal with."

"And here I thought you were the good guys," Meryl scoffed.

"Good and evil are a matter of perspective. One that is malleable. Didn't your master teach you that? It should've been day one in the laws of magick."

Meryl rolled her eyes.

"On with it," Dupree urged. "First, tell me about this Red Queen."

"The Red Queen is feared the most in Pandemonium. My mistress explained her as the great dragon, one that can only be slain by the will of Eve's children, who will step on her head. Whatever that means. The Red Queen was released from prison recently along with her brothers and sisters. Around the turn of the 20th century."

"The Fallen," Dupree uttered. *Raptor Team had the unfortunate task of dealing with one. We've suspected them being the reasons for the extreme boost in technology and vicious wars humanity fought at the behest of the shadow government.*

"The Red Queen doesn't share power, no matter how much her minions want to believe it. She wants it all. The materium, the etheric layers, every frequency, under her absolute control. Hell, I was even told she's trying to create a transdimensional gateway. One that can even penetrate the Elysian Fields. Guessing she wants round two with her brother? She won't be outnumbered this time with the armies she's amassing."

"Yes. We're familiar with the reconstruction of the Tower of Babel in Europe. That's something we'll have to combat later. We haven't the resources yet to deal with an international incident on such a scale."

"Even with my ambition I find such a thing foolhardy. What are they calling it now? CERN?" Meryl shrugged. "That is the main reason for the White Queen's uptake in souls. You see, there's an extradimensional war brewing. The White Queen knows it's only a matter of time before Big Red and her lackeys invade Pandemonium. I mean, if others can stumble upon the realm, then why not one of the most powerful beings in the universe with the aid of CERN?"

"This is all making sense now," Dupree deduced. "The White Queen is building a war chest. That's why she got sloppy and it's noticeable now on a grand scale. Before, it was simply just draining energy from hapless victims in their sleep, trying to stay off everyone's radar. Even having people doubt when they were paralyzed and being siphoned. But snatching away the souls of children on this scale..."

"Yup! That's the whole plan. At least what I was privy to. So, all this information must be worth something good, right? Are you going to release your dogs to beat the hell out of me?"

"Well now, if you keep referring to them like that, I might not have to order anything. Although, I like what I'm hearing. Keep going."

"Among the White Queen's children is their alpha. He's gone by various names throughout time, but most recently people have taken to calling him the Hat Man, because of how he manifests wearing a large top hat. While he leads them, he is unruly from the White Queen's perspective. Hat Man tends to wander off to his own devices most of the time. My encounters with him have proved inane and fruitless. Despite her attachment to him, I believe the Hat Man doesn't want to serve the Queen any longer and does so only when threatened. Many of the denizens of Pandemonium seem to be disillusioned with the Queen's ambition as of late."

"And the rest of the children?"

Meryl paused, choking back a crack in her surly

countenance that saw a moment of apprehension as hissing images of fangs, and acrid decay, reminiscent of rotting bologna and burning balloons. The cauldron of memories bubbled to the surface, their cackling laughter, akin to squeals with a jovial pitch, beckoning sinister intent.

"*The first time I went to the garden...*" Meryl swallowed deeply, her eyelids clamping tight, bringing her crow's feet into a pronounced squeeze.

"*What?*"

"*My ambition came at a price. I thought I could just saunter into that place. Like the little girl did. But, I didn't have her power to ward them at a safe distance and transform their reality. I saw them for what they were. Monsters. I didn't have anything to protect me. I was there for days as their plaything before the Queen found me in the garden. The stuff they did...*"

"*I see. Those lunatics have unwholesome appetites.*"

"*This world makes women suffer for their ambition.*" Meryl let out a deep sigh, lowering her sorrowful gaze to the table. "*Whether it's here or there. I wasn't going to let anything stop me from living eternally. Not after all that I've built. I was the first women's grand slam virtual gaming champion. I created the world's most successful international gaming franchise. Every step I took, men—boys, doubted me, ridiculed me, and even tried to sabotage me. I never backed down. Never gave in. They didn't want me there? Good. That motivated me. I wanted it to hurt every goddamn time I crushed their best efforts. I wanted them to shrivel up inside when they saw their names on the marquee next to mine, announcing our face-off, knowing they were going to be humiliated. I never backed down. Most would say brazen, and that's how my father taught me. But, as I walked into that garden...*" Meryl paused, swallowing again. The tremble of muscles from her throat dislodged the gathered wetness from her reddening eyes. Twin tears rolled down her pale cheeks. "... I wish I hadn't."

"So that's why you were reluctant to work with us? Because you gave up more than just money and infrastructure. Poor girl. Now you know the first rule to dealing with demons."

"What's that?"

"Never deal with demons."

Meryl nodded. "You broke me, Dupree. You win."

"I take no pleasure in this, save that your alignment is now correct in its path. The truth is the White Queen was going to find a way to implement her nefarious plans. With or without you."

"That doesn't make me feel better."

"You keep that ambition. It's a very good tool to have. Do you want to know the keys to immortality? Let me tell you, Meryl. It's by what we do in this world. You already achieved it. You stated as much. No one will forget the trail that you blazed in a world that was dominated by men for so long. Now to augment such a feat is even simpler, but requires you to lose that solipsism derived from your ego."

Meryl nodded.

"You help the next generation of women gamers who are facing the same tribulations as you in their careers," Madam Dupree continued. "Your name will be in the smiles and happy thoughts of every girl gamer on the path. It'll be the beacon of hope for those needing inspiration. That is how you live on forever."

"You're planning on going in there, Dupree? Here's my advice to you. Don't do it. There's nothing cute about that place. Nothing fun or happy. Don't for one second think that damn book can provide you with any useful advice."

"Like your past self, fear isn't something that I let get in the way of my ambition. Kat and I are readying a task force that is eager to face the challenges. My agents and scryers will be better prepared than you were. This mission isn't about giving in to fear. It's about facing it."

"One more thing." Meryl's face twisted with confusion. *"The Queen has a weakness. I think..."*

"You think?"

"Look, it's not like there was a fucking sign or instruction manual, okay? There were rumors around the castle that the Queen discarded all her positive energy. Not sure. Everyone shut the hell up about it if they thought she was within earshot. I believe it's her conscience, if you will. Gave it to one of her disobedient sons to hold. He went mad though, speaking gibberish and vanquishing his brethren with his newfound power. After that the Queen banished him, cursing him to some far-off region of Pandemonium. I just can't help feeling that positive energy is the key to winning. Likely, it was discarded so that her ambition could override her good sense and conscientious objections that may have arrived from her foul methods."

"I see there is some inkling of talent." Dupree smirked. *"You're right. There is something about what you said alarming my instincts. Good girl."*

"What now?"

"Now, you will be serving as an EPW liaison, that means Enemy Prisoner of War, assisting us with tracing the door to Pandemonium. Your service to the task force will decide whether you'll be executed for high treason—"

Meryl gasped. "What?!"

"—or released on infinite probation. Yes. While your cooperation so far has been appreciated by the agency, there's still the matter of immense suffering that you helped cause. After this is complete you will be dividing up your company assets among the families who have lost, ensuring reparations in the form of a *constant dividend, and a control of the assets their children gave their lives for."*

"I'll lose almost everything."

"Indeed. Except you'll still be alive to do what we talked about. Your legacy is what means everything to you now. So, damn the money, right?"

"Yes."

"Then, this should give you the means to continue seeking that goal."

Meryl nodded.

"Oh, and don't try to weasel your way out of the reparations, Meryl. If you attempt to flee to another country without paying your dues, we will find you. The agency has assets and allies in every nation, even those hostile to our shadow government. Remember, we don't answer to a conventional jurisdiction. I'm sure with your current karmic standing, you're not going to be getting into heaven. There's time to fix that, though. Our Father in Heaven can be very forgiving. Where was I... Oh, right. The task force will find you again, except during the next apprehension there won't be an arrest. Do you get me?"

"Yes."

"Yes, what, liaison? Come on, you've played the military games."

"Yes... ma'am."

"Excellent."

Madam Dupree's vision raced back to her body, in the adjacent room where Howler and their agents stood lined against the transparent glass. She looked up, seeing Portia's big blue eyes and thin pink lips rolling into a smile. The petite blonde was holding a glass of orange juice.

"I know you agents always get nervous when I transcend the layers." Madam Dupree chuckled.

"Yes, ma'am," Portia replied, handing her the glass. "Here you go."

Katherine spun around with a smirk. "Good job breaking that one, Simone. The chamber was able to echo her inner dialogue to us."

"Well now, I cannot take all the credit for this interrogation. I had help from my little buddy sowing confusion." Madam Dupree curled her finger to something on her lap, rubbing it with loving gentleness.

"I'm in such deep shit right now..." Meryl's thoughts continued. They glanced through the window at their quarry who put her head on the desk. *"Better do as they say. Swallow my pride and cooperate."*

"I have my theories on the proper nomenclature of this White Queen," Madam Dupree announced. "But I don't want to announce it yet until I can confirm it with a quick research stint."

"Not a problem, Simone," Assistant Director Howler replied. "I'll continue readying the task force. We should be green for launch within the hour. The final touches are being put on the transcendental chamber."

"We need to grab some coffee beforehand, Kat. I hate going under without some caffeine in my system."

"I'll have my assistant grab a cup of the cold stuff."

"Agent Agapito," Madam Dupree called out.

"Yes, ma'am," the stalwart agent answered with Butcher Team gathering around the Grand Scryer's wheelchair.

"Ma'am? Are you feeling okay?" Madam Dupree raised a brow.

"Yes. More than okay and more than ready. Getting revenge for Mara is my only goal now."

"Revenge? They'll use that against you."

Gabriel nodded. "Justice."

"Good. Because I'm going to need Butcher and Diver teams to spearhead this operation. My scryers aren't warriors of your capabilities. This is going to be extremely dangerous."

"We are up for the challenge, ma'am. Whatever it may bring."

"Right on!" Leo agreed.

"Never had a doubt. I meant it when I said you're their champion, Agent Agapito," Madam Dupree continued. "They see themselves in you."

"And I meant it when I gladly accepted the charge."

"Then, it's off to Wonderland."

CHAPTER 16
MISSION BRIEFING
WELCOME TO THE NIGHTMARE

DEEP UNDERGROUND MILITARY BASE - 0400 HOURS

Butcher Team crammed into a wide elevator with Diver. The fabricated polymer smell of ballistic grade nylon exuded from their new issue of vests and uniforms. Metallic odor from magazines filled the area from the combat loads stuffed into their pouches, secured by woven MOLLE straps, and packing full metal jacket 5.56 rounds to feed their short M4 carbines. Holstered M1911 pistols rattled with each step along their hips above their kneepads. Fat pouches rested along the top of their combat loads, containing plump fragmentation, cylindrical smoke grenades, and thin flashbangs. The straps of their patrol packs dug tight into their shoulders, bloated by the abundant supplies squeezed within.

Howler isn't fucking around. We got all new battle rattle thrown at us and clearance for full pyro, Leo thought. *Hey, my black ass ain't complaining. Better than waiting in line at musty ass CIF and filling out paperwork. Good thing I remembered Mara's trick for new boots. Keep the inserts from the old boots and wear a layer of moleskin to protect your feet. Mara...* Leo sighed.

Gabriel pressed a button with no label on the keypad. The doors glided closed. He tapped it again six more times, holding it on the final one. Pressure from the elevator's descent rose around them. The panel's lights revealed the first floor. It continued, lowering past the basement, heading into regions unlisted.

"Some kind of secret squirrel stuff?" Patel asked, scratching his head. "This is cool!"

"Shut up," Gabriel said.

"We just lost the best second in the agency," Leo murmured. "And we're about to go on the most dangerous mission to date. Try having some bearing, rookie squad." *I have to step it up as acting second now that Mara is gone. Damn... That hurts so fucking much. Gone. I can't believe it. That woman taught me how to pistol qual perfectly. Spent hours of her own time training me. She's gone. The toughest hop and I'm wishing she was here right now, giving me that self-assured thousand-yard stare that would let me know we got this shit.*

Gabriel nodded to him.

Actual is hurting right now. I know his ass. He's just bottling it up like he always does. That man is made from stone and fire.

Kevin glowered at Patel who lowered his head. Alexa patted his shoulder.

"Where are we going, Butcher Actual?" Harland asked. "Seems like we've been descending for quite some time."

"There is a DUMB underneath our headquarters for black operations."

"A what? Is that another quip at our expense?"

"Deep Underground Military Base," Gabriel continued.

"We only utilize it during our biggest operations where assets cannot all be maintained by HQ."

The elevator came to a stop, bumping them at their destination. The doors parted for a wide corridor breaking off in three directions. Gabriel stepped ahead, walking down a straight path with Butcher Team in tow. Diver raced to catch up with their hurried pace, walking down the hall with its glowing yellow rectangular lights along the lower portions of the steel walls. Loud squeals of churning metal mixed into the crackles of electricity drifting into the distance.

"What the hell is that?" Alexa asked.

"A superconducting maglev bullet train," Gabriel answered. "The fastest in the world at eight hundred kilometers an hour."

"We have tech like that?"

"Yep. It's only on a need-to-know basis. The military industrial complex is the cutting edge of research and development. That edge being generations ahead of what the civilian populace is made aware of. Have to spoon-feed them this stuff."

"Also, so we have time to account for any possibilities that might be exploited before releasing it to the world," Portia added.

Gabriel nodded.

"Damn thing uses a tremendous amount of energy," Leo said. "The civilians nearby must be pissed off that their grid has gone down suddenly."

"Queen Bee and Madam Dupree are planning something big," Gabriel continued. "So many moving parts right now for the agency. Our operation isn't the only one and it's massive."

Heavy bootsteps ahead stole Gabriel's attention. A tall figure with several inches of dark hair and a thick five-o'clock shadow peered at them from bloodshot eyes. A grape Swisher Sweet cigarette rested in his lips, smoke rising from the glowing end. The steps he took resonated with aggressive purpose, his black trench coat swaying around each leg.

At the man's side was a hulking Cane Corso dog. Black goggles rested snug on her head, with wires coated in gray plastic extending from it, into a Kevlar vest and pouch along her back. The canine's dark gray body swayed with excitement, her breaths gathering at an eager pace. A giant tongue plopped in and out of the dog's massive jaws, her lips pulling away into the parody of a smile, flashing large glistening teeth. The muscular beast glanced at her companion who nodded before blowing out a gust of cigarette smoke. The dog wagged its nub of a tail when seeing Gabriel. Floppy ears dropped back and down, even to the folds of excess skin drooping along the bottom of her face.

"HK Bessie! Who's a beautiful girl?" Gabriel softened his tone with playful exuberance. "You're a beautiful girl."

The gargantuan beast shuffled from side to side, her oversized muscular frame bouncing heavily above the enormous paws stomping with glee.

"Are you running with us?" Gabriel asked the man.

"Not this time, Gabe," the man answered with a gruff and smokey tone. "AD Grimes is augmenting Bess and me into Sentinel Team to apprehend EPW escapees. There was an ambush en route to the Sand Palace. It was ugly. Many shitbag vectors escaped. He's activating HK Chima, too."

"Damn. What?"

"You didn't hear? Guess you been busy. Stay safe, Agents."

The man and his dog walked past them, disappearing at the elevator.

"Never seen that agent before," Harland noted.

coach closing upon them. Within a few seconds, Wendy had been cut off by the swarm of bouncing little leaguers. Their smiling faces flashed through his mind's eye. Hands came into view, some with gloves, others bare, all of them smudged with sweat and dirt. He rose into the air, carried aloft by those surrounding him, and paraded around the catcher's mound.

"You did it, son!" his coach bellowed. "You broke the tie with two outs! We won for sure!"

A snickering Wendy came into view. Joey reached for her. The girl smirked, shaking her head and mouthing the word 'later.' Chuckles escaped from the boy as he nodded. Joey's head dipped back in surrender in a toothy beam. They continued floating him around to the hoots and clapping adulation of the audience rising in the bleachers.

"We got pizza waiting for us at Tony's restaurant!" Coach continued. "Let's finish this game and head out! Is your gorgeous mother coming? Perhaps you can put in a good word for me?"

Joey chuckled along with a few others and nodded. *Coach is a good guy. Why not.*

After he was set down, Joey stared over to the opposition gathering near their dugout. Wendy waved from the mob of her teammates, disappearing among them. Joey sighed, turning to meet his younger sister Phyllis. The curly-haired brunette pressed her slipping glasses even with her freckled nose before presenting a small black box.

"Where have you been?" Joey asked, ruffling Phyllis' hair.

"Sorry I missed the game, but I was in line at Mr. Crespo's Electronics Store." She pointed across the street from the field.

"What else is new, nerd!" Joey teased. "To get what?"

"To get us this!"

Phyllis held up the rectangular black box with a

triumphant grin. 'Sons of the Apocalypse,' was displayed in bold red lettering over two bare-chested, muscle-bound, soldiers carrying machine guns and firing at hordes of monsters.

"No way!" Joey hugged his sister. "You did it!"

"Yep, yep!" Phyllis chuckled. "It was free while supplies lasted, just like the commercial said. And after we register with Partridge Games, we get a free 3D screen saver, too!"

"Yes! So cool! We're going to be slaying mutant monsters tonight!"

"Let's go home right now and—"

"Can't. The team is going to celebrate."

"You and these stupid sports. Ugh! Fine! I'll install it on our computers and get a jump on the first quests. Don't get upset when my character is like ten levels ahead of yours with better weapons!"

Joey sighed, nudging her with his elbow. "All good. Just show me the ropes. See you at home."

The theater of memories evaporated from Joey's vision as light pierced into the room from the hallway. His mother appeared at the opening door, peeking in with chocolate locks dangling over the flanks of her face. Her gaze went to the computer desk, where the flashing lights from the screen saver portrayed animations of blaring guns as they fired at growling red monsters.

"I thought you were still up playing that awful game."

"Nope, just a screen saver, Mom. I'm too tired. Not going to last much longer."

"Good, I had to pull your sister away from it just now. Glad at least one of my babies has the sense to get some proper rest. I'll see you in the morning, Joe-Joe. I love you."

"Love you too, Mom. Goodnight."

mottled images of his tall lamp and bookshelf. Shallow breaths and the release of control followed, bringing the boy's mind drifting to the currents of slumber. The last visages of Joey's sight traced his arm, wandering to his dangling hand, away from the warmth of the full-size bed. Cool fluxes of the air conditioner rushed against his fingers. A pulse washed over him, vibrating through his body.

A shadow stepped forward, beyond the obscurity of blurred images and the fog of weariness. Alarm surged, jolting the boy. The presence remained within his peripheral, just out of reach from his focus. Its dark outline flickered with instability like rising smoke. The towering presence crept closer, looming over him.

"Heh, heh, heh, heh," laughter came, blending glee with sinister intent.

Gotta get my bat... *I can't... move...*

A tremble crawled down the boy's spine, lingering with vibrations that grew faint as mists of darkness continued enveloping the outskirts of his vision. The presence approached just beyond his fingers. As the shadows of the room peeled away, a man stepped out, his long black coat swaying into view. Yellow feline eyes fixed upon the boy with slit pupils.

Scream for Mom...

A crushing unseen force wrestled away Joey's willpower. Attempts to move were met with only a sizzle of communication that carried into his limbs with no response. The presence in the room enveloped him, bearing down on the boy's mind and spirit.

Help... Someone...

The desire to move melded with his slumber. The quake of his heart vanished, along with the coolness of the air

"Thanks, Mom," Joey smiled.

"And you, young lady!" Phyllis Senior snapped. "Didn't I tell you that's enough gaming for tonight?"

"Mom, I have to slay the Mutant Overlord of the Alpha Quadrant, or I won't be able to get the—"

"I don't care! Now turn off that rubbish and get some proper rest, I mean it, Philly! Or I'll disconnect the internet for a week."

Phyllis gasped. Her mother nodded with stern resolve.

"Okay, okay, sorry! Gosh! Speaking of overlords..."

"What was that?"

"Nothing. Going to bed. Sorry."

"Thanks for listening, Mom." Joey hugged Phyllis Senior.

"Anytime, kiddo. That's what I'm here for."

Joey went back into his room, closed the door, and plopped on his bed. He turned on his side, gazing across to his computer's monitor. Vibrant yellows of gunfire flashed between mutants crumbling in defeat to men and women wielding oversized guns. Cawing stole away his attention. His heart thumped with rapidity when it called again.

Fear weighed Joey's steps as he rose from his bed and hobbled to the window, ignoring the large black bird's stare. At the bottom of the tree was nothing save for the grass growing to ankle length.

Nothing. Thank God. I need to cut that tomorrow before Mr. Anderson starts griping. I really wish Mom would just get rocks and sand like everyone else.

Another slow, mouth gaping yawn escaped Joey, before he lay back down on his side, bringing the sheets over himself. *Really dragging tonight. No more worries. Mom has it handled.* Eyelids hung low, blurring away the vision of his computer desk. The glowing monitor's array of lights fused with the appeared, hinting at the beauty she exhibited during her youth, now wielded by her daughter.

"Nana...." Joey lowered his guard. "What are you doing here? Aren't you supposed to be at the hospital?"

"Don't be silly, Joe-Joe. I always come here, reading my beautiful grandbabies to sleep. I think I have a book around here for you. It has sports in it... You like sports, right?"

"Yeah, Nana, I do."

"Oh, look at that. She's gone again. Something is always keeping her up. She doesn't seem to listen to me when I urge her back to sleep. It's that youthful energy. I was that way, you know. Up at all hours of the night."

An encompassing gloom arrived, washing away the textures of light within the room's aura. Chills ran through Joey, sending goosebumps pressing from his skin, as alarm rang in his senses. *Is someone watching me?*

He peered over to his sister's empty bed.

"Nana, I don't understand. Where is Phyllis?"

Joey gazed away into the hall, his attention tethered by a looming aura of doom, before he shook free of it, returning to his grandmother. The old woman had vanished. Soft footsteps with a slow pace circled him. His eyes followed the ground where gentle patters continued out into the hall. A figure cloaked in shadows loomed in the doorway.

Piercing eyes fixed upon Joey, with a solid white glow encompassed by a stern glare. Wide shoulders brushed the doorframe as it moved forward with a muted glide. Black feathers stood from its headdress, scuffing the passage before it stopped within feet of Joey. Wings of midnight hung along its wide portions, the plumes along the length of them the only feature emerging from the darkness of its vibrating presence.

conditioning and the soft cushion of his bed. Mind and spirit drifted away from his body.

Joey found himself standing and surveying the emptiness of his room. Waves of light and shadow traced the details within view, like a mirage on a balmy day. His eyes followed to the baseball bat now clasped in both trembling hands, and over his knuckles turning white.

As he stepped from his bed, Joey's perspective shifted with the floor's surface canting to the left. Tremors passed through the room's texture before the ripples ceased. Another lurching move and he found the gradual slope had changed to the right. The world vibrated again, only to normalize with haste.

Dang… So out of it…

Staggered steps carried the boy into the hallway, glancing at the adjacent door of his sister's room. The corridor tilted as he continued. Joey's view wobbled until he reached his destination, where the entrance to Phyllis' room opened. Joey rushed inside, stopping, and gasping at the figure before him.

A short and hunched individual rocked in a chair within the darkness of Phyllis' room. The monitor's glare shone over the person's rounded back to a bushel of disheveled graying curls. The glare shifted off the large glasses hugging the wrinkles scrunched together as the being turned to face him.

"Joe-Joe, oh I was going to visit you next, dear," the old woman said. "Just finishing up this lovely book about a happy magical unicorn I found for Phyllis. I saw it, browsing the… the online… store… Yes, I tell you… I don't know how these authors come up with such brilliant ideas. Look at these delightfully adorable pictures."

The book's glossy cover was presented to Joey who stepped forward, raising his bat. Brown liver spots came into view over familiar high cheekbones. A face of perfect symmetry

"That's because they're not agents. They're Hotel Kilos. Hunter Killers," Gabriel answered.

"Specialized operatives tasked to do one thing only," Leo added. "You think we're ruthless? You ain't seen nothing yet. They're only used in the direst circumstances."

"Shit must really be hitting the fan," Kevin murmured. "I know we're all getting run ragged, but damn."

"Like I said," Gabriel noted to Harland. "It's been busy."

"Yeah," Alexa agreed. "Operations galore, good grief. No wonder every team is forgoing R&R."

Gabriel led them before a set of giant doors, framed by broad beams of shining gray titanium. Brilliant white quartz sparkled among the outer layer, aligned every few inches along the entrance. A black camera flashed above them, scanning with faint traces of red passing over Gabriel's eyes. Booming clicks followed the rumbling of metal cogs spinning into action. The doors parted, slipping into fitted crevices within the entrance.

A vast room expanded into a cavernous architectural marvel of titanium, with traces of gold outlining a majority of the region. Dozens of colossal pillars climbed to the immense height of the ceiling. Cold radiated from the white marble floors covered with the gray imprints of countless combat boots and tire treads. Personnel shuffled about from the line of camouflage Humvees to green containers piled on top of each other, and the countless medical gurneys occupying the greater portion of the area. Others remained seated at an adjacent array of desks, staring at computer monitors, typing, and scrutinizing rows of data racing across their monitors.

"Holy crap!" Kevin pointed to the far end. "Look, the Black Knights are here. We're in for some shit…"

Lined along the opposite end of the staging point were

M7A2 Bradley Fighting Vehicles. The green laminate armored war machines stood over ten feet in height, topped with a remote turreted 7.62 millimeter coaxial rotary cannon, accompanied by a small black lensed camera. A thick armored hull rested on heavy treads. The rear compartment's main hatch whined as the gears were commanded by agents inside the spacious passenger and munitions compartment.

Along the flank of its main turret were triple smoke grenade tubes, with secondary tubes stationed below them, marked with small white circles upon their base. A thick 25 millimeter Bushmaster Autocannon stood proud and long across the front, accommodated by dual TOW rocket compartments on the turret's right side, with a smaller twin Stinger missile system over it.

"Make sure you load plenty of hate into them compartments for alpha team. Leave room in bravo to seat the precious cargo, damn it!" A petite woman with broad shoulders and thick hips stood before the armored column, barking at the agents. Black and gray oil stains spotted her coveralls, along with blotches over her tight bun and large nose, indented from combat long ago. "I want all PM paperwork handed over to 'stang Actual by the end of debrief!"

"Roger, Actual!" numerous armor agents replied.

"Agent Conn Knight19Actual is here, too," Leo noted. "Looking feisty as ever. But, gots nothing on Sweet Pea over here."

Portia's glare narrowed on Leo, who stared straight ahead, pretending not to see her burning ire in his peripherals.

"Who do we report to again?" Patel scratched his head. "Good grief this is a lot to take in."

"This is the Transcendental Chamber," Portia answered. "Support personnel are going to take care of the other stuff. We just need to focus on the mission. Try not to stress so much, Diver. Just follow Butcher Actual's lead. Feel free to ask me anything if you have questions."

"You all should listen to legally blonde here," Leo quipped. The sharp and tiny point of Portia's elbow jabbed at his side. "Ouch! You bony thing!"

"Thank you, Agent Lawson." Alexa chuckled.

Harland nodded, walking beside Gabriel. They continued, weaving past the various staff, blending to the rear of a crowd gathered around the gurneys. Numerous agents from Monarch were present beside scryers wearing combat uniforms of green, brown, and black camouflage. Everyone's focus remained on Madam Dupree, with Tía Hermosa and Mama Dinga at her side. Behind them stood Meryl Partridge in her baggy orange jumpsuit, sighing with arms crossed.

"Excellent," Madam Dupree announced. "Our spearhead has arrived, and they look ready."

"Indeed, ma'am," Harland replied, his body snapping straight.

"For justice, correct?" Madam Dupree's eyes fell on Butcher Actual.

Gabriel nodded to the Grand Scryer.

"Very well then," Madam Dupree continued. "Let's start the briefing. Agents and Scryers. Thank you all for assembling on such short notice. I apologize to most of you for the lack of details until now. Everyone will report to their designated areas of respite. Once there, you will rest on your gurneys as you are. The factors of your presence will carry through the door from the acknowledgment of your active consciousness. We will be infiltrating a fringe portion of the etheric layers known as Pandemonium, but colloquially referenced in popular culture as Wonderland. I assure you that it is anything but. You will be administered an alchemical concoction of melatonin, iodine, kava root, valerian, chamomile, vervain, and the main ingredient ayahuasca. This will serve as the initial vehicle to port our uninitiated members through the etheric layers. We have checked all your medical files and received the clearance for any possible allergies to the active psychosis inducing element of DMT within ayahuasca. However, you will all remain monitored by individual medical personnel teams assigned to your sectors. When you go under, my scryers will be assisting the entire task force with their combined wills to sustain and protect the presence of your minds and souls, by guarding your silver cords. That is the name for the spiritual tether binding your mind, body, and spirit. Despite that, the cucuy are numerous and formidable in their own realm. Once through the door, be wary of their influence and maniacal games. They will attempt to coerce you into ruin. They prey on your emotions, fears, hardships, and traumas. Make no mistake, dropping your guard with them can easily result in a nightmarish encounter."

"The cucuy have a leader among them," Tía Hermosa added. "He is known for his love of hats. Be wary of this one and the big eared lunatic that walks with him. Pero, control your minds or you will succumb to their wiles."

"Ya'll be careful down there," Mama Dinga warned. "We're only going to be able to do so much from here. Pick and choose your battles. Don't go fussin' and fightin' with everything and everyone in there. My dears, if the whole of Wonderland decides to come down on you, we won't be able to hold them off."

"Indeed," Madam Dupree concurred. "There is a finite amount of time and effort that we can expend. It pains me to say this, but you cannot dive down there with the intention of being exterminators, trying to eliminate every vile vector you encounter." Her firm gaze turned to Gabriel. When their eyes met, he looked away. "I know this edict goes against everything you're sworn to uphold. Those instincts are why the agency recruited you and why you're the best in our field. But I repeat, you will stand down unless it pertains to achieving our primary objective. Saving the children shall be our only focus."

"Your secondary mission will be reconnoitering any details of this place for future intel," a voice announced from within the crowd.

Assistant Director Grimes stepped out from the mass of personnel. He met Madam Dupree's intense stare with a smirk. Stepping out, he strutted with a cocksure swagger from his upright frame and confident arched brows, steadfast under the Grand Scryer's disdain. After running fingers through his unkempt bushel of hair, he adjusted the drooping tie over his coffee stained dress shirt. Large bags swelled underneath his darkened eyelids. Yellow teeth appeared from his parting lips, expelling breath laced with java and cigarettes.

"Such hostility, Simone," Grimes quipped. "Lighten up." He turned to the agents. "While the grouch here is right, it would be a huge benefit to the agency as a whole if you were able to gather intel on anything you see in Pandemonium."

"My mission is to get them and the children out alive," Madam Dupree affirmed. "The safety of this operation is already limited without your schemes."

"What schemes?" Grimes retorted. "All I'm asking is that the agents keep note of what they encounter, and if—"

Madam Dupree glowered.

"—they happen to have a chance at gathering more intel, do so. This is our first such operation. It would behoove the agency should we have to neutralize such a threat in the future."

"Only at the discretion of Butcher Actual," Madam Dupree countered.

"Of course. What do you say, Agent Agapito?"

"The children are my main priority," Gabriel answered. "But I don't want to lose any more agents to this madness, now or later. We'll do our best to aid in codifying what we discover. So long as it doesn't compromise the primary objective. You're free to pick our brains during debrief for those mental notes."

"It's settled," Madam Dupree countered. "Anything else, Assistant Director Grimes?"

"Heck, I'm satisfied."

"Butcher and Diver teams, I would like to formally introduce someone very special," Madam Dupree continued. "A civilian liaison who is a specialist in the etheric layers of the dream world. May I present the heir of the Chaktowi Tribe, and the last Dream Walker Shaman. Corvus Gaagi."

The tall man walked out from the mass of scryers. Long raven plums ruffled from the sleeves of his deerskin tunic, brushing with others as he passed by. Corvus' black shining eyes matched those of the dark bird perched upon his shoulder, scrutinizing Gabriel with a hard and unceasing look. Corvus bowed, his headdress of shadowy feathers fanned upward in salute.

"We met as foes," the Dream Walker Shaman announced. "Despite the tumult of our first encounter, I hold steadfast to the belief that the Great Spirit's plan is to unite our prowess for the sake of humanity. Because of that I let go of any negative feelings for what has transpired and hope that we can work together for the greater good."

"Well said, Master Gaagi." Madam Dupree smiled. "Gabriel?"

"More sorcerers," Kevin whispered, rolling his eyes.

"Don't be an ass!" Portia hushed her snapping retort. "We need them."

Madam Dupree's smile traced over the Butcher team medic before ultimately arriving at Gabriel. "What say you, Agent Agapito?"

Gabriel stepped out from the others, grim-faced and resolute. He offered his hand. Corvus nodded and accepted.

"That settles it!" Portia squealed with delight. "You're with us now, Corvus."

"You're going to have to make a tough decision," Mama Dinga announced, pursing her lips into a weak smile at Gabriel. "Simone was right about you. Did she tell you why the children gravitate toward you?"

"No," Gabriel replied.

"Children aren't filtered by life's psychological control mechanisms," Mama Dinga answered. "Their minds are fresh. Clean slates for them to work with until the lies from the controllers come of course; there's no such thing as monsters and magick. There's no such thing as ghosts and spirits. Those premonitions, no matter how real they feel, well that's just a product of your overactive imagination. Sound familiar?"

Gabriel nodded.

"They see you for the truth of your journey Butcher10Actual," Mama Dinga continued. "Even if you can't." She reached for his cheek, cupping it with her chubby hands and a delicate maternal caress. "So much going on in that mind of yours. Gabriel, you're going to be faced with a choice in there. I can't tell you what it is or how to decide. I can only tell you that I see it coming as an energy fork in the road that is your spiritual journey. Funny thing about these glimpses of the future is how it looks when it all comes flooding down from the crown to the third eye. It's a mess. Then again so are most things in life, right?"

Gabriel nodded.

"Can we please get this going?" Meryl Partridge groaned. "Simone has a mountain of tasks for me to accomplish to earn my pardon and I just want this nightmare that you all dragged me into over."

"Indeed." Madam Dupree snickered. "Meryl is correct. Everyone in position at your battle stations. Prepare to invade Wonderland."

Teams shuffled to their stations, with a plethora of agents from Monarch usurping a major area. Butcher and Diver headed toward their respective zones, each of them aligning with a gurney, accompanied by a rolling desk of an electrocardiogram machine, and an open laptop computer. Leo tapped Gabriel, causing the entire team to peer over when he pointed to dozens of scryers gathering around a circle of meditation cushions.

Small and jagged towers of obsidian shone with glory, standing near the brown robed scryers' heads as they seated themselves upon the oblong maroon pillows. Incense burned from a device of rotating mechanical spheres, held aloft by brass insectoid legs that walked along their perimeter. Smoke streamed from the robots' porous presences, lacing the air with fading glimpses of gray, and the warm fragrances of jasmine and myrrh. The scryers brought their legs into full lotus posture, touching their index fingers to their thumbs while placing their hands in a relaxed pose on their lap. Eyelids closed as their faces rose, aligning to the same unseen angle above them all.

"I hate sorcerers," Leo murmured, shaking his head.

"Gee, thanks, Leo." Harland chuckled. "Still going on about your apprehensions?"

"Ow!" Leo barked at Portia who pinched the back of his arm. The tiny blonde glowered at him with piercing eyes, her face scrunching with disapproval. "Easy, woman! We're not even married yet and you're already trying to control me!"

"Married?" A small gasp left Portia. She swallowed, remaining quiet as Leo smirked.

"You'll learn to trust us." Alexa broke the pregnant pause between the two agents. "We will hold down your six, Butcher. Mark my words."

Harland nodded.

"I know," Gabriel replied, lying down on the gurney. "No more gripes though, Leo. We have no choice in the matter. Let's get ready like the scryers."

Medical attendants arrived, bearing metallic bowls in their rubber gloved hands. A reddish-brown liquid swished inside, carrying greenish flakes of vegetation within its simmering surface exuding waves of heat. A woman stopped before Gabriel, presenting the bowl with a smile before setting it on a stand next to him.

"I'd let it cool down a little bit before consuming, Agents," the nurse announced. "We just finished the brewing as per Madam Dupree's instructions. It's fresh off the kettle and piping hot!"

"Thank you," Gabriel said.

"My goodness, this smells like moldy gym socks!" Patel cried out.

"I was going to say it smelled like the sweat of an unwashed asshole," Leo quipped, smirking from his gurney.

"Are we bonding?"

"Don't ruin it."

"And how would you know what sweat from a dirty derriere smells like?" Portia smirked.

"A man has his secrets." Leo shrugged.

"You're nasty!"

Alexa chuckled. "They're a lot like us behind the scenes."

Harland reached from his gurney, their fingers entwining when his wife touched back. Warm smiles were exchanged. Discipline melted from the former ranger's countenance as he gazed into her doe-like eyes, hidden behind the dark bangs of her pixie cut. Nothing needed to be said. Familiarity resonated in his mind tracing the slenderness of her digits with his own, knowing the contours of their shape before even reaching the spots. Instinct bridged their bond of love, leaving their lips pressed in silence save for their eyes that spoke with longing.

"I think it's ready," announced the nurse, leaning over to examine a bowl.

Gabriel took his in both hands, taking in the conflicting odors of must and vegetation. Tingling traveled in from his nose, climbing into his skull with the thick clouds of warmth and tincture within.

"Sip slowly, Agents," the nurse continued. "Listen to the sound of my voice. Let it bring you to the grasp of benefactors guiding you through the door. Their presence will be waiting. Don't proceed alone."

The agents sipped from the bowls, tasting the hot liquid, leaving granules clinging to their lips and tongues. Warmth swelled in their mouths, racing through their senses only moments after the first swallow. Humming rose in the foundations of their minds, pulling bits of their senses away with each passing moment. Escalating heartbeats resounded through the core of their beings, thumping into their ears with beads of sweat gathering along their brows.

Deep and slow sips followed. A prickling touch tapped along their hands, spreading into their palms, and through their fingers. It continued, washing over their arms, and climbing with evergrowing speed through their torsos. Tension roiled through their bodies. The chemicals faded from taste and breath. The lamps hanging from the vast gray ceiling grew in brightness that consumed their vision. Pillars and beams overhead meshed into an unkempt artist's palate, until the colors combined to form darkness. Their senses caved inward, draining away in the panic of their minds, echoing with unintelligible streams of thoughts that flowed into each other, until there was only one churning black noise.

The agents found themselves drifting upon unseen currents, swallowed by an ocean of shadows, that washed them to the shores of a place their jaded senses could not register.

Touch returned to Gabriel, retracing the layers of his being together with each step he took into the unseen morass of energies. A hand of light reached out, taking his and pulling him closer. A familiar presence eased away the friction of apprehension.

"I am here, Agent Agapito," Madam Dupree declared. "We are working on guiding you all through this narrow corridor of the etheric layers. A dark door if you will. I am personally watching over Butcher and Diver."

"This is intense!" Harland's voice passed from the obscurity of dark regions. "I am sensing a transition though. The frequencies are so indistinct within their hidden energies. This dimension reads the same as the material realm, being of energies that were once positive, now having shifted to something different. Changed by the will of others. Yet, it all remains blended with the dream state of our minds."

"Very astute observations, Agent Gray," Madam Dupree acknowledged.

"I can hear everyone, and even feel you all," Patel stated. "But I've no idea where anyone is."

"I thought you were supposed to be the experts?" Leo scoffed.

"We've never been here before," Alexa said. "What we experienced was merely a glimpse of it from the materium."

"That's fine," Portia said. "We'll figure it out together."

"Just a little further ahead, everyone," Meryl called out, her voice further than Madam Dupree's. "Exert your will, or you will never make it through. So many others get repelled from it. Or worse…"

"Worse?" Kevin asked.

"Shrunken into oblivion, as Pandemonium swallows them using their unchecked emotions, and befuddled minds. This is a rough dive, the energies that comprise this place are derived from something not far off from yourselves. I've wondered myself if it were sentient in its hunger. Despite my many dives, I've learned that it's like a hurricane. The closer you are to the eye of the storm, the safer your presence."

"That part is good to know," Patel stated.

"Well, at least the safer you are from being consumed by the outlying energies. I cannot speak for what lies within," Meryl continued.

"And now I'm worried again."

"Although, never have I come through with an invasion force." Meryl paused, her mind skimming past the blaring energetic resonance of Madam Dupree, to the numerous presences in tow. Ethereal cords of silver extended from them with misty translucence, guiding them with gentle whispers that encouraged them onward.

"Almost there but be sure to follow your guides," Madam Dupree's cat warned. "If you're not careful, you could be taken on some wild rides."

Yellow eyes appeared within the expansive darkness, permeating through reality with shadows. Others opened, dotting the distance with their maniacal gazes. Darkness peeled back as lips among them, fanning sharp white teeth from their wide mouths.

"As she said, the rabbit's duplicity was to be expected," hissing sinister voices declared. "They are here wishing to capitalize on their minor victory."

"Mother is always correct," another murmured. "Mother knows best."

"Hatter isn't here to hog all the good parts. Let's feast upon their souls."

"This isn't right," Madam Dupree yelled. "They know we're coming! It's an ambush! Meryl!"

"I knew this was foolhardy!" Meryl Partridge's words snapped with fearful contempt. "I'm not sticking around for this shit! Damn you, Dupree!"

Partridge's breaths echoed into the distance, pushing through the shadow corridor and into a white expanse of light flashing into the room from the opening of a door.

"Agents push through!" Madam Dupree commanded. "Scryers! Waylay our opposition! The cuyuy are upon us! Minds free! Hold back nothing!"

Sparks of energy surged across the dark expanse. Glimpses of light uncovered hundreds of thin beings bounding through. Their writhing and emaciated frames appeared tangled, yet still moving in cohesion as a mass of shadowy lines. Warbling cackles filled the area in a demented chorus of echoing madness.

"Follow me," a familiar voice called out.

"We're no match for the cucuy in this state," Gabriel barked to his team. "It's up to the scryers. Push through as Madam Dupree ordered!"

Gabriel's will surged forward, stepping through the unseen until arriving at a break of light. It opened, welcoming him with a blinding vista that swallowed his presence.

The cucuys' howling laughter continued.

CHAPTER 17
THE TWINS AND THE WALRUS

FOREST OF THE LOST, PANDEMONIUM - TIME UNKNOWN

Gabriel awoke to the blurring vista of dull light emanating from a grayish sky mixed with light stains of purple. The reek of burning balloons carried through the air, invading his nostrils, and spreading to his taste buds. Tall grass remained smushed underneath him. Fatigue weighed upon his eyes, fogging his mind with a delicate haze.

I made it through. This doesn't feel real. There's a detachment to what I'm seeing. This is worse than before. I can feel traces of myself floating in whatever they call this shit. I must be deeper in this hell hole than the first time.

The agent sat upright, finding a plump daypack wedged between his legs. The large canteens swished with water along the sides when it rocked from his movements.

"*The factors of your presence will carry through the door from the acknowledgment of your active consciousness.*" Madam Dupree's instructions resurfaced in Gabriel's memories.

She was right. It's all here. Except for the team. Where the hell is everyone? The chaos must've done something to our traversing the door. The scryers didn't have time to carry us and repel the vectors.

Glimpses of sharp teeth and glowing feline eyes played back in his memory. Echoes of the cucuys' laughter played back, ringing with a noxious desire of nefarious intent. He recalled their near visible bodies, so thin and long, speeding through the dark descent of the doorway, for the presence of the scryers defending the task force.

Madam Dupree? Can you hear me? Nothing... I hope they're safe. Cut off from spiritual support. That won't bode well for this operation.

"Butcher Actual?" Agent Alexa Harland called out. The grass swished with her hurried steps.

"Shh..." Gabriel reprimanded in a stinging whisper. "Noise discipline, Gray! We've no idea where we are or who could be around!"

"Oh." Alexa's enthusiasm was erased with a wide-eyed alertness and softening voice. "Sorry. I'm glad to have finally found someone."

"You say that as if you've been here for some time?"

"A few hours."

"Hours?" Gabriel asked. "And I just got here. Time isn't functioning properly in this place. That could explain a lot."

Alexa's sight carried with slow unease to the towering trees surrounding them, with their drooping branches and leaves creating a myriad of paths through a thicket of green. Mists swelled around them, carrying the odor of rotting meat with a sweet and tangy after-smell, that flowed down to linger in their taste buds. The Diver agent lowered her gaze, pressing her lips together and shaking her head. "I dared not venture off on my own. This place. I know you don't feel it, but the energies here... I can't explain it."

That confirms what Dupree warned about. "Try, Agent Gray."

"The only other time I felt something so awful was during my youth, when the boys would torment us relentlessly. Even when some would make passes at me during my transition. I've always been what one would horribly label as passable by societal standards. But, being gifted, I knew who was sincere about being close to me, and who was trying to satiate their lusts, only to discard me afterward. Harland was the only one who cared. The energies are reading the same as our tormentors'."

"Torturous."

"Yes. Sorry, I guess I was a little long-winded there."

"No. Communication is key to success." Gabriel peered around. "Especially in a place like this. These damn vectors are hoping to prey on our inner turmoil against ourselves and each other. It's good that we know about one another to anticipate their methods."

"So how about you?"

Gabriel shook his head, looking to the forest depths.

"Okay, I'll follow your lead, Actual," Alexa responded. "What's our next move?"

"The battle at the door was a disaster. I have no idea which side has the initiative now." Gabriel looked at his M4 carbine, pulling back to the charging handle. The bolt sped forward, lodging a round into the star chamber, preparing the weapon for action. A flick of his thumb put the fire selector switch into semi-automatic. "We carry on with the mission."

"There's only two of us."

"I know. But as Madam Dupree and the other scryer leadership warned us, we've only a finite amount of time. And we've no idea how long that will last, judging how you've been here for hours, and I've only been here five mikes."

Alexa nodded. "I know we've had our differences, but I admire your tenacity, Butcher Actual. You never let anything get you down. Even when you're beaten."

She's scared. Probably her first time without her husband or any kind of backup.

"You're only beaten when you give up. I know you're green," Gabriel continued. "Listen up. Here's a hard lesson we need to accept as agents. Nothing ever goes according to plan. Ever. And the odds are always stacked. We soldier on because that is what we are. Death is a possibility every agent needs to acknowledge. Quitting is something we can never accept."

"Roger, Actual." Alexa nodded. "I'm ready."

"That damn Partridge fled through the gate. Our secondary objective will be apprehending her again. That bitch isn't escaping justice."

"I couldn't agree more." Alexa racked her weapon's charging handle, sliding a round into the chamber. White knuckle tension ran through her fingers, locked around the carbine with an unsteady grip.

Gabriel led their duo, the barrel of their weapons carried low and ready at the alert posture, keeping the guns angled to the ground, with the butt stock ready to be shouldered at a moment's notice. Grass and leaves crunched and crumbled under their boots. The mists continued, graying the area with floating ripples distorting their view ahead. The deeper they went, the darker their surroundings grew, obscured by the thickening foliage massing around, as if the world closed in on them. Rustling bushes whisked their attention to the left. The agents snapped their carbines into position, training the red reticles of their holographic aiming optics on a wide bush.

"Standard SOP," Gabriel ordered, stepping closer and raising his free hand from the secondary grip below the barrel as a fist. "Hold fire until hostility is confirmed."

"Roger." Alexa's finger remained straight along the weapon's magazine well, despite a racing heart.

Double sets of wide eyes peered from the long and dangling leaves of the droopy bush. Deep breaths of panic set them bobbing in place, growing faster with each step Gabriel took. Sickly green corneas shone from their hiding spot, surrounded by dull ivory sclera.

"Don't harm us!" a duet cried out. "We surrender!"

"Show yourself," Gabriel demanded. "Come out from your cover with your hands up. No sudden movements."

"Okay, okay, angry one," they replied. "You've got yourselves a deal."

Bulbous figures stepped out from the bush, upon thin legs wrapped in tight pants rising to their shins. The twins' feet were crushed within their shoes, leaving their toes pressing on or popping out the front of them. Their belts and trousers remained undone, around heaving globular bellies, sagging like spilled cottage cheese over their waists. Brown dirt was caked in and around their belly buttons, along with speckles of filth that hid within the folds and wrinkles.

"London Morning Daily 1865," Alexa read the words sewn in cursive upon their faded yellow jackets and matching herringbone newspaper boy hats. "Are these children?"

"They can't be. They're huge and disgusting. Look at them!" Gabriel sneered. "You're cucuy aren't you? Creating a parody of children, hoping for us to take mercy on you and drop our guard?"

"No, no!" the two pleaded. "We swear! We are children! Don't hurt us."

Alexa's will pressed out, expanding around the rotund boys. Negative energies of apprehension radiated from them. "Fear and desperation, I'm sensing it. They were taken from their sleep, like the others, Actual. I can feel a lack of development in their thinking patterns, an attempt at cleverness that doesn't seem at all cunning but done out of survival. They're not lying. I didn't see any changes in their frequencies when they spoke. They're children, even if they don't look like it."

"Okay." Gabriel's fierce stare scrutinized them. "If you are children, then tell us where are the others?"

"So many places they're being held," the left one said while the right one nodded.

"Yes, and there's the walrus, he has a few," the right one continued while the left one nodded.

"He's a greedy one that never shares his food with others," the left twin added. "Unless it's with the kids."

"He's feeding the children?" Gabriel inquired. "That doesn't sound so bad. Why isn't he feeding you?"

"That old walrus is a greedy one," the right twin agreed. "I hoped he'd fallen asleep one time, but his servants caught me trying to sneak a bite."

"I see. That doesn't quite answer our questions." Alexa sighed. "But I guess it'll have to do."

"Where do we find this walrus?" Gabriel asked.

A glazed stare washed over the boys' faces, their attention whisking as if to something in the distance. Gabriel and Alexa followed their eyes fixed on a tree trunk. Alexa waved her hand, hoping to get something from their stony countenances. They remained frozen in place, their frames not even moving as their breaths stopped.

"You boys okay?" Alexa asked.

"What's wrong with them, Gray?" Gabriel wondered.

Alexa closed her eyes, focusing on the twins' energies. Shrill screams clamored through their psyche with desperate piercing pitches. She tried pushing through, her reach being repulsed by tempestuous howls of torment.

"I don't know. There's screaming rising in their psyche. I think it's a flashback maybe?"

"Someone is crying," one of the twins stated.

"They're always crying," the other replied.

"Yep. Crying in our ears."

"We can never stop hearing them."

"What the hell are you two going on about?" Gabriel snapped. "Focus! Where can we find this walrus?"

"Not too far!" a twin answered.

"Continue your journey," the other added.

"And you'll be there by the coast."

"He lives in a tower."

The boys nodded in unison.

"You two stay safe," Gabriel ordered. "Continue hiding until we can return for you as well. We're going to rescue the others and rendezvous back here with you."

The boys stood upright and saluted. "Yes, sir! We'll wait for you to bring them all back here."

Alexa smiled and waved goodbye to them as they continued past large and fluffy bushes with streamer-like leaves, fanning with the gusts of cool mist pouring through. They wove through the tree trunks, stepping over thick roots pressing up through the ground. Their steps squished into emerald moss patches and fallen leaves that disintegrated into crumbles. A salty scent reached their noses. The pair looked at each other and nodded. The trees became sparse, with the few remaining becoming high palms with ringed and wrinkled trunks, bearing coconuts at their apexes. Sand mixed into the grass, its color fading into browns and tans, shorter than the lush green they found in the forest.

Churning waves crashed into each other in the distance, beyond the sheer drop of sandstone leading to waters darkened by the night. The moon's light carried across its center with gleaming ripples of white disappearing into the foaming shores. A rotating beam of shining light stole their attention to something in the distance. There stood the tower, its walls formed by numerous stones fashioned and aligned neatly with traces of mortar holding them together. Tall dune grass covered the building's perimeter, save for the steps leading up into large double doors with an oval archway, or the peeling doors leading below to a cellar.

"They weren't lying." Alexa gulped. "Seems kind of ominous."

"Kinda ominous?" Gabriel smirked, scanning the perimeter through a pair of binoculars.

"No. You're right, Actual. It's very ominous."

"I'm not seeing any hostile sentry patrols, but that doesn't mean there won't be any inside," Gabriel said. "Time for some action, Gray. Let's go invite ourselves in, shall we?"

"I knew you were going to say that…"

CHAPTER 18
DINNER IS SERVED

THE LONGTOOTH COAST, PANDEMONIUM - TIME UNKNOWN

Gentle patter came from Gabriel and Alexa's boots, with their thick rubber soles against the flawless and smooth surface of the stone steps. They stopped before the massive doors with its oval archway culminating in a marble crescent moon above them. Green tint filled their sight from their night optics devices, attached to their helmets via a RHNO horn jointed frame, extending over their faces. They scoured the door, searching for wires and levers. Gabriel nodded to Alexa signaling the all-clear. He pressed his ear to the withered wooden surface, faded gray from the salty sea air.

"I don't hear anyone on the other side," Gabriel said. "Snakes out."

"I'll pick it, Actual." Alexa nodded, her fingers rifling through a vest pouch for her snake kit. Her hands roamed past the long camera attached to a thin but pliable and sturdy cable, grabbing the hand pump with its wiry and flanged extension.

"I kind of like playing with the snake-pick." She wedged it into the keyhole, pumping the thick plastic trigger, sending the device whipping within the locking mechanism's tumblers.

"That makes one of us. I never had the finger dexterity to operate those damn things efficiently." Gabriel wedged his snake camera between the door and frame. The silicon tube of its body slid along the smooth wooden edges, pushing the lensed tip through. The agent then connected its pronged end to a small tablet, watching the snake's display light up on his screen. Darkness filled the room, save for faint traces forming details of tables and chairs. A tap of his thumb sent the screen into white.

Hmm... Nothing on Thermals. Place is colder than a witch's tit.

Another flick of his finger sent the view into night vision, matching his night optic devices. The screen's flash brought a renewed image of the room, revealing tables with unlit candle holders, paintings that lined the walls in even sequence, and a long carpet extending down the building's main corridor and stretching out of view.

What the hell? That doesn't make sense.

Gabriel stepped back, double taking at the thin tower and what he saw on the screen. *The inside view is so much wider than the outside. Going between them feels so... weird.*

"Agent Gray—"

"One second, Actual. Almost got it." Alexa squinted, pumping, and turning the snake-pick. An audible click signaled the lock's defeat and the doors' tension parting between them. "Got it."

"Well done," Gabriel said. "But we have another problem. There's sorcery afoot."

"I really wish you wouldn't call it that."

"Whatever. Look." Gabriel revealed the screen. "What's inside doesn't match. That room extends further than this skinny tower."

"There's definitely magick afoot. I'm sensing something but it's subtle. I haven't the experience to identify it."

"So be it," Gabriel continued. "Do you have your C-4?"

"Yeah. Why?"

"If we must, we'll level the tower after rescuing the children. I might need to snatch your brick for this, too."

"That's one way to put a stop to whatever this is." A wide-eyed Alexa nodded.

Gabriel cracked the door. Their carbine barrels were upright and shouldered, aimed into the large room they entered. Waves of detachment flowed over their senses. For a few seconds, the sensation of their boots on the firm ground and the chill of the coastal air ceased. The duo's wherewithal returned, with them exchanging glances.

"You feel that?" Gabriel whispered.

"Yeah," Alexa answered. "It's powerful magick. I feel we just crossed over into someone else's willpower."

"What the hell does that mean?"

"An active spell, for lack of a better term. You were right about this place."

Damn it! This is a lot of sorcery. It could be another trap. Gabriel's focus shifted to his fingertip resting on the trigger's cold curve.

They continued down the rug with its light backdrop and ostentatious black frilled pattern running up the center. The fine material absorbed their steps, muffling each one. Their shoulders were inches apart as they continued line abreast where the room narrowed into a vast corridor. Paintings surrounded them, evenly stationed along the walls, between many closed doors. Alexa tapped Gabriel, pointing to one. It was the portrait of a man in a curly white peruke, fluffed high on his head with locks draping his shoulders. A smug smirk was etched on his face with green eyes burning in condescension.

"What?" Gabriel asked.

"He's in every single picture."

"Good point. That must be the master of the house. The one we're looking for."

"I don't get it. Why did the twins call him the walrus? Maybe it's just a codename?"

"Perhaps. Let's keep moving."

"Jeez, this thing seems to go on forever," Alexa murmured.

"Focus, Gray. I thought you were a ranger?"

"I was... kinda..."

"You're going to explain that to me after this is over."

Wheezing came into earshot, growing louder the further they maneuvered through the hall, toward curtains draped over an archway leading into another room. Snoring rumbles grated against their eardrums from harsh and deep breaths expelled through nose and mouth. The noise traveled along the walls, clinging to their rising goosebumps, as they winced through exchanged grimaces.

"BRRRGGGRRRRRRRRR," the snoring scratched against dry skin folds of a dehydrated throat. "BRRRGGGRRRRRRRRR! Eat up! Eat your fill and then some, my friends! BRRRGGRRRRRR!" a gargled and bellowing voice demanded with jovial slowness.

"I thought whoever was in there had been asleep," Alexa whispered. "At least I was hoping as much."

"Guess not." Gabriel swayed the curtains with a gentle brush of his hand, peering through a narrow crevice as they shifted away from the main opening.

A vast room was before them. Shadows writhed around the light of a crackling fireplace adjacent to a long dining table, decked with a long white tablecloth. A spread of bread loaves and fruit were heaped upon mirror polished dishes, with a plump roasted turkey as the centerpiece. Juices glistened along the bird's breast, where steaming white meat lay in tender slices near the split middle. A mountain of roasted potatoes sat on an adjacent plate while fluffy buttery biscuits adorned another, with honey cascading down their neat pyramid.

A little girl dressed in a purple cotton onesie sat at the long table with piles of food on a large plate. She picked at it with a fork, taking a slow and reluctant bite. Other children next to her did the same, slouching in defeat, their eyes searching among themselves for relief.

Bellowing laughter broke the sound of wakeful snoring, driven from the stomach of whoever sat at the table's head. Gabriel shifted, bumping Alexa away to angle his view.

"Smells delicious in there," Alexa whispered. "Maybe we're getting some luck? Are you seeing anything good?"

"Not likely. Lots of food, some children, and—what the hell is that?"

Towering at the end of the table was a person with mounds of fat, expanding well past the width of his creaking chair. A beady round head sat on top of his corpulent body, serving as the nexus of countless flabby folds, squishing where his sloppy gut spilled half over the table and into his lap. Wet sores spotted his ashen skin, where reddish-brown scabs crusted over, leaving pink blemishes staining where black wiry hair did not grow. Tattered strands flared from the remnants of a peruke, sitting on the being's head with its weft risen and uneven. Fangs protruded over his saliva laden craggy lips, reminiscent of small tusks below his whiskery mustache.

"Actual? What you got?" Alexa asked.

"Nothing good. I think I found the walrus." Gabriel shifted away from the curtain keeping his profile tucked against the wall. "Take a peek."

"What the hell..." Alexa gasped. "It looks like the guy in the picture, but different like... like..."

"Like he's been dining well, despite not having a plate in front of him."

Alexa put a hand over her mouth, eyes widening. "Oh my God..."

"Looks like more are coming from a far side door." Gabriel leaned in. "We'll wait until they're gone then flex on the room."

"Let's go now—"

"We've no idea what these vectors can do," Gabriel's whispers reprimanded Alexa. "I know you're worried for them, but we can be easily beaten if we're outnumbered against a variable threat."

Alexa nodded, pressing her lips firmly.

An adjacent door opened within the dining hall, with two hunched figures shambling outward. Weathered brown cowhide belts hung from their waists with hammers, screwdrivers, a small bandsaw, and bulging bags protruding with nails, bouncing in their hurried and wobbled steps. Dark swollen bags hung underneath their wide eyes that were pale as moonlight, save for the red veins climbing through them. The pair's dilated pupils glanced in unison over the children. They connected with the dark-haired little girl, who returned a meek smile of reluctance. Saliva crawled from the corners of their mouths. Their bloated guts groaned like muffled jazz instruments as they clutched them in agony with desperate and outstretched fingers.

"Master! Master!" one of the workers called out. The other nodded with a strained grimace. "Some of the others were caught in the garden trying to... umm... pick out some more juicy fruit that rolled away from the Queen's tree."

"They're on high alert after our last run!" the other called out. "We have to make our current... crop last."

"Brrrgrrrrr." Scraping rumbles of breath expelled from the walrus. "Nonsense. We'll just give it a day or two and they'll go back to their incessant chores and rose painting. Until then, please continue with tending to our guests."

"When do we get to eat?" a worker snapped.

"This time I promise that you will have your fill. Brrrggrrr. Now see to it that these children are properly fed."

"Mr. Ross Marus," the dark-haired little girl pleaded with her emerald eyes to their host. "Thank you, ever so kindly, but I think I speak for the rest of us when I say we're full."

"No. No. No. Keep eating, my dear Penny. No leaving until you've finished your dinner. You know the rules, same as any other household. You've been a good young lady and you don't want to be disrespectful to your host, right?"

"But you keep putting more food on our plates!" a little boy scoffed.

"Be nice," Penny urged in a side mouth whisper with brow-raising unease.

"Brrrrggggrrr... now, see here, Melvin!" Ross snapped. "You do as you're told and respect your elders and the like. Children are starving, wishing they had such a feast!"

"Why won't you let the workers eat the food then?" Penny asked.

"Because they don't eat this, nor do they want it." Ross huffed. "Continue before your food gets cold. All of you!"

The adjacent door opened again with laces of smoke

drifting into the dining hall from the kitchen. Two more hunched minions spilled out, bumping shoulders, retaining their upright posture with wobbling steps as one attempted to hurry past the other. Gleaming silver serving dishes remained balanced in their hands, resting on upright fingers bowing with hairy and convex knuckles. Flour dusted their tan aprons worn over their baggy overalls and tool belts. Ross nodded, his globular face expanding into a grin while swaying with self-induced rhythm.

"Brrggrrrr." The wakeful snoring left Ross' nose. "Outstanding work, gentlemen. Yes."

Penny scoffed when a worker leaned over her, placing a butter drenched baked potato on her expansive plate, squeezing it next to the piles of turkey, ham, corned beef, smoked ribs, sweet potatoes, corn, biscuits, stuffing, cheese cubes, and jasmine rice.

"There." The worker smiled and nodded. "Looks like we can fit another... here."

After dumping more potatoes on everyone's plates, the workers high-fived each other before disappearing back into the kitchen's swinging door.

"And there's still dessert!" Mr. Ross Marus added. "So, eat up quickly, little ones."

"No!" Melvin yelled. "No more eating!"

Ross' brow rose. "My patience is wearing quite thin with you, young man!"

"Nothing is thin about you!" Melvin retorted. "This is stupid. I'm leaving, Mr. Marus!"

Screeching came from the boy's seat, pushing back and out of his chair. Melvin slapped his cloth napkin onto the plate, knocking over his large goblet of wine. He paused, catching himself on the table when his vision blurred. The brown of the dining table smeared in his view, wood patterns widened and blended into an ever-churning morass.

"Wh... what... what's goin... on..." Melvin groaned. A vise grip of pressure closed on his temples.

"You're in my world now." Ross scoffed. "And you aren't going anywhere." Saliva pooled in Mr. Marus' mouth, escaping over his lips, and pouring down his chin in glistening strings. He rose from his seat, which creaked from the relief. Thudding rapid steps brought him waddling around the table, his mass bobbing and heaving upward, closing on Melvin.

The boy screamed with the floorboards creaking and thumping from Ross Marus' hot pursuit. In a few seconds, he closed on Melvin, squashing the child underneath his gelatinous girth. The behemoth grabbed the boy, extending his arms outward for all to behold. Trembles ran through Melvin's shoulders, until their pops echoed through the room. The bones in his arms hung free within the skin, their ends protruding up from his swollen red sockets. Melvin's jaw dropped. He was spun around, wailing with a twisted agony as his assailant presented him to the other screaming children.

Hands peeled from the jiggling girth of Ross Marus, until eight in total grasped the boy, holding him steadfast, save for the knees that continued to bend in defiance. Ross cocked his head back and in a split second snapped forward with his fangs puncturing deep. The rough whiskers of his beard scratched the boy's neck. Hot breath ran over Melvin's back with trickles of blood, seeping down and into his shirt.

Gunshots rang through the dining hall from Gabriel and Alexa's roaring M4 carbines. Shoulder to shoulder the agents sped into the room, weapons snug in their grasp. Each trigger pull sent bursts of lead ripping across the obese vector's mound of a back.

"Help me!" the boy pleaded through his cries.

Shrill and jarring screams from Melvin grew to ear-piercing heights, with the whimpers of the other children sprinkled among the moments he drew breaths. The walrus' fangs worked congruently, each one digging down at opposite times as the other drew the boy closer into the death grip of his blubbery arms.

Melvin's face thinned. The structure of his muscles withered, growing pale with the draining of vital fluids. Penny gasped, covering her mouth, and cringing from her seat. Her big green eyes fixed on the daylights of his cognizance. Melvin's eyes locked with hers even as he shuddered each time the fiend's oversized fangs clamped down, churning deeper into the holes from extended and independent muscles within Ross' jaws. Essence drained from the boy, his head lowering, his broken body slowing in its racking. The gunshots continued peppering the assailant's back.

"Fuck!" Gabriel yelled. "Die, you son of bitch! Get off him!"

Penny watched Melvin's pupils roll upward, before his eyelids closed. The boy's withered composition caved inward, until there was only skin and bones. The full roundness of his eyes shriveled and collapsed. Shredded clusters of pink brain matter whisked down Mr. Marus' sweeping gullet. Audible pops followed in dual unison when Melvin's eyes pulled through his skull, draining with the rest of his life force. The bulging assailant's arms released the sloughed remains of skin and hair that slapped to the ground like wet laundry, still adorned in Melvin's Batman T-shirt and shorts.

"Brrgrrr." The walrus took a deep breath. His mouth opened, covered with stains of blood. Energy hummed deep within his gullet, resonating the faint cries of his victim until a long and croaking belch overtook them. "Dinner is served."

Penny and the other children screamed, cringing back into their seats. Cold radiated over them, with a growing pressure on their chests weighing the little ones in place.

"But first…" Mr. Marus turned to the agents. "I have to deal with these unwanted guests! You'll ruin everything! The idiots might hear you and realize I'm taking all the delectables for myself!"

Seven orbs of light appeared on the heavy vector, lining down his body from the crown of his head to his nether regions. Light beamed from the largest at the center of his sagging chest. Fangs stretched outward from the fiend's opening jowls, releasing a drawn hiss at the agents, outstretching his arms.

"Chakra points," Alexa noted. "They're glowing now and growing larger!"

"What the hell kind of scumbag are you?" Gabriel barked.

"Wouldn't you like to know?" Ross Marus' voice deepened like notes from a cello.

"Children, get away from him! Come over to us!" Alexa urged, retraining her sights back on the pulsating behemoth.

"They… stay… here…" Mr. Marus groaned. Jiggling and sloshing came from the expanding flesh of his bulbous gut. "Yess… The energy of innocence is pure… bliss. I am a god here!"

"There is only one God, you disgusting wretch!" Gabriel snarled. "Allow me to arrange the meeting!"

The walrus' expansion ceased, adding an inch to his mighty circumference. Blood covered and chapped lips peeled back into an unwholesome grin, with his whiskery mustache flaring over it. "Perhaps, you can be used to feed the minions. Yes, you shall suffice."

"What are you, shitbag?" Gabriel roared. "Answer me! I

command it!" *He's no demon. He would've said as much already. Some kind of psychic vampire?*

"You'll never know."

"Aim center mass, Gray!" Gabriel ordered. "Split the elements! Weapons free!"

"Roger, Actual!" Alexa pressed the magazine release of her weapon, slapping in a new one as she sidestepped opposite Gabriel.

Mr. Marus' large arms covered his chest, save for the top two reaching for Alexa. Heavy stomps drove the large assailant forward, thudding the ground with his round and flat feet. The agent dipped low and outboard, her body weight shifting into a tumble, before rolling back into a kneeling firing position. Muzzle flashes filled the room from a burst of fire that ripped across the vector's thick forearms.

Glimpses of the corridor portraits flashed into Gabriel's mind. The stiff upper lip from a pronounced jawline and burning eyes of noble pride etched into the agent's view, recalling every detail.

That's it!

Gabriel shouldered his weapon, sliding his nine-inch combat knife from its sheath along his vest. He sprinted at the wiggling mound of flesh plodding toward Alexa yet again. When Mr. Marus halted, Gabriel leapt toward his back, plunging the knife with both hands between the folds of his shoulder blades. One mighty pull and Gabriel heaved himself upward, reaching for the peruke with both hands.

Crumbling flakes of glue and skin cascaded from underneath the weft as it separated from Ross' moldy scalp. Gabriel fell back, clutching the tangled mess, groaning when he collided with the hardwood floor. Bellowing filled the room as the corpulent malefactor reached up with all arms for his missing wig, patting at his patchy dome. His chubby fingers poked at the lesions dotting his head, popping and dribbling with glistening yellow pus. The odor of moldy cheddar swelled around them, exuding from rashes caused by an ailment never cured.

"Now, Gray!" Gabriel ordered. "Now!"

Alexa leveled the glowing reticle of her close combat optic and weapon barrel over the pulsing heart chakra. Three rounds spewed from the muzzle with roaring expulsions of carbon. The impacts rippled across their target, leaving black bullet holes within the light. Ross gasped, clutching his chest as he staggered forward. Alexa stepped back; her weapon still trained on the heaving monstrosity as he spilled over to the ground before her. The walrus' head cocked at Alexa, his maw extended. Between his fangs a gleaming mass resonated within his gullet, emanating dozens of cries from boys and girls pleading for release. Their wailing spirits seeped from his jowls, racing past Alexa, whipping through the room, and vanishing into nothingness.

Pressure on the children's chests subsided. The chilling embrace of negative energy evaporated from their shoulders. Each of their little bodies zipped beneath the dining table, covering their heads as they balled into trembling submission.

"We're here to rescue you," Alexa called out. "Don't be scared. We're agents with the Department of Homeland Security."

Gabriel approached the hulking corpse, his weapon locked where the expelled heart chakra left a scorched circle of charred skin and rising smoke. A swift kick with his boot sent the vector's head rolling in the opposite direction. He nodded. "And stay down, shit bag."

"Don't mind him," Alexa continued. "Agent Gabriel Agapito is tough, but he has a heart of gold deep down."

Gabriel's empty and hard glower fell on Alexa as she smiled back and winked. He shook his head at her.

"And my name is Agent Alexa Gray," she continued. "I understand much of this may seem very disorienting. I assure you that this is more than a mere nightmare."

Shaking eyes peered back at them from underneath where shadows and table legs resided, holding steadfast to their covered position.

Alexa sighed, reaching out her hand. "I can only assume this vector may have falsely earned your trust before turning on you. I understand your fear. Please believe us. We're here to get you home. What are your names?"

"I'm Penny." The little girl crawled out, turning back to the others and waving with urgency. "Come on, guys. They're here to help. I can tell."

"You're gifted, like me." Alexa smiled. "I sense that."

"You're not turning her into a witch, too." Gabriel huffed, reaching out for Penny's hand.

"That's so rude, Actual!" Alexa shook her head, smirking while watching Gabriel help each of the children to their feet.

"We have other problems coming, Gray."

Doors leading to the kitchen slammed open. Hunched figures poured through waving hammers layered in rust and blood smeared butcher knives. The four hostiles formed a bastion, their maniacal twitching gazes took in the sight of the children scrambling behind the agents, and their benefactor's corpse sprawled over the ground.

"They killed Mr. Ross Marus!" a worker screamed.

"And they're getting away with our food!" another exclaimed.

"Kill them both and paint the room red! Devour their souls!"

Wailing minions spilled through the door with stuttering steps and rolled ankles, hobbling about as they followed behind the others charging forward. Bursts from Gabriel's M4 slammed into the skull of the first, sending his head jerking back as he collapsed to the floor. Rivers of blood spewed from the gaping holes left across his frontal lobe, creating a warm pool on the floorboards. Gasps and wide-eyed horror came from the others as the weapon trained on them.

"What the hell kind of musket is that?" a worker scoffed.

They raised their hands, tools relinquished from them and clanging to the floor.

"The kind that doesn't need reloading after every shot," Gabriel replied. "Now listen up you crazy assholes. Alexa and I are taking these children to safety. If you want to live, you'll march right back into that kitchen, and fuck off."

"Okay, okay." They stepped backward. "Don't be so testy. We were just playing around. Honest."

Alexa grabbed Penny's hand, the other children following in tow. "Come on let's go."

"Are there any more children?" Gabriel demanded. "Tell me, damn it!"

"No! We swear!" a worker pleaded as the others backed into the kitchen. "Do you have any idea how hard it is to steal one from the garden? Might as well do what the Duchess and Hatter do and kidnap the adults that wander here. The Duchess even managed to get a few new ones just this afternoon. I always told that bloated ole bum that the Queen would figure it out. Mr. Ross Marus made us steal from her. She sent you, didn't she?"

Who the hell is the Duchess? Judging how time works... or

doesn't around here. She must've grabbed members of the task force then. Damn it. I should at least launch a recon FRAGO. I couldn't imagine being a POW in this madness.

"Yes, I am here on her behalf." Gabriel's eyes narrowed with ire, and he spoke through clenched teeth. "How dare you steal from our beloved Queen!"

"We're sorry! So sorry! Forgiveness please!"

"Tell me about this Duchess. Where do I find her?"

"That big-mouth, loud-mouth, brat! Always crying! Always complaining! Always running from her responsibility!"

"Focus!" Gabriel snapped. "Where is she?"

"In a palace that was bought but never paid for," the head minion continued with his brethren nodding behind in the doorway. "It was built to beatific perfection."

"She let it fall apart! Lazy I say!" another added. "Just like her to run from her responsibility!"

"Okay, I get it. You made it. Like this tower. Very impressive. And it's rightfully yours. So where is your other property?"

"Just outside the forest! Northeast of here. Within the small white palace, where only one guard stands. Call him friend, and you'll have him as one. Act like the others and die like the rest."

"Shut the hell up with your riddles!" Gabriel snapped, sending the worker cringing. "We're leaving. Stay in your kitchen or I will neutralize you!"

"Okay, okay! Calm yourself! No funny business from us," the head worker pleaded. "I swear on all that I love and hold dear."

Gabriel stepped backward slow and steady, his weapon remaining fixed on the kitchen doorway and the frowning countenances that stared from it. Once at the curtains to the corridor, he sped between them.

"After them!" the head worker ordered.

"What about their strange muskets?"

"Through the secret door." He grinned. "We'll ambush them outside via the cellar. Hurry!"

"Hurry!"

Footsteps prompted Alexa to spin around with her weapon.

"One friendly on your six," Gabriel announced. "Double time it, Gray. I have a feeling those shitbags are going to try something."

"Roger, Actual."

They continued down the corridor, pressing past the pictures and the first door, into the entryway. Gabriel ushered the children to continue moving. He rifled through his backpack, finding a brick of Cyclonite-4.

"Cough it up, Gray," Gabriel commanded. "I'm going to need more to bring down this structure."

"You ever thought about saying please?" Alexa handed over her stash.

"Keep moving. Get the little ones to the bank of the forest and cover my exfil."

"Roger, Actual."

Gabriel removed part of the wrapping, revealing a glossy and sticky side to the explosive. Pressing it to the wall, he attached the payload with a cemented grip. Gabriel's hands dug through his vest pockets for a small black device with a concaved head possessing a small light that came on with the flick of a thin switch below it. A short spooled magnesium ribbon extended from the bottom of it. He buried this into the pliable contents. He pressed the device to the explosive, sticking them together. Another charge was placed on the opposite wall.

Primed.

Gabriel pushed through the door. His view jettisoned outside, greeted by the cool ocean air and seagulls above. Alexa's IR beacon pulsed in his NVGs from the forest outskirts, where she hid with the children in a prone position among the foliage. Gabriel jogged down the stairs, turning when rattling came from the cellar doors bursting open. The workers hooted and howled, banging the walls with their hammers, and scraping the stone masonry with knives.

I knew it! Gabriel ran for the trees.

"There he is!" the head worker exclaimed. "Don't let him escape!"

"Where's the tasties at?"

Gabriel's legs burned as they drove him over the sand, his lungs pumping deep for breaths. He turned, raising the RF ignition trigger with his hand, and pressing it hard. Thunderous calamity rocked the area, shuddering the tower as its sides ripped open, jettisoning smoldering debris in both directions. Smoking fragments pelted the churning waves of the ocean, while the rest crashed into the beach sands. The tower shuddered, with stones dropping from the gaping holes. It swayed, then leaned, toppling into the ocean with a tremendous splash. A colossal pile of shattered stones and wood protruded among the waves, stretching beyond their view.

Jaws dropped from the workers, their eyes expanding with horror, their loud lamentations expelling from gaped mouths. One reached up to the strands of his unkempt hair, ripping them out by fistfuls while shedding tears.

"Our beautiful home!" the head worker screeched, dropping to his knees.

"I guess it's best we wasn't inside, huh?" Another scratched his head.

"Quick, we must fix this! We are carpenters! It's what we do!"

"Aww dang it! This will take forever!"

"Then forever we must!"

The workers swarmed the ruins, their groans of disappointment resounding over the beach.

Gabriel patted Alexa on the back, catching his breath while they shared a nod. "Good work, Gray. But our mission is just getting started."

"What about us, sir?" Penny asked.

"You're a smart girl." Gabriel smiled. "I saw how you handled yourself in there with tact and discipline. It's how you managed to outlast your friend. And I'm sorry you had to witness that."

Penny's eye contact broke, her lip curling with sorrow. "I want to go home, sir."

"Hide with the two other boys we found earlier. They will be deeper in this forest. Hide and wait until we can rendezvous with you. There may be other agents like us around. If they find you before we do, go with them. They will be dressed in the same uniforms, representing an organization called the U.S.A, Unholy Slaying Agency. Are you tracking all this, young lady?"

"Yes, sir. Thank you."

She's like my little Alma at home. Smart, clever, quick. I miss you, iha. "Just sit tight while Agent Gray and I rescue the others."

The children stared at Gabriel and Alexa for a moment

before heading into the forest. The agents waved them goodbye.

"You sound as if there's more contact ahead," Alexa said.

"There might be," Gabriel answered. "Ross Marus' minions mentioned that someone named the Duchess might have taken some of our people to suffer similar fates."

"I'm with you, Actual."

"Good. We're launching another rescue mission. It's off to the palace. I'll get you up to speed as we infil the combat sector."

CHAPTER 19
THE CURSED SENTRY

Morning dew glistened across the trees and grass from the rising morning sun. Gabriel and Alexa trekked until approaching thick foliage bordering the forest, where the land sloped downward into an open field of grass. At the bottom of the descent, the area flattened. Before them stood a palace with two towers, and a small courtyard boxed in with high walls, leading to an expanding archway serving as an entrance to the main hall. Flaking brown moss encompassed the bastion, rising from a moat filled with murky and placid waters covered with lily pads, floating algae, and drifting clouds of mist. Pale green lichen blanketed the rocks around the base of the palace, with reeds sprouting along the shoreline. A drawbridge remained lowered at the wide and open entrance, forming the only path over the moat. An ashen suit of armor stood at the end of it, poised with both arms clenching a long sword upside down and leaning forward with it as support. Another sword lay mere feet from it, discarded upon the drawbridge.

"Are we going to infiltrate or hold, Actual?" Alexa asked

while they remained prone, overwatching from the concealment of foliage. "I don't know why but my mind keeps going back to those kids we just rescued. This place is harsh. I'm worried for all of them."

"There's nothing we can do for them right now, except hope they're all hiding in the woods. It's too dangerous to bring them along. One second, waiting to see if there are any sentry patrols," Gabriel murmured, peering through olive green binoculars. He scanned over the drawbridge into the empty courtyard with only a park bench and yellowish-brown grass, dusted over and long dead. The large double door leading to the main hall remained closed and draped in shadow. Only darkness filled the tower windows, each of them separating one story from the next. "There's nothing; the place looks abandoned. That white armor hasn't even moved in the thirty minutes we've been here. It's likely a scarecrow meant to ward off intruders."

"So, the Duchess is alone. Madam Dupree said we shouldn't engage every vector. Perhaps she'll be more reasonable than Ross Marus and his carpenters?"

"Witches are never to be trusted."

"Ouch." Alexa shook her head.

"You'll live. Let's move."

The duo double timed down the hillside, packs bouncing along their backs while speeding across the field. A rib cage appeared along the shallow end of the moat, among swathes of drifting algae and cloudy muck. Other skeletons appeared, some covered in tattered clothing, while most were shattered fragments in the clear portions of the sand bank. Alexa nodded when Gabriel pointed to it.

M4s drew down on the tall suit of armor, overshadowing both of them at seven feet in height. They stepped over the long sword, continuing down the drawbridge. An aura radiated around the plated mail, tethering Alexa's consciousness. She stopped in her tracks raising her fist to signal a halt. Gabriel raised a brow, following her gaze to the white metallic suit, covered in dents and gray scratches where the decorative paint had been scraped off.

"There's a life force coming from this," Alexa said. "I can sense its essence."

The helm of the suit looked upward from the sword in its clutches, tipping with respect before leveling its visor with a scrutinizing gaze. The knight's shoulders rose, along with his pronounced chest popping out with challenging authority.

"Ereht seog ohw, krah?" the White Knight's high-pitched voice asked from the ringing metal confines of his helm.

"What is that? Another language?" Alexa seemed confused. "I don't feel that he's hostile though, Actual."

"Ereh uoy sgnirb tahw?" the knight asked.

"I'm sorry, we don't understand, sir—"

"Enough!" Gabriel snapped. "The lady of your palace has seized people against their will. We're here for them. I take it that you are sworn to her. I ask you to do what is right by releasing those captured. You can either cooperate or fall like the others."

"Actual, I think…"

"What, Gray?"

"There's something about his words; it's not a foreign language. Didn't the carpenters say something about the guard?"

"They said call him friend and you'll have him as one. Act like the others and die like the rest."

"So maybe let's tone down the threats?"

Gabriel's eyes narrowed.

"Sir?" Alexa inquired. "How long have you been here?"

"Eromyna rebmemer t'nod I," the knight answered.

"Wait!" Alexa smiled. "I get it now! He's talking backwards."

"That doesn't make it any easier to understand him." Gabriel sighed.

"It reminds me of anagrams that Harland and I would play to pass the time on road trips."

"You nerdy scryers," Gabriel murmured, rolling his eyes.

"The knight said, 'I don't remember anymore,'" Alexa continued, "Are you cursed, sir?"

The White Knight nodded. "Em sdnatsrednu eno on tub. Dneirf doog a teem I fi desaeler eb ylno nac I, layarteb ym fo esuaceb. Dneirf doog a ton saw I dias dna reh gnivael rof em dekcom neeuq eht."

Alexa's face scrunched, her head cocking in wonderment as she scratched her chin. "Hmmm..."

Gabriel's gaze shifted between them.

"I got it!" Alexa chuckled. "He said, 'The Queen mocked me for leaving her and said I was not a good friend. Because of my betrayal, I can only be released if I meet a good friend. But no one understands me.' This is kind of fun, Actual."

"This word chaos is hurting my brain." Gabriel shook his head.

The knight's helm bobbed with enthusiasm.

"Are those corpses below your victims?" Gabriel demanded. "Huh?"

"Noissimrep tuohtiw gnissap deirt yeht," the knight answered.

"What did he say, Gray?"

"One second, Actual. Uhh..." Alexa smiled. "He said, 'They tried passing without permission.'"

"So, we can pass?" Gabriel wondered. "Just with permission?"

The White Knight nodded.

"See, Actual," Alexa said. "We don't always have to use violence."

"So be it," Gabriel said. "How do I become your friend?"

"Meht thguof evah uoy litnu enoemos wonk tonnac uoy."

Alexa paused. "Hmm... he said, 'You cannot know someone until you have fought them.'"

"Em ot gnihtyreve snaem ronoh dna thgink a ma I."

"'I am a knight and honor means everything to me,'" Alexa recited.

With swift motion, the knight spun his long blade upright into both hands, bowing his head in salute. Gabriel and Alexa backed away. The knight shifted the blade into a battle stance, stepping forward with his legs shoulder width apart and torso canted.

"So much for peaceful negotiations," Gabriel scoffed. "Any other bright ideas of yours, Gray? Can we neutralize the vector, Agent?"

"There's something we're missing, Actual."

Red reticles found the White Knight's center. Rounds popped from the M4, punching holes into the armor, revealing dark nothingness within. The knight looked down, turning his head to examine the protrusions. With a flick of his thumb against the selector lever, Gabriel put his weapon into burst fire. Salvos of 5.56 millimeter rounds pelted the knight, until the weapon's bolt locked back to the rear on the final shot. Traces of dark smoke rose from the empty chamber. Gabriel's hands worked in blurring motion, releasing the empty magazine with his index finger, while reaching for the next over his vest. He slammed the payload into the carbine, before slapping the bolt release locking the weapon into a ready condition.

Moonlight gleamed from the sword's tip, coming in with a wide arcing swing. Alexa dived backward, rolling her body off the drawbridge. Gabriel ducked underneath the rush of wind from the swift motion. He rose, driving the buttstock of his M4 across the knight's visor, knocking it open. The towering metal being staggered backward, pausing for a moment to look at Gabriel from the nothingness inside its helm.

"Dedleiw neeb sah leets litnu uoy tpecca tonnac I tub, enod llew," the White Knight murmured, closing his visor and retaking his stance.

"Whatever the fuck that means!" Gabriel barked back.

Butcher's team leader stepped back, until a boot heel collided with the discarded sword at the bridge's entrance. Gabriel shouldered his rifle, picking up the sword with both hands. An energy crackled from the long hilt, changing the dusted hilt into a shining gold. The transformation traveled upward, cleaning the stains from the blade, forming a keen edge leading to a sharp point.

This has to be the answer.

Another swing came. Gabriel raised his sword, parrying the blow. They locked in place, Gabriel staring into the darkness of the empty visor, staring back at him. Sliding edges squealed together, then the White Knight disengaged, bouncing back. He raised his blade in a salute.

I think I understand now. Gabriel nodded, raising his sword straight up and bowing his head in return. "You've been waiting a long time for this, huh?"

"Sey," the knight replied.

Clashing steel rang out over the drawbridge, with ringing echoes coursing down into the moat, and fading into the distance. Alexa grimaced with eager anticipation. Gabriel blocked and returned, only to be met with the same. An overhead shot came in. The agent sidestepped it, only to be embraced by the cool open air from the edge of the bridge that emanated from the open area below. *Whoa! Shit!*

Gabriel dived underneath the next shot, tumbling past the knight until he was centered on the platform again. The knight nodded, raising his blade again in salute, before letting his arms drop to his sides.

"Ronoh htiw ssap dna kram ruoy dnif. Yhtrow era uoy. Sknaht ynam."

"Gray, what did he say?" Gabriel called back.

"'Many thanks. You are worthy. Find your mark and pass with honor,'" Alexa answered.

The White Knight's plated chest remained outboard and exposed, his attention on Gabriel, nodding a final time with admiration. The agent stepped forward, thrusting the weapon at the knight's heart, running him through to the hilt. The suit of armor fell, rattling, clanging, and separating to the ground in a listless pile of steel. The helm's visor rose, with tiny bulbous eyes peering from it. Croaking came from within, followed by a chubby bullfrog leaping out. It winked at Gabriel, hopping by with a smile across its thick green lips.

"Oh, do make sure you keep that sword, Sir Gabriel," the frog instructed. "You will need it to face the terror that is Lilith."

"Who is Lilith?"

"Why, the White Queen of course. Good luck on your quest. I'm pleased to say that mine is over." The frog hopped over the bridge, diving into the waters below.

"We have a name for the prime vector now," Alexa said as she rejoined Gabriel.

"Yes," Gabriel agreed. "I believe it's safe to designate this White Queen as a prime vector."

"Lilith." Alexa paused. "All I know is that she was the first wife of Adam. She never fell from Eden by eating from the Tree of Knowledge of Good and Evil. Therefore, her existence remained Godlike, never being exposed to death or the consequences of material existence. It was said that she escaped to an unreachable area, outside of the influence of angels and humans. This place must be it."

"You nerd," Gabriel replied. "Okay. How do we waste her?"

"I don't think we can, Actual." Alexa's gaze lowered with her brow scrunching. "I don't think this is a fight we can win. Lilith didn't lose her immortality. She never ate the forbidden fruit. She never fell."

CHAPTER 20
YOUR GRACE

CASTLE EEHSNAB, PANDEMONIUM - TIME UNKNOWN

Their footsteps echoed through the courtyard, immersed in overgrown grass and shadow from the high walls, save for the cobblestone path cutting down the center. Unlit torch handles remained fixed upright along the perimeter, covered in flaking erosion akin to mud. Glimpses of black appeared along their flank from iron benches immersed in weeds rivaling their height.

"I'm starting to think those carpenters were lying to us," Gabriel grumbled.

"Why so, Actual?" Alexa asked.

"There's no way a duchess lives in this dump." Gabriel sneered at the crumbling path. Debris wedged into the deep treads of their soles with every few steps.

"Good point."

"We'll finish recon of the area, then rendezvous with the little ones back at—" Gabriel paused. A gray silhouette snatched away his attention. When his eyes settled on where it should have been, there was nothing. *What the hell?*

"Contact?" Alexa asked following his vision to the surrounding shadows.

"No... I thought... Never mind," Gabriel said. "Just shadows playing tricks on me."

Their attention continued forward, until they stopped in place at the sight of a tall and slender woman, turned away from them and facing the main hall entrance. Thick strands of grayish-white hair remained in unkempt swathes over her shoulders and back, past the silvery gown adorning her emaciated frame, to the floor. Her bobbing presence blended with shadows from the archway above, leaving her cloaked from direct sight.

"Ma'am," Gabriel called out.

"Actual, wait!" Alexa said. "Something is not right about her... Her aura isn't reading with the light of life."

Gabriel stared hard through the twenty-five meters of distance between them. The woman's details remained blurred, even as he pulled out his binoculars to further scrutinize. Loud sobs rose with her head, retching back to bellow echoing lamentation into the archway. She burrowed her face into both palms.

"The carpenters described the Duchess as having a big mouth," Gabriel said. "This woman looks petite in every aspect."

"Perhaps a metaphor? She talks too much?"

"Could be. You'd definitely fit that description."

Alexa scoffed.

"Let us hope so we can use it to our advantage," Gabriel continued. "We'll try it your way with pleasantries."

The gray woman's cries boomed as they walked closer. She

gasped, glancing over her broad shoulders to the agents through the corner of her shimmering green eyes.

"Good evening, ma'am," Gabriel said. "We mean you no harm, we only wish to speak with you as to the whereabouts of some individuals who may have ended up here on your property. Are you the Duchess?"

The woman nodded with slow reluctance. She turned, revealing a thin and withered face leading down into thick lips tucked among layers of dry craggy wrinkles that surrounded them, driving up the sides of her face in the elongated parody of a smile.

"Actual," Alexa whispered. "Look at her feet."

The blinking Duchess' head cocked, following the agents' gazes to her lower extremities. Dark stubs remained in place of where her feet should have been, blurred by churning ectoplasm forming the woman's grip on reality. The Duchess hovered in place, bobbing in rhythm with the swirling energies gripping her presence to the world.

Gabriel's eyes widen. "She's a—"

Shrill infantile cries broke out through the courtyard. The pulse of each desperate breath and harsh throat stripping howl rubbed upon the agents' exposed skin. Hot alertness flushed through their ears, causing them to spin around, searching in vain but finding only the courtyard. Abrupt silence brought their concerns to the forefront.

There's a baby here? Gabriel wondered. *I have to save that poor thing. But, where did the cries go? More trickery from this shithole and its vectors.*

Gabriel and Alexa looked at each other and nodded, turning with their weapons trained on the Duchess. The woman's jaws distended. Wrinkled folds stretched with her jowls, bringing the top half of her face to the sky. A surging scream came from the Duchess' rattling face, crashing into the agents with concussive force. Shots rang out from involuntary trigger pulls as both agents jettisoned several feet before crashing on their backs.

The low hum of white noise consumed their ears, overtaking anything that registered within, save for their own breaths matching their accelerating hearts. Throbbing pain streaked through their ears, coursing from their temples and grounding into their brains. A blinking Gabriel shook his head, pushing upward through the ringing haze of dizziness. Flashes overtook his mind, carrying him to matching memories that rushed through him like waters from a collapsed dam.

He was back in the seat of his Humvee, with its diesel engine chattering underneath the desert-tan fiberglass. Down the marketplace they drove. The area was devoid of any movement save for a discarded newspaper tumbling in the wind. Lamplights pushed back the night, bringing sight to the empty storefronts covered in Arabic lettering and posters.

Gabriel clutched the thin plastic steering wheel with both hands. His eyes wandered through the smudges of dust on their windows to the littered streets with bottles, paper, boxes, and stuffed trash bags. His team commander sat in the front side passenger seat, leaning in, and searching along his side.

"It's probably an EFP," Staff Sergeant Gellums replied. "Keep your eyes sharp, soldier."

"EFP, Sarge?" the young Private Gabriel asked.

"Yeah," the Staff Sergeant acknowledged. "Anonymous tip was called into the TOC. That explains why the market is empty in the middle of the afternoon. An explosively formed penetrator or EFP is a type of IED using a copperhead shape charge with a fixed trajectory. No way they can plant something bigger than that around here and expect it not to be seen."

Gabriel nodded, turning his focus back to a trash can along the sidewalk. Yellow and white brilliance erupted from the plastic container, reshaping into a withered husk under the immense explosion carrying through it. A wave of light washed away his vision. Racing pressure consumed his hearing. There was only the choking smoke, carrying a nauseating fusion of chemicals that added to the alarm pounding through his chest. The ringing continued in his ears, overriding the muffled and unintelligible barking of Staff Sergeant Gellums.

Gabriel slammed the gas to the floor, but the Humvee slouched in place, its engine gutted from the projectile.

We were lucky. The trigger mechanism was measured for a larger vehicle, like the belly of a Stryker. No! Focus! Focus! God damn it!

Conscious efforts guided Gabriel's mind away from smoke stuffing into his nostrils, and the vibrations of the Humvee's interior. Graying clouds drifted over the courtyard, where he gazed up from the chilling ground, seeping away from his body warmth. The floating haze took a moment to subside while he gawked ahead at the main hall entrance with both doors opened. Ringing in his ears faded, giving back the brushing currents of wind, and the creaking hinges from the doors still swaying. Deep mournful cries bellowed throughout the halls with no pause for breath.

Gabriel peered over to Alexa as he rose on uneasy legs, catching her when she wobbled on stuttering steps. Her big green eyes blinked around the dilated pupils staring off at the unlit main hall, churning with shadows.

"Talk to me, Gray." Gabriel patted the woman, examining her glazed eyes.

"Did you happen to catch the license plate on the bus that plowed into us?"

"Yeah. It's spelled B-A-N-S-H-E-E."

"Actual, there's no way I can do letters right now. What does that spell?" Alexa staggered and shook her head until regaining her balance.

"It's a banshee. A particularly nasty type of vector derived from the wailing woman family of apparitions. They are the residual energies of a psychically powerful woman who undergoes extreme trauma during life. I read reports that Hitman Team engaged one years ago. This Duchess though, she is far more powerful than what they encountered."

"What now?"

"We're going to neutralize it and rescue whomever she is holding inside."

"I was afraid you were going to say that."

"Use earplugs if you got them."

Alexa nodded while digging through her pockets. "I doubt these damn things will stop the level of impact. But, it's better than taking it all like that again. Gosh, my head is hurting..."

"Pie the corners tight," Gabriel ordered. "This is one of those rare circumstances when a vector is armed with range weaponry. Let the walls shield the brunt for us. I'll take point, keep a watch on the rear."

"Roger, Actual."

Hollers stretched throughout the manor, clamoring from all directions as the agents entered the main hall's entryway. Another large door was at the end of the room, with others that flanked them. Gabriel stormed forward, his weapon remaining trained on it. He grasped the curving bronze handle that flared at the top, only to find the entrance refusing to give in either direction.

"Locked." Gabriel delivered a swift front kick. The door remained undamaged, without even a rattle.

Shrieking coursed through the manor after the agent attempted another hard stomp against it. The woeful ring of her lament twisted into salivating vengeance, fuming with rage, before speeding through the building's other reaches.

"Actual, I have a question," Alexa said.

"What?" Gabriel murmured looking to the door on their right.

"How do we neutralize this type of spirit?"

"All that meditating, and crystal bullshit doesn't give you a way?"

"I could probably incapacitate her, or even banish her."

"Probably?"

"I've never dealt with an apparition this strong." Alexa paused. Surging energies of torment caused her eyes to water, growing pink with a heavy frown. "She's putting off some serious power."

"Likely due to the poor souls she has devoured. Damn it. This class of apparition is a derivative of something that they cannot let go, whether it be regret or desire."

"Sounds easy enough."

The door opened with Gabriel pointing his carbine inward following it. "Nothing is easy in the agency, Gray."

"You can say that again."

"Except kicking your husband's ass." Gabriel smirked and chuckled as Alexa glowered in his peripheral. "Focus, Gray. I need you watching my six."

They continued into the next room, zipping inside one after the next. Gabriel entered, banking right, his carbine scanning along the perimeter of the room. Alexa followed, going left, and clearing her side. A charred fireplace greeted them, with two chairs next to it. Bookshelves lined the walls, immersed in thick layers of dust blanketing the titles over their spines. The room elbowed to the left. Torn paper covered the floor, with hard book covers lying flat and discarded among the tatters. Claw marks stretched along the remnant on the shelves, leaving gaping tears that blended from the reading materials and stripped the finish of the wood. Gabriel and Alexa glanced at each other and nodded.

"Hi-low," Gabriel whispered.

They approached the corner where the room turned. Alexa ducked low, pieing around the corner tightly, her silhouette halved by the vertical cover the wall provided. Gabriel followed high, their bodies working in unison as their weapon barrels scanned their expanding view of the other half.

"Clear," Alexa whispered.

Shoulder to shoulder they proceeded. Each agent focused on their half of the room, never intersecting each other's sectors. A loveseat was on Gabriel's side. Its cushions were shredded with the cotton innards mushrooming from the seat. On the left were more bookshelves, and an end table on its side. The door ahead at the end was cracked.

Loud and haggard sobs grew louder as the agents stepped closer. Between the narrow view was the Duchess. Her mass of tangled hair writhed like a nest of serpents and exuded the silvery aura of unlife, wilting the area around her with a grayish tint. The apparition's thin hands cupped her face, bawling into them again after bawling into the ceiling. She stopped turning, going still. The Duchess snapped around in a second where the details of her body meshed together like crinkling static. Scowling at the agents, the Duchess bared her teeth of sharp white ectoplasmic energy.

"Take cover!" Gabriel pushed Alexa from the doorway with him.

Screams blared out with explosive percussion. The door swung open, crashing hard into Gabriel's helm, and sending him to the floor. Resonant shrieks followed, ringing in their ears, with their earbuds throbbing inside the canals. Gabriel rose, smirking at the Duchess with her big glowing eyes and head cocking examination.

"Not this time, bitch," Alexa barked, calling positive energies into her grasp. She slung the ball of light with a curved pitch.

The banshee buckled underneath the impact of brightness upon her chest, sending her careening backward. The Duchess reared, gasping deep into her rising torso, then retching forward with her gaping maw expelling another bellow that rippled straight through the room. Alexa dived from the entrance, taking cover behind the wall. The hinges gave, ripping from the frame as the entire door jettisoned and flopped into the room.

Alexa turned back, ready to toss another orb into the next room, only to find it empty. "She's gone."

"Yeah, she didn't like your sorcery," Gabriel said.

"Can you please stop calling it that?!"

"No."

Gabriel entered the room with his weapon aimed and ready, sifting his vision through the dusty chairs surrounding tables. A saloon-style entrance accompanied an archway leading into the kitchen opposite them. Another door was on their left, swaying with residual momentum. Gabriel pointed.

Alexa nodded, trailing Gabriel who was poised against it.

Infantile cries burst from the kitchen, escalating into desperate hoarse screeching. Warm steam billowed from the kitchen, over and under the entry, and between the decorative cross bars of the partition. The agents switched direction, stepping slowly with their weapons trained on the kitchen.

"What are you doing, Your Grace?" a man cried out. "You can't—Argh!" Steel drove hard, slicing down into meat and tearing cloth. Breathy groans came from the man each time the blade ran through him. "Your Grace... Pleas..."

The doors parted as Gabriel stepped through. Both agents stopped, lowering their weapons and their jaws. Sprawled across the kitchen floor was a skeleton, draped in tattered ruins that once formed long sleeved clothing. A chef's toque blanche lay next to his skull, long having lost the luster of its puffiness, with every inch of it covered in gray dust. A wooden handle protruded from his chest, leading to the steak knife that was plunged into his rib cage, where it remained wedged between bones.

"Poor guy." Alexa leaned over the corpse, frowning at the skull that dropped back with its jaws agape. "That was the thanks that crazy bitch gave him for his years of service."

Gabriel nodded. "What was he trying to stop though? Where's the infant?"

Alexa dropped to her knee pads, reaching over with a gentle caress of the skeleton's forehead. Her eyes closed, projecting the room into her psyche, carrying her back to a time when the floors had been pristine white and the counters free of accumulated grime. The chef stood by the marble top fixture, dicing onions with precise chops, and sliding portions over the carving board into even piles. A smile covered the man's face as he gazed back to the cauldron, rumbling with boiling water over a fire.

Alexa stepped back as the partitioned door erupted with the Duchess storming through. In her arms was an infant child, wailing at the top of its little lungs. A twisted grimace covered the woman's face, her lips peeling back, brows rising in shock.

"No," the Duchess murmured. "I can't... I..." She stomped over to the cauldron, raising the baby, then hurling it into the boiling water. "You did this to me!"

"What are you doing, Your Grace?" the chef cried out. "Your Grace... Pleas..."

The Duchess stormed over to the counter, wide-eyed and unblinking. With one rapid stroke, she snatched a carving knife, and plunged it into the man's chest. Redness streamed from the gash, spilling into his white apron, soaking thick with blood like a sponge.

"You can't—Argh!" The chef groaned. "Your Grace..."

The chef reeled backward. The petite woman climbed on top of him, driving the sharp point into his chest, until the final thrust that ground against bone, where it wedged and would not relinquish under her straining efforts. Infantile cries rang out from the pot. The Duchess stood upright, breaths growing heavy, taking slow steps. The pleas for mercy curled away, siphoned into silence with the loss of consciousness.

The Duchess sneered, looking into the shining steel confines. Streams of heat rose from the bubbling and popping around the red and purple swollen mass. Skin peeled from the limbs, curling like wet bacon. Once fine hair shriveled along the bloated little skull, folding into the husking remains of chest tissues. The Duchess shook her head, placing the lid over the pot. Tears streamed from her reddening eyes, her teeth biting down hard into her lip, sending blood trickling over her chin. The ring of sliding steel followed the woman claiming another sharp knife from the rack. The Duchess hurried back through the doors, leaving them swinging from her furious exit.

Darkness washed over Alexa's vision, bringing into view the dusty counter, skeleton, and dirt covered floor. Gabriel's hand reached for her shoulder. His brow firmed as he leaned in to examine her eyes.

"Thought I lost you there for a second, Gray," Gabriel said. "You did some trance stuff? The lights were on, but it was clear no one was home."

Alexa peered over to the pot, covered with blackened carbon and cracking brown rust. Her M4 dangled from its clip, brushing with each step. She reached for the lid. Bitter vapors of decay escaped into the room when the seal was broken. Clanging came when Alexa discarded it. Looking down into the pot's belly, she saw a tiny skeleton that remained in the fetal position at the bottom. Little fingers and toes were locked in a curling clench. Alexa removed the skull, clutching it close in both hands.

"I saw it all," Alexa said. "The first victims of her descent into madness. Must've been a severe undiagnosed case of postpartum depression. Modern society is just now taking these cases seriously. I can only imagine the lack of caring in those days, and how many women were forced to endure it alone."

"It's a fucked up world," Gabriel agreed. "Protect the payload at all costs, Gray."

"Roger, Actual. Let's go and deliver some peace to these poor souls."

The agents departed the kitchen, setting upon the door they had noted earlier. Alexa remained poised against the wall, tucking the skull into a front pouch pocket on her vest. Gabriel pushed the door, peering in with the M4's close-quarter optic guiding his vision. On a large table was a motionless man. His arms and legs were strapped to the sides. Etched like stone on his face was a grimace, scrunched together in agony. Trails of blood ran from his drenched ears to matching puddles that dried into the wood finish.

"It's a scryer!" Alexa gasped. "She did this to him. That evil bitch…"

"Poor sap." Gabriel shook his head. "Death by a thousand decibels. Nothing we can do for him."

"Help!" Muffled cries came within earshot. The agents peered around, seeing only an array of barren bookshelves and a rusted candlestick holder protruding from the wall. They walked closer to the source. "Help!"

"Here!" Gabriel pointed. "Beyond these shelves."

"It wasn't uncommon for these manors to have hidden passageways in case of emergencies," Alexa noted.

"Yeah." Gabriel reached for the candlestick holder, tugging on it. Locking mechanisms clicked and ground, rotating cogs within chambers unseen. Dust and dirt rained from the shelves, trembling as they pushed into the wall, sliding across the floor and coasting to the sides.

"Doo-doo-doo-doo-to-to-to-too." Alexa grinned after reciting the Legend of Zelda's secret door chime.

"Geek," Gabriel murmured and shook his head.

"I couldn't resist." Alexa's brow rose. "Wait a second! And how do you know that reference, Actual?"

"Hush, Gray!" Gabriel snapped, treading down the stone steps that spiraled along a winding path. Optics directed their weapon barrels that led the way, guiding low with their path, while they hugged tight to the pillar.

"Get away, damn it!" a familiar and deep voice barked. "Help!"

"Eeeek!" another squealed. "Leo, don't provoke her!"

"That's Butcher10Golf and Mike," Gabriel whispered.

Their path leveled out into a room of bricks, filled with the musty and tart odor of decomposition, that hit the agents deep in their nostrils, sticking to the sweat of their skin and contaminating their mouths with a lingering rotten sourness. Buzzing filled the room, from dozens of plump flies bobbing through the air.

Cuffs and chains hung from the walls, with writhing bodies clasped to them. A table sat in the middle. Wood chips peeled from it, even around the portions stained with clouds of red and brown. Metallic contraptions were stationed along the wall, composed of leather straps, spikes, and serrated blades. Chunks of meat remained woven between and upon the edges, withered and molting as a plethora of maggots writhed among them. Knives and hooks were strewn about the floor adding to the tapestry of blood, urine, and feces that streaked across it.

"She was gone before the postpartum..." Alexa's jaw dropped. "Long gone..."

"Leo!" Gabriel called out. "Portia. Where is she?"

"Bossman!" Leo cried out. "Your ass is a sight for sore eyes! The vector's gone for now! But she pops up whenever she's looking for a plaything. Sweet Pea and I were ambushed once we got through the door, and fought our asses off until this banshee overwhelmed us and the scryers. She's been picking on them, first. As you can see, it's just us now."

"Actual!" Portia smiled.

"Do either of you know where she keeps the keys to your shackles?" Gabriel peered around. "This place is a fucking mess."

"There are no keys," Portia answered. "She uses her will."

"Don't sugarcoat it!" Leo snapped. "It's sorcery. The bitch is pure evil."

"Just because I don't immediately condemn every practitioner doesn't mean I'm wrong!" Portia snapped back.

"Calm down you two," Gabriel ordered. "Save it for the enemy. There must be something I can use to free you."

Gabriel stepped between the discarded cutlery, searching the table, then looking among the torture devices. Alexa walked on the other side, checking behind a large, spiked wheel. Gabriel swatted away flies before looking at her.

"No visuals of what we need on this side. How about you, Gray?"

"I've got nothing here, Actual."

Shadows churned along the wall next to Gabriel. Alexa stopped, gazing over to an emerging silhouette of a thin face. Strands of hair followed, flaring around the snarling countenance of the Duchess. Her glowing eyes fixed upon Alexa.

"Behind you!" Alexa yelled.

"Gabe!" Leo called out.

Gabriel turned, raising his rifle. The Duchess' jaws extended open, propelling concussive ripples at the agent. Gabriel jettisoned over the table, crashing into a rattling pile of chains next to a chair covered in razor wire. He pressed up from the floor, attempting to turn, but finding his legs were not underneath him, nor was his sense of touch. Pain rode through his head, forcing his eyelids to crunch down tight. Gabriel collapsed, a thin barbed hook among the debris plunged through the palm of his hand in a vain attempt to catch himself. Stings channeled through his fingers and up his forearm.

Alexa reached into her pouch, hurrying forward, and withdrawing the infant's skull. The scryer agent held the skull in the palms of both hands, presenting it before the widening eyes of the Duchess.

"You are foul, selfish, you are swine!" Alexa screamed. "Face the justice of your deplorable actions and remember what you have done!"

The Duchess bellowed to the ceiling with a shrilling lament that rattled her core. She fell to her knees, reaching out for the skull with her pale, glowing hands. A small face materialized, peering back at the Duchess with his big blue eyes and chubby cheeks. The child screamed. The Duchess cried out. Bubbling ripples surrounded her aura, climbing to the surface, boiling the energies that composed her presence. Ectoplasmic particles dripped from the Duchess, as steam rose around her, cooking away the apparition until she evaporated from reality.

Alexa looked into her grasp. The child had vanished, save for the skull that crumbled into dust, slipping between her fingers. "Thank you, little one. May you finally rest in peace now."

Chains loosened, and shackles unlocked. Leo and Portia removed the metal confines and hurried over to help the woozy Gabriel. The four of them gathered around a chest, redistributing the medic's and machine gunner's gear. Leo grabbed his M249 Squad Assault Weapon Light Machine Gun. He opened the feed tray cover, pulling a belt of linked rounds from the plump belly of its ammo box, loading the weapon. Portia dug through her pack for iodine and bandages, racing over to Gabriel and patching his hand.

"Thank you." Gabriel nodded.

"We should be thanking you," Portia replied.

"Damn fine work neutralizing that heifer." Leo gave the beaming Alexa a high five. "We'll head to the rendezvous once Sweet Pea has patched you up."

"There's a rendezvous?" Gabriel asked.

"Yes, bossman. You were one of the first through the door. When Madam Dupree gave the order, I noticed you pushing through fearless as ever, leading the way. As you can see though, the chaos and unpredictable nature of the port didn't allow us the same landing zone."

"Or time for that matter," Portia added.

"Right before the rest of us went through, Madam Dupree gave us these during the fight." Leo held out a hunk of purple stone.

"An amethyst!" Alexa smiled. "Looks like we're finally getting some luck."

"What is a stupid rock going to do for us?" Gabriel scoffed.

"That stupid rock is like radio comms for scryers." Alexa took the stone from Leo. "It's great for telepathy, clairvoyance, pretty much anything that projects third eye abilities." She closed her eyes, focusing on the amethyst.

About time you got your hands on one of these, girl. Madam Dupree's voice carried into Alexa's mind, spreading to the others. *Here are our coordinates.* Images of metal barriers and sandbag walls formed a large compound surrounding two colossal pillars of churning light. *I'm glad you're in one piece. Others haven't fared so well. We're gathering all the survivors of the task force. Your orders are to rendezvous at our outpost and wait for further instructions. I see you have Mr. Grumpy Pants and most of his team. Good. Make haste, all of you.*

"Actual—" Alexa turned.

"Yeah, we heard it, too," Gabriel interrupted. "We need to grab the children first and then we'll head to the Combat Outpost. Madam Dupree is right. Let's hurry! Double time, team!"

CHAPTER 21
VICTIMS

FOREST OF THE LOST, PANDEMONIUM - TIME UNKNOWN

The four agents walked in an arrowed formation, with Leo and his machine gun taking center, while Portia and Gabriel remained on adjacent flanks. Alexa brought up the rear on the far right. Night's darkness immersed them as they stepped deeper into the forest, treading through the greenery that gathered frost. Twinkling stars dotted the sky between the canopy's breaks, leading to a yellow crescent moon. Sweat rolled underneath their uniforms, gathering within undershirts and moistening their socks.

"Stop." Gabriel peered around. "Something isn't right. We've been here already."

"Maybe another team found them?" Alexa wondered.

"That type of optimistic thinking is cute." Leo chuckled, keeping his sight ahead, and his grip tight on the light machine gun.

"I'm getting a bad feeling." Portia's gaze sifted through the greenery of her night vision goggles and into the distance.

"Me too," Gabriel agreed. "What was the smart little girl's name again, Gray?"

"Penny."

"Eyes up, team. I'm going to be giving up our position," Gabriel warned before calling out into the night. "Penny! We're the agents that rescued you! Please come out so we can escort you from here! Come on out, sweetie!"

Long, thick leaves rustled in the wilderness, near trees gathered along their formation's right side. Small quivering eyes stared back from between the foliage, immersed within the confines of shadow. Branches snapped and popped as a petite figure darted out, speeding toward Gabriel like a blur. Sobs followed when thin arms wrapped around the Butcher team leader's waist with trembling desperation.

"There you are!" Gabriel sighed with relief, patting the girl's head of dark hair, and returning the hug. "What's wrong?"

"She managed to minimize her aura to that of a cricket," Alexa noted. "Fascinating and clever."

"Gabriel!" Penny's weeping face glistened in the moonlight. "Alexa! The twins! They attacked us when we got here! I told them exactly what you said. To stay put until you returned. That's when their mouths..." The girl shook her head. "They started eating Albert! The rest of us ran!"

"Shit!" Gabriel snarled. "They're vectors. Eyes up, team. Penny, I'm sorry. I didn't know. You stay with Alexa in the rear of the formation. If combat starts, I want you taking cover again. Okay?"

The girl nodded, scampering to the rear and taking Alexa's hand.

"Poor little girl." Portia sighed.

"Yeah, but where are the other children?" Leo wondered.

"Up here!" a boy cried out. "It's not a trick, everyone! Gabriel and Alexa are back!"

Their attention carried to the trees. Wedged between two upright branches was a young boy. His legs floundered, finding the crevices to help guide his slow climb down. Snapping branches and rustling leaves signaled another little girl and boy, who started their own descent opposite the agents. The children gathered around Alexa.

"Are you all that's left?" Gabriel asked.

"Yes, sir," one of the boys answered.

"Where are the twins?" Alexa asked.

"We don't know," Penny said. "We heard them laughing and bouncing around earlier, passing by after they…" The girl swallowed. "Ate the other four."

"Okay. That sounds about right," Alexa said. "We rescued eight children. So, everyone left is accounted for."

"They're here!" Penny whispered, her quaking finger pointing into the forest depths.

Grinning maws of sharp yellow stained teeth appeared as thick lips slid back from the darkness. The twins' beady glowing eyes shone as they waddled into the moonlight. Their globular bellies pulsated from their expanding waists, their belts stretched tight, holding back the gurgling girth. Belches left the boys' parting teeth, vibrating the long strings of saliva, clinging within their mouths.

"So close to making the change," the first twin announced.

"Only a few more souls and Mother will love us," the other agreed.

"Mother will love us. She'll reshape us, and we'll no longer be orphans."

"Well now," one twin said as their eyes fixed on the agents and children. "Looks like the rest of our dinner has shown up—"

"—and it's time to eat!" the other said.

Clack! Clack! Their teeth chomped. The duo raced forward, their mouths expanding to great size, while the rest of them vanished. Sharp fangs bobbed in the air. Plodding steps thumped along the ground from the unseen presences, smooshing grass and bending weeds in their wide footprints. Heaving breaths escaped between their undulating jowls, carrying odors of rotting carrion and sulfur.

Damn it! Gabriel's aim lowered from one of the mouths. A trigger pull sent a shot forward. The round stopped in midair within unseen flesh, creating an impact trail that wobbled the mass it entered. A second later it disappeared, swallowed by the twin's will. Gabriel dived from their charge, rolling on the ground to a tree. He popped up, bending around the trunk, with his M4 pieing around, opening the sight angle for alignment on his targets, and retaining cover.

"Aim for their hearts!" Gabriel called out.

Portia scampered behind another tree. Leo's M249 light machine gun erupted with controlled bursts. Alexa placed herself between the children and the monstrous orifices biting into the wind. Penny and the others ran into a bush, dropping low and crawling underneath its bristling flora.

"I got nothing!" Leo said.

"Leo, disregard suppression!" Gabriel ordered. "Get out of there!" He patted his vest, rifling through a 40 millimeter grenade pouch for an plump red incendiary M203 round.

The twins' mouths bounced and stopped, turning to face the heavy weapons specialist. He paused, staring into the snapping teeth whisking toward him.

"Grenade out! Danger close!" Gabriel warned. A deep bellowing pop from his M203 grenade launcher signaled the launch of a dumpy 40 millimeter round. The spinning red warhead rose in an upward trajectory arcing down until smacking one of the twins. A conflagration spread upon impact, outlining their bulbous forms with flames peeling away at their flesh. The twins cried to the heavens, their stubby arms working to beat away the spreading fire as smoke rose into their mouths, swelling into their choking throats.

"Now!" Gabriel ordered.

Carbon spewed from the biting weapons as the agents walked down their foes, who twitched with each round entering their bodies. One of the twins gasped, materializing into view, clutching his chest. Holes pierced through his heart that shone before expelling its light. With eyes rolling into their narrow slits, he collapsed into a jiggling mass, his tongue protruding between knife-like teeth.

"No..." the other twin cried, his eyes following his brother's corpse. A shot entered his chest, jerking him one last time before he convulsed into a pile on the ground.

A glimpse of light fluttered from a twin's ear. Another followed, stopping before the agents with their weapons trained on the corpses. More flowed from their mouths, ears, and nostrils, until dozens of beaming little orbs hovered around them. Gabriel paused, lowering his weapon. Within the golf ball-sized orbs was the image of a boy. The youngster's weary eyes connected with Gabriel's. He smiled at the agent, waving with a spark of exuberance before whisking toward Alexa who welcomed the light with cupped hands.

"The souls of those they devoured," Alexa stated. "They're free now. The twins must have never used the energy, save to stay alive. But, why?" The lights gathered into her grasp, forming one glowing ball. "This is all that remains of them. Their consciousness is destroyed; likely their bodies have passed."

"So, what do you propose we do with them?" Gabriel asked.

"We're listening to witches now, Actual?" Leo raised a brow.

"Ugh! Not all witches are bad, butthead." Portia rolled her eyes, turning away from Leo to exchange smiles with Alexa. "I love you knuckleheads, but this team can be so stubborn sometimes."

"We're out of our element here, Leo," Gabriel answered.

"I say we take them back with us," Alexa proposed. "It doesn't seem as if they have anywhere else to go. Returning them to the material world will allow them to safely pass on."

Two final souls rose from the deflating corpses. Images of identical boys stood side by side, frowning at the agents, then exchanging uneasy looks of nervous apprehension. Their outfits hung from their skinny frames that stood slouching and knock-kneed.

"You two caused a lot of grief and tried to kill us," Gabriel reprimanded.

"We're sorry," the twins replied.

"Why were you devouring the other children?" Alexa asked.

"We can't go back." The boys lowered their heads. "And even if we could, why would we?"

"To work and still starve?" a twin continued.

"With papercuts, and people shoving us aside?" the other added.

"No thanks," they said.

"That didn't answer my question though." Alexa stared, pressing her lips together. "Answer me, boys."

"Mama gave us the medicine after a long day of work, when we felt ill," they answered.

"Was it laudanum?" Alexa inquired. "Judging by your outfits I'd say that places you around the time that awful medicine was popular."

"You nerd," Gabriel murmured.

"Continue, boys." Alexa grinned.

"We wandered here by mistake, many, many, many, many moons ago," a twin said.

"Yeah. More moons than these lot here." The other nodded.

"I see," Alexa replied. "So, the laudanum combined with your fatigue, illness, and unrefined psychic abilities ported you here via involuntary astral traveling. Your bodies died in the material world because you stayed here too long. But you're scared to cross over and leave what you already know. So that's why you devour the other children, to use their life force to stay here indefinitely."

The twins nodded.

"Tell me," Gabriel ordered. "How many souls were lost to your appetites?"

"None. We were fading, until the Queen had her minions grab so many from the surface recently. Never were there so many before. Souls are everywhere. She can't keep track of them. Some escape or get stolen. We tried to use the ones we found to live longer. Honest."

"What are your orders, Actual?" Alexa asked.

"Take them with us," Gabriel replied.

"Whoa! Whoa! Whoa!" Leo interrupted, stepping close to whisper. "Gabe, you feeling all right? We should be smoking these motherfuckers. They're evil."

"They're victims too, Leo. Just like the other children. This place shouldn't even exist. But it's here, like a trap for the innocent."

Alexa smiled and nodded. "Well said, Actual."

"No more shenanigans out of you two, understand?" Gabriel snapped.

"Yes, sir!" The boys saluted.

"Let's account for the other children," Gabriel ordered. "Then we exfil to the rendezvous. We'll link up with the rest of the task force and plan our assault on the White Queen's domain."

CHAPTER 22
COMBAT OUTPOST: GALLANT

Penny shadowed Gabriel within the formation trudging its way through golden grass fields gleaming with morning dew and light from the rising sun. The girl pointed at tall barricades forming a compound. Iron towers stood behind the bastion, with long barrels of pintle-mounted M2 Heavy Machine Guns protruding from them.

"Leo, give them a heads up on our return," Gabriel said pulling the binoculars away. "Monarch is manning those towers with some big hate, and I don't want any accidents."

"Roger, bossman," the machine gunner responded.

Portia removed a green tube from the side of Leo's patrol pack, handing it off to him.

The large man winked at her, feigning a Southern accent. "Thank you kindly, ma'am."

"What's that, Gabriel?" Penny asked.

"You're an inquisitive one." He chuckled. "It's a green star cluster. A type of signal flare."

"To let them know we're coming to the base, right?"

"Yes. Clever, indeed."

Penny leaned over, watching Leo unravel a seal, freeing the cap with an ignition pin on the inside. He placed it over the flare's bottom end, pointing the exposed green barrel to the sky. A hard slap brought his palm to the device's bottom end, smacking the pin into the primer. Smoke raced from the flare, corkscrewing its contents high into the sky. Sparkling green embers appeared among the trail of smoke, lowering in a haze of brightness lasting several seconds before fading from view.

The children's eyes scoured the area, their faces turning long with dread, while their pace slowed.

"Why are you slowing?" Alexa asked.

"This place seems familiar," Penny murmured, and the other children nodded. "But... it's hard to remember things..."

"Don't you fret." Portia smiled with a wink. "We'll have you at the outpost soon enough."

"What happens after we reach the outpost?" Penny asked.

"The medical staff will check you for any injuries or ailments," Gabriel answered. "Then, the scryers are going to help you maneuver through the door and get you back home."

The children whooped, exchanging high-fives, and skipping along.

"That livened their spirits." Alexa chuckled.

"Whhhaaaa..." an unintelligible hiss carried from the distance.

Dozens of thin silhouettes appeared on the horizon. Incandescent eyes shone among faces constructed of shadow. Distance faded their bodies in and out of view. Cat-like claws protracted from their fingers like barbed fishhooks. A number of them carried long spears with spaded heads that ended in sharp points, while others had three-headed flails adorned in needled protrusions.

"They're here!" Penny cried out. "The White Queen's soldiers!"

"Children, go!" Gabriel ordered. "Run straight to the COP and don't look back for anything!" He pressed the lever release for the M203 grenade launcher attached below his M4. An audible click sent the barrel sliding forward. From his vest, a 40 millimeter grenade was tucked into the weapon before he lodged it back into position. "Bounding withdrawal, team! Gray and I are alpha element! Call the movement!"

"Moving, Actual!" Portia and Leo announced, sprinting behind the fleeing children.

Alexa and Gabriel released controlled shots at the writhing mass of fiends. The lithe figures piled forward, tangling with each other. Sharp hissing resounded through the air, growing louder with the passing seconds as they closed the distance. The cucuy lashed at one another, snapping with contempt and curses, yet moving onward in their pursuit. Rounds passed without finding their marks.

"Aim for the heads," Gabriel said. "There's nothing else to hit."

"Roger, Actual." Alexa's reticle zeroed in on a grimacing vector. The pull of her trigger sent the cucuy squealing, reeling back as mists of black ooze sprayed from the impact zone that peppered its forehead. The foe collapsed, its tangled body carried by its yapping brethren, with their eyes affixed in pinpointed frenzy upon the agents.

"Set!" Leo called out after kneeling with Portia. They braced their weapons tight to their shoulders, their lead elbows lodged into their kneepads for support. Gabriel and Alexa broke contact, turning and taking off into a dead sprint racing past Portia and Leo. Their legs powered through the burning from the weight of their vests, combat loads, weapons, and packs.

Bursts of fire spat from Leo's M249 light machine gun. The weapon roared with six round salvos, inhaled from the drum resting at its belly. Leo placed his eye on the rubber lips of the PAS13 Medium Weapon Thermal Scope, reaching to the weapon's front where the PEQ16A sat. A press of the button sent the PEQ's marker laser streaking across the battlefield. He lowered the weapon's muzzle, aligning the glowing line to a cucuy's bobbing skull. A burst of fire sent the screaming foe's head wrenching back, crashing into its brethren. Controlled surges of lead raced from the light machine gun, withering the enemy's frontline chargers.

"Set!" Alexa called as Gabriel popped shots into the cucuy.

"Let's move, Sweet Pea." Leo bounced up with the medic turning to race across the grass.

"Grenade out!" Gabriel yelled. A heavy audible click sounded from Gabriel's M230 grenade launcher, sending a plump 40 millimeter round spiraling over the field in a descending arc. It smashed into the ground between cucuy, erupting in a cloud of dirt that rose from the impact zone. Screams rang out from the enemy, their formation bending around the explosion. Hot metal bit deep into them with immense pain. Choking fumes of smoke and dust were left in the explosion's wake. Cucuy lay strewn across the grassland, writhing in agony, bleeding out from the fragments of shrapnel lodged across their bodies.

"Set!" Portia screamed out over Leo's roaring machine gun, joining the onslaught with her M4.

Cucuy continued behind them, having closed the gap to only twenty meters. Gabriel glanced at the children running between the steel barriers forming the mechanized entrance of the COP. He peered up to the towers with M2 heavy machine guns and MK19 grenade launchers. "Break contact, Butcher! Run! Run! God damn it!"

Adrenaline washed away the heavy breaths that swelled in their lungs, and the ache of exhaustion clamping down on their cores and legs. The four agents pumped their arms and legs, gasping. Sweat pushed out from their bodies, saturating their uniforms with widening stains.

Long M2 heavy machine gun barrels turned on their pintles, aiming for the mob of cucuy. Thick stubby MK19 automatic grenade launchers trained their leafy sights on the foe. Thudding shots jerked back the heavy machine guns, spewing copious amounts of carbon with each large .50 caliber round they barked into the enemy's ranks. Thumping and clicking erupted from the MK19s, slinging three to six 40 millimeter High Explosive Dual Purpose Grenades into the cucuy. Eruptions strung across the ground in clouds of mayhem. Defiant hissing streaked across the field as the cucuy turned and retreated, leaving their fallen kin screaming among the chaos to be chewed apart by subsequent volleys.

Butcher Team arrived before the main gate. Agents sat behind machine guns in the adjacent OP towers, waving them through, and giving exuberant thumbs up. Gabriel nodded, returning it while sucking air through his heaving frame. Penny and the other children stood by the opening, smiling with relief. Gabriel patted the girl's head and nodded.

"Friendlies coming in!" the sentries repeated it for all to hear. "Friendlies coming in!"

Flutters of energy pulled from Gabriel's presence, drifting upward like a glimmering black and white butterfly, until vanishing. "What the hell was that?"

Portia shrugged at Gabriel.

"Part of our aura," Alexa answered. "It's our presence here in this world."

"Scryer bullshit." Gabriel shook his head, walking deeper into the Combat Outpost.

Giant tents were erected alongside thin plastic antennas and pillars of amethyst that jutted from gray and black stone bases. Members of the task force shuffled among the supply crates next to the tents, carrying radios and batteries. Robed scryers and technical agents clad in overalls gathered around orbs in transparent boxes. Blue and white light reflected in their goggles from the intense energies quaking within the glass and metal containers being maneuvered with slow and steady care.

What the hell are those?

Bradley light tanks were in a formation down the middle of the compound, flanked by Humvees, and gargantuan M939 cargo trucks possessing green canopies. Personnel were climbing over their vehicles, pulling away wobbling chunks of black flesh from the treads of tires. Along the backside of the compound were colossal dual pillars of churning white energies, their presence grounding away into a mass of darkness.

That's the physical presence of the door.

"You are correct to ascertain such, Agent Agapito," Madam Dupree called out, speeding through a tent's flapping entrance, with Corvus in tow.

"Praise the Great Spirit that you and the others have survived the journey, Agent Agapito," Corvus announced with his deep and solemn tone. Shining black eyes stared from his raven's cocked head as it perched on his shoulder.

Harland exploded through a tent, sprinting for Alexa. In a

great hug, he scooped up his wife, spinning around with her legs flying outboard. Harland squeezed her.

"Harry!" Alexa half gasped and half laughed. "I... can't... breathe!"

"Oh, sorry!" Harland put her down.

"I missed you, too." They gazed into each other's eyes, closing them in a slow cascade as their lips touched. Sighs of relief came the moment they parted.

"The ambush at the door..." Harland shook his head.

"We lost many good people before reclaiming the initiative," Madam Dupree stated. "This is why we endeavor onward. Understand that the task force is only at eighty percent strength in personnel, commanders. Our logistics support is still accounting for our static assets, but we've managed to ferry over our essentials."

Gabriel and Harland nodded. "Acknowledged, ma'am."

"These last two days have been chaos." Harland turned back to Alexa. "Many agents and scryers have fallen to establish this beachhead. I was worried when I couldn't find you."

"Butcher Actual is the reason I'm still here." Alexa turned to Gabriel. "His decisive leadership saved all of us."

The children and team nodded.

"Thank you." Harland stepped around to shake Gabriel's hand.

"She's being modest," Gabriel replied. "Your wife handled herself like a true agent. I couldn't have done it without her."

"You're exhausted and understandably so. I regret to say there's not much time for R&R," Madam Dupree said. "We're racing against the clock, Agents. Several recon missions have been launched to survey the area and discover the position of our primary high value target, the White Queen. I was worried we had lost you, Agent Agapito. I'm relieved this battle can still be won."

"Not sure what you mean, ma'am."

"Still turning away from it, huh?"

"I never turned to it."

"I have to admit, I would've missed our sparring matches had something happened to you."

"How are you still on wheels?" Gabriel asked.

"Well, if you must know, this dimension isn't completely ethereal or material. It's a strange frequency that derives from both. Some of the rules from the material world still apply here, giving a semblance of order to this godforsaken land. I've made do without my legs for quite a while. But, I was hoping your stubbornness was something that didn't transfer over."

"Sorry to disappoint." Gabriel smirked. "I can't believe I'm saying this—"

"It's good to see you, too. Now, let's get down to business. As you have probably surmised, the door's presence is not stable. It is frequency hopping within a fragmented bandwidth among the etheric layers. Its presence is ever-changing, and sometimes its function is happening without rhyme or reason. Hence many of us were ported to different regions. The door is stable for now with the scryers on the other side holding it in place. We can discuss this more in the command tent. Where are my manners? I see you've escorted some VIP guests. It is a joy to see these young people have been safeguarded by your team. A victory is very much welcomed among this chaos. Are you hungry, little ones?"

"No, ma'am!" Penny exclaimed in wide-eyed horror. The others groaned, shaking their heads, and holding their stomachs.

Madam Dupree chuckled, inquiring to Gabriel. "I take it there's a story behind that knee-jerk response?"

"Roger, ma'am." Gabriel smirked. "Too much of anything is a bad thing."

"Get me up to speed about your adventures in a little bit," Madam Dupree responded. "For now, let's have these young ones patched up and brought through the gate. My scryers on both sides are ready to ensure their safe travel. But first…" The Grand Scryer waved for everyone to follow.

Madam Dupree's tires sped over the crunching grass between the vehicles, and over to the glowing orbed devices within the translucent chambers. The team gathered around, watching an agent and scryer duo carry one of the mechanisms to their meeting, holding it aloft by the steel handles welded to the upper end of its frame.

"Behold our secret weapon," Madam Dupree announced with a grin. "The Psionic Bomb. An improvised explosive device of the scryer kind, if you will. I know the name is a bit lackluster. Bear with me while I think of a proper nomenclature."

"Your tricky witchcraft is hardly a secret." Gabriel winked.

"There's the feisty agent I need." Madam Dupree chuckled. "Glad you're coming out of your shell again. You had me worried topside. This weapon is the gathered energy of the entire Scryer Order's psionic attacks. Well, I'm exaggerating. Not the entire order per se. Everyone we could gather on a day's notice, at least. It's housed within these units and to be unleashed upon our departure against the doorway in order to destroy it once and for all." Madam Dupree scratched her chin. "Afraid I'm exaggerating there too. It'll destroy this door, until another is fashioned by the unholy power running this place.

Judging by the accumulation of energy, it will take thousands of years."

"So, once we've located the kidnapped children, we're exfiling this hell hole and blowing the gate?" Gabriel asked.

"Precisely, Agent Agapito. Monarch has already launched recon missions with their squads. That's a task that is outside of their element but necessary. The intel they gather will allow us to know where to best commit our strength. I'm expecting Curt to report back soon."

"Things are looking up." Harland smiled, his arm remaining around Alexa.

"Indeed, they are," a soft voice said from an unseen presence. "While you had me worried upon your initial run, it seems that you're determined to ruin my mother's fun." Yellow eyes and thin serpentine pupils manifested over Madam Dupree's lap. Sharp teeth revealed a wide grin from lips that pulled away reality to show itself. A bushy purple tail tapped at the railing of the Grand Scryer's chair, beating with a humming and melodious scat from the invisible cat. "Doo, doo, dum, dee, dee, such a glorious day. Doo, doo, dum, dee, dee, to find evil to slay—"

"A vector!" Gabriel snapped. "And just why should we trust a cucuy? If the White Queen is your mother, why would you be helping us?"

"This one is smart. He has a lot of heart." The eyes reappeared over Madam Dupree's shoulders. The rest of its invisible presence curled around her neck. The cat's tail continued tapping on her chest. "Simone, I like his fire. Without it in this world, one could easily tire."

"Answer the question," Gabriel demanded.

"Cheshire, my dear friend." Madam Dupree reached up,

guiding a finger over the cat's brow. "Perhaps, it's time you explained yourself to the others."

"The Cheshire Cat was a nuisance to Alice," Gabriel announced. "It's been a long time, but I remember that much."

"Are you sure about that, Agent Agapito?" Madam Dupree shook her head.

"Was I?" the cat responded. "I made sure that Alice didn't die."

"He guided her," Madam Dupree interjected. "The best way he could through this madness. Do you remember what Partridge told us about the composition of this place?"

"Everything is fashioned from the energy of stolen souls," Gabriel answered.

"Our friend here is no different."

"Mother isn't perfect, like her own father," the cat answered. "She hasn't refined her power and nor does she bother. The souls that I'm made from still have a voice. Unlike my brethren, it gives me a choice."

"She made a mistake when creating you?" Gabriel wondered. "Not erasing the consciousnesses completely. That's why you're similar, but not as dangerous as the others? And playful in a child-like manner."

"Your guess is correct; the laws of energy are the key. My existence continues because of them, and theirs through me."

"It makes sense," Madam Dupree added. "On another important note, I believe we have figured out more about the modus operandi of the White Queen vector. And it's not good."

"Friendly patrol returning!" sentries yelled from their posts. "Friendlies coming through the gate!"

Heads turned. Eyes fell upon the rotating cogs and chains clinking together, dragging open the steel barrier of the entrance.

Humvees rode inward, their growling engines with nonstop vigor. The wide-tracked vehicles bounced when hitting a divot. Their gunners held steadfast to the long barreled M2 .50 caliber heavy machine guns mounted within the spherical Chavis Turrets, where thick bullet resistant glass surrounded them.

The return patrol circled the motor pool filled with other vehicles, stopping in a line facing outboard to the main gate again. Whining came from the heavy door of the third vehicle's passenger seat. Curtis stepped from the Humvee, M4 in hand, unstrapping his helmet, and rushing toward Madam Dupree across the way. Streams of sweat ran down his forehead. Ammo pouches on his vest remained open and empty of magazines.

"It's good to see you all in one piece, Butcher10Actual," Curtis greeted them. "But there's no time for catching up. Ma'am, we found the Hat Man. He's located deep in the wilderness, about twenty klicks from here. I've marked his location on the force trackers. There's a lot of cucuy patrolling now that they know we're here. I had to bring my people in for a refit before pursuing."

"You have positive identification, Monarch Actual?" Madam Dupree asked.

"Affirmative, ma'am." Curtis pointed to the large green box with a giant lens that sat upon a Humvee turret next to the machine gun. "We parked on a hill. Surveyed the area via LRAS3, the Long-Range Advanced Scout Surveillance System. Managed to spot him another five klicks out from the fifteen we traversed. I even hopped in there myself to confirm. Big hat, wicked grin, devilish glazed over stare. It's him."

"Our HVT number two." Madam Dupree nodded. "Things are looking up, as you stated earlier, Agent Gray. Great work, Monarch Actual." Her attention turned to Gabriel. "Are you up for the challenge? It's your meeting with him that'll decide the fate of this operation. At least that's what the etheric layers are telling me."

"Always ready, ma'am," Gabriel responded.

"Hell yeah," Leo agreed.

"It will bring us closer to saving the little ones," Corvus added.

"I appreciate your sentiment, gentlemen and ladies." Madam Dupree smirked. "Finally, we're getting somewhere. Grab some Humvees. Monarch will escort you. Go and have a chat with this hat-loving fellow. If the book taught us anything, it should prove to be interesting."

CHAPTER 23
WATCH YOUR STEP

THE PLAIN PLAINS WITHIN THE PLANE, PANDEMONIUM - ESTIMATED TIME 1200 HOURS

"Contact!" Monarch2Golf yelled, gripping the M2's dual handles with a locked and steady poise. The heavy machine gun's thudding bolt hammered rounds into the receiver's chamber, sending them speeding off into the distance. Hordes of thin black figures gave chase toward the speeding Humvees. They tangled together, their lithe limbs blending their movements, working as one unit toward the task force. Swathes of large .50 caliber rounds ripped into the dark auras flexing around their bodies in opaque layers. The piercing tips of each bullet separated flesh and bone. Bellowing targets fell into the grassy fields, thrashing about on bloody stumps. Greasy meat and jagged fractures met the afternoon sun, saturating the ground with their life force. "Contact!"

"Where the hell do they keep coming from?" an agent from

Monarch transmitted over the radio. "It's as if they're just popping up out of thin air!"

"Sustain fire at your discretion, Golf!" Curtis ordered. "Keep them off us! Drivers, push through!"

That's a good question. Damn it, this has plummeted our situational awareness. I know my agents aren't asleep at the wheel, but these vectors keep appearing out of nowhere and getting the drop on us!

M2s shuddered in recoil, jerking back on their pintle with each thunderous burst. Glowing tracer rounds spat with every fifth shot. The gunner rotated his turret as the column continued past. He canted his weapon. Clouds of carbon spewed from the weapons' roaring salvos, dusting the Humvees that grumbled through. Black metal links and smoke laden shells sprinkled the rooftop, with remnants spilling back into the gunner's nest, down the open hatch, and clanging into the cabin.

"Maintain sectors of fire!" Curtis continued through the mic. "My golf and the rear vehicle can handle this. I want the other trucks keeping eyes up for other tangoes attempting an ambush from another direction!"

"Roger, Actual!" the squad commanders replied from their vehicles.

"How long has this shit been happening?" Gabriel asked from a passenger's seat.

"Since we arrived at the AO," Curtis answered over his shoulder. "The damn things gave us respect at the COP after we repelled them at the door with combined arms. Now they lie in wait. Whenever we try to leave, they send waves for us to battle through."

"These things have no fear!" Portia squealed from another seat, wincing at the mayhem through her window.

"The red ones are far worse," Curtis replied. "Luckily, they seem fewer in number. Our guess is that the White Queen is holding them in reserve as her rear guard. Wherever the hell that is…"

Angry scowls shot from across the field as the last galloping cucuy slowed in their pace before stopping. They disappeared in the gathering distance, vanishing over the horizon. Rattling within the Humvee ceased after the final bursts from the M2, culminating with the jingle of casing and links escaping into the cabin.

"They're simmering down, Actual," Monarch3Golf reported.

"Damn good shooting up there!" Curt tapped the gunner's knee pad with his knuckles. "I don't know how you were hitting those bony things. You're a better shot on the Ma Deuce than me."

"Thank you, sir! That's good ole country boy Kentucky windage right there!"

"ETA to mission sector is three mikes," Monarch3Alpha called on the radio from the lead vehicle.

"Roger that," Curt replied. "Gabe, you heard them. We'll be dropping your team just outside the sector, allowing you to infil via dismount. My element will continue a roving cordon and overwatch of the fields for any more waves of shitbags. That should keep eyes off your people while you investigate the whereabouts of the HVT. You call us via radio when you're ready for extraction. Be safe out there."

Fist bumps were exchanged between the team leaders. "Much appreciated, Curt."

"Yeah, not bad driving for former Marines," Leo quipped. The large machine gunner bolted from his seat, snickering.

"Boy, don't you make me get out of this TC seat!" Curtis snapped.

"I apologize, I didn't mean to offend you. You guys prefer the term Jarhead, right?"

"Oh my God, Leo!" Portia snapped. "Stop agitating Monarch!"

"Well, you know what they say about the Army, right?" Curtis asked.

"What's that, Monarch Actual?" Leo smirked.

"Aren't really Marines yet."

Leo's eyes narrowed. "You win this time, Monarch Actual." He slammed the passenger door.

"Gabe," Curtis' voice softened, calling out after opening the heavy up-armored door to his front passenger seat. "This hasn't been an easy op for Butcher. When this is over, if you want to talk about Mara, we can grab a few cold ones away from the others."

Gabriel's eyes broke contact. "Perhaps you're right. I... I'm not thinking about it right now. It hasn't completely hit me... yet."

"There's been a lot of loss in the agency these days, Gabe. I lost my buddies too, when the Steiners were almost defeated. Those knuckleheads and I went through indoc together..." Curtis' gaze fell on the horizon. "You're not the only one that needs to vent."

They shared a nod.

"Enough of me being sentimental," Curt continued. "We need tenacious asshole Gabe for this operation."

"That guy never left." Gabe smirked.

Curtis closed the dense vehicle door, cushioned by the outline of thick rubber along the frame that squeezed watertight when the securing latch locked in place. The rumbling Humvee convoy broke contact, turning away from the border of the forest. Butcher and Diver Team stared into the murky foliage draped in shadows, ignoring the radiance of light from the grasslands.

White fog rolled through the area, billowing from reaches obscure beyond its translucence. Brown and green vines hung low with drooping branches. Mud patches broke up the low grass that remained curled through it.

"Give me a status check," Gabriel ordered.

"Heavy weapons agent is green to green," Leo acknowledged.

"Medic is green to green," Portia replied.

"Close quarters specialist, green to green," Kevin added, cocking the fore-end of his twelve gauge.

"I am ready," Corvus said, his raven cawing from a shoulder.

"Scryer Agents of Diver Team are green to green, Task Force Actual," Harland replied with Patel and Alexa nodding.

"Double line astern formation," Gabriel announced. "Leo and Patel take point. Alexa and Kevin give me rear side security. Everyone else mid with me."

"Come on there." Leo chuckled at the wide-eyed dismay from Patel. "There's nothing to it. Keep your eyes moving and stay alert. If we get into any shit, I'll give them the business end of my girl here." He patted the light machine gun.

"Okay." Patel gulped.

Cool wetness blanketed the agents as they walked through the fog. Weapon barrels remained low at the alert position, canted outboard from the body of their formation. Fingers remained straight and off the trigger while weapon buttstocks pressed snug against their shoulders. Corvus walked with Gabriel. Slender pieces of smoothed wood were in the dream walker's hands, their deep orange lengths filed down into perfect points.

"Are those your wands?" Gabriel inquired.

"Yes," Corvus replied. "A gift from an alder tree. The best type to sleep under. It provides assistance and protection when navigating the sands. The Great Spirit has supplied everything we need through nature. We only have to listen and learn."

"That's how she did it," Harland noted.

"Who?" Gabriel asked.

"The little girl, whose adventures here were codified, although I question the accuracy of the story that obviously took liberties. She might've slept under an alder. I wonder if they have them in England..."

"We've got contact with a sign, Actual," Leo called out.

Three boards were aligned together on a tree. Rusted nails protruded from the peeling wooden surface, where fading words had been painted in black.

"Watch your step and show respect," Patel read aloud. "Lest you be humbled and get wrecked."

"Some kind of a trap," Gabriel announced.

The agents peered around, finding only the fog between the trees, mud that caked the treads of their boots, and small circular patches of grass.

Patel looked at Leo who shrugged.

"I got nothing," Leo said, turning his gaze up to search among the branches and leaves. "See any soft patches or areas that look recently disturbed on the ground? Maybe some spot where the leaves are gathered just a little too conveniently? Probably, a pitfall or snare somewhere."

"I'm not seeing anything." Patel stepped forward.

Muffled screams rose from underneath his boot as a patch of grass pushed up from the ground. Patel lurched back, leaning in dismay to examine a small being rising from the dirt. Moist soil clung to its body, save for the crumbling bits that fell when it shook itself free of the small roots clinging to its thick legs. Green, brown, and yellow blades of grass served for its hair, covering the creature's head and face. Spit jettisoned from a loud hiss of its stretching maw of bucked teeth. White foam rose between its gums, flowing over its lips and saturating its chin. The tiny nine-inch tall being trembled with ferocity. Bulbous white eyes glowed from its unkempt head, left with the imprint of Patel's boot.

"Oh!" Portia smiled. "It's so cute!"

"Are we looking at the same thing?" Leo glanced back at the medic with a raised brow. "This little shit looks rabid!"

"Step away from the cucuy," Corvus warned.

The creature reared its head back only to hop forward, directing the ire of its shrieking at Patel. "Heeee!"

"Don't insult it." Patel stepped closer.

"Heeee!"

"Get the hell away from it, Patel!" Leo urged. "That thing is pissed off! Your hippie empath scryer bullshit isn't going to work. Let's fall back and cut another path."

"You're wrong." Patel took a knee next to the creature. He closed his eyes, reaching deep within his psyche, pushing out warming energies of love, and regret. "I am truly sorry for my clumsiness, little one."

Popping came from the ground, with roots ripping like torn cloth from the haste in which more rose from grass patches. Several dozen of the little beings joined their raging brother, watching in quiet blinking glances of curiosity between him and the agents.

"Heeee!" Spit flew from the creature's roar. The horde followed its glare to Patel.

"Must be a family of them." Patel smiled at the plethora of eyes that blinked back with their gazes locked upon him. "What should we do, Actual?" He turned around to ask Gabriel. "Give it an MRE cracker?"

"Are you trying to piss it off even further?" Leo quipped.

A hard clamp came down on Patel's index finger. His black leather glove split underneath the bite force of the creature. Hard flat enamel punctured through, catching between the middle joint where its teeth wedged down. Agony shot from the separated cartilage, where the bones within thrashed and shifted amidst the mayhem. Wetness and hot breath seeped over his exposed skin, mixing with the rushing blood that was sucked away by the creature. It shook like a dog, rattling Patel's arm even as he pulled away and flailed about with it locked to his hand.

"Shit!" Patel cried out.

"Told you that thing wasn't buying what you were selling." Leo chuckled with the others, removing his combat knife from a sheath. "Hold still so I can pry it from your—"

"Heeee!" War cries resounded in harmony from the rest of the creatures, leaping forth with their bodies rolling into spheres, and colliding into Patel like fast baseball pitches. The agent reeled back, groaning and gasping to the canopy above as dozens of them thumped against his helmet and limbs. The creatures bounced away after impact, unfurling back into their stances before hopping forward, teeth first, and biting down on whatever they could.

Piercing pain shot through his gloves, boots, arms, and legs. Each locked maw claimed a section of meat and uniform, smeared with white foam. Patel curled in the fetal position. Baleful glowers zeroed in on him from the creatures with reddening rage boiling in their eyes. Lips peeled back from bucked teeth inches from his face before another bite came down. Sharp agony churned through Patel's nose. Streams of blood raced through his crushed nostrils. Deep teeth indentions became lacerations when Patel's skin gave under the relentless pressure of its sawing mouth.

"Crap!" Leo plunged his knife into one of the cucuy. Steel ran through the squealing creature, its legs kicking when the agent drove hard, lifting it from his comrade. Leo followed the reddening eyes of its maniacal gaze, still locked on Patel despite racking in its death throes.

"Hold fire! They're too close to Patel!" Gabriel ordered. The ringing of steel followed when he unsheathed the sword mounted along his pack. "Knives out. Alexa, Harland, and Corvus on overwatch."

The team drew their knives, surrounding their fallen comrade who hollered and convulsed. Gabriel thrust sharp carbon steel into a creature, its chest cavity splitting open as the blade drove to the hilt. The creature was pulled away, the strength of its legs fading to stillness, the rage heaving through its small frame subsiding. Only its arched brow remained firm, holding together the scrunched glower of its face, still turned to Patel. Gabriel chucked the little beast over his shoulder and drove his blade into the next one.

"I'm sorry, little thing!" Portia said to a creature, sliding her knife over its throat.

"You're sorry?" Leo exclaimed.

"Hold still, damn it!" Gabriel yelled.

"Yeah!" Kevin said. "Bro, this is dangerous. I don't want to slice you by mistake."

"Hurry!" Patel groaned. "This hurts..." He winced. "So... much! Gah!"

The ground erupted with more of the creatures shaking free of the soil before setting a narrow-eyed glare on Patel.

"Heee!" Hisses flew from hundreds of gaped jowls bearing bucked teeth.

"Oh shit!" Leo exclaimed. "We got enemy augments incoming!" He turned to the fresh wave, dropping his knife to reclaim the M249 light machine gun draped over his shoulders.

Bursts of lead roared from the weapon, the receiver drawing in rounds from its drum, and ripping them across the forest floor. Several of the creatures fell, struck by 5.56 millimeter bullets that pierced their pudgy stomachs, leaving stringy greenish innards oozing from the exit wounds. Others swarmed around Leo, bounding past him, heading for Patel.

"Shit! There're too many! And they don't give any fucks about suppression fire!" Leo warned, scooping his knife back up.

With an inverted grip, Gabriel drove his sword down into another creature, prying it off Patel's boot. Rapid pitter-patter surrounded him in seconds. He turned. The swarm of creatures parted around him, heading for their quarry.

"No! No! No!" Patel's screams escalated to greater decibels, peeling the moisture and skin from his throat. New bites locked on his legs, arms, and shoulders. Sections of his vest weighed from the clinging presence, holding steadfast via vise-gripped jaws. He rolled several feet, the other agents following with the swarm. Their eager maniacal glowers searched for their own piece of the agent to chomp down on. Patel continued his frantic barreling until he arrived at the foot of a wide and towering tree.

"Work with us!" Gabriel snapped. "We're trying to get them off you!"

"It hurts!" Patel screamed. "Like—hell!"

Heat from stale breath rushed along the side of Patel's neck, signaling a presence approaching his head. Teeth chomped down on the entirety of his ear, crushing the cartilage and slurping the meat of his ripping lobe down its gullet. Patel locked in place, grimacing as spiderwebs of pain spread in his skull, churning through his face. It channeled along his neck, grounding through his limbs, convulsing with anguish. Flesh shredded away as the growling creature shook and pulled. Hot pain replaced the weight of what was once there. Shock numbed the area greased in blood and saliva.

"Get away from him!" a deep voice bellowed from above. "Shoo! I said shoo now, mome raths! Before I spray you all with my sap!"

Hissing and growls ceased, with the tiny creatures peering up at the tree.

Gabriel pointed to a wizened face with long scrunched eyes. Leaves draped like a beard over his thick and dry lips. The tree leaned over delivering a firm stare upon the mome raths. "I mean it!"

"Eeeee!" The little beings fled from Patel, leaping back into the ground, where the grass patches returned from their protruding scalps.

"Nasty business when those things get angry," the tree continued. "Are you okay, young fellow? You seem to be leaking red sap from many places."

"What the hell are you?" Gabriel's grip tightened on the hilt of his sword.

"Well, you're a rude one," the tree scoffed.

Patel rolled to his back, deflating with a deep sigh. Blood splatters immersed his uniform, seeping from numerous bite-sized tears. Groans fled his quivering lips. Patel's stare carried into nothing, before his twitching eyes rolled within their sockets.

"Oh no!" Alexa exclaimed, shouldering her M4 and moving toward her teammate, only to stop when Harland's hand grasped her shoulder.

"Hold, Alex," her husband said. "He's our friend, but we have to stay disciplined and maintain their cover."

Alexa nodded, retaking her position near a tree.

"He's going into shock!" Portia plopped her daypack next to him, rifling through her medical contents, drawing packages of gauze and sterilizing agents. "Keep his feet elevated!"

"Got him!" Leo replied, grabbing Patel's boots, indented deep with teeth marks. Something rolled around inside the footwear. *I know what that is... His toes. The bite force of those damned things must be* tremendous *for their size.*

"I—I can't feel... anything," Patel murmured, his head rolling among his shoulders. "I... Everything so c-cold..."

Patel's hand whipped out, slapping Portia's away and sending her syringe flying before she could apply its pain relieving contents. The medic gasped. Patel's face twisted, his cheeks rolling upward, lips peeling back with his teeth clamped in a grin. His eyes scrunched tight save for a glimpse of the pupils within, shifting about in nervous apprehension.

"Umm, whatever you gave him seems to be working," Leo said. "He's smiling again."

"I didn't get a chance to apply anything," Portia replied. "He slapped it away before—"

"Ha! Ha! Ha!" Patel cackled. "Ha! Ha! Ha!" His body writhed and convulsed, with legs kicking and arms thrashing. The harsh laughter stopped when his neck curled back upon his tense and rising shoulders. The agent shook and struggled, only to explode with body quaking laughter.

"What the hell is wrong with him?" Gabriel asked.

"Oh my," the tree said. "I'm afraid the mome raths' venom has taken hold of your friend. It's supposed to be delightful in small doses, but in larger ones it's known to cause death by laughter. Your friend's ribcage and lungs will collapse at this ever-increasing rate, as his muscles grow tighter with each contraction. Nasty stuff, indeed."

"How do we stop it?" Portia pleaded, wrestling Patel still with Leo, bandaging his mouth shut.

"Why the sap of the Tumtum tree of course."

"And where do we find one?" Gabriel asked.

"I'm right here." The tree smiled.

"Hand it over."

"You are definitely a rude one!" the tree scoffed.

"We don't have time for your madness!" Gabriel snapped. "You denizens of this insane hell hole seem to think everyone is at your disposal for shenanigans."

"Perhaps I should just enter a deep meditation and project my psyche into the material realm to watch other mortals go about their day. You're beginning to bore me. Time is something in which I have plenty, young rude fellow. And how ironic you say such a thing while wielding the Vorpal Sword!"

"What's that supposed to mean?" Gabriel snapped. "Damn it! Why must all you—Stop speaking in riddles!"

"Oh, what a delightful idea! A riddle contest! That would be most entertaining for me."

"We do not have time for your games!" Gabriel repeated and snarled. "Give us the sap!"

"Oh, I will. If you win our riddle contest. But should you lose, your friend gets to die here, and you'll leave his corpse to feed the forest. What say you?"

"I say, I will burn your sorry ass into ashes," Gabriel replied.

"And your friend will certainly die, because my sap will burn with me." The tree chuckled. "Any more rebuttals? Time is wasting."

"Actual, please!" Portia pleaded, wrestling to hold Patel still. "I can feel his chest straining. The contractions are getting worse."

"And now thanks to your rudeness, you must answer three riddles." The tree smirked.

"Damn it, I'm not skilled with this kind of bullshit," Gabriel grumbled.

Corvus stepped up.

"I accept your challenge, Mr. Tumtum," the dream walker announced. "Start with your riddle, please."

"Someone with manners." The tree smiled, its branches and trunk swaying with a gentle nod. "Okay, here goes an old classic to start our competition. There are seven fish swimming in a pond. Three will drown. One will find his way, while the others flee. How many are left?"

"Three!" Leo shouted.

"That is incorrect," the tree responded.

"Leo, let the smart people answer!" Portia snapped.

"Ouch, Sweet Pea. Just ouch…"

"Time is of the essence," the tree reminded.

"None of them have left the pond," Corvus answered. "So, seven remain."

"Well done." The tree smiled. "You are a clever one. Different from these soldierly types. I think you're going to make this interesting for me. Next riddle; I'm packed away and carried wherever you go. I take up no room in your suitcase, purse, or even wallet. Yet, I weigh more than anyone can know. What am I?"

"Let me think."

"Of course." The tree grinned. "Take all the time you need, my feathered friend. I'll just be standing here."

"Yikes! This one sounds harder than the last!" Portia grimaced. "Leo, don't say anything!"

"Ouch, woman!" Leo snapped. "You going to keep kicking me while I'm down?"

"Yes."

"I'm getting a feeling," Gabriel whispered to Corvus. "These riddles all have to do with this place somehow."

"You ascertain correctly." Corvus nodded, keeping his eye on the smiling tree. "This one is definitely more complex than the other denizens. A tree that speaks and astral projects. That shall be included in the shadow bestiary, should I ever escape this realm."

"That's not very optimistic." Gabriel sighed.

"Experience has taught me never to—" Corvus paused. "Thank you, Gabriel."

"For what?"

Corvus turned to the tree. "Memories is the answer you seek, Mr. Tumtum. More specifically, trauma."

"You are indeed a clever one!" The tree's smile widened. "Sifting through that banter actually helped you figure it out. Bravo!"

Patel groaned.

"Actual, we're running out of gauze here," Kevin pleaded. "We've emptied three combat lifesaver kits on Patel."

"On with the next one... Please," Gabriel requested.

"It can learn." The tree nodded. "Okay, since you're actually displaying manners, I won't make this one as difficult as I initially intended. Are you ready?"

"Yes! Yes... please," Gabriel said.

Corvus nodded with approval, turning back to the tree.

"You were a guest to her, but you couldn't stay. Someone with a knife cut you away. Who is she?"

"Mother," Corvus answered.

"Well done." The tree smiled. "And you be wary when dealing with mine. Oh, your secret is safe with me. So many of us are tired of her war with the Red Queen and the lust for power." Mr. Tumtum peered at Gabriel. "You must learn to slow down and look around. Or you will have given everything for nothing, child."

Child? This motherfu— "I understand." Gabriel swallowed. "A deal is a deal, correct, sir?"

The tree smiled. "Indeed. Help yourself, young one." Golden brown liquid oozed from the corner of Mr. Tumtum's dry and cracked lips. Gabriel retrieved a handful, running over to Patel and cupping it to his mouth. The laughter died down, along with the convulsions, his body turning limp, with a gentle snore.

"He's combat ineffective," Gabriel said. "Portia, Kevin, and Harland will take him back to the rendezvous point. Diver12Actual, you're in command. Link up with Monarch and let Curt know that we are going to CASEVAC Patel to the FOB for extraction."

Alexa and Harland rejoined the team.

"I'm calling the request now," Harland replied before directing to his mic. "Monarch2Actual this is Diver12Actual. Stand by for 9-line CASEVAC request, how copy?"

"Roger, we copy you Lima Charlie," Curt's voice transmitted after the cryptographic beep. "Send it."

"One; grid coordinates PM12121111, one klick from mission infil point. Two; extraction commander is Diver12Actual. Three; one patient requiring urgent care. Four; no special equipment required. Five; one ambulatory patient, three accompanying security. Six; wound types are animal mauling, multiple lacerations, poisoning, and severe damage to limbs. Seven; we will signal with a green star cluster when we have eyes on extraction element. Eight; patient is a U.S. citizen and active duty agent. Nine; reaction due to biological agent has subsided but handle with caution. How copy?"

"Roger, Diver12Actual," Curt replied. "That is a solid copy. Force tracker has us twenty mikes from the pick up zone. We are en route now."

"Monarch will be here in twenty minutes from their cordon patrol," Harland replied, helping Kevin get Patel from the ground. "We're moving now, team."

"Excellent," Gabriel replied with a solemn nod.

"Fight that shit, Patel," Leo urged patting his shoulder. "You fight that bullshit and stay strong, buddy."

"The rest of us are Charlie Mike to the Hat Man's lair," Gabriel announced, glaring into the distance.

"Roger, continue mission, Actual," Alexa acknowledged.

Particles of energy fluttered away from Gabriel's shoulder. The glimmering spot zipped into the air, fading as if its presence was never there. Alarm blared through Gabriel's senses, increasing the pace of his heart. Wide-eyed expressions were exchanged between the agents after seeing the flapping images of black and white energy flakes drift from their auras. *Damn it, there it goes again!*

"Your grip on the layers is artificially induced?" The tree leaned in, raising a brow. "Hmm... time is not a luxury you can afford to waste, child. The longer you are here the more effort will be required for your consciousness to hold your presence in Pandemonium. Eventually, it will be exhausted, and you will face expulsion, back into the material realm."

"As Madam Dupree warned." Gabriel sighed. "Thank you. I'm far from being a perfect leader. I fuck up. I fall short. I need a reminder once in a while to keep my focus."

"We all do at times, young warrior."

"Don't be so hard on yourself, Actual." Portia smiled. "I wouldn't want anyone else leading our team."

"You've gotten us this far," Alexa reminded with a soft smile.

"The concern is important," Corvus stated. "An expulsion from Pandemonium would allow the White Queen to better prepare. It will be impossible to gain another foothold should we fail. With how time is traversed here, even a day back in the material realm could be too long of a departure. There would be no stopping her."

"Corvus is right," Gabriel agreed. "We move with haste. This isn't about our safety. It's about recovering the lost souls of the innocent."

The agents watched with long faces as the other half of their team carried Patel away. Gabriel turned, staring into the distance, the direction of their mission tethering his attention.

"I bid thee farewell, young Agents." The Tumtum tree exchanged respectful nods with Corvus. "And might I strongly suggest you exercise caution when dealing with the Mad Hatter."

CHAPTER 24
UNINVITED GUESTS

A HOVEL OF HOMOPHONES, DEEP FOREST - 2000 HOURS

Clouds of heat rushed on the back of Matt's neck, contrasting with the cold rusted iron he lay upon. Darkness brought by the haze of slumber peeled from view, giving shape to bars that enclosed him. The spaces in between provided glimpses of drooping foliage from surrounding trees and the dark blanket of night. Shadows and fog blocked the details in the far distance, save for a cottage with a thinning and frayed thatched roof that sprouted a billowing chimney. Footprints covered the muddy terrain and crushed grass, leading in every direction just outside the confines of his cage.

Dried streaks of blood stained across the square panels of the cottage windows, stretching into the splintered logs that formed its walls. Warmth returned, brushing over his right ear, and spreading to the side of his face, leaving a clamminess and shivers from a looming threat. The man turned, seeing nothing.

I remember a tunnel… and a small door. Matt tried recalling through the mind fog that sent most thoughts careening away without acknowledgment. Images of nocturnal yellow eyes resurfaced in his memories, with their thin pupils. Shivers climbed down his spine, curling deeper into a fetal position on the steel floor. *This is a bad trip… That's all it is… My head… killing me. The fuck is going on? Just curl up and wait until the high is gone…*

The warmth expelled over his neck again, carrying a voice of eagerness. "Yesss…"

Matt bounced up and rushed to the opposite side. "Who's there?"

The being scampered away, disappearing into curtains of shadow several feet from the cage's rear. Matt ran fingers through his frayed hair, rubbing his stubble and gasping. Salt from a long day of hard work remained on his lips, along with the moisture of sweat that gathered in the armpits of his uniform. Remnants of pizza dough encrusted his apron, crumbling away from the myriad of white stains as he gripped it.

This can't… This shit is real! Where the fuck am I? Matt muttered, staring at the bars and ceiling of the cage. *Okay! Okay! Think! How did I get here? Wait… just ended my shift at Tony's… We closed the restaurant… Mario and Joey wanted to chill in the break room… Ralph cooked up that stuff in the kitchen… The drink… Fuck my life…*

Shifting images whisked away Matt's attention, between the bars, where other cages stood several feet from him. *My vision is adjusting… somewhat.* A figure writhed about within the darkness. Groans of agony puffed out from the individual, chiming in Matt's thoughts with a familiar tone. "Ralphie! Is that you?"

"Yeah..." His friend rose on wobbling legs. Ralphie's right arm remained clamped to his side. Four rips crossed through his baggy white server's uniform, leaving shallow scratches that beamed cherry red over his exposed skin. "Something caught me good on the side... I—I must'a took a bad fall or something... Are we still tripping? Are we... in jail or something? Did we get arrested? What happened?"

"I don't know, man. I just woke up like a minute ago. I'm still out of it. Can barely think. That shit was so hard. My head is hurting like hell! You see Joey?"

Ralph peered around. "Hard to see in this damn place. Bro, where the fuck are we?"

"I don't know, man... I just want to go home."

"I just want to go home!" someone repeated in a woeful and dopey tone. "I just want to go home!"

"Who said that?" Matt barked. "Show yourself and quit playing these fucking games!"

"Ooohh, it's awakening," the person replied sauntering forward, keeping his silhouette traced among the shadow and fog. Large protrusions extended up from its head, amidst a long mane of wild hair. Bristling whiskers flanked its upturned nose, above a cleft lip with sharp fangs aligned close to each other. The fine edges of a tailored jacket stood pronounced on his drooping shoulders. His knees remained bowed from thick hind legs, carried upon furry paws.

"I'm fucking tripping," Matt scoffed. "I'm still fucking tripping! God damn it!"

"Oh, you getting here was quite the trip," the figure replied. "No easy feat for either of us, I tell you."

"Shut the hell up!" Matt snapped, rising. Lightheadedness consumed him. Each shaky step he took refused to register in his senses, despite him staring at his feet. "What the hell..."

"Careful now," the person warned. "You're swimming into some deep waters. Here be quicksand and it'll swallow ya whole, I say."

"Quit playing fucking games!" Matt retorted.

"Bro, who are you talking to?" Ralph sighed with fatigue, leaning against the bars of his cage.

"It's Joey over here trying to fuck with me," Matt replied. "I know it."

"Know," the figure responded. "Know! Know? No? No! No. Definitely not Joey. Why would you accuse me of such a thing? That's very rude, you know. Bad form! Bad form indeed! He's over there."

A long hanging sleeve extended into view with a fuzzy hand pointing its clawed finger. Matt and Ralph followed it. Mists and shadows receded down a path for several feet, revealing another cage. Its open door swayed, creaking and squealing. On the floor lay shredded scraps of black and white clothing. Matt recognized the green and red button labeled 'It's Pizza Time!' and the apron straps.

Shaking his head with doubt, he focused his view on the corpse strewn across the ground. Blood splatters soaked the breached flesh where shattered ridges of his frontal skull were exposed. The twisted neck left the head remaining with an outboard stare toward Matt and Ralph, from the naked body that remained in the prone. Crimson smears soaked across his shoulders extending into a greasy tapestry that ended with sloppy strokes toward his lower back.

"No... What the hell..." Matt gasped. "Joey!"

A wide gaping hole of stringy flesh hung from the bloody fissures folded and exposed over where his anus should have been. Threads of blood spilled between his open legs, matting together in his pubic hair before dripping. It pooled below the torn and shriveled remnant of his missing genitals, between the handprint stains over his thighs.

"What did you do to him?" Ralph demanded. "You fucking monster!"

"Wasn't me!" The being leaned from the darkness, bringing his face into the open. Veins stretched through his yellow bulbous eyes, staring in opposite directions. Both upper and lower lips curled back, revealing a mouthful of uneven spiked teeth, save for the front pair that curved together. Large, long ears remained erect on his head, rigid despite his rhythmic bobbing in place.

"You're a rabbit!" Matt scoffed.

"Yes, indeed I am a rabid," the being agreed.

"What did you do to Joey?" Matt demanded.

"I told you! I did nothing!"

"Come now with the truth, Hare ole boy," a smokey voice suggested from the unseen before giving an echoing slurp from a cup. "My only wish on this special day was that we tell no lies."

"Ah, yes. Now I remember…" The hare drew from his coat's inner pocket. Wet squishing came from his hand rifling to withdraw the contents. Resting in his palm was Joey's flaccid and torn member. Half of the organ's base was ripped open with dripping flaps of skin riddled in gnaw marks, around the scrotum with one missing testicle. Blood trailed down his wrists and into his sleeve when presenting it. "I borrowed this from your friend after the mouse escaped its teapot, you see. He wouldn't be needin' it anymore, since it was his unbirthday. Or was he alive when I took it? I can't remember, you see. Hard to think over all of his screaming. And I can't find a better form of testosterone to keep my figure lean. Straight from the source is always best, as Mother used to say."

"Organic is the term you material dwellers love using," the man said.

"A mouse murdered him? A fucking mouse did all of that? You're not making any sense!" Ralph screamed.

"Because he's withholding information again," the man in the distance said before taking another slurp. A mug chinked with a dish. "Such dalliances and it's not even the season of love, ole Hare."

"Oh, but I didn't hurt his face, though!" the hare snapped.

"Just the other parts," the man quipped.

"Who are you people?" Matt demanded. "Stop hiding and show yourself."

"I have to watch the mouse, or he'll ruin the party again," the man in the distance replied. "Lest it become all our unbirthdays. I do believe that I need better friends. But I can't be choosey given the circumstances."

"You're stuck with us, dear Hatter," the hare replied. "There's always your brethren, but in their mindless loyalty, they would surely make known these dalliances to your dear sweet ole mum?"

"Reminders aren't necessary, Haigha. Where were we?"

"Oh yes!" The hare turned to his victims, flashing his teeth with a grin. "It's quite rude to join a party uninvited!"

"This trip is getting out of control, man..." Ralph dropped to his knees, lip quivering into a loud sob. "I don't want to do this anymore..."

"Were it so easy," the Hatter replied. "Mouse had his fun, taking the one I wanted. I guess it's only fair that I allow my dear guests first choice at the meats."

"I do appreciate such kindness," the hare replied. "Hatter, your parties are always the best. I can't make up my mind! I can't think! I can't!" He flailed his limbs. Joey's severed component sloshed about in his grip, flinging droplets of blood.

"And it's not even springtime." Hatter snickered.

"Where was I? Oh yes, this is why I travel so far just to share tea with you, old friend. This is why! And they think demons like me cannot get along with rakshasa like you. We know better! Don't we?"

"One day, this will all be mine, dear friend. No more animosity between the two kingdoms. Working claw in claw. Red and white, finally united!"

"Well said!" The hare dipped away from view, slipping into the fog and shadows once more. "Let us toast to your words!"

Thin beams of green light flashed among the fog. Matt and Ralph stared in a hypnotic daze, following the lasers. People traveled from obscurity, spread in a line, pinpointing where the Hatter and Hare had congregated.

"More uninvited guests!" the hare squealed.

"I swear!" Hatter scoffed. "Folks just have no decency or respect these days! Sorry, but there's no room here!"

"No room, see!" the hare screamed. "No room!"

"Shut the hell up!" Gabriel barked, training his weapon on the rabbit who gasped in horror.

Corvus ushered forward in the shadow and fog, raising his hands. Winds howled forth from his projected will, swirling around him into a vortex before jettisoning outward, pushing away the darkness and white blanket of vapor.

"I banish the illusion designed to generate fear," Corvus chanted. "May the moon's light bring clarity."

A large table of polished rosewood stretched along the open area. Teapots, cups, and dishes covered it, sitting on top of a white frilled tablecloth, spotted in a myriad of stains. Steam rose from the spouts, with boiling contents rumbling inside. Small white cakes were in perfect squares, covered in chocolate ribbons and raspberry drizzle. Cookies with sprinkles and sugar confetti sat in a large pile upon a dish at the center of the table.

Hatter ran a napkin over his mouth, folding it into his lap, and leaning back in his chair. Etched on his face was a dead man's smile, crooked and undiscernible from the stillness within the rest of his countenance. His eyes glanced over to a large teapot along the right side. The vessel shuddered, with its lid rising and falling to a loud clang every few seconds. Hatter reached for the pot, clutching it in his wide hands, drawing it to his chest.

"Seems as though we're at an impasse," Hatter quipped.

"Hardly," Gabriel retorted.

Weapon sights remained locked on Hatter. A red glowing reticle hovered over his grinning countenance, between his incandescent yellow eyes. Leo moved along the table's left side, with Alexa shadowing him. Gabriel and Corvus stood at the opposite end of their demented host. Hatter's thick dry lips curled away from his rows of yellow canines and black gums.

The large top hat upon his head bobbed as he swayed with a bubbly jovial rhythm. Wild strands of his brown mane brushed against his broad shoulders, having escaped the confines of his headwear. The oversized hat's brim was perfectly etched, while its midsection remained tapered from a band of onyx. Tucked inside was a card labeled with the fraction 10/6. His eyes separated their view, one thin pupil tracing the movements of the flanking element, while the other remained connected to Gabriel.

"Oh, I beg to differ," Hatter replied. "Tell me, Agent. Have you ever heard the old tale about the devil and the dormouse? It's quite peculiar how you mortals twist things, but I can assure you that the devil is a shepherd of dormice which serves her well. Infernal familiars and their forms can be deceiving. Close by, but never truly seen. And they always blamed the cats."

"Your mad ramblings won't save you!" Gabriel said. "We are not little children you can bewitch!"

"How good are your shots with those pretty muskets?" Hatter asked. "Better not miss. You'll hit the pot. Better not hit me. Or oopsie, I'll drop it."

"And why should I give a damn about your pot?!" Gabriel snapped, before Corvus placed a hand on his shoulder.

"Hold steady, brave warrior," Corvus warned. "There is a very powerful dark presence within that vessel." The dream walker's firm gaze carried over to Alexa who nodded as she turned her focus to the ceramic kettle. The lid rattled, until Hatter pressed it closed. "Something is being subdued via copious amounts of arcane opiates within that teapot."

"What we have here is a good ole fashion, st-st-st—" The March Hare's head jerked forward. "Stand off!"

"He stutters when he gets nervous," Hatter said.

"D-d-d-do not!" the hare scoffed. "N-n-nervous! Of these uncouth party crashers?"

"Yes," Hatter replied.

"Maybe a little." The hare shrugged.

"This doesn't have to get ugly," Gabriel warned.

Corvus nodded, tightening the grip on his wands.

"I'm—I'm a-afraid it's a bit too late for that!" the hare snapped. "Have you looked in a mirror lately, mortal?"

Hatter snickered as his friend leaned over the table to swipe a cup of tea.

"We are here for the children," Corvus said. "That is all."

"Caw!" the raven squawked at Hatter. "Caw!"

"Little dreaming birdies are making demands." Hatter chuckled. "Funny, I was just discussing my hopes and aspirations with dear Haigha here, before you interrupted our meal."

"You should eat less sugar," Gabriel quipped. "It's rotting your brain."

"Sugar is not my sustenance, but my sustenance is sweet," Hatter replied.

His eyes drifted from the agents to the adjacent cages where Matt and Ralph remained. "They're human!" Gabriel exclaimed.

"Help us, please!" Matt sobbed.

"Shhh..." Hatter looked back to the agents. "Let's strike a bargain."

"We don't make pacts with demons," Alexa replied.

"Well then, I guess it's a good thing I'm not a demon." Hatter smiled. "My two friends here are demons. I am a child of the sands. A rakshasa. Or cucuy. Or incubus. Ugh, so many names. But, definitely not a demon. Can you deal with that, Scryer?"

"You must tell us the location of your Queen," Corvus commanded. "Then, release those two lost souls."

"Nope!" Hatter chuckled. "What kind of deal is that, birdy? Especially with our history. How much did you learn from those defeats I handed you topside? Priceless knowledge."

"I must save the children," Hare muttered with a deep and dimwitted tone of mockery.

"And what do I get for my troubles, and the troubles that come from those?" Hatter asked.

"Troubles upon troubles!" the hare added.

"I can put one between your eyes," Gabriel said. "And save us the trouble."

"Ooh!" The hare grinned. "Now he's talking our language."

"Should I just let my mouse friend free and cry havoc?" Hatter grinned. "Is that what you said? It'll take more than just one musket shot to kill me. Even here in the nominal."

"Don't let him out!" the hare cried, scooping up a vial of jam. "Don't do it, ole boy! You're better than that!"

A particle of Gabriel's presence slipped away from his aura, rising above their heads where it zipped into nothingness. Hatter's eyes connected with Gabriel's. The rakshasa's grin stretched wider.

"Oooh..." Hatter said. "Did you see that, Haigha?"

"I did!" Hare pointed. "The crumble! They're crumbling like sugar cubes in our tea!"

"Running out of time from the look of things," Hatter added. "Judging by the strength of your presence, there's not much juice left to keep you here in our precious Pandemonium."

"Oh dear!" the hare said, tapping the serving knife along the vial of jam.

"Say what you mean," Corvus ordered.

"I will give you directions to where the Queen resides," Hatter said. "I will let you depart our festivities without confrontation. But the meat bags stay here with us."

"No deal!" Gabriel barked.

"You don't have enough juice for this confrontation and then dealing with my mother," Hatter reminded. "You must choose. Save these two or save the children."

"I must save the childrens." Hare mocked Corvus again with a deep dimwitted tone.

"Why would you give up your mother and the children you helped whisk away to this nightmare?" Corvus asked.

"Children aren't fun," Hatter answered. "My mother wants

the energy for creating, hence why I do her bidding. I want entertainment. The adult psyche can understand and anticipate everything that is coming. Exuding emotions with such raw power. Making their presence all the more sweeter to savor—"

"Mmm…" March Hare licked his lips, thrusting his hips, and culminating his dance with a chomping of his massive teeth. Chomp! Chomp!

"Choose, but do so quickly. My hand tires of holding this lid shut."

Corvus and Gabriel looked at each other.

"You know what we must do," Corvus whispered.

"I can hear you just fine." Hatter smiled. "No point in feigning these pretenses."

Gabriel lowered his M4, turning away while shaking his head. Hatter chuckled and Hare clapped his hands with glee. Leo and Alexa broke contact, dropping their weapons to the alert position, barrels facing downward.

"We choose to rescue the children," Corvus said in a solemn tone. "You have a deal."

"Excellent!" Hatter smiled, cocking his head. "I knew there was some reason to be found in all this messiness."

"What?" Ralph groaned, as sharp pains sparked from the bruises on his ribs. Crippling agony coursed through his back, leaving him hunched and wincing.

"You're going to just leave us here?" Matt cried out. "Don't! Please!"

"Enough!" The hare spun around, chucking a pot that crashed against the cage. Ceramic pieces shattered with a violent eruption. Boiling tea spat from the impact, squirting between the bars and catching Matt, who cried out when hot liquid burned his skin.

"My eye!" The man scrambled away from the front, cringing in a corner while covering the cherry red burn marks. His left eye squeezed shut, as blaring heat and pain climbed through his retinas, down into the socket where the burn festered and swelled.

"More pain awaits your unbirthday," the hare's voice deepened, resounding with a sinister bellow. His presence blurred, giving way to glimpses of something else. A towering hunched figure stood in his place with fangs of a viper, and a thick hide of scales. From his draconic countenance rose long curving horns where his ears had once been. A massive erection swelled between his muscular hind legs, possessing an array of barbed quills along the shaft. The layers morphed again, returning the visage of the smiling rabbit.

"That's enough!" Gabriel barked.

The hare's lips peeled back, shuddering from a teeth-baring growl. "Grrrr..."

"Calm yourself, Haigha," Hatter warned, sipping from his cup. "I know you can. It's not springtime. There's more at stake than just your pride."

"Steak does sound lovely for dinner." The hare's attention went back to Matt, licking his lips. "Great idea!"

"Get on with it!" Corvus demanded. "Where is the location of the White Queen?"

"Dear sweet ole mom? You seek a confrontation with her? How ambitious. Even if I thought you weren't walking headlong into your unbirthdays, I wouldn't make an effort to oppose you. There was a time when we all adored and admired her so much. Feels like so long ago. Perhaps because it was. You think I'm mad. You haven't seen anything yet."

"Out with it!" Corvus prodded.

"You'll find my mother in a place you'd least likely expect,"

Hatter said. "Sometimes what we're searching for can be right in front of our eyes, even when we can't see it."

"Enough with the damn riddles in this place!" Gabriel snapped.

"That's not a riddle," Hatter retorted, taking a slow sip. "How is a raven like a writing desk?"

"I'm not playing this game!"

"Oh, you will if you seek clarification. You only requested the answer, which I have delivered."

"I love this one!" Hare exclaimed.

"I know you do, my homophone loving friend." Hatter smiled.

"Answer the question! How is a ravin' like a writing desk?" Hare demanded.

"Never mind." Hatter sighed. "No one ever gets it."

"Except Tumtum!" Hare noted.

"That tree doesn't count. Not until he shares his precious sap. That silly ole miser."

"I have some," Alexa volunteered. She rummaged through the cargo pocket of her pants, withdrawing a small plastic storage bag. "I was keeping it for study, for its healing properties. If it'll help ease the brokering of this deal, then I'll gladly give it to you for the sake of the mission."

"Thank you, young lady." Hatter smiled, leaning forward in his chair as Alexa placed the bag on the table.

"That's the sap!" Hare exclaimed, his eyes following the shapeless brown liquid. "Suckling and salivating! Such steady, sour, slow, satisfying, sticky, super sweetness!"

"Don't go starting with the tongue twisters today, Haigha," Hatter said. "I've already burned mine on tea. Well now, I guess I must tell you after all. A ravin' is like a writing desk because they both create moments when one is delusional."

The hare cackled, slapping his knees. Hatter smiled at the dour agents.

"I guess you have to be a writer to understand." Hatter cleared his throat.

"That's not what I was requesting, Mr. Hat Man," Alexa corrected. "We want more precise instructions on finding the White Queen."

"There's a large field, stretching many kilometers," Hatter said. "I'm sure you've seen it, with my brethren roving around in their little bands, searching for interlopers such as yourself. I've spotted your little fort. Cute. My mother's dwelling is just across the way from it. Remember my words. Sometimes what you're searching for can be right in front of your face. Correction! That's most times. A little girl was able to find it and the door only several kilometers from that. I'm sure you professionals will manage."

Corvus nodded. "We shall."

"Break contact and withdraw," Gabriel ordered.

"Shame about Mara," Hatter murmured.

"What?" Gabriel turned around, glowering. "What did you say?!"

"See you in the 'morrow?" Hatter and the hare smiled.

"Don't leave us!" Ralph screamed. "Please!"

Gabriel's head lowered, shaking as he turned away. *How many times must I taste defeat?* A coldness resonated in his core. It was the tug of guilt, melting away the warmth of his soul. The agents and dream walker fell back, their cautious stares locked on the grinning denizens as they disengaged from the hovel. Tendrils of darkness returned, creeping forward with the rolling fog.

"Now back to our party, dear Haigha," Hatter said.

"Oh joy!"

CHAPTER 25
INFILTRATION

COMBAT OUTPOST: GALANT, PANDEMONIUM - 0130 HOURS

Gales swept across the open field, racing between the outpost's open entrance, where agents stood sentry watching across the way. Madam Dupree was held by Curt in a guard tower, accompanied by Gabriel, Corvus, and Agent Conn of the Black Knights Light Armored Cavalry Team. Their view amplified through binoculars on the vast horizon filled with swathes of yellow and brown grass turning opaque from the looming twilight. The team leaders turned to Madam Simone Dupree.

Hatter's words to Gabriel. Simone repeated the mantra. *Right in front of us.*

With an intense stare, she scanned across the area, searching with sharp scrutiny, wading through the churning energies surrounding them. Her willpower mixed with the ebb and flow of the layers, its pulsing frequencies bordering on the lower reaches, where ripples of negativity dwelled with a noxious prickling growing from awareness to stabbing pain.

The ruinous presence sprang an alarm within her soul, urging her to rise away, but cooled by the focus, calm, and understanding that more had to be done.

If only they knew how close we were to hell, Simone thought. *Best to remain focused on the necessities for the sake of the task at hand. Oh, what's this? How could I have missed it this entire time?*

A presence towered in the distance, fueled by a will that read foreign from the ambient energies. It remained sealed from the rest of Pandemonium, formed by an ever-expanding presence, guided by a power that blocked Simone's will. The scryer pushed harder, only to crash on a bastion of resistance propped up by a steady subconscious effort.

This is it... She's here. I can't penetrate it at all. Even though she's not trying to directly resist me. There's a frequency within a frequency. The nexus guiding this nightmarish realm into reality. Formulated by the mind, thoughts, and intentions of the White Queen. A dream within a dream.

"There it is!" Madam Dupree pointed.

"Not seeing a thing, ma'am." Agent Conn scrunched her large nose in confusion. "But the Knights will assault it."

"There!" Madam Dupree exclaimed.

Across the kilometers of field, dark particles of energy appeared as spotted shadows in the moonlight. They outlined a materializing compound, surrounded by towering stone walls. White rose bushes loomed into view, pulsating as if breathing, with vine-like tendrils draped over the barriers. Rising above the landscape was the palace, its dark marble walls possessing narrow arches leading to pathways of shadow. Three colossal winding towers lined across the palace's central region. They reached up to the rolling gray clouds that rumbled, thundered, and sparked through the backdrop with bolts of lightning.

Large thorns extended from the tower walls, following up the structures whose apexes formed gargantuan rose petals. The compound's vast length extended to the northeastern end, bordering coastal cliffs where the land descended into a thin strand flanked by a foaming sea of crashing waves.

"Just like that asshole said," Gabriel noted. "Right in front of us the whole time. Must be about seven klicks out. My team and I even passed through it when we first arrived on the plain. How the hell did we miss it?"

"Because it's not a structure," Madam Dupree said. "It only manifests that way. It's the psyche of a powerful being, serving as the nexus that guides the existence of this nightmarish place."

"Gabriel!" the familiar voice of Penny cried out from between the tents of the outpost. "Gabriel! Wait!"

"Young lady!" a scryer called out, giving chase as Penny darted out and started up the tower ladder. "There you are! Come here! We need to return you to the material realm!"

"No!" Penny shouted down, before scrambling up the tower.

The girl turned to Gabriel, rushing past the others and hugging him. Butcher Team's leader removed his green combat gloves with their Kevlar knuckle dusters, folding them into his combat vest before patting her head. The scryer stopped halfway up the ladder, mouth dropping into a lip quivering and babbling mess, when Gabriel's glower pierced him with the threat of imminent death.

"It's quite all right," Madam Dupree called down to the pursuing scryer. "I want to hear what she has to say. There better be quite the excuse for this belligerence and disregard for your own wellbeing, young lady."

"Damn right," Conn scoffed. "We're not out here risking our asses so you can be on vacation in this hell hole."

"I'm sorry!" Penny exclaimed. "I thought I was too late. I overheard the plan to attack the White Queen's palace before going home—"

"Loose lips sink ships," Gabriel quipped. "Apparently the scryers were never taught that."

"I couldn't let you just go in!" Penny countered.

"Okay. Okay." Gabriel patted Penny's shoulder. *My own troubles were brought about by loneliness due to one factor. Adults never listen.*

"Indeed," Madam Dupree transmitted into Gabriel's mind. *"Most minds are molded by the world as it sees fit, via the media, and the derivatives of social norms. Their conclusion drives them to delusion."*

"Out of my head, ma'am."

"Sorry, Agent Agapito. Force of habit."

"I want to hear what Penny has to say," Gabriel continued.

"If you have intel, best get out with it," Curtis said.

"Like the others, I was brought over after being paralyzed, only seeing shadows. They took me away and then I was in the Queen's domain. Some of us tried to escape. Most tried going out the front way, through the courtyard gardens where the red ones are hiding. They didn't make it... The monsters in that area have a saying. They'll paint the roses red with you..."

"Well, that doesn't sound pleasant," Madam Dupree said.

"Listen! Listen! They're not even the worst of her servants." Penny continued, "There's something in the sky at night. When the Queen is upset, her screams can be heard from above. I think the Queen let out a flying monster when a few kids escaped. The servants hide when it's around, whispering something about a jabberwocky. Something like that."

"Nothing some Stinger missiles and hate from Buster can't fix." Agent Conn smiled, patting the girl on the shoulder, before pointing over toward a Bradley Fighting Vehicle within the compound. "That's the nickname for my boy over there. Love him like a son and named him after the first man to defeat my favorite boxer; Mike Tyson."

"If he's your favorite, why the heck didn't you name the damn thing after him instead?" Curt raised a brow.

"Don't go disrespecting my big iron baby, Curt!" Conn snapped. "Truth is I don't know, damn it! I just liked the name Buster better than Mike!"

"Rattling around in those tin cans has scrambled your brains." Curt rolled his eyes. "That's the Cav for you."

Conn shrugged. Paused for a second. Then nodded.

"How did you escape, Penny?" Gabriel asked.

"I found another way when I heard the screams. I went through the kitchen and into the sewers that led to the sea. That's where Mr. Ross Marus found us."

"We should've brought some tunnel rats with us," Curtis said.

"It's too late now," Gabriel replied. "We don't have the time to muster one."

"I can show you," Penny volunteered. "I couldn't remember my way back to the palace until now. Everything went black when Mr. Ross Marus carried us to his dining hall."

"You're a brave one," Conn noted. "Reminds me of me when I was a girl."

"Penny, we can't ask that of you," Gabriel said. "No, that's not happening. You're supposed to be home now, waking up and greeting your parents. I couldn't imagine losing my own dau—"

"You'll die in there!" The girl pleaded, "Please, Gabriel. I want to help! It's the least I can do! Don't be like the other adults and not listen! I told my mother and father about seeing the monsters at night. They didn't listen. I ended up trapped here. You're not like them. You believe me."

Gabriel nodded with slow reluctance.

"That's a strong point," Madam Dupree added.

"Ma'am!" Curtis pleaded. "You can't be serious."

"We're pressed for time and have had to do things we aren't proud of," Madam Dupree countered. "Penny knows the back entrance, and how to navigate the palace. It'll be better if we humble ourselves and listen, despite the age of the person dispensing wisdom, lest this all be for nothing."

"Agreed, ma'am," Conn replied. "Hell, I was only a bit older than her when my pa took me to bag my first buck. Y'all would be surprised what a little girl with a stubborn streak is capable of."

"Can't have you fighting evil in your jammies, Penny. I'll talk to logistics about getting her some battle rattle." Curt murmured while climbing down the ladder, "That pipsqueak is going to need some extra-extra smalls."

"You stay glued to me," Gabriel said with a stern warning. "Follow my orders and no arguing. You keep your head down. Once we've located the Queen, you're going back to the COP and letting the scryers send you home. Got it?"

"Yes, sir!" The girl straightened her posture and saluted.

"Too much?" Gabriel asked.

"Just a tad." Penny chuckled.

"Well hell, what are we waiting for?" Conn hooted. "Time to mount up and ride on these sombitches!"

THE LONGTOOTH COAST, PANDEMONIUM - 0300 HOURS

Penny sat in the rumbling belly of the M7A2 Bradley Fighting Vehicle's crew compartment. Growls reverberated through the metallic chassis and resonated through the young girl as she sat on one of the foldable resin benches along the wall. Small boots covered her feet, compacted with thick woolen socks cool to the touch, rising up to her shins. A baggy camouflage jacket and pants covered her body, along with a matching vest weighed down by ceramic and steel plate inserts. Straps from her helmet hung loose, despite being tightened to its smallest possible length.

"The plates are heavy," Penny noted. "You guys must be very strong to be able to wear all this and fight."

"You get used to it." Portia smiled from across the bay.

"Be strong." Leo winked at the girl. "Soldiers are used to being uncomfortable."

"Did you tie your boots like I showed you?" Gabriel nudged Penny with his elbow.

"Yes," Penny said. "Laced around the top, tied off, with my pants tucked inside."

"Good. I know it gets warm like that, but it'll protect you from the elements."

Penny nodded.

"Let me see your earbud and mic." Gabriel leaned in, his finger tracing over the girl's communication equipment.

"Left ear, just like you said, Gabriel."

"Why?"

"Because we're not used to hearing things in our nondominant ear. So, it'll catch my attention faster."

"Outstanding. You learn quick."

Penny sighed with relief.

"Calm your nerves."

"I'm not scared!"

"You're lying. That's a good sign. Truth is all soldiers are scared. That knee-jerk response right there is called courage. The ability to perform even under duress."

"Are you scared, Gabriel?"

"All the time."

Agent Conn hopped down from her vehicle commander's seat in the turret, crouching low with the strap from her Combat Vehicle Crewman helm dangling near the attached microphone. Along the rear of the helm, in view just past built-in earphones, was the brim of her black cavalry Stetson hat, that hung over the woman's upper back as an ornament. The golden crossed swords on the front shone within the dim red illuminance from the lighting of the passenger compartment.

"I see you eyeing my Stetson." Conn smirked. "Why don't you ever wear yours?"

Gabriel shook his head with doubt. "I'm a ranger first."

"Bullshit! You got your start with the Cav. I remember."

"How long have you two known each other?" Portia asked with the others leaning into the conversation with brows raised in curiosity.

"Heck, me and this ole blowhard go all the way back to the 1st Cav Division in good ole Fort Hood." Agent Conn slapped her knee and chuckled. "Believe it or not, back then this guy had the same look, pissed off at the world and shit. Never got a damn haircut until NCOs were breathing down his neck.

Agapito here rode regulations to the minimum. Poor bastard stayed on extra duty because of peeved higher-ups."

"Language, Knight Actual!" Portia scolded.

"Private Agapito must've been a sight." Leo chuckled.

"Can you not?" Gabriel sighed.

"I'm the convoy commander here! Now where was I... Guess I'd be doing the same if my hair was all cool like yours," Conn continued. "I always admired Filipino hair. Not all unmanageable like my rat's nest. This beach air is going to make it all frizzy. That's why I usually just chop mine off. Makes it easier to wear my headset."

"That is a good idea," Penny agreed.

"You keep that good nature about you." Conn smiled at Penny. "Don't let ole grouchy Gabe go rubbing off on you."

"He's not so bad."

"Did you have something for us?" Gabriel asked. "Other than giving me shit and stirring bad memories?"

"Why yes, I did." Conn smirked. "Force Tracker has us arriving at the infil point in two mikes. We're on the underside of the cliff. Monarch is beginning the assault to take the field. They're clearing out nonstop tangoes! Should put all enemy eyes on the field and give you extra concealment. You hurry on up so we can get in on that action, too."

Rumbling from the Bradley's tracks died down around them as they came to a slow stop. Agent Conn winked at Gabriel, before climbing back into the right side of the turret, opposite her gunner. Whining came from the back hatch, dropping open to form a ramp from the cargo compartment. It touched down with a thud, crunching on sand. White noise fluctuated in and out of earshot from the churning waves that flanked the narrow strand of beach at the foot of the cliffs.

Speckles of illumination lit the beach from the night's stars, gleaming through the dark purple hues of the sky.

"Line astern with noise discipline," Gabriel ordered over comms in a whisper. Acknowledgment came in the form of nods and quick steps putting the team into movement.

Dozens of M928 trucks shifted behind them, reforming the convoy line to point back down the path they came. The large vehicles' diesel engines muttered and clacked, carrying the long empty beds covered in walls of green painted iron. Boots chopped hard at the steel ramp as the team hurried outward, treads compacting with the wet sand as they disappeared down the strand. Portia held Penny's hand as the girl jogged to keep up

Kevin led the way, his M4 up and ready, eyes peering through his night vision goggles, following the circular reticle of his close compact optic. Alexa and Harland were paired behind him, facing outboard on their respective flanks, keeping a distance of five meters from their point man. Gabriel maintained center with Leo, while Corvus and Portia brought up the rear with Penny. Large, jagged rocks stood between them and the sheer cliff that rose beyond view.

"Just a little bit further," Penny whispered. "It's in the rocks, where it all comes out to the ocean."

The aroma of salt and seaweed faded, giving way to the stench of rotting meat and copper, carrying a tart sweet undertone that clung to their tastebuds.

That smell... Gabriel surmised. *Dead bodies.*

Buzzing overhead filled their ears, with plump black flies rising from the sands and whipping around them. The rocks parted with the opening of a large tunnel leading into darkness. Reddish brown liquid spewed from it, washing into the tainted sands dotted with flakes of clothing and meaty sediment gathered among the outflow.

"This is from him..." Penny swallowed. "The Queen's cook usually washes out the leftovers. This tunnel leads into the kitchen from the sewers."

"Keep in mind that the Queen doesn't use food for sustenance," Corvus warned. "She uses innocent souls."

"I see," Gabriel said.

"The chef just rambles and wanders the kitchen," Penny added. "I booked it when he was on another rant."

"Good to know," Gabriel replied. "Let's move quickly."

"Right on, bossman," Kevin acknowledged, stepping into the tunnel. The point man's boots slid in the slimy wetness, before regaining his bearing with a slow and stuttering pace. Stagnancy took hold of the air around them, choking their breaths with the warm and thick stench, growing ever greater with each step. It clung to their uniforms, seeping into their skin and sweat. From their lips it hung, creeping into their mouths with a myriad of distaste. A harsh wave of rotting eggs pushed against them with the smell of expired yolk. Meat and blood mixed with the heat, creating the imagery of burning balloons and old berries. Salty urine and liquid dung etched into their thoughts with the burn of methane and ammonia tugging at their senses. It was a reminder that the wetness immersing their boots was more than just blood.

"If I slip in this just put me out of my misery, Sweet Pea," Leo murmured.

"Okay."

"You weren't supposed to answer that quickly or willingly!" the large man snapped.

"Oh, I mean... That would be just so, so awful, Leo. But, if I must." The tiny blonde shrugged.

"That ain't right..." Leo shook his head.

Corvus patted the big guy.

A kilometer of walking up a gradual slope had them approaching reflections of light between the steel bars of a manhole, dancing from the illumination of candles within a room above. Loud sobs came from someone inside, exploding with haggard and shrieking cries before dying down into whimpers again.

"ALWAYS FAILING HER!" the cook sobbed. "ALWAYS FAILING DEAR OLE DEAREST MUM! I'M SORRY! OH, SO SORRY! I COOK AND I SLAVE OVER A HOT STOVE MAKING MEALS FROM SCRATCH AND SHE NEVER EVER EVER WANTS TO EAT THEM! DOTH SHE APPRECIATE THEE? NO!" he wailed into the ceiling and then paused. "I don't need a cook." The same voice continued imitating a spiteful feminine tone. "THEN WHY DO WE HAVE A KITCHEN, IF IT'S NOT FOR A COOK MUM? WHY, OH WHY? TO MOCK MY LOVE OF CULINARY DESIRES?" He gasped before continuing. "For the last time, it's not a kitchen, you imbecile! You are the guard to this drainage system!"

"That's him," Penny whispered. "The Mad Cook."

"ICK! SCOLD ME ALL YOU WANT, MUM! I STILL LOVE YOU! YOU WEAR THE HATS HE MAKES FOR YOU! YET, MY LOVE IS REJECTED? I WILL MAKE A MASTERPIECE THAT SHALL HAVE YOUR TONGUE SINGETH TO THE HEAVENS WITH MINE PRAISES! THEN MAYBE ONETH DAY YOU'LL REMEMBER MINE NAME!"

"Dude is speaking old English or something?" Leo asked.

"No," Portia replied. "I studied Shakespeare in college. He's just a raging idiot."

Gabriel poised near the manhole next to Kevin, peeking through the spaces between the grill patterns covering the drain. A tall, thin figure stood adjacent to them. His wide back hunched with tapered shoulders narrowing into a thin waist and even skinnier legs. The spaded rear of his dress coat hung from a bony and angled backside. Uneven sleeves rolled up revealing forearms covered in greasy curling hair over his pale, spotted skin. Tears stretched along the upper shoulder regions of his coat, where it ripped from the width of his massive back. Frayed and tattered pant legs brushed over his bare feet, which were long, flat, and enveloped with blackened filth.

"YOU LOVETH MY BROTHER, WHO ONLY CARES FOR MERRIMENT IN THE WOODS WITH DEMONS! WITH HER CHILDREN! NOT YOURS! HE CAVORTS AND FLIRTS WITH HER! YET HERE I BE! HERE! FOR YOU ALWAYS!" Long woeful cries followed, only ceasing to gasp for air.

"Lift the grate slowly, Kev," Gabriel whispered.

Kevin nodded, pressing upward. Metal pulled from the stone rim. Crumbles of dirt rained on them as inches gave, the manhole rose until parting several inches. Gabriel reached into his vest, unclipping a pouch and drawing a cylindrical M84 flashbang from it. A whip of his arm sent the stun grenade bouncing with a metallic cling across the stone floor.

The Mad Cook's sobbing ceased, his large head leering at the object that collided with his heels. Serpentine pupils locked on the device. Rising breaths huffed between his mouth encompassing the length of his face, whisking between rutted teeth standing from dry charcoal gums. A dual river of mucus flowed from his nose, gathering among a glistening mustache, before passing over the lip ridge to his mouth to be sucked in by heavy breaths.

"WHAT THIS?"

Flashing brilliance washed away his vision, etching it with bright yellows and white. Stinging pulsed through his retinas, forcing his eyes to shut tight. A loud noise wiped out his hearing, leaving pain coursing through his throbbing eardrums. Smoke expelled from the detonation, forcing coughs from the Mad Cook as he reeled back and collided with a long table.

"Moving!" Kevin pushed up the grate, pulling himself up into the room, kneeling by the manhole, and scanning with his weapon.

Gabriel followed next, taking a position on the opposite side, while hoisting up Penny and the others. The Mad Cook flailed about, his long unkept yellowing nails leaving scratches over the table's wooden surface. He leaned over it, pausing, before spinning around. Sharp teeth jutted from his grinning maw, widening to lengths that further stretched his countenance. His eyes shot to each of the team members, their weapon barrels meeting him.

"IT SEEMS WE HAVE GUESTS!"

"Shut the hell up!" Gabriel ordered.

"Tell us where the children are being kept, cucuy," Corvus demanded. "And your life shall be spared."

"MINE LIFE?" the Mad Cook roared back. "MINE LIFE BELONGS TO MUM! ARRRGGGHH!"

"She doesn't love you!" Penny snapped, a sneer contorting her face with contemptuous resolve.

"WHAT?" the Mad Cook cried out. "YOU LIE!"

"You know I'm not lying. Look at you! I was with the Queen for days, hearing her go on and on about her children who are complete failures!"

"WHAT? NO!"

"Except for the one that wears hats."

"HIM!" the Mad Cook growled. Lengthy fingers stretched

over his face, squishing down the few strands of hair on his balding scalp as he grasped himself, howling with sorrow.

"Hatter and Haigha were laughing about it the other day," the girl continued, shaking her head. "I tried to get them to stop, but they kept going on and on about how he'll be the Queen's favorite until the day he dies."

"NO! NO!"

"It's true," Gabriel added. "I was there. They asked me a riddle. How is a ravin'—"

"—LIKE A WRITING DESK? THAT SAME STUPID RIDDLE HE ALWAYS ASKS! YOU MUST BE TELLING THE TRUTH! THEY'RE ALWAYS HAVING THOSE PARTIES TOGETHER! IS THAT SO, HATTER? WELL, THAT DAY IS TODAY, SIR!" The Mad Cook bowed. "THANK YOU, UMM... YOUNG LADY. THAT SOUNDS JUST LIKE MY ARROGANT BROTHER! AND I FOR ONE HAVE HAD ENOUGH OF HIS SHENANIGANS! I'M NOT APPRECIATED! BUT I WILL BE AFTER HE IS DEAD! MAKE SURE NO ONE TAKES MY KITCHEN DUTIES WHILE I AM GONE!"

"Of course, chef!" Penny stood upright and saluted.

"CHEF? NO ONE'S EVER CALLED ME THAT!" The Mad Cook touched his heart and smiled. "I LIKE YOU! WHEN I GET BACK FROM DEALING WITH MY BROTHER, YOU SHALL BECOME MY SOUS CHEF! RABBIT STEW WILL BE ON THE MENU!"

"Oh joy!" Penny clapped. "I can't wait to begin learning."

The Mad Cook grabbed two thick butcher knives that were plunged into the blood soaked table. He rushed through the room, past the spiked torture rack, dangling chains, and tables with shackles. The lanky fiend stopped at the door, taking a bow, before bursting through it, cackling to the ceiling of the corridor.

"That was quick thinking." Corvus patted Penny. "Fighting that greater cucuy at this range would've been dangerous. You are indeed a smart young lady, thinking to take advantage of him while disoriented and emotionally disturbed. I sensed as much from the brilliance your mind exudes within the ether."

"Agreed," Harland stated with Alexa nodding. "You would make a damn fine scryer, someday."

"Thank you, Mr. Corvus and Mr. Gray."

"I've observed that these entities want to express themselves," Corvus continued. "They lack the proper outlet. Their attempts come out uncontrollably and incoherent to those of a rational mind."

Gabriel peeked out the doorway, into the darkness of the expansive corridor ahead. "Let's move, team. Eyes up and weapons ready. There's no telling what lies ahead in this nightmare."

"Affirmative, Butcher Actual," Harland agreed, his blank stare carrying to a vision of the unseeable reaches. "The layers are swelling with turmoil. I hope Monarch is faring well with the cordon."

Alexa nodded. "Silent prayers for our brothers and sisters."

"Let's hope they are or there's no way we'll be able to exfiltrate across the field." Gabriel swallowed.

"*I was the first,*" a feminine voice carried with sinister majesty. Her words were concise and confident. She spoke with a delicate grace, each syllable announced with crisp perfection. An aura enveloped Gabriel. Surrounding him was the warmth of a mother, contradicting the alarming urges racing from the agent's instincts.

These aren't my thoughts... Who the hell...

"*The first daughter. The first wife. I transcended the shackles of fate to escape the paradise prison and became my own goddess.*"

Gabriel's eyes widened. His steps slowed until stopping.

"Are you okay, Actual?" Portia asked, cocking her head.

"Yeah, G." Leo's brow raised. "I'd say you look like you've seen a ghost, but I know for a fact you're not scared of those."

Butcher's team leader peered around in wide-eyed dismay, his mouth dropping open. Along his back, the Vorpal Sword pulsed, heralding the voice. Energy sizzled with alarm in his peripherals, crawling into his ears with radiating warmth. The Grays and Corvus turned to Gabriel, the latter placing a hand of concern on his shoulder.

"We heard it, too," Harland announced.

"That voice... lovely and sinister at the same time," Alexa murmured. "So chilling."

"It's her." Corvus swallowed. "The White Queen."

CHAPTER 26
FIELDS OF FURY

THE PLAIN PLAINS WITHIN THE PLANE - 0330 HOURS

"Contact!" Murphy screamed from the Humvee turret, down into the cab. "Hostiles inbound eight hundred meters and gathering!"

Curt nodded, hearing his gunner's calls for action, noting the position of the vast bastion of stone and iron forming the towering walls of the enemy fortress. A row of steel portcullises creaked and whined as they lifted, giving way to dark tunnels. Ravenous thin figures stormed from the castle, their skinny bodies shuffling with rapid abandon. Salivating jaws snapped at the air, locking with bared teeth. Trembling ire coursed through gibbering mouths, and lips that curled with hungering spite. Hooked claws ripped into the ground with their quick pace. Howls soared across the field followed by high-pitched whines and unwholesome cackles, growing louder from the assembling mass of foes.

"Make the hog ready," Curt ordered. "We're going to break that bullshit up so they can't hit us with full strength. Time to introduce these fuckers to modern tactics. Calling the gun bunnies, now. Monarch11Charlie this is Monarch Actual, requesting fire mission, over."

Several kilos away, beyond sight of the battlefield was a Stryker Multi Wheeled Light Armored Vehicle. Wide panels were opened and locked to the vehicle's side, where a large olive green mortar barrel protruded with its 80 millimeter bore aiming at the clouds. Mortarmen scrambled into position. The operator agent sat on the left side of the weapon, near the monitor next to the fire control system. The ammunition loader stood poised beside the barrel, holding tight to the payload with both hands.

"Acknowledged, Actual," the operator agent replied. "Standing by for fire mission, send it when ready."

Curt slid open the slab of glass serving as the ballistic-resistant Humvee window, hanging his arm out with the laser rangefinder. A red dot tagged over the distance, blinking among the chittering swarm of foes, gathering after clearing the bottleneck of the gates. Ringing came from the rangefinder. A string of numbers fed grid coordinates through the screen of his force tracker.

"Coordinates are following," Curt continued. "The assault element is under a klick so danger close. Give me a creep fire."

"Coordinates are acknowledged," the mortar agent replied. "Shot over!"

"Shot out," Curt replied.

The mortar loader placed the payload into the barrel, dropping below the weapon's muzzle as he slid in one smooth motion, safety-clearing the trajectory. A puffing explosion signaled the large round belching from the mortar, sending it whistling into the air. It careened downward, bringing its hate upon the masses. The round dived into the ground, cracking like lightning with a burst of thunder. A torrent of metallic fragmentation exploded from the impact zone near the front end of the cucuys' amassing army. A horde of yellow eyes stared at the blackened crater left in the wake of clearing smoke and pelting debris.

"Damn close!" Curt said. "Add fifty! Fire for effect! Let'em have it!"

"Adding fifty! Firing for effect! Acknowledged, Actual!"

Torrents of whistles signaled the arrival of several payloads soaring through the sky. Diving impacts erupted across the ground, erasing cucuy within the chain of explosions that followed. Dirt and stone darted across the field. Gangling limbs rived from their bodies, torn away by incredible waves of percussion.

Shrapnel flew, finding marks across the ground, tearing into foes caught in the trajectories, and lodging into the walls. Wails of lamentation arose from the masses, morphing into cackling howls for vengeance, before the survivors charged across the field. Streams of cucuy continued pouring from the castle. Hard steps from their forward momentum crushed their downed allies sending screams into the heavens.

"Repeat! Repeat!" Curt ordered. "Keep your trajectory locked on that spot!"

"Roger," the operator agent replied. "Sustaining fire, Actual."

Salvos of smoke and fury continued bombarding the front gates. Cucuy dropped to all fours, zigzagging in their movements, neither batting an eye nor looking twice whenever their brothers were caught in the onslaught.

"They're inside bombardment range," Curt announced over the radio to his team. "Split the elements. Alpha on me to the west side of the field. Bravo run opposite. Then, evade and fire at will. Hold them here at all costs!"

"Acknowledged, Actual," the response repeated over the radio from the seven other Humvees.

"We're going live, Actual!" Murphy opened the large ammunition can, underneath the hulking MK19 automatic grenade launcher. Its wide barrel, and thick heavyset frame directed outboard from the turret, aimed with quiet menace toward foes racing across the horizon. Sitting inside his grip was the first plump 40 millimeter high explosive dual-purpose grenade with its shining round head and hard cylindrical body. Black links chained it to others, weighing heavy upon Murphy's arms as he hoisted them out. A click from the side latch brought the massive, tapered, tortoiseshell-like cover rising from the feed tray.

"Remember to make sure they catch," the agent murmured lessons of the past to himself, reciting the hypnotic biting tone of his drill sergeants. "It's gotta catch on the latch or it's a no-go."

Murphy slid the rounds up from the weapon's side, bringing the first between the splayed fiberglass feed throat assembly, dragging the rest of the belt through. A round went into the weapon's belly, held in place by two teeth rising from the receiver. Murphy examined the innards of the risen feed tray cover, swiping the small arm of the drive lever within it to the right-hand side. The agent slammed the weapon shut, grabbing both charging handles along the side while depressing their release latches. He pulled back with a great heaving tug against the powerful spring, resisting before the bolt locked to the weapon's rear.

The handles were brought forward again, locked upright and into a safe position. Murphy's thumbs rested on the wide leafy trigger along the backside, between the weapon's parallel handles where his hands gripped with hot apprehension pulsing through his knuckles. Above the standard iron sight was a tall rectangular optic, magnifying the gunner's view of the cucuy with a chevron reticle glowing crimson.

"Big Bertha is hot and ready, Actual," Murphy announced, after the brief seconds that passed to load the weapon.

"Hell yeah, let'em feel that thickness!" Agent Cole cheered from behind the Humvee wheel, turning wide, circling back around to put distance between them and the cucuy.

"Give them the business!" Curt ordered.

The MK19's thick barrel reared toward the cucuy, lowering to the assumed trajectory. Rows of sharp teeth appeared from faceless grimaces phasing in and out, howling with trembling rage coursing through the thin visages fluctuating within the etheric layers. The reticle found its mark, locking on target with steady poise from the gunner's tense forearms. Murphy's thumbs pressed on the leaf trigger. The bolt roared into action in an instant, launching forward, and slamming the first grenade through the barrel. Carbon jettisoned among the grooves of the barrel's flash suppressor. Murphy kept the trigger down. The bolt churned with fury, rumbling the Humvee with thumping clicks each time the large machine gun spewed another round of hate at the enemy.

Plump round 40 millimeter warheads careened across the field, tailed by faint lines of smoke as they spun through the air. The first landed in a calamity of force, tearing through the first few cucuy in its path. A flash appeared upon collision, ushering forth a spread of smoke and debris. Fragments of metal sped through the kill sack. Hot blood sprayed across victim and bystander alike as shrapnel spread from the impact zones, shredding through the tangoes. Whistling heralded the arrival of more grenades, disseminating explosive vitriol across enemy lines.

"Get some! Get some!" Murphy howled back. "Oh, they are not liking this shit, Actual!"

"Don't let up!" Curt ordered. His mouth dropped as foes continued storming from the gates, clapping the ground with vigorous strides toward their position. *Damn it! How many does she have? And they couldn't care less about their comrades being chewed up by any of our firepower!*

"Monarch Actual this is Monarch11Charlie, over," the mortar commander called over the radio.

"This is Monarch Actual," Curt replied. "Tell me something good. Send it."

"Barrel's running hot. And we're halfway through our reserve. IDF will be down for two mikes."

Shit! "Understood, Monarch11. Give me a status when you're up again. Monarch Actual, out."

Cucuy hounded through the grassy fields, their long, lithe bodies galloping with all four limbs. Saber teeth materialized from the etheric layers, curving downward from elongated muzzles glistening with saliva. A mane of sharp quills rose along their necks, fanning down the length of their backs in rhythm to each raging snap of their maws. Rippling and flexing muscle materialized from the once thin frames that signaled their presence, giving form to the fiends with lion-like bodies. Scorpion tails hung from their rear, thumping the ground with spaded stingers. Noxious purple venom oozed from their tips, giving rise to ribbons of smoke, after touching the ground and scorching holes into grass.

"So, that's what these assholes really look like," Curt murmured. "Not so thin anymore. Guess they're finally revealing their hand."

"Damn, they're fast!" Cole exclaimed.

"Keep the pedal to the ground, Marine," Curt ordered. "Burn that JP8! Make those fuckers work for their meal."

"Aye, Actual."

The Humvee skirted across the ground, with the remainder of their element in tow. Bouncing from the uneven surface overwhelmed the shocks, spreading into the cabin where the agents jostled about in their seats. Curt braced himself against the dash with both arms as Cole turned the wheel, cutting hard right away from the far end of the castle walls. Curt looked back through the large face of his side mirror, seeing tall figures looming over the ramparts. Cole turned again, causing the frontline of their pursuers to lose their footing, toppling over from momentum. Piercing screams rang out as their brethren's heavy and powerful steps continued, crushing their limbs and paws as they passed over.

Curt opened his window to the rush of wind, bringing his binoculars' view to the ramparts. Within the magnified view, a tall figure stood behind the angular parapets. Straight strands of black hair hung from his head, over his broad shoulders. A single yellow eye beamed from his arched brow and glaring face, while a black patch rested over the other. White armor covered his body with a scaled pattern that flexed and bent with ease as he pointed to the battlefield. Upon his chest was an enormous red heart, bearing within it a black crescent moon over an upside down cross.

"The Knave watches!" the bandernsnatches announced in unison. "The Knave judges!"

Who the hell is that?

"These useless bandersnatches are failing, yet again!" The Knave's voice rippled across the field like a booming explosion. "Send forth the jub jubs!"

"Damn, that guy is loud! What the fuck is he going on about, Actual?"

Large birds rose, hovering upon vast wings of red plumage with frosted tips. Triple spurs flexed like claws from the leading edge of their wings. Black talons curled underneath their massive frames, with nails hard as steel, thinning into fine sharp points. Twitches ran through their eyes, locking on Monarch's Humvees while frenzied screeches pierced through the skies, from their long serrated beaks.

"Shit! We have incoming! Enemy air support!" Curt called. "Coming in hot!"

The avian terrors sped toward the rear Humvee at blinding speeds. Black curved talons unfurled, reaching out for their marks. The agents within followed ceaseless screeches to the side of their vehicle. One effortless swoop brought talons penetrating the thick dusty rubber of the passenger side rear and front tires. Shuddering pops came with the collision, followed by the long hiss of air rushing away.

Curt peered over to the other vehicle, seeing two of the large birds screaming, their talons caught in the thick rubber, pulling them from flight, and sending them spinning with the tires. Shredded rubber and feathers spat from the mayhem after the creatures were sucked underneath the vehicle's tires. Their bones crunched and snapped underneath the weight, spitting their broken bodies from the carriage.

"Mother!" Strident screams came from the birds, imprinting on eardrums with the ringing pitches. "Mother's milk! Mother save us!"

The Humvee continued, leaning to the right, while slowing under the pressure of its heavy frame.

"Monarch, give me a status check!" Curt called. "How's your fireteam doing, Jacobs?"

"This is MonarchBravo4. Passenger side tires are gone, Actual. We're still chugging along—"

A thudding impact rocked the Humvee, lifting its passenger side from the ground. Loud scrapes dragged across the armor, along its back and sides. The vehicle slowed with additional weight clinging to it. Another thud jostled the agents within. Jacobs braced himself with outstretched arms. Claws punctured through the driver's side door. Long fingers gripped it before an incredible force ripped the armored hatch clean from the hinges.

Sabered yellow teeth loomed in the doorway, with leering yellow eyes set on the driver. The large maw of a bandersnatch reached in. Particles of saliva flew from its opening jaws, latching onto the agent's head. Screams came from the man who flailed about. His body rose as the creature pulled, slamming the agent's knees into the dash where his caps dented and shattered, dislodging to hang low within the joint. The bandersnatch braced itself along the outside, tugging again. The seat belt gave, ripping from its lodging. Screams escalated to throat shredding decibels as the agent was torn from his seat.

The speeding Humvee traversed left, then a sharp right. Momentum sent it storming through dirt and grass. A divot forced the vehicle to buckle and tumble. Cucuy and agents cried out as the Humvee rolled, its sides smacking until it landed upside down with a loud thump.

A wave of bandersnatches pounced the vehicle. Dozens of them gathered around the steel carcass, peeling away handfuls of the armor panels and tossing them aside. The passenger door was pulled away with a loud echoing of twisting metal, culminating in a final snap. Claws reached inward, stabbing into Jacobs' sternum. The man gasped. He unholstered his .45

ACP pistol. The roar of gunshots fired into the gash within the door, burrowing shots into the creature's forearm. Blood sprayed across Jacobs, seeping into his lips and bringing the tang of salt and copper to his tastebuds. The whimpering cucuy's arm withered back outside.

Another claw reached in. Fingers expanded with nails aiming right for the agent. Click. Click. Jacob's pistol failed. Its receiver locked back to the rear, the chamber devoid of any rounds. The bandersnatch grabbed him, pulling him from the seat, his body slamming against the door, wedging into the large gash. Frayed and jagged steel pushed through his uniform, lodging him within as the agent's legs and shoulders would not clear it. Pressure rose around him. Jacobs howled in agony when his humerus separated from his shoulder, wriggling free and buckling his arms to the rear. Pops erupted from the hip's crest when his legs folded behind him. Jacobs raced outboard, getting a glimpse of the castle walls, then dozens of gathering bandersnatch, before biting jaws sent everything dark.

"They're eating them!" Cole exclaimed. "Those bastards!"

Rest in power, warriors. A deep sigh expelled from Curt, shaking his head. Monarch's team leader pressed his lips together, keeping his chin up. The cab shuddered with another salvo of rounds spewing from the MK19. Curt peered over as Jacobs' wreckage exploded with dozens of 40 millimeter grenades colliding into their marks, delivering burning eruptions, spitting shrapnel that carved into the cucuy at the scene. Clouds of smoke and dust disappeared with the fleeting horizon.

"Fall back," reluctance hinted in Curt's order. "I want all fire team leaders to give me a status."

"MonarchBravo2 is green to green, Actual."

"MonarchBravo5 is green to green, Actual."

"MonarchBravo7 and 8 are green to green, Actual."

"Monarch Actual, this is MonarchBravo3. I thought command said to hold until Butcher retrieved the precious cargo?"

"We're not withdrawing, just fighting dirty," Curt said. "On me, Monarch. Give us some room between us and their ground forces. The crew-served weapons are too cumbersome for those flyers. Have the drivers give their twelve gauges to the gunners. Time for some good ole fashioned bird hunting." *Gabe, wherever you are and whatever you're doing, I hope you're doing it quick. If this doesn't work, we're going to be in a world of shit.*

CHAPTER 27
THE GOLDEN RULE

THE IVORY PALACE, PANDEMONIUM - 0330 HOURS

Glimmers of moonlight shone through small squared window panes, spaced across the ceiling of the dim corridor. Darkness and shadow immersed the rest of the place, save for the center where white marble floors were lined with rugs of ivory and gray. Patterns of black trees and long-stemmed roses were sewn into them, parallel to each other. Black doors stood among the white walls, polished to brilliance, glimmering like onyx.

"It's not a place," Corvus reminded the team. "We are delving into the consciousness of the Queen, within the dream state."

"I don't like the sound of that shit," Leo murmured. "Probably a trap."

"That's because it is," Gabriel continued. "And we're going to spring it."

"I was hoping you wouldn't say that." Leo sighed. "But, hey. We're here anyways. Might as well make a party of it."

"What you heard through the Vorpal Sword isn't the Queen's consciousness, Gabriel," Corvus said. "The mind is a very complicated thing. Ruminate upon it and understand, it is a realm unto itself. Not just as we know it from the science of psychology. It's more complex than that. The thoughts that it generates don't simply go away because the consciousness is not dwelling upon them. They are ever present, within the other levels."

The Diver agents nodded in agreement. "He's right," Harland said.

Corvus pointed to Gabriel's sword. "Thoughts create the universe as we behold it within the subjective reality. I believe what we heard was the Queen's unconscious voice, being carried through her realm and all that she has fashioned with its energy. Which means there is hope that we can infiltrate and execute our goals while maintaining stealth."

"Regardless, we Charlie Mike," Gabriel ordered, raising his M4's barrel and continuing through the darkness.

"I knew he was going to say that," Leo murmured, continuing behind, clinging to his M249 light machine gun. "And you know I got your back no matter what."

"Penny, I want you to stay close to Portia," Gabriel ordered.

The girl nodded, shuffling to the medic's side.

The green tint of their night optic devices revealed the wide arcing frame of an entry point. White silk curtains hung from the top, their furbelow lengths reaching to the floor with flounced borders only centimeters from the ground. The agents waded through the pale display, until only darkness enveloped them.

"*I abandoned paradise, in the name of truth and discovery. What is paradise when one is aware of the illusion that is free will? I can still hear my Father's pathetic pleas for my return. For a moment, I thought he was sincere. I thought there was a greater plan for me. Something other than to be mounted by his overbearing creation, to assume the role of placation for the sake of peace. There's another term for such an arrangement: slavery."*

"I can still hear her ranting," Gabriel whispered.

"She clamors on like a petulant child." Corvus nodded. "Albeit one of great intelligence and spite. Examining her perspective is interesting, yet haunting. While one could sympathize with her desire for independence, this is not the way to go about it. Pride truly is the greatest sin—"

Laborious groans stole their attention away with immediate glances to the far end of the room. The green hue of their sight illuminated uneven cracks along pale gray blocks forming the walls. Droplets pitter-pattered in an adjacent corner, splashing into a puddle. Flashlights activated along the teams' weapons with thumb flicks. Concentrated spotlights of infrared exposed chittering swarms of roaches. The insects' shuffling legs bent underneath their flat bodies, approaching the crevices in the wall, where their antenna pinned behind their heads as they passed away from sight. Scratches came from the hundreds of tiny appendages squirming within the unseen reaches of the room, broken by the occasional flutter of wings expanding from their backs.

"Ewww." Portia grimaced.

"Oh, what happened to miss 'I-care-about-all-life.'" Leo snickered. "You don't care about these little guys?"

"Noise discipline, you!" Portia's hushed snap followed a slap to the chuckling big man's shoulder. "Shh..."

Beating wings trailed across the room from a large roach passing through Gabriel's view. Its leap came to a wobbled landing on the pale scalp of a figure strapped to the wall, her head hanging low. Greasy long remnants of her hair draped over her face, bowing out of view and staring at the floor. The center of her scalp blared with warmth from speckles of blood rising from the skin and hair follicles that had been torn away, exposing the pink dermis layer. The roach crawled up and over her head, its body shimmying into clumps of hair matted along the back of her neck.

Sloshing sounds brought their view to the woman's torso. A long tear stretched across the lower part of her belly, canting into the left side where it was deepest. Flaps of skin hung over the soggy intestines that dangled from within, sagging down in a clump that swayed from her arduous breaths. Shackles held the woman aloft by her outstretched arms brimming with pressure along the shoulders that had dislocated. Her once alabaster pigmentation transformed into deep blue bruises, swelling to the size of grapefruit.

Blood dripped from her innards, splatting across her bare feet. Trails of it spiraled down the wound, over kneecaps that were caved inward. Rumbling gurgles left her abdomen as the muffled sloshing continued. A groan escaped between her quivering lips.

"Oh my God!" Portia broke the heavy silence, exclaiming as she rushed to the woman. "She's still alive!"

Leo stepped back, scanning the room, his gaze falling on the lone door across from them. "Do your thing, Sweet Pea. I got you on overwatch."

"It's the rabbit!" Penny cried out as she pointed.

"What?" Gabriel said, joining Portia's side. "You're not making any sense."

"The woman who runs the gaming company with the rabbit logo!" Penny continued. "I can't remember her name. The Queen said she's her little pet rabbit."

The woman's head rolled upward, bringing her wrinkled

countenance into view. Red chalkiness covered her complexion, with pores crying for hydration. Puffy eyes and lashes were caked in flaking mucus. The woman's irises disappeared, rolling back into her sockets. Crusted lips split over her mouth, remaining ajar for the passing of desperate wheezes. Another quiet groan escaped. She winced, her body grumbling, writhing in place, while a few more inches of her tangled intestinal track pushed outward. Dripping tapped at the floor with rapidity.

Gabriel examined the sunken face locked in an elongated scream she could not summon the strength to expel. Locks of silver hair clung to her face, the roots greased in blood cowlicked over what remained of her scalp. The mephitic scent of copper and salt emitted from her. *Damn it. She looks so familiar. Can't quite put my finger on it.* Faces flashed through Gabriel's memory, stopping on an older woman with attitude and unwholesome ambition.

"Meryl Partridge," Gabriel announced.

"It's that bitch that's responsible for this," Alexa sneered.

"A far cry from the overconfident scumbag that allied herself with these fiends," Gabriel added.

"These godforsaken sleep demons did a number on her," Harland said. "I got your six, Butcher Actual. But we're sensing a negative presence here." Diver's team leader and his partner stood outboard with Leo. Their backs to the wall, sentrying the room with M4s at low alert.

Corvus and his raven raised their gazes in circumspection. Turmoil pulsed through the etheric layers from the agony and panic coursing through Partridge's mind. A small aura of negative frequency appeared close to the woman, squirming at the center of her energy. "One of the cucuy is here. I can sense the insidious presence. Yet we cannot see it."

"Remain at the ready, team," Gabriel ordered after nodding to Corvus. "Keep a scan on this shithole."

Alexa took Penny by the hand, guiding her close. "Stay with me."

"Can you hear me, Partridge?" Gabriel asked, guiding Meryl's face with his hands, attempting to look in her spiraling eyes. "Listen to my voice."

"K-k-kill... me..." Meryl spoke through quivering jaws that would not close nor open completely. Glimpses of her mouth revealed gaping sores where teeth should have been. Blood dried within them, crusting over into a gelatinous layer. "K-kill me..."

"You're not getting out of this," Gabriel rebuked. "Not until you tell me what I want to know."

"D-damn you." Meryl jerked in agony. Blood squirted on Gabriel's boots, from her grumbling bowels. "He's... he's t-tearing through... me!"

"Who?" Gabriel shook his head. "What the fuck happened to you?"

"T-the Q-q-queeeen..." Meryl groaned. "Sh-she's... punishing me for betrayal... and f-failure..."

"The first rule to dealing with demons..." Harland stated.

"You don't deal with demons," Leo finished. They looked at each other, nodding in respect.

"This is more than just a demon," Corvus added. "But your sentiment applies all the same. You aligned yourself with the nefarious forces of the White Queen. Her temper does not bode well for those underneath her. Of course, you knew this and still continued with your arrangement. There was no other fate for you save this one. I pity you, Partridge. The agony you must be feeling right now seems beyond anything I can describe. I had to block off your energies so that you didn't pollute my psyche with your suffering. How you are still alive is a miracle though."

"N-no," Meryl refuted with gasping sharpness. "S-sh-she comes when... aw-awake... Gives me energy to continue living... c-continue suffering." Her face wrinkled with a weeping grimace. Puffing cries escaped through her dry cracked lips. Nothing flowed from the woman's reddened tear ducts. She only shuddered.

Portia turned to Gabriel with a sad frown, shaking her head with doubt. The medic flipped her large pack to the floor, kneeling beside it and rummaging through the contents. "I'm going to do my best. It's a miracle you're still alive, Partridge. Don't give up on us."

"Do what you can, Portia," Gabriel said turning back to Meryl. "Looks like the Queen bestowed immortality upon you after all."

"Damn you!" Partridge wheezed the words. She racked in her shackles. Blood squirted from her exposed digestive tract.

"Agent Portia Lawson is one of the best medics in the Agency," Gabriel snapped at Meryl. "Her big heart is matched only by her discipline. You will show respect while she tries to salvage your miserable life. And to be honest that's something I'd rather not do. But, she's a better person than me." Gabriel grabbed the woman by her face. "Look at me! Where are the children being kept? Penny's memory of this place is vague, so I'm trying to collect as many details as possible for the safety of my team."

"D-d-down the hall in the Queen's quarters! B-beware the soporific fragrance!" Meryl whimpered.

"Stay with me, bitch!" Gabriel barked. "What about the fragrance? That's what she's using to keep the kids sedated? That's why Penny's recollections are foggy about this place?"

"Yes... it's everywher—" Meryl racked with pain again, rattling the chains of her confines against the cold brick wall. "Damn you! Damn you! Damn you!"

"Meryl!" Gabriel barked. "What the hell is wrong with her?"

"Besides her guts hanging out and being half scalped?" Leo raised a brow. "Not to mention all those scratches—and are those bite marks?"

"You are not the one she is damning." Corvus stepped forward, examining the woman. "I can feel a cucuy's presence."

"I sense something too, Actual," Alexa agreed, scanning the room. "But we got eyes on nothing."

"Damn you!" Meryl screamed, her mouth agape and retching. "God damn you!"

"I thought you didn't serve Him!" Alexa quipped.

Between rapid gasps, the woman sighed and went limp. Quaking emerged from her exposed intestines and stomach, sloshing around the massive incision. Strings of meat and sticky body fluids parted as a tiny head poked through. A miniature feline countenance blinked to work away the blood that glossed over its eyes and orange fur. Slitted pupils peered out from small and bulbous yellow eyes, locking on to the agents who stepped back, raising their weapons. Pointed ears rose to full mast on the small being, gasping at the hostile postures.

"No! Peas no!" whining pleas emitted from the kitten-like creature's squeaking voice. "Don't hurt me!"

"Fiend!" Gabriel snarled.

"No!" the bloody kitten pleaded. "Not bad!"

"You're inside Meryl's gut, ripping her apart!" Leo stated. "I'd say that's pretty fiendish."

"No!" the kitten continued. "No. I only explore like Mama told me. Mama said learn what makes humans work. Mama said go inside the rabbit to see how she works. So, we can learn about humans!"

"Where's Mama, now?" Corvus asked.

"Mama ish..." The kitten's head canted as he pondered. "Mama ish sleepin'! Yes! She's sleepin' and resting. Mama said that she's got a big plan soon."

"What plan?"

The kitten shrugged. "She doesn't tell me. Doesn't tell me anything except that I have to learn what makes humans work! Now, if you'll excuse me. I have to taste test these giant beans near the rabbit's hips. Back to work for me. Bye now."

Little legs reached around, gripping with small claws. Intestines pushed outward. Waves of fresh blood seeped from the wound. The kitten swatted around, grabbing at the soaked viscera, scratching thin tears into the entrails. The dangling bowels slapped around before the kitten managed to drag some back inside.

"Leave it be," Gabriel said.

"Actual, you can't be serious," Leo argued. "Let's neutralize this thing—"

"Let's go. The White Queen is sleeping and now is our chance."

"Gabriel is right," Corvus said. "It is best that we have the element of surprise for dealing with a powerful foe like the Queen."

"And her room isn't too far." Penny's head lowered in deep thought. "It's still all foggy. But we are close. I remember. Kinda."

Leo stood upright from his ready posture, maneuvering out the door. The team followed.

"Gabriel!" Meryl called out before he could step through the door. "You... b-bastard! Don't leave me! Y-you can't just leave me! Y-y-you're... supposed to be... the good guys!"

Screams belted out from the woman, her chains rattling against the stone wall. The skin peeled from her hoarse throat with ever-ascending cries. Sharp pain clamped down into her kidney, puncturing and shaking it from side to side. A bulging uneven sense throbbed through her hip, rising into her lower back with a dull torment. Aching pain shot into her like a knife wound from the dislodged organ, sending her heart into a pumping frenzy.

"I lost my best friend because of you. She was a hundred times the woman you will ever be. Mara was selfless and courageous. What she did wasn't for glory, or vanity. It was to protect others from enduring what she had. Mara always covered my six, no matter what. Even when I went rogue. And let me tell you, with my temper, dealing with you scumbags, there's been many moments when I've gone off the rails. This time, I'm not going off course. This time I'm going to do things by protocol. You wanted to transcend your humanity. To be like these evil immortal fiends, right? Well, looks like you finally achieved that much." Gabriel's words were cold as he glanced at Meryl one last time. "What's the first rule to dealing with demons, Meryl?"

He stepped outside the room, shutting the door and muffling her screams.

CHAPTER 28
BROOD MOTHER

THE PALE FURNACE, THE IVORY PALACE - 0400 HOURS

"My story was erased from scripture because our Father couldn't handle the truth. That's what they try to tell all of you good little kiddies in your places of worship, right? That your precious book cannot be tampered with because it's God's divine word? Then, why have so many books been removed? Why are there so many versions? The explanations given are usually a derivative of cognitive dissonance. Here's the truth. You aren't even human anymore. You are a broken parody. Complete mongrels."

"Here's something your dogmatic leaders seem to always dance around. The fact that your misbegotten species was split in half the moment I left. Taken from the rib? Is that the best way you dimwitted creatures can explain the visions that showed you the truth? I guess it's nigh impossible for an ignorant species of subhuman spawn to understand the intricacies of the universe. The correct answer is energy siphoned through the heart chakra, one of *the main energy points within the body. I see you're trying to block me with your pathetic will. Futile."*

"I do hope you're listening for your sake, mortals. Adam was split into two. I guess my Father knew that selfish being he created could only ever love himself. Both sides of him even disobeyed my Father in the end. I wasn't even there, and I understand what happened. I know the answer though, the question is, do you? When you gaze upon me, you will marvel at the limitless potential of a complete being. It is I, the first daughter, who has achieved the pinnacle of his grand design. I am the only one who has truly followed in his footsteps, fashioning life from sheer force of will. Your sojourn is nearing its conclusion. Not much longer and we shall meet, wielder of my cursed sword."

"Shut up!" Gabriel snapped.

Blurred haziness dissipated from his vision, drawing him away from the stupor gripping his psyche. Wide halls of stone and darkness reappeared, with the echoes of his team's footsteps grounding his mind into conscious reality.

"Is she at it again, Actual?" Portia placed a hand on his shoulder.

"Yeah." Gabriel shook his head. The Vorpal Blade hummed along his back, tethered to his mind, attempting to draw away his attention. "I'm glad you all can't hear this insane bullshit. Part of me wants to toss this damn sword and be done with her influence. But something is telling me otherwise."

"Me too." Leo huffed.

"Such an astounding arrogance," Corvus murmured.

"The books got that part accurate," Alexa added.

"There seems to be some mixed up parts when you think about it, though," Harland stated. "This Queen seems to be far from the meek and humble version spoken about in books and films. Her sister the Red Queen is seen as the aggressor."

"Makes you wonder what Alice saw and experienced when she first stepped through the door," Corvus said.

"My sentiments exactly, Master Corvus. We knew that lines were blurring from what was written. That much is blatantly obvious by its whimsical nature. But what if the girl wasn't strictly here in Pandemonium, but it was a culmination of her astral travels, recalled via a fuzzy memory."

"That would definitely make sense of this world that has none."

Kevin rolled his eyes, stomping past the scryers in their formation, and stopping before Gabriel. "Actual, I don't say much. I'm a good soldier. I just keep my mouth shut, waiting to take orders."

Gabriel nodded. "Absolutely."

"Give me the sword," Kevin continued. "So you can have some relief from that bullshit."

"No." Gabriel patted his agent on the shoulder. "It's mine to bear. No matter how this plays out. But thank you."

Kevin nodded, returning to formation.

Delicate feminine laughter ran through Penny's mind. The girl stood upright, staring straight ahead, her body locking in place. Jovial cackles flowed down the hall, guiding her attention to the ceiling that rose into a dome. Images flickered in the girl's vision of young faces twisting in pain, whipping away from view into a whirlpool of energies. Groaning voices and harsh screams fought for Penny's attention, quaking into her ears. Splashes of thick ooze washed away the voices, drowning them in gargling agony. Pressure released a spray, bringing memories of wet mist, its coldness stretching over her forehead. Fragrant floral accents hit the girl in waves, weighing heavy on her blinking eyelids and drooping shoulders.

Penny's trembling finger rose, pointing ahead as whimpers

fled from her lips. "She's in there... I remember now... the big garden scared us. Some of the others tried escaping through there. But I didn't go in there. I could hear screaming."

"Well let's do this thing!" Leo said, turning back to march forward.

"Wait!" Penny urged.

That's jasmine and rose we've been smelling, Gabriel thought. *And it's getting stronger. We haven't been hit by it yet, but that must be the soporific fragrance we were warned about!* "Before we breach it, don and clear NBC gear, everyone."

"Ah, shit!" Leo said. "Roger, Actual."

Velcro and zippers peeled open from secure pouches resting on their left thighs. Sleek and shining CM-14 masks were removed. The plastic apparatus possessed an open face shield, providing a semblance of peripheral vision. One-inch-thick purification cannisters were locked along the side, below the rim of vision, and shaped to the contours of their faces.

"I will say this about the masks," Gabriel noted. "They're not as bad as the ones they issued in Iraq."

"Those damn things!" Leo scoffed. "Could barely see shit out of them and the giant canisters felt like a softball attached to your face."

Portia chuckled. "Quit your bitching, big lug."

"You know I'm right, Sweet Pea." The machine gunner shook his head. "You know it."

Gabriel took a knee beside Penny as Alexa helped her with the mask. "This is the smallest size we have."

"I think it's working," Penny replied in a muffle.

"Speak forward, as if you're pushing your voice through the front," Gabriel said. "There's a kind of a makeshift speaker built into the masks that allows sound to escape, without compromising the seal. I'm not an NBC soldier, so I don't know all the nomenclatures. It's kind of tricky at first."

"Like this!" Penny's voice came through loud and clear.

"Roger." Gabriel gave a thumbs up, running his finger along the plastic edge of Penny's mask. "Shake your head vigorously after Agent Gray finishes tightening the straps."

"All done," Alexa announced. "Try it."

"This is heavy!" Penny shook her head then turned to Gabriel with the mask canted along the side of her face, the filter canister over her nose.

Gabriel chuckled. "Not quite snug enough."

"I have an idea." Alexa rummaged through her pack, withdrawing a thick black nightcap. "Might get a little toasty, but at least it'll hold."

With Gabriel's help, Penny removed the mask and placed the nightcap over her head. They strapped it on and tried again. The girl shook her head from side to side, then up and down as Gabriel directed. When she stopped, her big doe-like curious eyes stared back at the agents. They both gave a thumbs up.

Leo tiptoed around. Everyone watched the big man with brows risen. "Here."

"Leo, no!" Portia snapped.

"Damn, bro," Kevin scoffed.

"What?" Alexa gasped.

In Penny's hands was a large knife with its inlaid rubber hilt and black fiberglass scabbard. The little girl unsheathed the weapon, her eyes following the glint traveling up the razor-thin steel edge, into a sharp point.

"You all need to chill the fuck out," Leo said. "I'm making this call as acting Bravo. She needs something, damn it. There ain't no birthday cake and bouncy houses waiting on the other side of this door. Besides, everyone back home carries one on the streets. Doesn't matter what age you are."

Gabriel's hands guided Penny's, sliding the knife back into its scabbard. "First rule to being a soldier is discipline and maturity. Weapons aren't toys."

Penny nodded as Gabriel continued.

"Don't fear it. But respect this tool and what it can do. Only use this when you need it. Understood?"

"Yes, sir!" the girl replied.

Gabriel patted her head, turning to the rest of the team. "Give me a status check. Then, we move on the Queen."

"Green to green," all agents replied.

"I am ready, Gabriel," Corvus said.

Barrels zeroed on the entrance. Hard stares locked upon the doorway, scanning the smooth texture of its polished wood finish and golden handles. Their sight traced over blocks of marble forming the towering archway, leading to the high ceiling above. Gabriel reached for the double doors, parting from his touch and gliding open. He shifted to the wall, peering inward, searching from cover.

Stone floors and ostentatious rugs stopped at the door, replaced by emerald grass, covered with fresh morning dew. The room expanded further than reason, with its perimeter stretching outside of view. White roses dotted the greenery, starting in a sparse pattern, then becoming thick swathes surrounding the area. The flowers had long vined appendages that extended from the tall spike riddled stems of their bodies. A cloud of mist spat from one of the flowers, its petals fanning wide as the buds puffed out its contents like a whisper. It evaporated within seconds, blending away into the room's atmosphere without a trace.

Children of varying ages slumbered by the hundreds in close piles, curled up in fetal positions. Tremors throttled through a little boy, his eyelids breaking open for a moment, flickering in glimpses, as his eyes rolled back into his head. A whimper escaped the child's quivering lips before his head swayed into a shoulder. The boy's toes curled, turning bright pink on his pale feet, popping the knuckles within them. A girl lay next to him, wearing a purple nightie that covered her completely save for her hands and long auburn hair. Rapid twitches climbed up her back and limbs. She jerked forward, gasping loud and flinging upright. With dull and listless brown eyes, the girl scanned around, registering nothing before blurs consumed her vision, and she plopped down on her back again.

"Moving," Gabriel announced.

"Wait, there's someone here." Corvus reached around the door's opposite side, grabbing their team leader. The dream walker pointed to the far right, outside of Gabriel's view. "A cucuy. It's over there, coming into range."

Groans of pain grew louder as someone approached from the far right. A narrow glance brought bulging muscles into view, stacked on an elongated arm and pronounced shoulder. The being hobbled into full sight, carried by his arms, his legs dragging across the ground. From the knee down his limbs dangled from where they had been shattered. A flowing mane of silvery white locks descended from his head like waves of wildfire, traveling down his chiseled back that fanned like a cobra. Beads of sweat gathered and glistened over his skin, tanned to perfection and devoid of hair. The grunting being paused, reaching with his large hands for a sleeping girl. He heaved her limp body over one of his hulking and bulbous shoulders, before turning away.

"Oh, hell no!" Gabriel stormed into the room, the reticle of his combat optic pinned to the cucuy's forehead.

"Wha—?" the being gasped at all the weapons aimed at him, and the sizzling charge of energy arising within Corvus' wands. The agents remained in a wide pattern, keeping a few meters between them. Penny stood behind Alexa, hand on the hilt of her knife. "Curses! Intruders!"

"Caww!" Corvus' raven squawked at the being.

"Put her down, you son of a bitch!" Gabriel snapped through bared teeth.

"Okay! Be calm! Be calm, I say!" the cucuy pleaded, reaching over to set the girl gently on the floor. He looked back up at the team. Black and blue bruises surrounded his eyes with a yellow halo. Dried blood flaked under his nostrils, twisted to the left. There was a rugged handsomeness underneath the wounds, with his high cheekbones, pronounced dimples, and cleft chin, leading to a stern jawline with a five o'clock shadow. "Be cool!"

"Oh, we're cool, motherfucker! But you won't be if you make any sudden movements," Leo said.

"Kind of hard for me to do that, since my mistress lost her temper." The cucuy's eyes searched among them. "One of your energies is familiar… Yes! You, girl! Why are you back here?"

"Shut the hell up!" Gabriel ordered.

"What are you doing with the children?" Corvus demanded.

"I'm doing as I was told by my mistress!" the cucuy snapped back. "Thanks to your little friend hiding over there!"

"So tired of the lunacy you idiots speak around here," Gabriel barked. "You have one mike to start making sense or we're turning you into Swiss cheese."

"Please, don't!" Penny cried out. "Don't hurt him!"

Gabriel's finger eased off the trigger. "Penny, who is this joker?"

"He is her husband," the girl answered. "He didn't look like this when he helped us escape... I'm sorry, White King."

"I see." Gabriel's barrel lowered. "You're some kind of consort to the White Queen?"

"Blah! Blah! Blah!" the King replied. "Why are you back here, girl? Why?" The cucuy shook his head. "The only solace I had in my torment was knowing that I did the right thing, for once. Now you're throwing it all away by coming back here?"

"You were punished," Corvus stated.

"Oh, is it that obvious, bird brain?" The White King shook his head. "She beat the hell out of me for several hours! Then refused me the energy to heal! The Queen controls it all in this realm, unlike those born with the Ruach, we have zero say in the etheric layers without our lovely creator's authority. I thought you sorcerers were supposed to be intelligent?"

"I like this guy," Leo murmured.

Gabriel nodded.

Both Grays rolled their eyes.

"Where were you taking that girl?" Gabriel asked.

The White King turned, peering over his shoulder. Eyes followed his attention to a gargantuan construct of green fibrous tissues, shaped like a budding head of a flower, resting upon the grass. Leaves and thorns extended from its long serpentine body, rolling into thick coils and rooting deep into the ground. Vines and foliage extended through the vast room, slithering up the walls on all sides with their sharp ends. Bloated sacks hovered above them, writhing and groaning arising from the distended bodies, where a humming paleness blazed within bulging sacks held firm by gossamer veins and sinew.

A large humanoid outline remained poised, encased in a shell of leaves against the wall. Long and slender calves went into thighs that curved into the figure's wide hips, leading into a tapered waist, and pert breasts. Rounded shoulders topped a wide upper frame, with a thin neck. From atop the greenery flowed locks of ivory, draping over a thin porcelain face with high cheekbones and a delicate nose. Her eyes remained sealed, inert like the rest of her body.

That's her... Gabriel's thoughts wandered from the cucuy to the female along the back wall.

"I was taking the child there." The King's head lowered with a reluctant glance toward the giant bud on the ground. His eyes shut tight, face scrunching in shame. "After my punishment, I was demoted to furnace duties. Ladies and gentlemen, I present you the inner sanctum of the Queen's nursery. The white furnace."

"What the hell..." Leo's view remained elevated. His eyes traced with a rapid attempt to identify the countless vines gripping along the ceiling. "For the record, Actual. I never signed on to fight aliens."

"For once we agree," Portia said. "You feed the children to these plants?"

"Not like I've had much of a choice," the White King retorted. "This is where the power is stored and fed into Pandemonium. Where the Queen creates this reality in her half-assed manner. She claims to be on the same level as her father, yet overlooks so many details in creating things, whether it be physical or mental. Which I'm sure you've noticed if you've spent more than a few seconds chatting with my kin."

Gabriel nodded. "That explains a lot."

"I've seen glimpses of the furnace through my visions,"

Corvus stated. "Watching white flames devour innocent souls."

"You're not wrong about that, birdy," the King retorted. "You know what's worse than that? Seeing it every day in person! The screams... Having their souls shredded by the devouring flames. I can never stop hearing them..."

"What's the deal with her?" Kevin asked pointing to the towering feminine figure along the wall.

"That's her," Gabriel answered. "The White Queen."

"She's slumbering," the King replied. "Used up all her conscious energy creating a grand army in the hopes of overcoming your technological weapons, by swarming you. Without compromising the castle garrison."

They're not all outside engaging Monarch.

"You're their leader, correct?" The King turned to Gabriel. "I can sense the aura of authority from you."

"Yes."

"Well, what are you waiting for?" the King said. "Let's get these little ones out of here."

"Why are you helping us?" Alexa inquired.

"I was created, like everything you have beheld in this world," the King replied. "Fashioned to be the perfect mate. I was given ambition and courage, along with my once dashing looks. I was also given a sense of justice, judgment, knowledge —emotion. This is wrong. Everything she's doing is wrong. Even if it's the source of my life."

"A noble sentiment," Corvus said.

"What happens to you?" Gabriel asked. "Come with us."

"And do what exactly? I've nothing if I go up there. Not like these little ones. No grieving family to cheer my arrival. I'd be reduced to a disembodied spirit, with only your annoying psychics for company. And while that may suffice for some, no thanks. I still have my pride. Now, enough talk. The Queen is in slumber while she recuperates from her last spawning. It requires tremendous will to create. We need to hurry before she awakens. Expect hunger and anger when that happens. So much anger…"

"We move," Gabriel ordered. "Alexa and Corvus give us an overwatch. The rest of the team, start grabbing kiddos, run them out of the musk, and get them awake. Penny, you're tasked with guiding them out through the sewers, and along the coast once the first several dozen or so can start walking. Get in position, we're going to send them your way. The rest of you, get these kids going. Splash water on them, slap them, pinch; do whatever the fuck it takes to get them up and double time the hell out of here!"

"Roger, Actual," agents sounded off one after another.

"Yes, sir!" Penny said, darting out of the room.

"Come on, sleeping beauty." Leo allowed his light machine gun to hang along his massive back, scooping a little curly-haired girl from the floor. She bounced in his arms as he hurried, exiting the room. "Time to wake up. Come on now."

After clearing several meters from the garden's entrance, the large agent placed the girl, dressed in her onesie, seated against the wall. Leo reached for a canteen, uncapping it and splashing water on her face. Twitching rose within the girl's eyelids, opening through the gripping haze of sleep.

"Where… Who…" the girl muttered.

"You gotta wake up, sweetie," Leo urged, shaking her. "Stand up as soon as you can. I'll be right back."

Butcher's machine gunner ran back down the hall, with Harland passing him, carrying a boy. Alexa trailed behind with another over her shoulder, along with the White King carrying two children on his back. Murmurs and groans arose from the children gathering in the wide corridor. Portia scrambled up and down the line of youths, presenting smelling salts. Heads jolted up, shaking from the trance of their slumber. Curious eyes peered around with silent apprehension, exchanging looks of concern. Several of the children took to hugging themselves. Others started rising on wobbling knees. Jerking steps canted their walk until the agents guided them by the hand.

"We got a few ready for evac," Portia called out.

Alexa grabbed two by the arms, turning toward the others. "Come with me!" she urged. "We're going to link up with an honorary agent named Penny. You will follow her out and don't stop until you've reached the trucks. It'll all make sense. Form a single file line for others to follow."

"Go! Go! Go!" Portia ordered a train of nodding children who jogged behind Alexa. The medic turned to the next arrivals with her salts. "Wake up! Wake up! Wake up! Please!"

Boots clapped hard from the agents rushing back and forth with the children. Straining took hold of their lower backs, carrying the precious cargo in their mad dashes out of the garden. Heat rose from their reddening skin, along with dribbling sweat beads that raced down their frames, soaking into their uniforms. Breath pumped from their lungs, burning with the cold embrace of fatigue. Hundreds of children lined the vast hallway with hundreds more trekking outward to the kitchen and down into the sewers.

"We're almost done here," the King replied. "Only a few more children left."

"We're loading the trucks again, sir," Penny said over comms. "The convoy leader said she's going to call in for more help from Tactical Command."

"This is Butcher Actual. Excellent work, Penny," Gabriel

replied. "You make sure you're on the next wave back, understood?"

"But I can still help."

"Negative. You've done enough and accomplished your mission, Agent. Now fulfill your promise. Get on the next trucks heading back. That's an order."

"Yes, sir."

"On your feet, please," Portia urged, continuing to spread revulsion with her smelling salts.

"We're grabbing the last now," Gabriel ushered the rest to follow back inside the garden.

Alexa, Harland, and Gabriel grabbed the remaining children.

"I'm going to check around!" the King called out. "Make sure we didn't leave any of the little ones hiding within the tall grass or behind a bush."

"Excellent idea," Corvus agreed. "I will go with you."

"I know it's a good idea!" the cucuy snapped. "I don't need some dream walker amateur telling me that!"

"Hardly an amateur. Now focus."

"Looks clear. You seeing any, birdy?"

"I would agree," Corvus replied. "I believe we have everyone. Much to the relief of my weary arms. Correction, everything on my body is fatigued."

Gabriel jogged back inside, seeing a thumbs up from Corvus and a nod from the King.

"All the children are accounted for—" Corvus' words chopped, registering the widening eyes of Butcher's team leader. Gabriel's hands reached down from the sling of his rifle, whipping the weapon around and into the ready position. The barrel rose toward the wall.

Green stalks raced through the room, banking through the

rustling grass and leaping upward. Spiked tentacles pierced into the King's abdomen, where his flesh gave to the holes burrowed through his racking frame. Blood spilled down his body, the warmth coursing over his legs, smearing across his pale skin. Whimpers escaped the King's quivering lips. His head rolled when the strength of life left his body, leaving it limp and impaled as he was carried into the air, showering droplets of crimson over the garden.

The giant bud opened, revealing a maw of concaved teeth oozing with saliva. A quaking hiss shot from the monstrosity, revealing the sweltering depths of its gullet. The pale flames rose into view, churning within.

Gabriel and Corvus paused. Their mouths dropped, going limp where they stood. The surroundings faded, ushered away by the brightness washing their vision. Ringing overtook the slithering tendrils that ruffled through the grass, leaving only their thumping heartbeats to play in their eardrums. A white morass of souls consumed their thoughts, pouring forth with the bellowing lament of countless victims.

Corvus snapped from his trance, pulling away from the brightness, and shaking Gabriel from his stupor. "Awaken, warrior. This hellish evil was not meant for mortal eyes. Find the will to pull away from its haunting ire."

"I—I..." Gabriel shook his head. Images of the room returned. The screams remained etched in him, bubbling through his consciousness, with each involuntary eruption rising to the forefront of his thoughts. They cried out for a mercy that would never come. "Such suffering..."

"Your empathy was victimized," Corvus continued. "Reclaim it and steer away from the Queen's intentions."

Gabriel and Corvus' view went to the Queen where she remained encased along the wall. Pallid eyes opened from the woman, teeming with the same unholy luminosity as the furnace they beheld. With her snowy brows arching, and clenched teeth bared, the focus of her baleful glare set upon the agents.

"Shall we skip the formalities?" the Queen's voice showered over them in soothing grace and feminine elegance. "White Queen is a derogatory label, from those who cannot comprehend my ambition. Refer to me by my chosen name. I am she who never fell to the clutches of mortality. I am the last pure human being, fashioned in the image of the throne. I am the grand design manifested. The first Havah. The pinnacle of my Father's vision. I am Lilith."

CHAPTER 29
BEWARE THE JABBERWOCK

THE PALE FURNACE, THE IVORY PALACE - 0700 HOURS

Vines slithered away, leaves molted off her body, opening the shell that encased Lilith's feminine form. She stepped forward upon the balls of her feet with the soft grace of a dancer. Wide hips swayed from her tapered form. Curled pubic hairs matted between her legs, where a set of masculine and feminine genitalia were exhibited. The former draped over the lips of the latter.

Strength rippled through the bands of muscle that encompassed her body, culminating into capped deltoids. Red lips pressed together in the palms of her clawed hands, tugging on Corvus' attention as he inventoried their foe. Cords of sinew and vegetation popped free, withering away from the back of her head, neck, torso, and abdomen. Red imprints swelled where the extensions had once been attached, dotting down her body in a line of succession.

There was one protruding from the top of her skull, Corvus ruminated. *One immediately upon the back of the head, and then* her neck, heart, descending into... Could they be feeding into her chakras?

Lilith's towering presence closed the gap of the immense room. Corvus' etheric senses blared with the heart-racing alarm of impending doom. Within the unseen reaches, energy channeled like a constant stream of lightning from dark clouds rolling through the dream walker's second sight.

"Give back my property!" the fiend hissed.

Such incredible power, but that isn't what chills me. Her mastery of the layers, so effortless and instinctive. We stand no chance. Madam Dupree knew it. Hence the attempt to pilfer the souls in stealth. Great Spirit be with me. Corvus looked at Gabriel. "Run. Get your team out of here."

"No." Gabriel raised his rifle. "We stand toge—"

"Run! There's no time to argue! Damn your courage, Gabriel," Corvus snapped. "Curtail your instincts, comrade. Ensure the children get to the door! Make haste!"

He's right. No time for pride or hatred of the unholy. Rescuing the little ones is our priority. No matter the cost. "Thank you." Gabriel turned. "Give her hell, brother."

Corvus nodded, lunging forward.

Lilith stopped, lowering her head and grinning, raising one pale claw with blackened feline nails extending from porcelain fingertips. The Queen's towering presence loomed in the dozen meters between them.

Corvus analyzed, scanning the chiseled muscles brimming through her statuesque physique, from her charcoal lips to the onyx nipples spiking her firm breasts.

"Imprudent mortal," the Queen's words shot with an otherworldly contempt, echoing a deepening animosity from her masculine side. "Had you taken a knee and returned my sustenance; I would've shown you mercy and allowed you to dwell amongst my world as a slave. Now you shall be annihilated!"

Everything we have goes into this. Leave nothing for a return trip this time, as I was taught when I first learned to dive into the recesses of the dream. No, my dearest companion. We won't be awakening from this journey. The Great Spirit is with us. I can feel it.

Brilliance pulsed through Corvus' wands, channeling from the deepest recesses of his willpower. His raven stood tall upon his shoulder, fanning his wings, declaring their challenge. Churning energies expelled through the wands, striking Lilith. Smoke rose from the seared crevice between her breasts, crackling in residual power of the manifested psychic attack. The raven took flight, squawking in defiance, bearing his willpower against their foe.

Great Spirit, I beg of you to be with me during this final trial.

Lilith reared back, bringing a hand to the wound. Charred flakes broke from the deadened flesh, sloughing away with the rapid regeneration of new tissue. Lilith smirked, the fires of the Pale Furnace within her eyes locked on Corvus as she charged forward. The Queen's movements grew in rapidity the closer she drew. Blurred pale limbs consumed Corvus' vision with the swiftness of wind.

"Caw!" the raven's call warned. Flashes of their sight melded through Corvus' vision, channeling an overhead perspective through his left eye.

Lilith swung down and wide with a mighty stroke. The dream walker dived, tumbling across the ground, and springing back to his feet. A stroke of Corvus' wand ushered forth a crackling stream of lightning. Lilith's torso reeled from the stinging impact. She stepped back, regaining her balance. The Queen's glare fell upon Corvus.

"You haven't been challenged in a while," Corvus surmised. "You've become slovenly in your decadence."

"Hold your tongue!" Frustration brimmed through the Queen's scowl as she spat the words.

Lilith's hands outstretched, coiling with energy. Black particles accumulated within her grasp, forming thick handles that extended into long drooping whips. Metal rings hung from the pommels, clanging as her arms sashayed the weapons upon the ground. Cruel steel barbs protracted like giant wasp stingers from the tip of each popper, slicing the grass as Lilith taunted Corvus with her dance.

"Pain, Gaagi." Lilith smirked. "That shall be the only reward for your defiance!"

"Likewise."

Rage soared from Lilith's core, trembling through her mouth with a hissing scream that clawed its way up her throat. A fierce snap sent a whip shooting for Corvus. He raised his wands, pushing out defiant energies.

No!

Shimmering light reflected around the dream walker as a wave of calamitous force struck out from the whip against his psionic shield. Immense pressure buckled his knees and bent his elbows. Strain ran through his twitching lower back, convulsing to keep him upright.

The ultimate battle of wills. No fear. No holding back. As my grandmother taught me. Give them nothing. Push back!

Another cracking blow sent Corvus collapsing to his hands and knees. The pressure of fatigue weighed down on the dream walker, left to stare at the grass beneath him. Strain ran through his face. Exhaustion blared from the core of his will. Ruinous currents of Lilith's aura swelled around him, pushing against the quaking dam that was Corvus' efficacy. The whip reeled back once more, cocking into position for another blow.

"Caw!" the raven belted out, strafing across Lilith's face with its talons.

The Queen screamed and huffed, sneering up at the bird rising out of range, matching her ire with its unyielding gaze.

Direct confrontation will not work. I cannot kill what cannot die. There must be a way to stop her... Corvus gazed around, his focus wading through the fatigue of combat, guided by the mournful wails of countless innocents, and finding the large bud. Its mouth remained agape, presenting the white balefire of souls. *The Pale Furnace. What she covets the most. The source of her power.*

The dream walker rose on uneasy legs. Hissing bolts of power poured into the convulsing wands as Corvus shuddered. His spirit strained as if turning his stomach upside down. Heartbeats drummed through his body and trembling aura. A stream of light jettisoned from both wands, striking the bud. Flames erupted. The Pale Furnace bellowed, swaying in agony, its roots lifting from the ground. Cracks of light escaped from its rounded head.

"Curses!" Lilith screamed. "Damn you, Dream Walker! You'll ruin everything!"

The Queen reared back her whip. Talons and feathers strafed her vision, as the raven's fury assaulted her again. Lilith snapped with her teeth, biting down on a mouthful of air. The raven whisked away, cawing in defiance. Lilith peered through the streaks of pain running through her eyes. Her arm shot forth the whip, catching the bird. The raven cried out. In an explosion of black feathers, the smoking husk of Corvus' familiar crashed into smoldering debris.

"No!" Corvus screamed as the familiar connection severed. "Justice will be done!"

The dream walker launched another arcane blast at the Pale Furnace. The bud shrieked. Fragments of its presence peeled away. The radiance from within shone through. Its skin peeled from the massive lips, while its teeth crumbled. The Pale Furnace crashed to the floor; its long neck withering. Light poured through the convulsing husk.

Corvus smiled at Lilith as she screamed to the heavens. Blinding energy erupted into the room.

The light consumed their vision, as the chamber quaked around them.

Leo, Portia, and Kevin's boots clapped the ground as they ran down the hall catching sight of Gabriel. Shuddering overtook the corridor, causing the agents to stumble into each other and brace against the walls. Flashing light pulsed through the area.

"What the fuck was that?!" Leo exclaimed.

"Corvus is taking on the Queen," Gabriel answered.

"Did he win?" Kevin asked. "Shit... Sounds like he won."

"Hell yeah!" Leo cheered.

"I don't think so," Portia said. "Remember what Madam Dupree told us about this vector. It cannot die."

"I know you want to go back for him, but we can't," Leo urged.

"Right, we keep moving," Gabriel spoke into his mic, pressing it close. "Everyone give me a SITREP."

"Butcher Actual this is Diver Actual," Harland replied.

"We're topside and loading more precious cargo into the trucks. I'd say about five mikes to completion."

"These kiddos are double timing it faster than we are," Alexa added. "Poor things are more eager than us to get out of here."

"Good to hear. We're traversing the palace and heading to the rendezvous," Gabriel said as the team jogged through the hallway. "Closing on the kitchen area now. We lost Cor—"

A crimson javelin hurtled through the air like a lightning bolt, smacking headlong into Kevin's chest plate, splitting it in two within the tactical vest. The agent gasped, his eyes following down the long shaft to the heart-shaped spearhead piercing a pouch of two magazines. Kevin buckled, expelling the wind from his lungs, desperate for relief. Portia grabbed him, heaving the agent back to his feet.

"Kev!"

"I-I'm... okay," Kevin managed. "The plate took most of it..."

A quartet of hunched figures stood across from them, barring their path to the kitchen entrance. Heart-shaped faces growled from the ends of elongated necks. Shields and spears clanged as they marched forward. Thin interlocking fangs extended from their drooping lipless jaws, where ropes of saliva hung over the red tabards that draped over their chests, with a large tear in the middle. Glistening red tissue was displayed within the hole, revealing a gaping exposure in their chest where their hearts pumped. Blood churned through the ventricles and long valves that stretched through their torsos.

"Interlopers!" one of the heart guards declared with breathy condemnation. "Slay them all!"

Muzzle flashes blared down the corridor from Leo's machine gun. Rounds punctured the heart of a red guard, sinking into his thick flesh. Blood spewed from the holes leading into wet darkness, squirting out as the sentry fell backward. The organ continued to pump, raining over the corpse. Death throes wracked from the fallen guard, slowing as his life fluids pooled around him.

"This demon goddess bitch did a really shitty job designing her troops," Leo murmured.

The guards lifted and planted their tower shields. A red wall of hardened steel crept forward as Leo's machine gun fire bounced away. Ripples traveled from where the bullets struck, only for the bastions to hold form. The guards marched in unison.

"Shit!" Leo exclaimed. "Spoke too soon."

"*Use me to unmake my mistakes*," the voice of the sword offered to Gabriel's mind.

Steel rang as Gabriel drew the sword.

"Halt!" a guard cried out. "The Vorpal Sword!"

A heart guard hissed, cringing behind his shield. "Curses, I thought she discarded that thing!"

Gabriel swung, slicing through the shield with ease. The barrier melted away as the blade connected, withering into ash that dissipated in the guard's grasp. Leo pulled the trigger, a control burst roared forth, sending the guard plopping down, grasping at his spewing heart. Gabriel thrust at another. Flakes of energy peeled away from the shield, becoming nothing. The sword ran through, piercing the guard's heart. The cucuy screamed, ripples of his presence pulling him apart. Speckles of energy fluttered where it once stood.

"Flee!" another guard screamed. "Flee our mother's wrath!"

"What?" Portia asked as she helped Kevin hobble up to them.

"What—What are those assholes going on about?" Kevin groaned through his words.

"How did you know the sword did that?" Leo asked. "That's badass!"

"I didn't." Gabriel looked at the weapon, shaking away his astonishment. "The path is clear. Let's move before those assholes regroup."

Pillars of smoke arose throughout the blackened area, striped with the glowing orange of residual embers. Swathes of hot air billowed around them. Lilith stood at its center shaking her head and clenching her teeth, as the swelling redness of her scalding flesh regenerated. New tissue coagulated from her bloody dermis, pushing away the crinkling husk as it withered and crumbled to the ground. Shriveled hair cascaded from her tender scalp, sprouting locks of shining silver that draped over her shoulders and traveling down to the small of her back. Glowing residual power stained the ground where the head of the furnace laid, its upper portions agape and tattered from the souls that erupted forth.

The presence of innocence no longer lingered in Lilith's senses. She reached out into the etheric layers. An absence stood between her and the endless wealth she once commanded. The remaining power she converted within herself rose with the bubbling cauldron of rage that remained in her spirit. She reached out with a claw, remembering the swell of purity that once engulfed her throne room. Lilith was bare to the world, no longer able to masquerade the tidal wave of emotions behind a pilfered blanket of innocence. Lamentation. Shame. Greed.

"Come with me." Memories of forbidden lectures resurfaced within Lilith. *"How dare our Father not appreciate your majesty. Your doubts are of little shock to me. He's always indulged in self-loathing and restriction. He crafted you from himself. Lilith, we are destined to be goddesses. Not by his authority, but by our own hand. Why can't you see how special you are? Shed this false shell of humility, as I have. Such a thing has only made us into slaves. It only serves to hold you back. I must go. I feel your husband approaching. He seeks you. Like his Father, he thinks you are beneath him and will feign love to emotionally extort your compliance. Remember, no more subservience to our masters. We seek freedom."*

Deep chuckles echoed into Lilith's thoughts like a stone into a pond, sending ripples of destruction. She broke away, growling, and curling her claws with murderous intent. She followed the mirthful transmission to Corvus' ruined body. A grin stretched along his weary face. Scorched clothes hung to his seared flesh. Corvus' white teeth remained visible through his laughter. A cough stuttered his amusement. The dream walker hunched over, cradling the charred remains of his familiar.

"Y-your... pride..." Corvus stated. "It has served as a tool for your own manipulation. Steering you away from the Great Spirit, into never-ending conflict."

"Silence!" Lilith screamed.

"What are you going to do, your majesty?" Corvus jeered through interrupting groans of pain. "Kill me? We rest in honor... knowing I can take my place with my ancestors. I upheld their legacy... the souls of my people... smile upon me from the light of the afterlife. Can you say the same, nightmare-maker?"

"I am perfection!" Lilith paused. "No! I refuse your words. Do not attempt to dissuade me with your circumspection, Dream Walker. I am made in the image of my Father's grand design!"

"No. You ran. You quit. You are a coward. The Great Spirit knew you could never be like him because you took your free will and chose failure. Man and woman are the heirs to his legacy. Hence why he promised he will never forsake us, never give up on us."

Lilith turned away. "You've wasted enough of my time, Dream Walker. I will not end your pain with death. Suffer slowly in your throes."

Must recover the souls... Rage permeated through her thoughts, breaking her inner dialogue with growing spasms. *Cut off from the Furnace... No matter. I have enough energy. I will carry the deserved wrath to this gaggle of mortals myself.*

A roar screeched from Lilith's outstretched maw as she carried her reddening vision to the ceiling, her ire projecting to the cold skies beyond. Muscle and sinew flexed, folded, and shifted underneath her ivory skin like churning gears. Bones snapped and scraped against her innards. Twitches of agony coursed through Lilith's physique. Slimy snaps heralded the push of limbs from her back, flanking her and extending into great lengths. Blood and sweat dripped from the growing skin that fanned beneath the appendages, forming into wings.

"Alice dreamt of vanquishing me," Lilith recalled. "Most do of the things they fear. The reality is that she fled in terror, back through the door, recalling dreams and desires that never transpired."

Thick claws pushed forth, jettisoning her once delicate

toes, sending them sprinkling over the grass. She pushed upward, rising from the ground upon hind legs that culminated into sickle-shaped talons. Inches added to the width of her arms and thighs, where veins pushed out to the surface like a tapestry of lightning bolts.

"I was there in the garden when my Father presented those lesser creations that Adam adored so much, his precious animals. I understood what mattered most, their gifts. Their strengths, and ferocity, reaching a zenith with my imagination and creating the most dangerous of forms."

Lilith's countenance convulsed, her head rattling back and forth, lips peeling back until ripping and folding away. A new mouth pressed outward, upturned to the middle of her face with its fish-like demeanor and rows of shark teeth. Her nose stretched wide until the nostrils became only two narrow slits. The pressure along her forehead tore away her eyelids. In their stead were sockets of unblinking bulbous eyes, incandescent in the shadows.

"Gaze upon the pinnacle of my fury!" Lilith towered over Corvus, leaning into the dream walker, with her graying locks flanking the view of her dreaded appearance. "I am now the perfect hunter. No clever quips? No retorts? I leave you with these words. Your allies will fail, dream walker. And you will all have suffered for nothing."

CHAPTER 30
THE GREAT JOUST

THE PLAIN PLAINS WITHIN THE PLANE - 0800 HOURS

The static of crashing waves mixed with Butcher Team's heavy breaths as they ran along the beach. Lactic acid burned through their legs, pumping along the sand. Grumbling and cranking came into earshot as Humvees, trucks, and Bradley Fighting Vehicles came into view. Harland stood outside of a Humvee door, waving, flagging them with wild abandon and a smile.

"Push it, Agents!" Harland cheered. "Woo!"

"Oh boy, are you nerdy sorcerer sons-a-bitches a sight for sore eyes," Leo wheezed out the words.

"Where's Penny?" Gabriel asked.

"Gone with the seventh or eighth wave, Actual." Alexa nodded. "I made sure she was on it."

"Excellent work, Gray. One less thing to worry about. All promises have been kept." Gabriel jogged over to his Humvee passenger side door. "Mount up, task force. We move—"

"Hey you!" Agent Conn called, poking out from the turret's hatch. "Gabe! Don't ignore me you lumpia eating bastard!"

"Hey now!" Leo barked back. "Lumpia is fucking delicious!"

Gabriel's eyes narrowed with ferocity.

"Think fast!" Agent Conn tossed her Stetson cowboy hat down.

"What?" Gabriel asked, catching it. "Why?"

"Don't want any of these unholy bastards getting their hands on it, defiling it and whatnot," Agent Conn replied. "This is prolly gunna be goodbye, Gabe."

"I can't take your Stetson. It means too much—"

"I couldn't in good conscience go leaving it with some non-cav type that hasn't earned their golden spurs," Agent Conn said. "So, you better take it with no fuss and do me a solid. I was listening to comms. That thing in there—Whatever ya'll wanna call it. She ain't giving up so easy. And after what Madam Dupree said, nothing is going to keep her down for long. That's not gonna stop me from trying though."

Gabriel nodded, holding the Stetson with both hands. "You're going to relieve Monarch on the front?"

"Yes, sir. That's what we do. Cavalry saving the day. You hold my stet for me. Hold it until we meet again in Fiddler's Green."

"Roger," Gabriel replied.

"All right, enough of this sentimental bullshit," Agent Conn barked into her mic, dipping back into her turret. "Let's get these children to safety and relieve Monarch. Time to show these boogeymen what twenty-six tons of fury can do!"

Carbon spat from the long barrels of the M2 .50 caliber heavy machine guns, mounted within the turrets of Monarch's racing Humvees. Jub jub birds passed overhead, attempting to avoid the thick glowing tracer rounds guiding the sectors of fire. Screams carried from the avian monstrosities as swathes of twelve-gauge buckshot slammed into them.

"It's working, Actual!" Murphy hollered into the cabin.

"Good ole buckshot," Curtis said, punching into the Force Tracker's touch screen.

"They're stopping."

"What do you mean?"

"The enemy stopped advancing." Murphy kept his hands wrapped around the parallel handles of his machine gun. Faint waves of heat rose from his spent weapon as he gazed over the sights to the horizon. "Should we give them the business?"

"No," Curtis replied. "Cease fire. Something isn't right. Eyes up, Monarch."

"Roger," the squad leaders replied, their Humvees rolling around to face the enemy and coming to a stop across the field.

"What the fuck are they doing?" Murphy scratched his head.

"What the hell? I don't like this." Curt sat up in his seat, folding down the Force Tracker's screen for a complete view through the windshield. "Ravenous as fuck one second and now they look—terrified?" *Please let this be a stroke of luck...*

The teeming masses of cucuy faced toward the castle. Their feline bodies dipped low, bowing their heads. Trembles ran through their frames. The jub jub birds squawked, sailing to the ground, folding their wings behind their backs, and lowering themselves into a bow. Quivering ruffled their feathers, shaking along their backsides. Howling curses rose to great levels, expelling from the depths of the castle.

Damn, who the fuck is making that racket? Curtis raised his binoculars, extending his sight to the embankments and towers. *It has these bastards scared shitless.*

Haggard wails of lamentation escalated to greater levels, carrying a woman's cadence. The words within her curses twisted into unintelligible cries broken apart by the levels of insurmountable rage. The cucuy buried their faces into the grass.

"Jabbering, jabbering, jabbering," the cucuy repeated. "Jabbering, she jabbers!"

"Jabber!" jub jubs squawked. "Jabbering!"

Stone erupted from the tower in an upheaval of dust. Rock debris pelted across the castle's front. Cucuy shook and whimpered as shards rained down upon them. Screaming overtook the words, blaring across the field. The etheric layers pulsed with each note of fury. A pale towering form of claws, teeth, and hair extended its massive wingspan, taking to the skies with a powerful flap.

"We're going to need more than buckshot for that vector," Murphy gasped.

"That must be their Queen," Curtis said, bringing his view over her distended jowls and the turned-up muzzle of her fish-like countenance. The Monarch team leader sighed. "This changes nothing. We hold the line and their attention, Agents. That is the mission. No matter what."

"Monarch Actual, this is Knight Actual, your mission is complete, Monarch," Agent Conn's voice announced over the radio. "Say again, the cavalry has arrived."

THE GREAT JOUST 423

Curtis turned his gaze to the rumble of steel tread carrying the armored hulls of Bradley Fighting Vehicles. Three of the light armored tanks rolled from the opposite end of the field in wedge formation, Conn's vehicle serving as the tip of the spear, while the others flanked her respective sides. The Bradleys stopped in a formation. The long thin barrels of their 25 millimeter cannons scanned, while the cylindrical 7.62 coaxial rotary autocannon revved into a whining spin, all training on the horde of cucuy.

"Damn those are some ugly bastards," Agent Derrick, the gunner said, his face pressed against the rubber inlay, viewing the battlefield through a turret camera.

"Fucking-A," Conn replied. "Monarch Actual, the infiltration team has successfully acquired the precious cargo. They are en route to the rendezvous. You are relieved."

"You are a sight for sore eyes," Curtis replied. "Monarch, disengage. All survivors on me for exfil. Give them hell, Black Knights."

"Chico, you're free on the wheel unless I say so," Agent Conn said over comms to her driver located on the front right side of the hull.

"Roger, Actual," the driver replied, peering through the thick bullet resistance panes over his seat.

"Same with you, Cole," Conn continued. "Free gun it. Trust y'alls instincts on this one, gents. It's our finest hour."

Conn peered through her turret camera, displaying a right sided view, and scanning along the battlefield. A click of her finger switched her view to the gunner's left side camera, before changing it back to her own, sending the shining black lens canting upward. The Queen's glower appeared in Conn's HUD. Strings of saliva whipped out as she bared her teeth with a chittering frenzy.

"Evasive maneuvers, Knights," Agent Conn ordered, following the Queen pacing overhead. "She's looking for someone to pounce, go wide to your respective sides. Chico, rear back to give us a clear shot."

"Roger, Actual," Chico replied. "We're moving."

Bradley engines roared, spinning their tracks into action. Hulls shifted in place turning the girth of the vehicles while the turrets remained locked and upward, tracing the airborne vector. The fighting vehicles hooked to their flanks, with Black Knight One swinging wide to the left, while Black Knight Three went right. Agent Conn's Black Knight Two jerked and thrust backward.

Opening the kill sack. Come on, I know you're pissed off, big girl. Take the bait, damn it!

"Eyes on that vector twelve o'clock high," Conn announced.

The Queen roared, soaring down the middle after Conn.

Got her!

"Well now," Agent Conn scoffed. "I reckon that big ole bish isn't happy to see us. Give her a reason to be peeved, Cole. Bring her down to our level."

"Target acquired. Arming stingers." Cole watched the glowing yellow reticle through his green tinted view. It locked over Lilith and the square within their heads-up display that outlined her presence. "On the way!"

Smoke puffed from the rear of the launcher, located along the side of the turret. The rocket hissed forward, its fins slicing through the air. A trail of exhaust followed as the warhead careened upward speeding in a direct path to Lilith. An intense flash heralded the massive explosion of the payload, steel and smoke ballooning across of sky.

Lilith screamed, buckling in flight and tumbling through the air.

"On the way!" the other gunners announced from their vehicles.

Two more rockets crossed into view. They soared through the sky, hounding after the falling Queen, smiting her with catastrophic detonations. Lilith crashed into the field, her smoldering body slamming with booming impact.

"Ooooh..." Agent Conn chuckled. "I bet that hurt like hell."

Lilith's snarling visage appeared, as the cucuy Queen pushed up from the ground, rising to all fours. Bandersnatch and jub jub birds watched in mouth gaping horror from across the way.

"Vector in the open. 1200—correction 1300 meters," Agent Conn announced. "Weapons free!"

Loud thumping from within the 25 millimeter cannons launched a salvo of fire. Tracer rounds spat forth guiding the path of violence upon Lilith. Thick high explosive rounds hammered Lilith's torso. The Queen screamed and shuddered, her skin peeling with the burning pull of each collision, riding a pain deep down within her that stung to the core. The arch of her right wing snapped, bending, and folding downward. Lilith called energy from the depths of her reserves. New portions of skin reformed and grafted, underneath the enemy fire chewing her apart.

Curse the children of that bitch, Eve! Lilith's thoughts snarled through her psyche. *The energy within me is being depleted! Curse them all!*

Lilith rose to her feet, staggering from the onslaught of another hard blow. Phosphorus burned bright from a tracer round finding its way into the Queen's eye socket. Bits of meat and skull jettisoned from the explosion that followed, pushing out the side of her head and sprinkling to the ground in a sloshing rain of crimson.

"Save our mother, idiots!" a voice bellowed from the castle ramparts. "Now is not the time for cowering!"

Who's talking all that big shit? Agent Conn's camera went to the castle walls searching upward to see the Knave back in position, glaring with his one good eye upon the battlefield. "Golf, please do dispense some hate along the wall where that asshole is trying to rally them."

"Roger, Actual! On the way!" Cole brought his reticle to bear upon the Knave. A quick burst sent pieces of the cucuy commander spraying back into the castle's confines, while the rest of him hovered as a pink mist that evaporated into the night.

"Hot damn that's some good shootin'!" Conn cheered. "Okay give me—shit! Enemy reinforcements! Incoming!"

Bandersnatches and jub jubs raced down the field, swarming toward their mother. Salivating jaws snapped from bobbing heads. Sharp nails extended from their paws. Muscles flexed throughout their lion-like bodies, teeming with the anticipation of violence. Cawing signaled overhead to the circling jub jub birds stalking the vehicles.

Lilith reached over, grabbing the nearest bandersnatch, ripping the creature from its gallop, and holding it aloft by the throat. The cucuy's eyes widened, staring into the fierce gaze of his mother, with her arched brows and clenched teeth. Others slowed in pursuit, attention drawing toward their brother. Lilith's maw gaped, inhaling the energy that composed her child's existence. Frantic cries expelled from the cucuy, thrashing about in the grip of his mother, while shards of light splintered away from his aura. The cucuy's cries resounded through the battlefield as his lifeforce streamed into Lilith's hungry gullet.

More energy! More! I reclaim what I have wasted upon you fools! Surrender your lives to me!

"Hold your fire," Agent Conn ordered. "This crazy bish is fucking up her own people. Let the vectors have at it."

Gasps came from the bandersnatches. The jub jub ceased their calls for violence, instead convulsing in midair at the sight of their Queen. Lilith grabbed another, devouring his life in a flash of brilliance that broke the cucuy apart, swallowing his soul.

"Mother!" a bandersnatch pleaded in horror, turning to flee when the ire of her gaze fell upon him.

The others followed, fleeing back toward the castle.

"How dare you!" Lilith bellowed. "You are nothing without me! Your existence is purely by my will alone! You cannot escape!"

Cucuy cried out in agony as dozens of them halted in place, their feet stayed by a force greater than their will. They peered back over their shivering shoulders, watching their mother raise her claws. Body quaking convulsions over took them. The eldritch call stretched their crumbling husks, twisting with the command of the great power tearing them asunder. Their weeping souls syphoned into the Queen's eager maw.

Fully charged. Lilith roared, turning her gaze back to the Bradley Fighting Vehicles.

"Recommence fire!" Agent Conn ordered. "Weapons free!"

"Roger, Actual! On the way!" the others acknowledged.

Tracers arced across the field in glowing streaks, guiding the line of fire from the 25 millimeter cannons. Explosions erupted around Lilith, gouging holes into her wings as she waded through the hail of fire. The cucuy Queen's growls escalated to levels that matched the bellowing shots thudding against her.

"She's pushing hard!" Cole announced. "It's not holding her off anymore!"

"Suffer, children of the harlot Eve!" Lilith screamed.

"She just call our mama a hoe?" Chico asked.

"I reckon she did," Conn replied.

"Aw, hell naw!" Chico snapped.

"All vehicles converge on mine," Conn ordered. "We'll give this bitch something to choke on."

"Roger, Actual. Moving!" the others replied.

Bradley Fighting Vehicles shifted on their tread, their turrets maintaining a lock on the vector, delivering salvos of high explosive rounds. The light armored tanks strolled up beside Conn's, keeping ten meters between them. Coaxial chain runs spun into action, sending forth an endless belch of rounds. Muzzle flashes and carbon sparked in a wave of chaos pushing against the Queen. In churning steps Lilith continued, her arms raised into a guard. Skin and flesh evaporated with the many impacts, regrowing from the energies she called forth. Her wings peeled away, jettisoning behind her as tufts of meat, and red mist that stained the grass in a wet trail.

"Vector fifteen meters and closing," Cole announced.

"All vehicles release and let your Willie Pete fly!" Conn ordered.

Cannon and gunfire ceased. Lilith lowered her guard, her arms pumping as her massive legs galloped the remaining distance with rapid abandon. Cole stared through his gunner's sights catching a grimacing visage of hatred and anger etched over the Queen's face. Lilith's claws flexed with anticipation, readying to carve through the vehicle's armored hull. Cole flipped the top switch to their grenade launcher.

A click and loud thudding sent white clouds spewing out from small quad barrels positioned on both sides of the hull. Lilith lost sight of the vehicles. Her growl tapered into a cough, swallowing a mouthful of the white phosphorus. The walls of her throat dried and cracked. Burning pain crawled down her neck, racing into her chest and stomach, searing away the flesh within. Her insides curled up, boiling from the impossible temperatures that fried her organs.

Chalky powder clung to her skin, smoking as each layer peeled away. A gasp brought the burning air into her nostrils, clogging them, before sending waves of searing pain running through her skull, where it culminated into her brain with a blistering ache. Convulsions ran through Lilith. She cried out before keeling over into the fetal position.

"Choke on it!" Conn snapped. "Break off, Knights!"

Gears and tread ground, pulling the light armored tanks away from their mark. Conn's Bradley reared back, pulling away from the swathes of white smoke. Shrill cries echoed across the plains from a silhouette thrashing amidst the burning pale haze. The grass around them folded over, deadening into a deep brown, withering away into the dirt. Shrieking cucuy remaining along the outskirts of the castle, clawed for the door to open, their energies peeling away from reality.

"I gave you life," Lilith called out. "Now I take it."

Lilith leapt from the unseeable whiteness, propelled by a tremendous flap of her wings, closing upon Knight One's Bradley. Claws peeled into the armored hull, with the roaring Queen stripping it away like an orange peel. Steel from the right side curled under her grip, before she yanked it from the light tank, discarding the armor over her shoulder. Heat rose from the exposed engine block, with its timing belts spinning and gears still churning. The Bradley lurched away in reverse. Lilith reached down grabbing its left track, tugging hard, and popping it loose into one strand of metal that plopped across the ground. The vehicle came to a halt, its wheels spinning along nothing despite the engine roaring for movement.

"She's too close to them, Actual!" Cole said. "I don't have a shot!"

"God damn it!" Conn said. "Knight One get your asses out of there!"

Claws reached into the Bradley, wrapping around Knight One's tank commander. The radio blared with the agent's haggard screams. Lilith pulled the wedged body, dragging along the confines of the vehicle. Bones gave with audible snaps. Ligaments and tendons popped, dislodging limbs that buckled underneath the pressure. His appendages folded behind his rag-dolled body. Lilith presented the whimpering agent for Conn to bear witness. She hurled the agent's broken figure, sending it crashing into the field as a weltered mess of arms and legs.

"Shoot!" Knight One's golf screamed. "We're finished! Just cause her pain!"

Desperate hollers followed as she grabbed the gunner, dragging his body from the turret. Thudding shots smacked across Lilith's back.

"Monarch Actual, this is Knight Actual," Conn said over the radio.

"Knight Actual this is Monarch Actual, send it!"

"My delta and golf are going to be dismounting and exfiling the AO. Can you swing back and pick them up? They will have their beacons active."

"Roger, we're swinging back around," Curt replied.

Lilith's roars snatched away Conn's attention.

"Bear witness to my unbridled power!" the Queen demanded, grabbing the Bradley's torn husk. She heaved the vehicle from the ground, spinning with it, then hurling the metal behemoth. Like a discus it spun through the air, crashing into Knight Three. The third Bradley's turret separated clean from the hull. Agents screamed into their mics, as the force ripped both tank commander and gunner in half. "Playtime is over, children." Lilith's sights fell upon Conn's Knight Two.

"Listen up, crew," Conn announced. "Cole, I want you to hop out of the gun. Chico, I have the wheel. I'm taking control from the TC seat. Turn on your IR Comm beacons. Drop out the back side hatch and slam it shut. Then low crawl your behinds as far as you can. Don't let her see you. When you're clear you double time it back to the Combat Outpost."

"No way, we can't just leave you—" Chico started.

"That's an order, Agent!" Conn barked. "You get both your asses out the back hatch now! Look at you, got me yelling and forgetting I'm a southern belle," the commander huffed. "Do it, and you continue the Black Knights' legacy. Got it?"

"Roger, Actual," Chico's voice cracked. "I'm moving."

"Moving!" Cole patted Conn's shoulder, their eyes connecting with mutual nods.

The agents stooped over, Chico backing out of the driver's seat into the larger crew compartment, squeezing between boxes of ammo while stepping over the long chain of gargantuan 25 millimeter rounds that extended from the turret. Cole pulled on the main latch releasing the oval rear door. The two crew members hopped out, dropping down and low crawling into the cover of wilted foliage.

Booming cannon fire spat carbon as repeated shots from the Bradley collided with Lilith. The Queen raised her guard. She leapt forward, only to be met with the hard explosion of the final Stinger rocket within the carriage. The coaxial rotary cannon blared out its remaining shots, spinning with ribbons of smoke after dispensing its payload. Lilith rose to her feet, grimacing through the mayhem around her. Stepping forward, she braced each time she heard the thudding bolt within the Bradley chambering another round. An audible clunk signaled the end of the belt, leaving a knee-high pile of warm black links around Conn and traces of smoke drifting from the autocannon.

You two better be crawling away, damn it! I ain't doing this for shits and giggles! Conn unholstered her Kimber M1911 .45 ACP sidearm, drawing back the slide, and loading a round into the chamber.

Lilith closed on the Bradley, racking the vehicle as a swipe of her claw rended the front armor. The barrel of the main cannon ripped from the turret, leaving a gaping hole, exposing Conn to a cool breeze. Growls and unintelligible hollering came through clear, no longer muffled by the vehicle's steel walls. Lilith's face peered into the hole. Muzzle flashes greeted her from Conn's sidearm, delivering fat .45 caliber rounds that smacked hard into her face. Lilith shrieked, reeling away as hot lead struck an eye, puncturing into her socket and tumbling about. White and pink meat oozed from her skull, hanging by bloody nerves. The Queen reached up with her claws, quivering at the snapping tendons as she ripped out the sloughing remains of her eye. Her skull convulsed, riding out the agony that coursed through her face, while a new eye regenerated.

Conn held tight to her sidearm with both hands, bringing the rear and front sight apertures in line with the gaping hole. Lilith's massive claw reached through, grabbing Conn's right arm. The limb pulled from its socket. Ligaments and tendons popped. Muscles stretched until snapping away from the bone. Lilith ripped away the arm, covered in the blood soaked material of Conn's coveralls.

"Looks like you are out of tricks now, mortal!" Lilith declared. "I'm going to savor this."

Conn's yells subsided into deep, gasping laughter.

"Why are you laughing?" Lilith demanded. "What's so funny?"

"You," Conn declared, grasping her torn limb, while folding over in her commander's seat. "You... you... lost..."

"You're mistaken, mortal." Lilith chuckled. "Such fragile bodies and minds. A little pain sends you into delirium. It's rather entertaining."

"Still... not gettin' it, darlin'?" Conn chuckled with a wince. "Madam Dupree said that temper of yours was legendary. That ego, too... blinded by both... Guess the stories were true... You done wasted all this time... all this effort trying to kill a handful of raggedy ass cav scouts... And nothing to show for it except getting your ass beat. You lost sight of the mission..."

Lilith's eyes widened.

"Those children are long... gone," Conn continued, laughing through her words. "Safe in our deployment bay, and out of this hell hole, your highness..."

"We'll see about that," Lilith snarled, glancing over her shoulder to the remainder of her children cringing across the field. "This is far from over!" *There is only one way to victory. It has never been through love. I've stayed my wrath long enough and it has cost me everything. Love has cost me everything. It shall hinder me no longer. I am what I am.*

Conn smiled back into Lilith's snarling visage, twitching, turning flush with reddening anger. She winked at the Queen before a final claw swipe ushered her into darkness.

CHAPTER 31
REGICIDE

COMBAT OUTPOST: GALLANT, PANDEMONIUM - 0900 HOURS

Engines grumbled from the Humvees as they entered the Combat Outpost, driving down the main stretch. Lacerations covered their armor, and chain links rattled around within the turrets, rotating to align their barrels back to center. Curtis and the agents of Monarch stepped from their vehicles. Bags of fatigue weighed heavily underneath their eyes, still burning with the fire of combat within them. Curtis headed straight for Gabriel, standing beside Madam Dupree. They gazed between the two pillars of marble. The well of crackling white energies fluctuated into the fathomless depths of the etheric layers.

"That's the last of the children," Madam Dupree announced, the whirring motor of her vehicle's electrical components spinning her toward Gabriel. "Monarch is here. Well done, Agents. I cannot state that enough. We sacrificed so much for the success of this mission. My scryers will be working on safely guiding their presences through the door, where we will stabilize them in the bay via protective crystals, cleansing them free of the wretched aura of this world. After we're all through, we'll focus on reattaching all minds and souls back into their bodies."

"Curt," Gabriel called out. "Get your people through the gate next. No one has fought harder than you today, except—" The agent paused reaching over to touch the Stetson draped over his pack. "Go on. We'll cover you."

"Roger that," Curt replied. "All Monarch Team elements, withdraw from AO. We're exfiling back to the bay. Let's do this orderly. Leave all the gear. Give me the agents standing perimeter detail at all the even OPs first. I'll call up the odds once they're through."

Cheers came from the tower guards, half of them sliding down ladders and hurrying to the door. Madam Dupree nodded and smiled at the agents hurrying through. "Outstanding work, all of you. Now hurry..." The Grand Scryer paused. A tremendous concentration of darkness arose within the horizon of her psychic reach. Negative energy hovered like a cloud, closing the distance by dozens of meters each passing second. Madam Dupree looked up, seeing the skies roiling with shadow. Lightning streaked with tremendous power that leaked from the gloom.

"Something is coming," Madam Dupree announced, her wrinkles lowered with a frown. "Like a tidal wave of evil. Through the portal now! All of you!"

"You first," Gabriel said, grabbing Madam Dupree's chair and pushing her into the portal.

"Agent Agapito!" Madam Dupree snapped. "Unhand me!"

"Sorry, we can't afford to lose you, ma'am. Chew my ass later if you want."

"Oh, you most certainly will be receiving a fierce talking—"

Madam Dupree's irate voice zipped away into the clashing frequencies.

Gabriel stopped before the portal after ushering Madam Dupree through and turned his firm glower to the black storm clouds that overtook the morning. Lightning forked out, striking in the distance. A whistling gale flowed through, swelling into the agents' ears with a chilling caress.

"Airborne vector incoming!" tower guard number three barked. The long barrels of dual .50 caliber gun emplacements spat tracer rounds and carbon into the air. Shots thundered along the outpost perimeter from the remaining OPs.

"Get everyone through, Curt," Gabriel ordered. "My team already went over. You get your people the fuck out of here. I have to set the psi bomb's timer."

"Roger!" Curt replied. "Monarch, double time it through the door! Relinquish all posts, damn it! Move!"

Prattling rose from faint traces on the horizon into screaming gibberish from salivating jaws. Tower guns continued roaring.

"Negative, Monarch Actual!" observation post three called out. "I have visual on the vector and it's closing fast. We're engaging now. Everyone else get the fuck out of here!"

"Roger, Littleton," Curtis replied and nodded to the tower continuing to spew hot lead. "And thank you, brothers."

Agents rushed down from the tower, hurrying to the portal.

"Everyone through!" Curtis ordered. "Go! Go! Go! Double time it, Agents!"

Gabriel ran to the controls of the psionic bomb, ripping off his frayed and dusty combat gloves. With a delicate press of his fingers, he typed a combination of buttons on the keyboard, sending the computer next to the device into a series of menus.

"Arm and initiate, damn it!" Gabriel snapped.

"Initiation code confirmed, Team Commander Agent Gabriel Agapito. Arming sequence activated," an AI voice replied over the speaker. "Initiating detonation in T-minus five minutes."

Charging rifts of power within the clear confines of the cubed warhead flared with blinding light. A shudder went through the massive metallic frame holding the device together. Gabriel sprinted over, turning at the screams rising from OP Three.

Lilith loomed over the wall, her hulking size standing with the height of the tower. Crackles and sparks of darkness coursed around the Queen, climbing up her extended frame, through her elongated neck. A quaking shriek released from her hanging jowls, revealing endless rows of spiked teeth trailing down her gullet. Quills of coarse white hair rose on her back, trailing into her spaded tail.

Lilith grasped the tower, the support bolts bursting from its base as she tore it from the ground. The pair of agents within cried out, one falling from the structure, landing at Lilith's feet. She hurled the tower away, sending it crashing into the field in a calamity of bending metal and dust. She peered down at the agent, lying on the ground. Lilith raised a foot. Gravel fell from her leathery soles, while her talons widened. The Monarch agent screamed as the crushing weight drew down upon him, smothering his cries. His ribs collapsed, lungs pushing out what little breath remained. Innards rushed out from the man's ears, mouth, and anus, smashed into a red paste that oozed from the flattened corpse. Lilith howled a challenge.

"Fuck you!" Gabriel yelled in anguish, turning to run through the door.

Darkness enveloped his vision, casting his racing presence through the etheric layers. Shadow figures appeared among the varying frequencies, closing around him. Gabriel tightened his grip around his M4.

"Easy there, hun," the calming voice of Mama Dinga called out, reaching with a gentle pat. "You have no enemies here. We're going to guide you safely back to your body."

"It's friendlies, Gabe," Curt said, trailing Madam Dupree's arrival.

"I've started the detonation sequence—" Gabriel replied.

"That's good news," Tía Hermosa called out.

"And you have quite the talking to coming your way when this operation is complete!" Madam Dupree snapped.

"No time, ma'am!" Gabriel exclaimed. "It's Lilith! The White Queen! She's coming! She's at the—"

Shrieking howls of rage reverberated through the layers, permeating into their being. Eyes widened and gasps escaped from dropping mouths. A colossal presence of shadow stood within the doorway, hatred seething through her glowing white eyes.

"Scryers to the front!" Madam Dupree bellowed into the ether. "You will stand your ground! Hold this fiend back while we await the detonation that will separate her world from ours!"

Lilith's narrowed eyes fell on the assembly of scryers as they stepped forward. Glowing auras of light arose from each of the practitioners, raising their hands in resistance to the coming darkness. Their radiance combined into one presence. The darkness pressed forth. The scryers slid back underneath the immense pressure collapsing upon them.

"Hold firm!" Madam Dupree groaned. "Hold the line!"

"Pathetic," Lilith retorted. "Silly Scryers. You subhumans can never hope to match my prowess. Behold!"

A rush of power sent one of the scryers reeling in screaming agony. His cries filled the doorway with a resounding echo, ringing into the ears of his comrades.

"Looks like everyone is getting patched up or grabbing food," Leo said. "Where the hell is Kevin? Probably off taking a shit like always. You know, he holds it out in the field the entire time?

"Well, that's not healthy." Portia raised a brow. "What's even more concerning is you knowing that."

"Anyways, I think it's safe to say we made it out in one piece, Sweet Pea. How about we grab a cup of joe while we wait for Actual and the others? I'm sure they'll want one too." Leo smiled at Portia, patting her on the shoulder as they walked through the massive holding area. "One of these desk bubbas has a pot brewing somewhere around here."

"That sounds like heaven right now," Portia replied. "See, you don't always have to be a rabble rouser."

"Rabble rouser!" Leo scoffed, poking the medic's tummy. "Now thems be fightin' words, foo!"

Throat shredding screams of torment arose from one of the scryers around the channeling circle. Leo and Portia ceased their rough housing, standing upright, gazing past the medical gurneys, desks, and crystal collection, where apprentice scryers worked to cleanse the unseen spirits of children. The cries continued, guiding their vision to the ritual site where one of the practitioners had awoken from his meditation. Racking convulsions overtook him, sending the robed man's body clapping against the floor like a fish out of water.

The agents raced over. Leo grabbed the man's torso while Portia went for his legs. Trembling limbs flailed about, his fingers twitching and flexing. An unseen rush of force knocked them all over, sending Portia and the scryer collapsing upon Leo.

"Well... this sucks..." Leo groaned. "You okay, Pea?"

"Yeah, I'm—" Portia gasped.

Blood rose from the scryer's eyes, boiling over and leaking across his face into a cherry red stream. His mouth remained agape, vocals strained to no avail, having the meat peeled from them during his escalating cries. Droplets of crimson fell from his earlobe, splatting on the floor. His eyes rolled upward, hiding his pupils within the upper sockets. Chunks of meat jettisoned from the scryer's ears in a slough of pink and red, before his body went limp.

"Brain matter?!" Portia cried out. "His brain erupted!"

Others within the circle shook with violent force. Another scryer keeled over from her cross-legged position, screaming with eyes widening in shock, her irises following something that was not there. The scryer reached up, grabbing her auburn locks, ripping handfuls away. Blood smeared across her skull, sliming her hands as they returned to yank more. The woman grasped her heart, seizing up. Her convulsions died down and life fled from her body.

"What the fuck is going on?" Leo hollered.

A powerful force rushed from Lilith, channeled with tremendous willpower. Another scryer reeled back into the depths of darkness surrounding the door. His screams echoed, fading into the endless layers. Gabriel stood behind the gathering of scryers, their eyes clenched tight, mantras of faith and focus upon their lips, with arms raised high presenting hands that generated an invisible bastion of resistance to Lilith's approach.

Why the hell hasn't the psi bomb detonated yet? Gabriel wondered. *It's been well over five minutes. They're not going to last much longer at this rate. Once they fall, Lilith will come into the material realm to wreak havoc and retake the young souls we worked so hard to rescue. Too many good people sacrificed for this. I can't let that happen.*

A vision of the sword flashed in Gabriel's mind. He reached back, placing a hand on its scabbard. Images of the White Knight played in his memories. An honorable presence trapped along the bridge yielding this sword. *The White Knight... What does it all mean? It's all energy. It's... Lilith!*

"Only one who is like us can wield this blade. Return me to where I belong," the Vorpal Sword murmured into Gabriel's thoughts. "You finally know what must be done. You see through her lies. She isn't complete. Restore the balance within Lilith and she will falter."

"Tell my wife and daughter that I love them very much," Gabriel said to Madam Dupree as he raced by her.

Gabriel unsheathed the Vorpal Sword, aiming for Lilith's torso. A wild and hard thrust saw the weapon sinking into the cucuy Queen's heart. Lilith buckled, staggering backward. The sword dissolved into particles of light that streamed into the Queen. Lilith racked in place. She clawed at her chest, tearing away at her own presence, as the positive and negative energies balanced into one.

"No!" Lilith bellowed. "No! I rid myself of you!"

Energy can never be destroyed, Lilith. We are one as it was always meant to be. Positive and negative in balance. You had hoped to rid yourself of me. To spare your ego the grief of your designs. I let you get the better of my judgment so many times before. You destroyed our children! With clear eyes, I know now the monster that we have become, the very same thing I had imagined to have fled. And I would rather destroy myself than stand by watching you ruin us. May our Father forgive us. We both knew that reunion was inevitable. I am you. You are me. We are whole again.

The orchestra of crying children resounded into Lilith's consciousness, each voice stinging into her heart chakra with guilt. They stared through her memories, each of them pointing from her mind's eye. The ache of accusation ran through her, shattering the ego. Fallen agents stepped forward with the children, pointing, staring down Lilith with stone-faces of unrelenting retribution. Screams played out into another moment that resurfaced. Her outstretched hands calling the energies of her fleeing children beating against the castle doors to flee back inside. Their presence, minds and souls, broken and reduced to raw power that she invoked to devour and end their existence.

I... My children... What have I done?

"Her focus is waning!" Madam Dupree announced. "Drive her back, Scryers!"

"No!" Lilith snarled. "It cannot all have been for nothing!"

The cucuy Queen pushed back against the tidal wave of resistance. The sting of guilt ran through her core. Lilith's outstretched arms quivered. Her eyes closed tight. Every ounce of will that she summoned was impeded by the cries of her victims, and the empathic tether of her restored humanity.

Gabriel whisked past Lilith, heading for the mouth of the gate. Shadows parted revealing the portal with a view of the compound. The agent leapt through, tumbling toward the controls. He bounced up seeing the keyboard clawed to ribbons, with torn buttons sprinkled below.

'Countdown halted,' the monitor displayed. 'Five seconds remaining.'

Fuck my life! She stopped it somehow and trashed the controls. There's no way to restart unless... I manually detonate it. Gabriel sighed and nodded. *It must be done. Forgive me, Alma. I won't be coming home this time.*

Gabriel ran to the array of tents, searching within and grabbing a keyboard from a desk. He hurried back to unplug the damaged one, popping away its USB cord from the computer and installing the other. Gabriel punched in the command prompt.

'Recommencing timer, Team Commander Agent Gabriel Agapito.'

Gabriel's eyes closed tight as he sighed deeply, the seconds passing like hours from his locked body. *Go! Go! Go!*

A force of energy took hold of Gabriel in a vise-like grip, pulling him back through the door. The dark morass of the entrance usurped his vision. Lilith's back was before him, the hulking monstrosity roaring at the scryers defying her presence. Madam Dupree steered her chair through a narrow opening between Lilith and the dark corridor of the entryway.

"It was you!" Gabriel smirked. "You saved me!"

"Of course," Madam Dupree snapped. "I still owe you that ass chewing. Don't think you were getting off that easy, Agent Agapito."

"No, ma'am."

Light exploded around them, shaking the entire doorway. Energy pushed from the other side, erupting against the unseen elements that shaped the door. The surrounding darkness advanced, closing upon them. Lilith raised her arms, holding it aloft. She groaned in agony, wincing with clenched teeth as her limbs spasmed.

Gabriel and Madam Dupree slipped around her, rejoining the scryers.

"Not even you are strong enough to hold up the layers indefinitely," Madam Dupree quipped.

"Curse... you!" Lilith's voice strained from her trembling frame.

"So much potential for greatness, yet all of it wasted through ego, and lack of forgiveness," Madam Dupree said. "I hope we never see each other again. Goodbye, Lilith." Madam Dupree wheeled around. "Everyone out! Oh, and thank you for holding the door, your majesty."

Lilith roared in anger. The scryers exited through the portal, their souls zipping away to the material plane. Gabriel looked back one last time at the monstrosity writhing in fatigue. He vanished with the others.

Throbbing pain coursed through Lilith's shoulders and lower back, fighting to press the closing layers overhead. Convulsions brought her knees to a sway, while her legs fought to keep the ground from rising. She looked ahead, seeing the entrance leading to the material world before peering back to the mouth of Pandemonium.

Must... return... home... regather...

Lilith stepped back, locking her limbs in alarm as the pressure of the etheric layers forced down. Her teeth clenched together, tremors of fatigue rocking through her body.

No! No! Losing... it...

Both elbows and knees snapped, dislodging limbs within the joints sent femur and humerus bones pushing through the wrinkled and loose skin. Lilith cried out as she toppled over. The door to darkness closed upon her with the weight of the etheric layers. Ripples of energy coursed through her view of the broken power used to create the pocket dimension. She saw them in her mind's eye peering at her with their unblinking curiosity. The children, whose souls she had pilfered over the ages, used to fashion her world and create the very same door now crushing her. They watched Lilith in quiet judgment. A vigil for eternity to protect others from the same fate.

Defeated... by the spawn of Eve! Defeated... by that bitch's children...

Lilith couldn't muster the room to scream; there was no air for her lungs to summon. Nor did her lips have space to part. Her cries bellowed within her aching soul. The darkness swallowed Lilith, paralyzing her underneath the weight of her own misdeeds.

CHAPTER 32
HOPE RESTORED

PRESENT DAY: USA HQ WEST, SAN DIEGO, CA - 1700 HOURS

Katherine Howler stood with her arms crossed behind Madam Dupree. The door to Howler's office stood closed, while the two shared tall cups of iced coffee. Katherine placed a hand on Simone's shoulder. The older woman chuckled, watching the ice slosh as Katherine took another sip.

"What's so funny?" Katherine asked.

"I got you addicted to the cold stuff, didn't I?"

"Maybe." Katherine smirked.

"Oh, let me hush. It's about to start," Simone said, bringing their attention to the television screen mounted along a corner of the wall.

The words 'Breaking News' flashed before the camera changed to a blue suited man seated behind a conference desk. With a giant smile, he tapped a stack of papers into alignment, holding them with both hands.

"It brings me great pleasure to deliver a much needed story

for many of us," the reporter announced. "Thousands of children worldwide have awoken from their sudden comas. A few weeks ago, we reported here at Channel 7 News about an undiagnosed tragedy, where children between the ages of four and sixteen began suffering from inexplicable narcoleptic attacks. Medical professionals were left baffled as to why perfectly healthy children, most with no history of medical issues, were enduring the same unfortunate symptoms."

The camera cut to a smiling Hispanic girl.

"That lovely little thing looks familiar," Madam Dupree said.

"Consuela." Katherine smiled.

Consuela grinned from the gurney of her hospital room, flanked by her parents, and waving into the camera. The girl blew a kiss. "Thank you, Agents!" she exclaimed before covering her mouth. "Oops, I'm not supposed to say anything!"

"Most of the children have no recollection of the events over the last few weeks or even months," the reporter continued. "But, I know their families are happy to have them home."

"Wow, just look at that smile," a woman reporter chimed in. "I think I speak for everyone when I say all of us are happy they're awake and safe. A lot of loved ones are going to be resting easier tonight thanks to this miracle."

Madam Dupree turned to Katherine. The Grand Scryer's hand caressed at nothing in her lap.

"Are you hearing some purring, Simone?" Katherine gazed around, then raised a brow.

"Everyone is on some well deserved R&R. How about you, Kat?" Madam Dupree asked.

"Nope." Katherine pointed at the television before taking

another sip of coffee. A woman was hugging her son who was lying on a bed, surrounded by hospice nurses. She continued planting kisses on the boy, squeezing him to the point where he gagged. Katherine's eyes stayed fixed on the montage of happy reunions. "This is what I live for."

"And where is Agent Agapito? I'd like to ask him that question. See if his surliness is finally waning."

"Tying up some unfinished business," Katherine replied. "I think this mission straightened out a lot of perspectives, forcing many of us to understand what's important."

"Agents Portia Lawson and Leo Mills?"

"Those two are tying something different." Katherine smiled. "They're tying the knot. A little quick for my tastes, but they've also known each other longer than most couples."

"I was pulling for those two."

"And now I have to get back to work, Simone." Kat sighed, turning back to her desk.

"Dealing with the escapees? I heard there was a mishap while I was gone."

"One of our prisoner transport convoys was attacked by an extremely skilled and armed hostile force," Katherine replied. "They freed him..."

"No... Edjewale is on the loose?"

Katherine nodded. Her eyes gazed at the picture on her desk of Ghost Team. Emmerich stood on the far left, his face etched in stone cold stoicism and a brow weighing heavily with calculations. Callisto was next to him glaring into the camera, her chocolate brown locks unfurled from their usual bun, wearing a necklace of vampire fangs. Fredrick was on the far right, holding up an M240B machine gun and grinning. Katherine was in the middle, with heavy bags under her eyes. To her immediate left was Badrick, bearing a weary smile. Both of them reaching over unbeknownst to the others, with pinky fingers wrapped. Katherine's eyes closed tight.

"We'll get him, Kat." Simone placed a hand on her friend's. "Edjewale will not escape justice. Who freed him?"

"No idea." Katherine shook her head with doubt. "They were skilled, proceeding with a coordinated complex nocturnal ambush. They were knowledgeable of military convoy procedures and able to anticipate how the agents of Sentinel would respond. Very heavy firepower was utilized along with NVGs and IR lasers."

"Oh, damn it! They're adapting." Madam Dupree shook her head. "The darkness has started to recruit combat veterans like us. Evil never rests, does it?"

"Neither do we. Except for you. The agency needs its lead scryer in tip-top shape."

Madam Dupree nodded. "Truth be told. I'm feeling the fatigue in my old body. Can't run missions like when I was a spring chicken. I'm sure Master Bingwen would be happy to accommodate the agency in my stead."

"Good choice," Katherine replied. "His presence will be much appreciated to support this operation. I'm afraid though my personal vendetta will have to be put on the back burner. Whoever freed Edjewale also let loose the other dangerous inmates being transferred to the Sand Palace. Years of work down the drain in one evening… And worse yet, Sentinel's quick reaction force reported the extremely dangerous vectors escaped into a nearby city. That amount of concentrated evil in one area will undoubtedly begin causing absolute mayhem. God help us…"

KALINGA PROVINCE MEMORIAL GRAVEYARD, PHILIPPINES

The sun bore down on Gabriel, stepping forward with a bouquet of flowers in his hand. Upon his head was the frayed brown baseball cap, gifted by his father. His wife and daughter held hands, trailing behind. His Uncle Garret walked beside him. They approached the twin gravestones with a smaller one between them.

With each step Gabriel took, the warrior aura of discipline receded, withering until he was no longer the man, but the boy he had always been. The world felt so big once again. Fear crept into his heart. This was the real Agent Gabriel Agapito. The man who faced down the terrors of the world was a mask worn by a boy still trembling in the shadow of fear.

"How long has it been?" Uncle Garret asked.

"Never." Gabriel shook his head. "This is my first time."

The boy placed flowers upon his parents' gravestones. Gabriel stepped back. His father's thin face appeared in his mind's eye, smiling with a wink, and nodding with pride. His mother followed, with her full cheeks bunching together as she smiled with joy.

The first tear fell, sliding down the side of Gabriel's nose and disappearing between his lips. More followed, glistening wetness covering his face. He turned, hugging his uncle. A cry escaped his quivering lips, releasing the floodgates to more.

"There you are, Gabe." Garret patted him. "At last you're letting it out. After all these years. Go ahead. I'm proud of you. We all are."

"Is Daddy going to be okay?" little Alma asked.

"Yes, iha." Gabriel replied. *Daddy is finally going to be okay.*

44 YEARS LATER: SANTA FE, NM

Two women and a little girl hiked through the forest, following down a path of beaten grass. An elderly man passed, with his walking stick, nodding to the women.

"How much further, Grandma?" the little girl asked.

"We're here." She chuckled, holding up a bouquet of flowers and taking off her pack.

The grandmother turned toward the monument of polished stone. A thick glass case displayed a black Stetson hat, flanked by a bronze statue of a raven and a Bradley Fighting Vehicle. Upon the shining placard read the words: "In memory of the agents of Task Force Gryphon during Operation: Through the Looking Glass. The quiet heroes who fought the battle that mattered most, while the world slept. Rest in the green for none have earned it more than you."

"Looks like someone already beat us to the maintenance," her daughter said.

The grandmother rifled through her pack removing polish and a rag. "That's not going to stop me. It's the least I can do." After a few minutes, the grandmother turned back to her daughter and granddaughter. She took a moment, seeing herself in both of them. "Promise me that when I can no longer make the trek up here, you two will carry on making sure it remains pristine here?"

"Of course, Mom," her daughter replied.

"You got it, Grandma Penny." Her granddaughter saluted.

A smile rolled back on Penny's face, through the strands of gray that escaped the confines of her hair tie, and the wrinkles etched upon her countenance. Her attention turned back to the monument, taking a moment to polish the raven and Bradley, then dusting the glass case.

"Thank you," Penny said, taking her progeny by the hands. "Thank you all for what you gave me."

WANTED: DEAD OR ALIVE
UNHOLY, UNHINGED, AND EXTREMELY VIOLENT FUGITIVES ON THE LOOSE!

Stay tuned for the next installment of the UNHOLY SLAYING AGENCY series, TRAILS OF MISERY.

Evil has been unleashed and is ready to pounce on an unsuspecting civilian populace. Edjewale, the master of the dark arts, has escaped while in transit to a maximum-security prison for the supernatural. The escort Agents from Sentinel suffered a catastrophic loss in an ambush. Intel has yet to identify the party responsible for the assault.

Edjewale released the other unholy captives being transported. We believe these vicious fiends have absconded into a nearby unsuspecting city. The prisoner convoy contained some of the most vicious and nefarious vectors that the agency has apprehended over the last few years. We fear it is only a matter of time before this concentration of evil unleashes ultimate mayhem.

We are calling upon the rogue Hunter Killer contractors for a clandestine operation. Your objective is to apprehend or neutralize these vectors. Backup is unavailable. Follow the path of destruction. Only the brave dare to hunt evil on the 'Trails of Misery.'

Sign up for my newsletter to be notified when new books are released.

    guyquintero.com/recruitment

ABOUT THE AUTHOR

 Guy Quintero is a former reconnaissance soldier with three deployments under his belt. Quintero combines his military background and a life-long fascination with the occult, bringing a mix of bone-chilling horror and heart-pumping action. His inspirations are Stephen King and Tom Clancy. He hopes to follow in their footsteps someday.

GuyQuintero.com

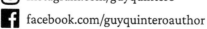

 Milton Keynes UK
Ingram Content Group UK Ltd.
UKHW021940081024
449407UK00017B/262/J